Heels over Head in Love

A Novel by

John Butler

Herndon, VA

Published in the United States
STARbooks Press PO Box 711612 Herndon VA 20171
Printed in the United States

Many thanks to graphic artist Emma Aldous for the cover design. Ms. Aldous
may be reached at emma@starbookspress.com.

Herndon, VA

STARbooks Press Publications

By John Butler:

Novels

model/escort
WanderLUST: Ships That Pass in the Night
Boys Hard at Work – and Playing with Fire
This Gay Utopia
Teacher Is the Best Experience
The Boy Next Door (in the anthology *Any Boy Can*)
The Year the Pigs Were Aloft (in the anthology *Seduced 2*)
Heels over Head in Love

John Butler Editions

Seduced 2 (Co-editor)
Wild and Willing (Co-editor)
Living Vicariously – The Best of John Patrick (Editor)

Short stories in the following anthologies:

Seduced 2
Fever!
Taboo!
Fantasies Made Flesh
Wild and Willing
Virgins No More

AN APOLOGIA

This is fiction, in spite of what I say in the body of the text. I didn't make it all up, though.

I will admit there are a number of minor characters in this story who are entirely figments of my obviously fevered imagination – so sue me! Do you think Melville really knew Ishmael and Queequeg? Surely you don't think Dickens was actually acquainted with Wackford Squeers or Tom Gradgrind, do you? The several orgiastic parties chronicled in these pages are also, I am extremely sorry to say, products of my invention; how wonderful and rewarding it would have been if they had taken place in reality, rather than only in my fancy.

Otherwise, all characters, locations, and situations are remembered from my real life, although I have of course changed names and places to protect innocent bystanders. Cary, Mike, Mark, Richard, Dean, Thom, Billy, Bob, Hal, etc., were real guys, but with real names. If these relationships didn't quite go where I say they went in this book, there is one simple reason: Life isn't always fair. I have also taken the liberty to rearrange a few dates, but just a few – and only a little bit.

These unforgettable men actually played smaller parts in my life than described here, but they did each play a part. The following pages detail, however, the parts I wanted them to play.

DEDICATION

This one is also dedicated to Derek, an astonishingly talented young man, who continues to make my senior citizenship fun.

A NOTE TO THE READER

My first book of sexual memories was *Boys Hard at Work – and Playing with Fire*. The following pages fill in the gaps in that accounting, which was published by STARbooks Press in 2001. If there are slight discrepancies between the two books, they can be attributed to lapses in memory; the events described in both books actually happened and are described as best I can recall.

CONTENTS

1. TWO CHALLENGES AND ONE CONQUEST

In a certain sense, Freshman Orientation was something like window-shopping in a candy store. Here sat hundreds of young men who only a few months before had been undisputed kings of all they surveyed – their high schools and environs – but who were now reduced to the least common denominator on the college scene, the incoming freshman class. In general, their last year's cockiness had now become an eagerness to please, but young men don't generally need to do anything for me to find them very pleasing indeed. The simile of the candy shop arises from my personal view of young men as delectable goods to provide the sweetest and most enjoyable part of the diet of living. The young men who sat in the auditorium that fall looked particularly toothsome to me – especially after an entire year of what I regarded as far too little indulgence in that particular variety of sweets!

To be sure there were female freshmen (not "freshpersons," however politically correct that might be) present in this new class, but they were vastly outnumbered by the males. Dowd College had been a military school from its founding as Dowd A&M in the last few years of the nineteenth century, until the late 1950s, when the military system was abandoned and a coeducational student body was instituted. Now, in 1965, the total student body of some 5,000 included only a few hundred coeds. So, the freshman class that I surveyed from my seat on the stage that fall afternoon was overwhelmingly male, and – not surprisingly – that suited me fine.

I had come to Dowd in the summer of 1964, as an Assistant Professor of Music and Director of Bands. This was my first experience as a college professor, although I had a number of years' experience at the public school level. After one year of full-time teaching in Texas, and two years in the Navy, I had entered the University of Alabama, and stayed there through four years of graduate study, eventually receiving both my master's and doctoral degrees from that institution. For three years, I had returned to directing a high school band as I finished writing my doctoral dissertation and sought a promising position at a college or university; Dowd seemed ideal. It was a middle-sized State college, and there were a number of those in Alabama, but Dowd, because of its football notoriety, was – like its sister in the state system, Auburn University – only barely subservient to the University of Alabama in statewide prestige. The band program was well established, and even though there was no degree offering in music there, I felt lucky in securing my appointment.

A year earlier, I had sat on this same stage and surveyed the incoming freshman class; at that time I had been pleased to note the enormous pool of attractive young men, but had been dismayed to think how I should feel compelled to practice a policy of "no fishing" in that pool, since, I must confess, I had experienced a few professionally ill-advised liaisons with young men in the student bodies at schools where I had served before.

During my first year of full-time teaching, in a very small town in the panhandle of Texas, I had fallen in love with Billy Polk, an eighteen-year-old high school senior Adonis, and had enjoyed a wonderful sexual relationship with him, and, peripherally, with a few of his friends. Although circumstances and distance separated us, Billy and I had remained very close friends – still lovers, really, but without sexual contact; he had married a year before I came to Dowd, and his wife was now expecting their first child.

Among the young sailors I dealt with during my two-year tenure in the Navy, I had enjoyed a very active sexual life – mostly casual, short-term contacts, but two intense, extended relationships with beautiful young men who were members of musical organizations I directed. One was the dark, sexually explosive Chicano, Fernando Soto (during the year I spent in San Diego), and the other the blond, "down-home" Tennessee stallion Ron Daniels (during the year I spent on an aircraft carrier). Both Fernando and Ron had been strictly tops, and both were hugely endowed, so I had been extremely well-served during those years in a passive role, regularly and frequently thrilling to the huge volume of cock and cum with which the two had filled my hungry ass. But I had found a plentiful supply of other young sailors – and a surprisingly large number of Marines – who were eager and ready to play bottom to my role as top. If I couldn't give them as monstrous a dick as the ones I was regularly taking up my eager, insatiable ass, I drilled their voracious holes with one as hard and as cum-filled as those magnificent ass-reamers Fernando and Ron were using to fuck me.

My four years at the University had been a sexual paradise, with hot, handsome young men ready and willing for all kinds of sexual activity, but nothing lasting had developed. I had sex with something like 500 young studs during those years, including quite a few who sported really monstrous dicks: one who regularly filled my ass or mouth with five or six loads each time we met; another who always brought his very well-hung partner along for our meetings, so that he could get double-fucked by both our cocks at the same time; and one who was not only marvelously built and very well hung, but who was one of the most perfectly beautiful men I had ever seen. This last-named Adonis was talented at all forms of oral sex, passive or active, and loved to fuck butt endlessly and savagely, and with amazing frequency, but would permit nothing up his own asshole except my tongue. Although I enjoyed giving him my load in his mouth as much as he obviously relished taking it, I loved every minute I spent sucking his generous cock and rounded tits, and thrilled to his hungry kisses and ferocious fucking. I was so frustrated at not being able to fuck his very sweet ass that the long-term relationship I would otherwise have cultivated with him was not a possibility.

The proximity of the University to the small town where I taught for three years as I finished my dissertation allowed me to continue that wild life back on campus, without being tempted by the younger students I taught.

Life at Dowd was very different, however. Although the college was large enough, it was located in a very small town, and one's life was pretty much an open book – one that was read by everyone. Fortunately, I was able to get up to Atlanta for the occasional weekend fling, so the pressure wasn't too great. Furthermore, almost as soon as I arrived there I had fallen desperately in love with Richard Austin, a very handsome, magnificently hung student who exuded the most passionate kind of sexual charisma. Shortly after I was shown nude pictures of him with an enormous erection of astonishingly succulent appearance, I arranged for a meeting, wooed him assiduously, and he became my first live-in lover. While our affair had only lasted a couple of months, it had been wonderful and unbelievably intense, and I glowed in the indelible memory of Richard's huge endowment servicing me at least nightly – and usually more frequently – with a passion and a savagery I had only occasionally experienced before, and of the copious draughts I had drunk from his magnificent organ.

There were any number of very attractive guys around campus, but there were only two young men during that first year whom I actually lusted after following the dissolution of my affair with Richard; coincidentally, both were trumpet players, and both played in the band I conducted. Cary Adams was a gorgeous blond freshman, and Mike Sharp was a dark, fairly ordinary-looking sophomore.

It had been while I was working my first freshman orientation session at Dowd that I first spotted Cary and had been blown away by his good looks and air of cocky sexual assurance. I made it a point to speak with him and was delighted to find that he was planning on playing in the band. I cultivated his friendship during his freshman year but was unable to direct him toward a possible sexual liaison. I had made it a point to visit his dorm room frequently and, if possible, at a time when he would be going to the shower. I had often been treated to the sight of his nude body as I chatted easily with him while he showered, and it was so exciting, I always developed an involuntary erection, which I had to hide from anyone else in the large communal bathroom. I never concealed my obvious arousal from Cary – I wanted him to know how much he turned me on. He was fairly trim, but extremely well-muscled, with a broad chest and narrow waist, a firm, rounded ass, and a nice-sized cock surmounted by a thatch of golden pubic hair. Furthermore, he was not shy about letting me see him walk around nude in his room, and I felt sure he was more than aware of the throbbing bulge in my pants every time he displayed himself to me – and I felt that was what he was doing. I had taken him to movies and out to dinner on a number of occasions, and while I made tentative sexual overtures, he responded to none of them. I did not give up, however – Cary was far too sexy and cute to abandon.

Only at the end of that first year did a few potentially sexual situations occur with Cary. We were playing a concert in a small town, and during the intermission, while I was standing alone outside, smoking a cigarette, Cary came up and said, "Look what happened." As he said this, he held the crotch of his uniform pants tight for my inspection, and I could see that a fairly sizable hole had developed just below the fly. Since he almost seemed to be inviting me to examine it, I reached down and put a finger into the hole and was really excited to find that he was apparently wearing no underwear, for my finger encountered his bare cock and balls. I tickled his cock, and he did not draw back, but giggled and said, "Guess I'd better get that fixed." To my amazement, he let me keep my finger inside his pants for a few more moments, and I could even feel his prick beginning to get hard; my own cock was by this time straining hard against my own fly. Then he backed away and left, saying he was going to go find a safety pin. Cary said nothing about the incident later.

A few days before he left for summer vacation as we were riding around in my car, I worked up the courage to put my hand on Cary's leg. He allowed me to keep my hand there, even spreading his legs and sitting back. After some time, I moved my hand to the inside of his leg, brushing his crotch, and asked if any more holes had developed. He laughed and said all his other pants were in good shape, and only after that did he take my hand in his and remove it from his leg, without comment. I was heartened to note that he had been in no real hurry to remove my hand, nor had he sat up or closed his legs to hide the inviting bulge at his crotch – which I was sure he knew I was aware of. While I was not encouraged, I was not discouraged either, and spent the summer hoping something was going to develop that fall.

The situation with Mike had been much more rewarding. I had not particularly thought about him as a potential bed partner at first. He was good-looking, but not unduly so, and it was only when I began to hear guys tease him about the size of his cock that I began to get interested. He was of average height, and wore fairly strong glasses; I soon discovered that without his glasses he was actually quite handsome. I inferred from the comments I heard that Mike's cock was enormous, and I naturally developed a strong urge to see it. On my visits to Cary in his dorm, I also made it a point to watch for Mike going into the shower and was soon rewarded with the sight of his prick. It was dark, uncircumcised, and huge, even when flaccid. It flopped and swayed between his legs as he showered, and I could hardly take my eyes from it. Nude, Mike was more attractive than I had thought – considerations of his mammoth equipment aside. He had a nice body, smooth and hairless, and a cute bubble butt to set things off.

I had begun cultivating Mike's friendship and seemed to be progressing much better than I was with Cary. Joe, the student drum major of the band, with whom I had developed a close, platonic friendship, asked me to join him and his roommate on a weekend trip to Atlanta to see a Dowd-Georgia Tech basketball game. Since Mike was the younger brother of Joe's roommate, I suggested he join us, and Joe agreed. As I hoped, the hotel room where we stayed had only two double beds, and I made sure that Mike and I wound up in one together. We

4

had all drunk a good bit that evening, but I had made it a point to hold back somewhat, hoping to be in good shape to seduce Mike somehow.

After waiting until heavy breathing and ample snoring seemed to suggest everyone was sound asleep, I began to move up against Mike, and soon had an arm around his waist from behind. He murmured a little, and I began to play with his bare chest. My cock, although contained by my shorts, was painfully hard, and pressing against Mike's ass. After lying like this for some time, I began to quietly move my hand down, and soon encountered the bulge of his crotch. His cock was not hard, but I cupped it through his shorts, and squeezed it gently. Soon I was rewarded with the knowledge that Mike was not only awake, he was beginning to murmur his pleasure at my attentions and gently humping against my hand. As I continued to squeeze and fondle him, his prick began to grow beneath my hand – and grow, alarmingly and wonderfully. He murmured "Mmm-hmmmm!" and pulled the front of his shorts down to free his huge prick, now fully hard and throbbing in my grasp. I held the mammoth shaft in my hand and stroked it gently as he finished removing his shorts.

It was a wonderful cock, not the largest I had ever held, but not far from it – close to nine inches in length, I guessed, and very fat. Mike shifted his body to lie on his back. He took my head in his hands, and guided it to his chest. I began to kiss and suck his nipples, then moved down to lick his belly and kiss his navel, all the time fondling his magnificent cock. Still holding my head, he pressed it lower, steering my mouth to the magnificent gift he was about to give me. I had thought all along I was being rather subtle about hiding my attraction to him, but he had obviously been well aware of it.

I had to open my mouth very wide to admit Mike's fat monster, and I was unable for a time to take all of it into my throat. I did my best, however, sucking greedily, and driving my tight lips up and down the long shaft. Mike's ass began to hump, and he was soon plunging deep inside my mouth. I gradually was able to relax my throat, and soon he was burying every thrilling inch in it. He seized my head roughly, and with a particularly savage series of thrusts, drove his glorious shaft all the way into my throat and began to shoot spurt after copious spurt of his hot cum into my worshipping mouth. I swallowed greedily, and continued to suck and lick his now-softening prick for a long time. Finally, he withdrew and whispered into my ear, "Get a towel." I went to the bathroom and came back with it. Mike whispered, "Take your shorts off and kneel over me." I did as I was told, straddling his chest and fondling his rounded pecs. He took my throbbing cock in his hand and began to masturbate me ferociously. Even though his prick was only now partially erect, its bulk was impressive as it pressed against my ass while he jacked me off and I played with his tits, dreaming how wonderful that enormous cock would feel if it were still as steely hard as it had been only a few minutes earlier and I was riding up and down on it. Soon I began to shoot my load all over his chest, and he continued to stroke and shake my prick until he had extracted every drop. Then he took the towel, cleaned us both off, and as I collapsed on the bed, he curled up behind me, with his soft prick pressing against my ass, and we went to sleep; we had been almost completely quiet as we made love.

As it began to get light, Mike shook me awake and again guided my mouth to his prick – which was hard and huge again. Once again he fucked my face savagely and deposited an enormous load down my throat – even bigger and better tasting than the first one he had given me. He whispered, "Do you want me to get another load for you?" I did, and he beat me off again, after which we both put our shorts on, and returned to sleep, on opposite sides of the bed.

Nothing was said about our experience in Atlanta, but during the rest of the year, I had probably six or eight occasions to be alone with Mike, and he invariably wanted me to suck his huge prick, but he had little interest in my showing too much affection for him. The few times I tried to kiss him on the mouth, he averted his head, and I did not press my luck – but he welcomed my kissing him anywhere below the belt. Usually as he was cumming, he would caress my head and my face, cooing his satisfaction, and occasionally when we rolled around on a bed, passionately fondling each other, and I kissed him everywhere except the lips, he would kiss my leg or my stomach or my neck – but at that point kissing on the lips seemed remote at best. He did allow me to hold him in my arms, to stroke his body, and even play with his pretty ass, but I could tell he was just "putting up with it" until he could get his hard prick inside my adoring mouth – usually with him grasping my head as I knelt before or over him, but a few times with me lying on my back as he held himself over my face and really fucked my mouth. On a couple of occasions he jacked off on my face and into my open mouth, so I could watch him cum, but he particularly enjoyed the wonderful sensation of exploding his enormous load deep inside my throat – probably almost as much as I enjoyed it. The one other time we were able to spend a whole night together, he deposited four huge loads in my mouth.

We never talked about what we were doing, and aside from his usually masturbating me to climax – which he seemed to enjoy – he had so far never come close to real reciprocity. I was still waiting a signal that might indicate he was interested in fucking my ass – and praying it would come soon, knowing how I would thrill to that fat nine inches of throbbing meat driving in and out of me.

I was extremely busy during that first year at Dowd, but between busily lusting after Cary and occasionally administering a mutually satisfactory blowjob to Mike, the relative torpor was not unduly problematical.

2. CARY DELIVERS AND UNLOADS

Now as my second year began, and I looked out over another new crop of freshmen, I spotted a real beauty. This one was fairly thin, apparently of slightly over average height, fairly short brown hair, wide set and intelligent large eyes, a generous mouth – with a really captivating smile – and prominent, high cheek bones; the total package was extremely attractive. Even now I cannot quite say why I was so particularly attracted to this one boy, but he struck me at once. It was no doubt a combination of the fact that he was gorgeous, and that he sat in the very front row, so I couldn't miss his beauty. He sprawled there, with his legs spread out before him, and had he been wearing tight jeans, I might have been able to assess his hidden charms, but the loose trousers he wore gave nothing away concerning his endowment. I watched him closely, and as I spoke to the group, orienting them to musical activities at Dowd, I often caught his eye. During a break for refreshments, I made it a point to speak with him. Unfortunately, he was not wearing a nametag, and even though I talked with him and introduced myself, he did not offer his name. I was frustrated, in a way. Anyone this attractive, and I thought him among the most attractive young men I had ever seen, should have a name I could use when I fantasized about him – and I knew instinctively that I would be evoking his beauty when I masturbated. Unfortunately, it was to be many months before I learned this beautiful boy's name.

Over the course of that year, I frequently encountered the stunning young dreamboat from orientation, but never had a chance to speak with him, other than casually saying, "Hi," in passing – to which he invariably responded with a small smile and a like greeting. Fortunately, things were progressing much better with my first-year orientation dreamboat, Cary. Over the summer, I had acquired a new car, a very sexy Chevrolet Impala convertible, and Cary – like everyone else – was mightily impressed with it. With my hot new wheels, it was never a problem to coax him to go out for a beer or a cup of coffee, and he was especially pleased when I threw the keys to him and told him to drive. He permitted the occasional hand on his leg as he drove, but if I began to move it to his inner thigh, or up toward his crotch, he always gently removed it. A couple of weeks into the semester, as we were driving around one night, I had ventured to squeeze his leg, and he had permitted me to move my hand closer to "the promised land" than ever before. He pulled into a highway picnic area, cut the ignition, and turned to me.

"What exactly do you want?"

I looked into his eyes a long time before I replied. "Cary, I think you know full well what I want."

"Look, Dr. Harrison ..."

"I thought we agreed you'd call me John when we were together."

"Okay ... John. Look, I think I do know what you want. You want to pull my dick out of my pants, don't you?"

"That would be great, as a beginning."

"Suppose I let you do it, what then?"

"Look, I'm going to ask you, as a friend, to keep this strictly between you and me, okay?"

"Of course I will. So you do want to play with my dick?"

"Okay ... Yes, I want to play with your dick. Hasn't anyone else ever played with you that way?"

"Well, a few girls have ... and I loved it, but I've never let a guy play with me before. Well ... I take it back; when I was growing up my cousin and I used to mess around some, but that was just kid stuff."

"Well, I'm interested in man stuff with you. Kid stuff doesn't mean anything to me."

"I didn't think it did. So ... you want me to get my prick out and let you suck it? Or what?"

"Would you like that?"

"I guess I'd like getting sucked off. Hell, I'd love getting sucked off, but I'd rather a girl was doing it."

"Cary, I know what this makes me in your eyes, but I'm going to level with you. I'd like to suck your cock, I'd like to get you naked and hold you in my arms, I'd like to kiss you, I'd like to play with your ass while I jack off, I'd like for you to shoot your load in my mouth. And if I could have my way, that would be just for starters. Straightforward enough?"

To his credit, Cary laughed. "That's straightforward enough all right!" His laugh broke the tension. "Look, John, I really don't go for that. I don't mind that you're that way ... that you're ...well ..."

"Oh hell, Cary, say it. That I'm queer." Gay was still a few years away as the adjective of choice.

"Okay, right, that you're queer. Well, I don't mind, but I don't want to have sex with you. I like you a lot ... really, a whole lot ... but just as a friend. Can't we still be friends even if I don't let you suck me off?"

"Of course we can. I like you a lot, too, and not just because I'm hot for you. If you won't let me ... well, just promise me you'll think about it, okay? That can't hurt anything, can it?"

"Look, I'll think about it, but I can tell you I'm pretty sure nothing's going to happen. Okay?"

"Fair enough. Just understand I really want you, but I also like you a lot, and whatever happens, that's not going to change. And if you don't mind my saying so, I think you're one of the most handsome and attractive guys I've ever seen."

"Well, thanks. It's nice to know you admire me, but let's just leave it there right now, okay? But I promise I will think about it."

Cary had allowed my hand to remain on his leg as we talked. He now took hold of it, and removed it. Then he changed his mind and put it back – over his crotch! "I guess you can squeeze it a little bit, if you want, but I'm not taking it out of my pants. Okay?"

I began to gently squeeze his crotch, and was rewarded with a considerable growth inside. Cary sat perfectly still, saying nothing, but his cock was getting hard, and bulged along his pants leg. I stroked it as I said, "Jesus that feels wonderful!"

"If you want to jack yourself off while you feel it, I don't mind."

"You're sure?"

"Hell, it's not gonna hurt me. Go ahead, if it will make you feel better." I unzipped my pants, took my cock out, and began to stroke it as I returned my hand to Cary's prick, which was by then rock-hard. He spread his legs and stretched out while I played with him and beat my own cock frantically. As I neared orgasm and began to pant heavily, Cary began to hump gently, and I was actually masturbating him at the same time, but through his trousers.

"Stop for a minute," Cary said, and unzipped his pants. He pulled his cock out and said, "What the hell, you can suck it while you beat off." I dove for his lap, and took his luscious prick in my mouth. It wasn't especially big, but it certainly wasn't small, and as I began to suck, he began to fuck upwards into my mouth. His hands grasped my head as he fucked me. "You want me to cum in your mouth?" I nodded as I continued to nurse eagerly. He began to moan wordlessly and stepped up the pace of his fucking. Soon he began to pant. "Here … take it!"

His cock shot a long series of copious spurts of hot cum deep inside my throat. "Oh shit, that feels great! Take my load, John … take it all." I continued to suck greedily long after he stopped ejaculating, and while he calmed down he allowed me to lick him and suck his cock gently as it grew flaccid. At the same time I continued to masturbate, and soon Cary put a couple of Kleenex in my hand, saying, "Here. Sounds like you're gonna need these." In just a minute I did need them, and I shot my load into the tissue as I continued to make love to Cary's now-soft cock. After I calmed down, Cary gently pulled his prick from my mouth, restored it to his pants, and zipped up. "Was that what you wanted?"

"God yes! Thank you, Cary … it was wonderful!"

"I don't know why I let you do that. I guess you really got me horny. And I don't think it's gonna happen again, but if you really liked it, well, I guess it was all right this one time. But don't you dare ever tell anyone about it."

"Of course I won't … and I hope you won't tell anyone either." I put my hand on his crotch and caressed it; I was especially pleased to note that he did not stop me. "Thanks again, and promise to think about letting me do it again, okay? Didn't it feel good?"

He put his hand over mine and pressed it to his cock. "I think you can tell I enjoyed getting off … and your mouth felt great when I fucked it, but it just doesn't seem right."

"That's okay ... it felt right enough for both of us, as far as I'm concerned. I can't tell you how much I enjoyed eating your load."

"Hey, that's okay. I guess once in a while, that's what friends are for, right?" He ruffled my hair and laughed as he said it.

"Right. Thanks again, friend." I squeezed his crotch and laughed as I replied, and he let me leave my hand on it as we drove back to campus – a very promising sign.

About halfway through the football season, Cary asked if he could borrow my car for a weekend, so he could go up to Knoxville, Tennessee, for a very special date. He figured the flashy convertible would impress the girl mightily.

It would certainly have been possible for me to do without my car for a few days. It would have been only a bit inconvenient, but I told Cary my insurance wouldn't cover him and offered to go along with him and stay in a motel while he went on his date. I said I would pay for the motel, where I assumed we would both stay. I obviously hoped for an opportunity to get him in bed.

He agreed to the arrangement, adding, "But I'm dating a girl, you understand. I'm not going to be dating you, right?"

"Of course not. You're probably going to get some pussy, and I'm probably going to be frustrated as hell, but I guess I can deal with it."

Early that Saturday morning, we headed for Knoxville and checked into a motel on arrival, around noon. I booked the room, and told the woman at the desk we would only need one bed, since that would be cheaper. She said she'd give us two beds for the price of one. "Two nice young fellows like you should each have a bed."

Cary laughed when I described the desk clerk as a meddling bitch as I told him about her giving us two beds. I told him, "I know you're not going to allow anything to happen between us, but I was hoping I could at least sleep next to you."

He laughed again. "Hell, John, it's an imperfect world. Besides, I'm probably going to be all used up when I get back to the motel, if this date is half as good as I'm expecting."

"Well, you can at least sit on my bed and tell me about it, okay?"

"That's a deal." He prepared for his date and left me behind at the motel, where I spent a long day and evening reading and thinking about Cary. And hoping that somehow something would develop between us that night.

It was after midnight before he came into the room. He seemed happy enough. "How was the date?"

He sat on the edge of the bed. "Well, it was fine. She really liked the car and told me to tell you thanks for letting us use it."

"I was glad to do it, and I'm glad you had a good time. Did you have a really good time, or what?"

He laughed. "Well, I didn't get any, if that's what you mean. She'd only go so far, and we hardly ever got away from her roommate and her roommate's date. So, you might be happy to hear I'm horny as hell."

"I'm not going to lie to you and tell you I'm sorry you're horny, but I am sorry your date wasn't all you expected it to be. So ... you're horny; does that mean ...?"

"No, I'm tired, John. I'm supposed to meet her for breakfast at nine o'clock, and I need to get some sleep." He put his hand on my chest. "You okay with that?"

I put my hand over his and squeezed it. "Sure. I'd love to do something with you, but I understand. Will you do something for me before you go to bed, though?"

"Look, it was really nice of you to come up here with me, and let me use your car. I appreciate it, and I really am sorry I can't return what you feel for me. But ... sure, I'll do something for you if I can. What is it?"

"This may seem queerer to you than letting me suck you off, but ...will you kiss me before you get in that bed all the way over there?"

Cary smiled at me for a long time, then leaned over and planted a very sweet, chaste kiss on my lips. "Goodnight, John. Thanks again." Then another short kiss, and he stripped down to his shorts, climbed into his bed, and turned out the light.

Even with the lights out, it was easy to see in the room; there was ample ambient light from the motel's large neon sign to see Cary's form as he lay in the bed across from me. I had napped a bit during the early evening, and was not remotely sleepy. Furthermore, I was very horny, thinking about the beautiful, sexy man who had just kissed me, but who did not want anything further to develop between us. I lay on my side watching him. He tossed and turned for a while, then was quiet, and then again began to stir under the sheet that covered him. Finally, he got out of the bed, and I watched him walk across the space between the beds, where he stood and looked down at me. I was thrilled to see that his shorts were pulled down below his balls, his prick was standing straight out from his body, and he was stroking it gently as he looked at me. Shadows in the room made it impossible for him to see if I was awake or not.

He stood that way for three or four minutes, and then I threw the sheet off my body, raised my legs, and slipped my own shorts completely off. I lay on my back, completely naked. Cary simply stood there for a minute or so longer, then slipped his shorts down and stepped out of them. I got out of the bed and knelt before him. Without a word he stepped toward me, dropped his hands to his side, and said, "Do you want me?"

His prick looked perfectly beautiful as it bobbed before my eyes. I reached up and took it gently in one hand and kissed the tip very gently. "I want this as much as I've ever wanted anything."

11

"You can have it tonight. I want you to make love to it again."

I put my hands on his hips and held him as I moved my mouth below his balls and began to lick them. He murmured his satisfaction and held my head in his hands as I took his balls in my mouth and began to suck – they were quite large, and tasted wonderful. I began licking the underside of his prick, licked all the way to the end, then began licking up and down slowly.

"Take it in your mouth, John. Take my big fucking prick down your throat again." He held my head tightly now as he drove his cock into my eager mouth. "Suck it for me. Suck the cum out of my cock … I want to fuck your mouth again!" I sucked hard and Cary drove his cock deep into my throat, fucking me eagerly. My hands sought his fiercely driving buttocks; then with one finger I began to play with the opening of his asshole, and with the other hand I cupped his balls while he fucked my mouth. His breath was coming fast, and his voice was growing hoarse. "Oh shit, that feels so good! Suck me, take my big prick all the way inside!" Cary's prick was larger than I remembered it, and while it wasn't the monster size that Mike had been giving me, it was a real mouthful – and he was burying it in my mouth with such savage thrusts that it seemed almost too big to accommodate.

I released his prick and stood to put my arms around him. "Kiss me again." He put his arms tightly around me and this time he planted a very passionate kiss on my lips. I opened my mouth, and our tongues began a frantic interplay, both of us murmuring in ecstasy and grinding our pelvises together. My hands sought his undulating ass – rounded, velvet smooth, very muscular, very exciting – and caressed and kneaded it. He held my ass as I humped.

I broke the kiss. "Lie down on the bed." I took his hand, lay on my back, and pulled him down on top of me. "Fuck my mouth, Cary; I want to eat your big cock." He kissed me again, and I slid my body down below him so that his cock was directly over my mouth, and he drove it all the way into my throat. I reached up and held his ass as he raised his body with his arms, and did push-ups over me.

He was driving his prick as deep into my mouth as it would go. I gagged some, but was able to relax my throat enough that I could accept even his deepest thrust. He murmured a breathy, passionate litany of approval: "Oh God, your mouth is so fuckin' hot! Suck this big prick for me! Gonna fuck your mouth like it's never been fucked!"

To say that I was enjoying this would be an understatement of truly epic dimension. This beautiful, hot man I had been craving for over a year was concentrating every fiber of his being on fucking me – and he was a truly masterful fucker. He pounded my mouth for a long time, until I held him away so I could speak. "Don't cum too soon, Cary; please make this last … I've wanted it for so long."

He sat back and took my head in his hands. "I've gotta get my load …
but I swear I won't quit. Just let me cum in you, and then we'll have all night to
play. I won't quit after one load, Okay?"

"That's a deal. Give it to me, then … fuck my mouth and let me drink
that hot cum again."

He gave me a quick kiss, then raised my head from the bed, cradled it
in both his arms, and shoved his cock deep into me again as he started to fuck
wildly. His ass felt magnificent as it writhed beneath my hands, and his moans
of pleasure were wonderful to hear. After about five minutes of frantic mouth-
fucking, he accelerated his pace to a frantic level and called out, "Take my load
… eat my cum. Here it is, John … take it, take it!"

His last words were said as his cum shot violently into the back of my
throat. It was all I could do to avoid gagging as he filled my mouth with his
enormous load. I didn't want to lose any of it, and managed to swallow just
enough as he was shooting to avoid that. His prolonged and plentiful orgasm
filled my mouth when he had finished, and I savored every delicious drop of the
wonderful lotion, bathing my tongue and tonsils in it. Finally, keeping his prick
as far into my throat as possible, he fell on his side, still cradling my head in his
arms. "Oh shit, that felt wonderful. God damn, but you're a great cocksucker!"
He began to gently hump my mouth again, with his now-softening prick
swimming in the mouthful of cum I still retained; at the same time I teased his
prick with my tongue. He panted, "Jesus, that is so wonderful … you are one
great fuck."

I finally released his cock and swallowed his generous offering. "Jesus
Christ, Cary – you are a great fucker. No, you're a stupendous fucker! That was
a huge load."

He released me and fell on his back. "Man, you wore me out."

"Don't forget you promised me ..."

He laughed. "You're not through. I've got a lotta cum left, and you're
not getting out of this room until you drain me dry." He raised himself on one
elbow and kissed me quickly. "I'm gonna have this cock back in that hot mouth
of yours before you know it."

"Your date doesn't know what she missed."

"No, and you're gonna get every bit of it."

"Jesus, Cary, I ... thanks so much for ..."

"Look. I'm incredibly horny. We're fucking. It's great … and it's
gonna be greater, but that's it. Okay? I don't want you to make something out of
this that its not."

"Just give me your prick and I'm happy. I'll just settle for tonight right
now."

"Fair enough." He got up and peed, and before he could get back in the
bed I stood to intercept him, holding and kissing him where he stood. I ran my
hands all over his body, licked his broad chest and sucked his nipples, then

13

turned him around to kiss and lick his adorable ass. He leaned forward and used his hands to spread his asscheeks while I buried my face in the heaven between them. I kissed his asshole, and then began to penetrate it with my darting tongue. He wriggled his ass and moaned, "God that feels great!"

I was encouraged to put as much of my tongue into him as I could, and tongue-fucked his writhing asshole to the best of my ability while his hands reached back to pull my head into his busy ass When I stopped, he turned around, and his cock was again standing straight out. "Look what you did. Guess I'm just gonna have to ask for another blow job."

I stood and held him in my arms and kissed him. "You don't have to ask."

"You want me to pump another big load in you?"

"You know I do." And we returned to the bed.

Cary lay on his back as I knelt over him and sucked, but then he rolled over and raised his ass so that I could kiss and eat it again. As my tongue penetrated him, he raised up on his knees and he gasped in absolute delight. Then I drew his prick behind him, through his legs, and sucked it that way as I played with his balls.

He collapsed to the bed and rolled on his back, his legs between my knees as I knelt over him. He looked up at me and grinned, "Jesus, but you are good at this."

I raised his legs up to my shoulders, with his stiff prick almost in my face. I sucked it for a few minutes, and then pressed his knees down to meet his shoulders so that I could again bury my face in his ass. As I did so, I began to masturbate him at the same time. He groaned in ecstasy as my tongue drove fiercely in and out of his tight asshole. Shortly, I lowered his legs to the bed and again began to suck his cock. Moving up where I was lying directly over him, we began a long session of very passionate kissing. Cary was humping his cock against me and fondling my ass as eagerly as I was fondling his head while we kissed.

He rolled us over, so that he was now on top. "I can't believe I'm actually kissing a guy."

"You're making love to a guy. The kissing's just part of it."

"I'm fucking a guy. This isn't love, John … it's just fucking. And I never thought we'd be doing this, but I gotta admit it's a helluva lot of fun."

I raised my legs, and rested them on his shoulders, so that Cary's prick was poking up against my asshole. "Okay, no love. Just shut up and fuck."

He laughed and humped my asshole with his cock. I feel sure he had no idea of actually fucking me that way, but gradually his cock began to seek entrance to me, and I encouraged him to fuck my ass. With some patience and a little spit, he soon had his prick buried deep inside me as he lay over me. "Now I'm really going to fuck you." He knelt and held my legs up as he began a really savage assault on my ass.

14

"That's it, Cary. Fuck me … really fuck me!"

"God damn, yes," he gasped, as I threw my legs back, and he fell over me. He drove his ravenous prick as deeply into me as he could, pulling back almost to the point of removal with each reverse stroke. He was panting and grunting, and crying out in passion as he delivered a stupendous fuck. He seized my cock as he fucked, and masturbated me with as much enthusiasm as he was bringing to exercising his own.

"God, Cary, I'm gonna cum."

"Shoot your load … here comes mine, too." And with that, my cock began spewing all over his hand and my face and chest, and I could feel Cary's violent eruption deep inside me. We were both almost screaming with passion, and after several final thrusts and shudders, he collapsed over me and buried his tongue in my mouth, holding me tight and kissing me – wildly at first, but gradually gentler and more sweetly.

We lay in embrace for a long time until he said, very quietly, "Jesus, that was incredible!"

"I've never been fucked better. Thank you, Cary."

"No … thank you, John. I wouldn't have believed that I could actually fuck you, but I'm so glad you let me. And it was really hot to see you shoot your load, too."

I turned around and snuggled back against him – my ass up to his now fairly flaccid dick. "Just hold me in your arms." He cradled me, and we drifted off to sleep. At one point I awoke, and his prick was very hard and pressing against my ass. I backed up onto it, and Cary murmured his delight as he gradually filled my eager hole again, still so full of his cum that he had no trouble inserting it. We returned to sleep with him inside me.

As it was just beginning to get light, he got out of bed and peed again. He returned and stood over me. "I cleaned my dick off. Wanna taste it and see?"

"Get over here and shove it in me."

Cary knelt over my face and sank his hard prick in my mouth. "I've got another huge load to give you." He plunged himself into me with the longest strokes he could manage, but slowly, and – I felt – lovingly. All the time he murmured endearments: "God, your mouth is hot, Take every inch of this big prick. I want to fill you up with cum again. God I love to fuck your mouth." Then, after a long time of delighting me this way, he cradled my head in his arms and drove his prick as deep in my throat as it would go, and held it there. "I don't want to cum yet. Just suck me while I stay in you."

I sucked slowly, but with maximum vacuum, using my tongue to stimulate the big shaft he held buried in my throat. He almost purred his satisfaction, whispering in my ear, "God, John, my cock has found a home in your hot mouth."

I took my mouth from his cock. "Welcome home, Cary." and I returned it to its rightful place and recommenced my worship.

Finally Cary pulled himself from me. "I'm almost ready to cum, but I don't want you to stop loving my cock yet. Let me get you off. How do you want to do it?"

"Can I cum on you?"

"Sure ... that would be hot." He rolled on his back, and I straddled him as I began to masturbate. He reached up and took over for me. "You wanna give me another big load?" I murmured my assent as I fucked his hand, keenly aware of his hard prick pressing up against my asshole.

"Let me eat your ass again, Cary." He threw his legs in the air, and I pressed my face into him to tongue-fuck his asshole as deeply as I could, while he almost whimpered with delight. At the same time I was jacking off, and soon I could hold back no longer. I raised up, and held my prick over his asshole as I masturbated it. "Gonna shoot my load on your beautiful ass."

"Do it. Give me your load!"

I began to shoot violently, directing most of it onto his ass, but much also splashed up onto his chest. He rubbed the cum on his chest, "God that's hot ... give it to me!" As I finished cumming, Cary swiped his hand over his asshole, scooping up my cum. He spread his legs wide, so they fell to the bed on either side of me, and he spread my cum all over his cock. "Suck your cum off my cock, and don't stop until you get every drop of mine."

I leaned down and opened my mouth to Cary's violent thrusts. He locked his legs around my neck, grasped my head tightly in his hands, and fucked upward into me. At the same time I was driving my mouth up and down his prick, lips locked tightly around it. Our joint efforts paid off in just a few minutes as his cum began to explode inside my mouth – and kept spurting as he continued to fuck. "Suck it, eat my cum, God damn that is so fuckin' hot!"

I sucked every drop of cum from Cary's softening prick, swallowed it, and continued to hold him inside me as I fondled his ass and murmured my contentment. His legs were still around my neck, and his hands still held my head, but now gently, and he ruffled my hair as he continued to hump very quietly into me. "Damn, John. I've never shot a bigger or a better load. Jesus, I love the way you suck cock."

I moved up, took him in my arms, and lay over him. His arms went around me, and we looked meaningfully into each other's eyes for a long time. He eventually broke the serious look we were exchanging and grinned. "And I was planning to fuck your ass again." We kissed for a long time, our tongues intertwining slowly, but very erotically. Cary held my face in his hands. "That's my cum I taste in your mouth, isn't it?"

It was my turn to grin. "Tastes great, doesn't it?"

"It's not too bad at that."

"So, if you were planning to fuck my ass again, why don't you do it? I'll bet we can get that big cock of yours hard again in no time."

16

"Shit, I could have it hard and inside you in a minute, but I've got to meet my date for breakfast, and I'd better get moving. We'll do it another time, okay?"

"You promise?"

He grinned. "I promise; I'll fuck your brains out." He kissed me quickly, winked, and headed for the shower. As he left, he agreed to be back by noon – checkout time – and asked that I pack his clothes for him, so we would be ready to go.

As he got ready to go out the door, I put my arms around him. "Thanks again for last night ... and this morning was even better."

He held me tightly. "I can't believe we did what we did. But I have to admit I enjoyed the hell out of it. Thank you. I don't know why I didn't give you what you wanted a long time ago." He kissed me for a long time – sweetly, but at that point it meant more to me than a passionate kiss. "You're a helluva guy, John." He was gone.

I passed the rest of the morning with a leisurely shower, packing, and reading. Shortly before noon, I was ready to leave, waiting only on Cary. He appeared about five minutes before checkout time.

"I made it. Let me take a leak, and we'll hit the road." He went in the bathroom, and I could hear him pissing loudly. Then he was quiet for a time, and called out, "Checkout time is noon?" I said it was. He came out of the bathroom, his pants undone, his shorts pulled below his balls, and his prick fully erect. "I think we need to do something about this." He called the front desk and asked if we could check out an hour late; they agreed. By this time I had knelt in front of him and had taken his cock in my mouth.

He fucked me gently as I dragged his pants down and played with his humping ass, and his hands held my head tight. He raised me to my feet and kissed me. "Get your clothes off. I told you I wanted to fuck your ass again." He was already stripping his clothes off. I was naked in a matter of seconds, and managed to unpack a tube of Vaseline I had in my shaving kit. We fell onto the bed and began a long session of passionate kissing and writhing – our hands all over each other. Finally he told me to get on my knees. I knelt on all fours, and handed him the Vaseline. He greased himself up, and applied it liberally to my asshole, using two or three fingers to massage it deep inside me. He grasped my waist in his hands and positioned himself behind me. "You want my prick inside you?"

"Fuck me as hard as you can, Cary, shove that prick all the way inside me, and fill me with your cum again."

He drove himself deep into my asshole with one fierce lunge, and began fucking me savagely. "God damn, John, your ass feels so fuckin' good." He fucked wildly for a long time, grunting in passion, and urging me to take his cock.

17

"God, Cary, you are so fucking beautiful and hot; I want your cum in me again … deep inside me. Fuck me with that huge prick, baby, fill me with your cum!"

With a wild cry he shouted, "Here it is!" and I felt his prick discharging another massive offering deep inside me. I rose to my knees, and Cary's arms went around me to hold me tight. I began to jack off, but he took over, and as I put my arms behind me to pull his ass in and keep his prick inside me, he squeezed my balls with one hand, and masturbated me savagely with the other. He nibbled on my ear, and gasped into it, "Shoot your load for me again!" I began to spray cum all over the bed, and Cary encouraged me. "That's so hot … shoot for me. Show me your cum!"

"Oh Jesus, Cary … you make me so fucking hot! Your cock still feels huge in my ass."

"Your ass feels so fucking hot, I can't believe it." He began gently humping, and within minutes he was fully erect again, and fucking me in earnest – his driving prick bathed inside me in his own cum. "God damn, I wanna keep fucking you. Is that all right with you?"

"Jesus, I can't think of anything I'd rather have than two loads of Cary Adams' cum inside me at the same time." He pulled out quickly, took my hand, and led me across the room, where he sat down in a straight chair as I straddled and faced him, He pulled me down, and my distended ass settled down immediately over his prick, which I began to ride frantically. His arms were tight around my neck, and we kissed hungrily as I rode, and he humped me as best he could from his seated position. My feet were planted firmly on the floor, and the leverage allowed my ass-ring to travel the complete length of his prick with every stroke as I pistoned up and down his hot shaft.

Cary buried his face on my chest and began to suck my nipples; in a few minutes his breathing signaled the onset of another orgasm. "Oh fuck! Here it comes … take it, John!" He raised his ass off the chair, and I felt another explosion inside me. His hands held me tightly, and he almost whimpered in passion.

"No one has ever fucked me twice in a row without a break, like you just did. God, Cary … you're so fucking beautiful, and you're such an incredible stud."

"Shit, John … you inspire me. I've never shot two loads in a row like that. Your ass is so hot … I love fucking it."

"I hope you're going to be fucking me a lot in the future."

"Get used to the feel of this prick up your ass. I've got a feeling it's gonna be there a lot."

"And in my mouth?"

He grinned and kissed me. "Oh, yeah! You're gonna eat a lotta my cum, too,"

"I can't get enough of your cum to satisfy me, however you give it to me."

I began masturbating as I sat, still impaled on his prick. He continued humping me as he panted, "Shoot on me, John ... get your load again." In only a minute or so, my cum shot all over our two stomachs. We sat and kissed for a long time before breaking I stood and Cary's prick slid out of my ass.

When we were fully dressed and about to go out the door, Cary took me in his arms, kissed me and nibbled my neck as he said lovingly in my ear, "Look, I never would have believed this could happen, and I sure as hell wouldn't have thought I'd enjoy it like I did."

"But you did?"

"I loved fucking you, John ... and if you want, I'll fuck you again and again."

"Oh God, Cary ... I want it. You know I do."

"Okay, but understand that I date girls, okay? And what we do is because we're friends, and we both enjoy it. Right? You're not gonna fall in love with me or anything, are you?"

"I'm gonna love your cock, and I'm gonna love your fucking me, and I'm gonna love being with you, but I promise it's just a special kind of friendship. But whether you like it or not, I'm always going to think you're beautiful and incredibly attractive."

He kissed me. "Fair enough. And thanks for thinking I'm attractive. That kind of turns me on, you know?"

"Great. I'm for anything that will turn you on!"

The trip back to Dowd was almost six hours, and Cary was exhausted. He fell asleep with his head in my lap, and I fingered his fine blond hair and caressed his body as he did so. I was about as happy as I could be. The weekend had exceeded my wildest hopes to an unbelievable extent.

Two incredibly hot young guys now seemed to be lined up for my sexual gratification. It was hard to decide which was more exciting, Mike's unbelievable endowment, or Cary's blond beauty. Of course I had yet to get Mike's meat up my butt, and I had never been able to kiss him, but the size of his cock made up for a lot of shortcomings – and hopefully, I was going to be able to broaden the scope of Mike's participation soon.

Both were masterful lovers, each in his own way, and I really should not have thought past that, although I must admit I also desperately wanted to be doing to someone else's ass what Cary was doing to mine, and I also longed for someone to be performing the same service for my cock that I was providing for both Cary's and Mike's. Still, I should have been satisfied – in my opinion, it's a lot better to receive than to give, if you're talking about fucking and sucking with hot young men. But I must confess I also love the giving part of it.

Even with the wonderful, if not completely idyllic situation I now found myself in, the occasional encounter with the handsome young man I had seen at Orientation that fall served to make my imagination run riot. I still did not even know his name, but was absolutely fascinated by his beauty. I was usually able to greet him when we passed, and he was always friendly, but I never had occasion to stop and talk with him.

He was taller than I remembered, probably close to six feet, and had an easygoing, assured walk that I found endlessly sexy and fascinating as I trailed admiringly after him when the opportunity presented itself. He frequently wore rather brief walking shorts, and his legs were extremely well muscled, and wonderfully, sexily, long. He never seemed to wear really tight clothes, so I could only guess at the contour of his ass – I suspected perfection – or the bulk of his cock and balls. I regularly guessed about those features as I fantasized over him, however, and in my dreams he had a darling bubble butt, and was hung like a mule. His chest was not massive, but his shoulders were broad and his waist was narrow. In short: a fine body. But, the face – my God, the face! He seemed more perfectly beautiful every time I saw him, and his wide smile showed wonderfully white, even teeth.

This so-far nameless beauty made my heart beat a lot faster every time I encountered him. I needed a name for him, since I regularly wished to call out his name when I thought about his beauty as I jacked off. Murmuring "Oh, God, What's-your-name, fuck me!" seemed more than a little strange as a masturbatory mantra. I settled on "Danny" as an appropriate name for him, in honor of the first real crush I had ever experienced.

Danny Morales had been an unbelievably handsome guy I worked with when I was fourteen years old, and who would always occupy a special place in my life – his having been the first ass I ever played with, his prick the first I ever sucked, his cum the first I ever tasted, his mouth the first I ever fucked, etc. So my latest crush, for the time being, bore the same name – although, aside from his also being a stunning beauty, he seemed to resemble his fantasy namesake only bodily. Would I ever get to meet him, and share at least some of the thrills I had with the other Danny? I certainly hoped so; my luck seemed to be running pretty well, after all: the only two other guys I was really lusting after at the moment had both shot their hot cum inside me, and the promise of a steady diet of that delicious fare seemed likely. But I desperately wanted the new "Danny" on the menu as well.

3. PHONE SEX AND A PROMISE

If I had expected Cary to be unusually friendly when I saw him the Monday after our trip to Knoxville, I was disappointed. If anything, he was a bit cool. I tried to catch him as he left band rehearsal, but he got away before I could speak with him. The same thing happened for the next two successive days, so I called him at his dorm room; fortunately, his roommate was out.

"Cary, I've really wanted to talk with you, but you seem to be avoiding me. Are you mad at me about last weekend?"

"No, but I have to admit I'm confused about what happened, about how I acted."

"I thought you enjoyed it; you sure seemed to."

"I did, John, and that's what confuses me. I know I shouldn't have enjoyed myself, but you've got to be aware of how much I enjoyed it. I've never had any experience that was so ... intense, and I sure never shot that many loads in that short a time."

"Look, if you don't want to get together with me again, I'll understand. I can't tell you how disappointed I'd be, but I would understand."

"No, no, that's not it. I want to be with you again ... hell, I've got a hard-on now just thinking about it, and I'd love to give it to you ... but I just need to think things through a bit. Will you be patient?"

"Of course I will. And I've got a helluva hard-on myself, thinking about you having a hard-on."

"Do this for me: go jack off and pretend my prick is all the way up your butt while you do it, and I'll go jack off and pretend I'm there giving it to you. Okay?"

"God, Cary, of course I will. In fact, I'm jacking off right now."

"Go ahead and jack off while we're on the phone." He lowered his voice, speaking softly and suggestively, and I could tell by the breathiness and hoarseness that developed as he talked, that he was stroking his cock as he spoke. "Think of what it felt like when I was fucking your throat ... and your lips were tight around my prick, riding up and down every inch of it." I was masturbating frantically. "Did my cum taste good when you ate it? Could you feel me shooting my load up inside your ass? Don't you wish I were fucking your ass right now? Deep strokes ... in and out, in and out, shoving all the way inside you, then almost pulling out, then all the way back in ... fucking you with my hard prick, deep as I can. How would that feel? If you could only see how hard I'm stroking my own prick right this minute." He was now panting so hard he could barely speak. "It's so hard and so big ... suck it for me, suck all the cum out of it and swallow it for me."

"Oh God, Cary, I'm gonna cum!"

Just as my orgasm began, Cary gasped, "Me, too. I'm gonna shoot a huge load, and soon I'm gonna give you another one in person ... soon ... up your butt and down your throat ... oh God, here it is! Oh man, so much cum ...

I'm gonna give you so much more cum! Oh John, my cum, my cum! Ooooohhhh! … oh, it's so hot! Oh God, oh God ... it's all over me."

"Jesus Cary, I wish I were with you. I'd lick up every wonderful drop of it"

He gradually stopped panting. "Shit, I should have been giving that to you in person, John ... and I will, and soon. Look, I'm confused about what I'm feeling, okay? I know I'm feeling a way I never thought I would, so just give me some time, and if you do that, I'll give you plenty of cock and plenty of cum. I don't know what that's going to mean, you understand, but if it only means we're good friends who fuck, at least we'll have that, okay?"

"Of course, Cary … I'll give you all the time you want."

"And I'll give you all the cock you want."

"And all the cum I want, too … remember!"

"And plenty of my hot cum for you to eat. Thanks again for the weekend, John, and actually, thanks for this phone call, too … I wound up having a good time."

"If you're in the same condition I am, you'd better go clean up."

He laughed, "I sure need to. We'll talk soon, but let me tell you when we can get together, okay? I'll let you know as soon as I'm ready."

"I'll be looking forward to it." And, as it happened, I didn't have to wait long for a break-through. In fact, a tremendous experience was right around the corner.

Mike called late one night a week or so later. "You want to come and get me? I've got something I'd like to deliver to your house."

"Wow, a house call this late?"

"I believe this delivery is gonna take all night long."

"Is long the key word there?"

"Well, along with hard, and fat, and juicy … yeah."

"Damn, I don't know which sounds better. Fifteen minutes, in front of the dorm?"

"You got it. Turn down the bedspread."

"Mike, I'm not turning anything down tonight."

"I know you're not gonna turn down what I've got for you." He laughed and hung up.

I immediately got in my car and headed for campus. The last sex I had was with Cary, but only by telephone – and I was horny as hell. The thought of having Mike's monster cock in me was even more welcome than it would normally have been.

The trip into town took about fifteen minutes. I had built a small house out in the country, on a large lake, where my only neighbors were a married couple, good friends of mine, who only used their lake house on occasional weekends. Their large swimming pool was available to me at all times, and although by this time of year it was not usable, it served to enhance my life-style

22

considerably in warm weather. We were now well into November, and any activities Mike and I engaged in tonight would be strictly indoors, although on a particularly warm night less than a month earlier, I had knelt over Mike's nude body as he lay spread-eagled on a blanket next to the pool, romantically moonlit, with his monster cock straining for the stars until my hungry mouth engulfed it and sucked a memorable explosion of cum from it.

Mike was waiting as I pulled up in front of the dormitory. He opened the driver-side door, said, "Slide over," and got behind the wheel. Before he put the car in gear, he undid his belt, unbuttoned his fly, and took his cock and balls out. He stroked his prick only a few times before it was hard, and truly formidable. "Man, I'm horny. Think you can take care of this for me tonight?"

I reached over and took him in my hand. "You know I want it. God that looks great!"

"Look good enough to eat?" He reached over and pulled my head down into his lap, where I took his cock in my mouth and sucked hungrily as he put the car in gear and began to drive. His hand played with my head while I fed on his massive organ. "Jesus, that's what I need!" My tongue lapped his shaft and played with the huge head, and my lips drove up and down as Mike murmured satisfaction. Finally he pulled my head away from his prick. "We'd better hold off … I'm about ready to cum right now. Wait until we get to your house, and get ready for a huge blast down your throat … and that's just gonna be for openers."

"What's come over you, Mike? All the times we've been together, you've hardly ever talked about what we're doing. You let me eat your cock and you give me a couple loads, and that's it. Not that I'm complaining, you understand."

He laughed. "I've been thinking more and more about what we do together, and I'm having to admit to myself I enjoy it more all the time. I got so hot thinking about ... about us today, I just had to see you … and I'll even admit I want us to ... well, expand out activities, I guess you'd say."

"Man, sounds great to me … you know how I feel about you."

"Well, that's the thing … I really enjoy being with you, too, you know, but I've never thought I was queer, and what we've been doing certainly is queer … so I haven't wanted to think about it. I've just got around to admitting to myself that when I'm with you I want more than just getting my cock sucked … I want to really have sex with you, to ... to make love with you, if you want to call it that. Look, I'm not talking about us being in love, or getting serious, or anything, but I sure as hell want to keep having sex with you, and I want to ... bring more to it. I guess what I'm trying to say is that I want us to have something like meaningful sex. You know what I mean?"

"I do, and I'm very happy you feel that way, Mike. Every time I've been with you it's been meaningful to me, though."

"Well, it really has with me, too, but I just figured it's time I admitted it to myself." He laughed. "And to you, too, I guess!"

As he parked my car and got out, his cock was still hard, and protruded from his pants (I had been playing with it during our entire conversation). I knelt in front of him in the driveway and he held my head tightly while he fucked my mouth eagerly for a while. Then he pulled me to my feet and put his arms around me. "Let's get naked and fuck!"

"Or maybe make love, huh?"

He grinned. "Yeah ... let's make love! Of course, it might seem at first like I'm just fucking you in the mouth."

In the house, we didn't even make it to the bedroom before we were both naked. On the carpet in front of the fireplace I crouched over him as he lay on his back and drove his huge prick eagerly up into my mouth. I pushed my head down so far that my nose was in his pubic hair, with my throat relaxed enough that his entire gargantuan shaft was inside me when he humped. He locked his legs around my neck as he pulled my head down onto his frantically driving cock. Soon I was rewarded with a huge spurt of his hot love in my throat, followed by a long series of lesser eruptions – all of which I savored and swallowed as he rolled us on our sides. He cradled my head in his arms and kept his cock in me while he relaxed and his erection subsided somewhat. "Jesus, John, you are good."

I finally released his cock, moved my body upward, and we put our arms around each other. I nibbled his ear and whispered. "You're the one that's good. That is the biggest, hardest cock I've ever sucked ... and nobody ever gave me a load like that."

That was not entirely true, of course, but it seemed like a reasonable thing to say at the time. To be sure, Mike's cock was one of the biggest I'd ever sucked – in the same league as my first lover, Bob, my most recent real lover, Richard, and my Navy studs Fernando and Ron, but still lacking the unbelievable size of the incredibly fat, ten-inch monster tool – ten-inch-plus, more than likely – that the unforgettable Hal Weltmann had repeatedly used to plumb my depths so astonishingly during my last year in college. And it would be impossible to tell whose cock was hardest or whose load biggest: I had entertained some extremely hung young men, who had delivered many truly copious love offerings to my worshipping mouth and hungry ass.

"Make us a drink, and let's get in the bed. I want to fuck your mouth all night long. I don't know how many loads I'm gonna give you, but I'm gonna break my track record tonight. Okay?"

I put a hand behind his head and pulled it in so that we our lips were almost touching. "I can hardly wait." I began to kiss him, but he put a finger over my mouth.

"Make a drink, okay?" He stood, and pulled me to my feet. "Where's the bedroom?"

24

"In there," I said, pointing toward the open door. "Drinks coming up." I turned back after I had taken a few steps toward the bar. "God damn, Mike, you are an incredible stud."

He grinned and winked, "I'm your stud tonight." I watched his cute ass as he headed for the bedroom.

"And your ass is as cute as your dick is hot," I called after him.

He stopped, looked over his shoulder, and wiggled the cute feature under discussion. "Play with both of 'em all you want."

"Wow! All I want?"

He laughed. "Well, play with my dick all you want; my ass may have to be negotiated. Make our drinks and get in here. I can see you're as ready as I am," and he went through the door. It was true. My cock, while not in the same size league as the beautiful monster that protruded at a near-ninety-degree angle from Mike's sexy body, was fully as hard.

He was lying on his back, idly stroking his huge cock when I got to the bedroom. I handed him his drink and sank to my knees at the side of the bed. "Jesus, I love your dick."

He took a sip of his drink, put it on the nightstand, and raised his body so his back rested against the headboard. "Show me how much you love it."

I got on the bed and buried my head in his lap, opening my mouth wide to engulf his challenging monster. The fat shaft began plumbing the depths of my throat again. He held my head and fucked slowly and sensuously, while I deep-throated him and let my mouth more-or-less act as a static receptacle for him to fuck. He murmured his contentment, and his legs spread, rose, and circled my neck. "Suck that big prick, John … make love to it."

I continued to suck for some time, then came up for air, and spent a considerable period of time sucking his large balls while I stroked his cock. I raised his legs, spread his buttocks, and buried my face in his ass. My tongue sought his asshole. He raised his legs higher, all the way back until his toes were touching the top of the headboard, and he whimpered with ecstasy as I began to fuck his ass with my tongue.

Mike gasped breathily, "Shit, that feels incredible. Eat my ass, baby … make love to my asshole. Give me that hot tongue as deep as it'll go!"

I rimmed him until I was too tired to continue, with Mike continually moaning in ecstasy, and encouraging me in passionate terms. Finally, I stopped, and again took his cock in my mouth. It was incredibly hard and seemed impossibly large. His legs fell to the bed on either side of me, and keeping his plunging prick inside my adoring mouth, I dragged his body down where I could kneel over him to suck then reversed my body so that his head now lay beneath my cock and balls. I drove my head as far up and down the considerable length of his magnificent shaft as I could, and he met my downward plunges with upward thrusts of the hot ass I cupped in my hands – driving my nose into his pubic hair, and burying his enormous tool completely inside me.

25

Mike's hands held my waist as he fucked my mouth, and soon he moved them back and began to fondle my ass. In a moment, his finger began to play at the opening of my asshole. "Do you like that, baby? Shall I play with your ass?"

"God, yes, Mike ... fuck me with your finger."

"I'll do better than that. Suck me hard now." And with that, his hands spread my cheeks, and he pressed his face into me and ... unbelievably ... his mouth sought my asshole, and he began to tongue-fuck me as eagerly as I had done to him. I stopped sucking long enough to encourage him to continue, but he stopped rimming me when I did, and he said "Suck!" before he returned to servicing me.

His tongue was darting in and out of me, licking the opening, and moving sinuously around inside me. This unbelievable stud had never kissed me, much less fucked me or sucked my dick – and I doubted he had ever done those things with any boy or man – yet he was eating my ass as eagerly and expertly as anyone ever had. I was ecstatic, and my sucking grew frenzied. He had begun stroking my prick eagerly, and I could contain myself no longer. I shot a load all over Mike's chest as he continued to rim me. Soon he levered his body high above the bed, and it grew rigid as an enormous explosion of cum filled my throat. I continued to suck greedily as Mike tongue-fucked me with equal avidity. We both collapsed, panting heavily in ecstasy, and very gradually his cock grew relatively limp, and he removed his tongue from my ass.

His arms circled my body, and mine his. His face nestled against my ass, and his prick still stayed inside my mouth as I nursed gently on it. Neither of us said a word for some time, until finally I reversed myself and lay over him, face-to-face. "Jesus, Mike."

"I don't know what came over me," he said. I've never been that hot in my life before. Christ, John, I can't believe it ... I just ate your ass. I've never even thought about doing anything like that, but it felt so damned good when you ate mine. I've never felt anything like that before, and I just wanted to please you the way you had me ... and the way you were pleasing me with that hot mouth all around my cock."

"It was wonderful ... you can't imagine how wonderful it felt with your tongue in me, and your load shooting in my mouth at the same time."

He laughed, "Hey, it felt pretty damned good to me, too." He put one hand behind my head and pulled me to him. "Come here." He kissed me, chastely at first then opened his mouth, and our tongues began a passionate intertwining. We rolled on our sides, arms around each other, and necked for a very long time, without saying anything. Then he asked, "You've wanted to do that for a long time, haven't you?"

"God yes, Mike. I've dreamed about kissing you almost as much as I've dreamed of sucking your cock. You're such a hot man, and so damned attractive … and I want to do everything with you, but I didn't think you were going to let me do anything but suck your prick, wonderful as that is."

"I surprised myself. Kissing just seemed so damned queer to me, but I've wanted to. I just held back." He laughed again. "But now ... well, it seems like if I got hot enough to eat your ass, we might as well start kissing, right?" I nodded eagerly. He pulled me tight, and fondled my ass as he said, "Kiss me again, and be my lover tonight … my baby, my piece of ass, my hot fuck!"

After another prolonged bout of alternating passionate and tender kissing, we talked for some time. Mike confessed that he had often been sucked off by other guys – mostly boys his own age, or thereabouts.

"The word seems to be out that I've got a big dick, and a lot of guys have wanted to see it. Some came right out and said they did, and others hinted around until I just asked them if they wanted to. About half of 'em asked if they could feel it, too, and I had to invite the others to feel it if they wanted. But every one of them wanted to handle it. Once they started feeling it, it always got hard right away, and every one of them began to stroke it and play with it. A couple of them just played with it for a while, and then quit, and a few of them played with it until I got a load, but I could tell that most of them wanted to suck it … and all but a handful of them did. I asked some if they wanted to suck me, but most of them didn't wait for an invitation … they just knelt, or bent over my lap, and gobbled. There were quite a few of 'em who pulled their own dicks out and started to beat off while they were jacking me off; I didn't play games with those … I just pushed their heads down and shoved my cock in their mouths.

"Probably forty or fifty guys have sucked my dick, and only two of 'em quit sucking when I started to get my load. One just watched the cum shoot out my dick, and land all over his face and chest. The other one changed his mind when my cum started coating his face, and he opened his mouth to finish me off. The rest have all sucked me all the way off, until I came in their mouths. A few spit my load in their handkerchiefs, but the rest all swallowed every drop I gave 'em.

"For some reason, I was hardly ever tempted to play with any of those guys' dicks when they were sucking me off … I just stood there, or lay there, and let 'em blow me. There were a few who had even bigger dicks than mine, and one who blew the biggest load of cum I ever saw while he was sucking me off. One of the guys with a really big dick asked me to play with him while he came, and I did. I gotta admit his prick felt really good while I stroked it, but when he started to cum, I wasn't tempted to suck it." He laughed," Besides, I don't think I coulda opened my mouth wide enough to get that thing inside.

"I was really surprised when you started sucking me in the hotel room in Atlanta that night, but you gave me as good a blow job as I've ever got. It was the first time I ever got blown while I was really in bed with a guy, and it seemed to be more ... I dunno, more meaningful that way. Hey, I like girls, but ... well, I really enjoyed getting it on with you." A quick kiss and a grin. "And you obviously enjoyed getting it on with me. I was assuming since you were blowing me, you were queer, and I wasn't, and I still don't think I'm queer, but here I am, doing ... I don't know what, with you."

"It's called making love, Mike."

He kissed me and smiled. "Yeah, I guess it is, isn't it? So, do you think I'm queer, or what? You're queer, right?"

"I love making love with you, Mike. I love sucking your cock, eating your ass, kissing you, swallowing your cum. I want you to shove your huge cock all the way up my ass and fill me with as many loads of cum as you can shoot in me. I don't want anything like that with a woman, so yeah, I'm queer. You want sex with women, and you enjoy sex with me. All that makes you in my book is Mike Sharp, not queer, just a good guy ... a very, very handsome guy with a great body, who has a huge, hot cock he enjoys giving to a friend who appreciates it."

"Fair enough. So ... you want me to fuck your ass? Really?"

"Jesus, yes, Mike. I want every inch of that big thing all the way up my butt."

"Can you take it?"

"I'll take it if you'll give it to me ... and believe me, I think you'll enjoy it, too."

"Well, we'll just have to see about that, won't we? You want me to suck your cock, too? You want to fuck my ass, too?"

"Mike, I ..."

He laughed. "I don't know about all that yet. I told you, my ass is negotiable. I didn't necessarily say it was available."

I kissed him and put my hand against his asshole. "I certainly want to open negotiations, though. Remember what my tongue felt like in there? Think about that feeling multiplied a hundred times. I remember what your tongue felt like in my ass, and if you fuck me with that big thing of yours, it's gonna feel like it's multiplied two hundred times."

He smiled lazily. "I've got a feeling you're gonna get two hundred times as excited tonight as you were a little while ago."

I put my arms around him. "Fuck my ass, Mike ... put that incredible monster inside me and fuck me as hard as you can."

"You got it John. Get ready for the fuck of your life!"

And when it happened a bit later that evening, it might not have been the fuck of my life as promised, but it didn't miss it by much – if at all,

I started on my back, with my legs spread and Mike lying between them on his stomach – his head rested on my chest while we talked and he occasionally kissed my nipples as I fondled his head. He pulled his body up on the bed to kiss me, and I could feel his cock nudging my balls. As he sank his tongue into my mouth, I raised my legs, and wrapped them around his waist – placing his cock right at my asshole. "Fuck me, Mike."

He grunted, "Oh, yeah!" and began to push against me as we kissed feverishly. The head of his cock was actually almost penetrating me, but there was no doubt lubrication was going to be in order if that monster dick was going to invade my ass – no matter how eager I was for it. "There's Vaseline on the stand there."

Mike reached over and opened the jar of lubricant, raised himself to his knees, and smiled sexily at me as he smeared his throbbing cock with it before applying it liberally to my ass as well. He took my legs in his hands and raised them to position his cock for entrance. As he began to insert himself, he leaned over me, hands on either side of my head, and whispered in my ear, "God, I'm gonna love fucking your ass!" He began to kiss me again. While his tongue searched my mouth and danced passionately with mine, his massive prick entered me inexorably, and I thrilled to the huge bulk filling me so wonderfully. My whole body felt warm, and I murmured my satisfaction around Mike's probing tongue.

As the last inch or two of his prick began to enter me, I panted hoarsely, "God, Mike … I can't believe how big your cock feels. Fuck me with it … fuck me, Mike, I love it!"

He rammed the last inch so into me with a violent thrust and nibbled my ear. "Oh shit, this feels so good … I'm gonna fill your little ass with my big load tonight." He was now pounding away at me – his ass, which I held cupped in my hands, was driving his cock fiercely in strokes so long that it almost emerged with each backstroke, and his balls slapped audibly against my ass as he reached maximum depth.

He had cum fairly recently, so I was able to revel for a long time – a wondrously long time – in the wild fucking the hot young stud gave me. "God damn. You're a great fucker, Mike. Fill me up with that big hot cock … bury that stupendous meat inside me!"

"Jesus, yes … you're so tight it makes my cock feel three feet long, and I want to drive every inch of it all the way up your ass."

"It feels like three feet to me, too … and I want every inch of it as far in me as you can shove it." He complied with my wish, and his fucking went on and on, with unflagging intensity. His huge cock was pumping me unbelievably deep and fast. He grunted his pleasure while he pounded my ass … as I did, loudly and often … and his assault was perhaps the longest sustained effort I could remember in a long time. After a very long period of truly hard fucking, with unfailing excitement and apparently boundless drive on Mike's part, he cried out wildly, "Take my load, baby! Aaaaaaaahhh!"

His eruption was incredible! His prick was in me as far as it could go, his hands gripped my shoulders almost painfully tight, his head was thrown back and his eyes squeezed shut, and his rigid body was absolutely motionless as I felt violent spurts of cum coursing through his fat shaft where my tight asshole gripped it, exploding deep inside me. He looked like a god as his body loomed over me, he felt like a giant inside me, and I was in absolute heaven.

Mike stayed frozen inside me, and I was so close to orgasm that I grasped my cock and began to masturbate wildly. "Stay in me while I get my load!" I reached my orgasm in only ten or twelve frenzied strokes. My cum shot out onto my chest, and all the way up to my chin and onto Mike's face. I moaned as I spewed all over us, and just a few seconds later Mike lowered his head and licked my cum from my chest and chin before he drove his tongue into my mouth. We kissed passionately for a very long time, while our bodies gradually relaxed and our arms held each other tightly. His prick was still buried in me, and even though relatively soft, it was still a wonderful, formidable assful.

His head nestled in my shoulder, and I played with his hair. I said, "You're the hottest fucking man I've ever known. You'd never believe how good your cock felt when you shoved it in me, or how exciting it was to feel that huge load shooting all the way inside. Nobody ever got fucked better than that, Mike ... you are truly a wonder."

"No girl ever felt like that to me when I fucked her, John. Fucking your ass was ... well, honestly, it was the best. It was so much tighter and hotter than a pussy, and you know exactly what to do to make me feel ... well, to feel big inside you, and ... I don't know, to feel really wanted I guess, and appreciated. Jesus, I could tell you really enjoyed me fucking you ... more than I've ever been aware of before when I was fucking a girl. I can't believe I wanted to eat your load when you came, but I just had to take some of you into me when I was giving mine to you." He smiled and kissed me. "And it tasted great, too!"

"If you only knew how much I enjoyed you inside me. And wait until you feel how it is when you fuck a guy from behind, or lie on top of his ass, or when you lie on your back and he rides you. The guy's ass you're fucking can do a lot to make it even more exciting. If you will, Mike, let me be the one to prove that to you."

He grinned. "Jesus, I can't wait! I may have to give myself a few minutes though ... I seem to be a little tired at the moment." We lay on our sides, holding each other and cuddling. Quietly: "Does getting a cock up your ass really feel as good as you make it sound?"

"It's the most exciting, and wonderful feeling I know, Mike, really."

"You can play with my asshole if you want. I know how great your tongue felt in there, and I'd like to feel something a little bigger." I began to probe his asshole with a finger, but he reached back and moved my hand. "But we're gonna wait a little while. We've got all night, and I need a break. I think I just put the biggest load inside you I ever shot."

"And it felt wonderful, and we're in no hurry. Just hold me, and kiss me, and let me think about filling your pretty ass ..." I kissed him quickly, "and sucking your big prick, and licking those huge balls. But especially, let me think about how lucky I feel to be able to make love with you."

"I feel pretty lucky myself. You're a helluva lover, and kisser, and cocksucker ..." A big grin here and a return kiss, "and the greatest piece of ass I've ever had. When I came out here tonight, I knew we'd be having sex, and I was looking forward to three or four of your fantastic blowjobs ... and that was going to be it. You know, I guess, that I love the way you suck my cock." He laughed, "I know you can tell I do, and I wanted it bad tonight, but I never thought it was going to turn into ... well, whatever it's turning into. I've fucked you, I've eaten your cum, I've sucked your ass – Jesus, what next?"

I grinned and closely into his eyes, nose-to-nose. "How about getting fucked? How about giving a fantastic blowjob?"

"I guess I really owe you a blowjob or two, don't I? Shit, I just tasted your cum, might as well suck it out of you next time, huh? And man, if your cock feels as good in my ass as your tongue does, well ... I don't know ... the way I feel now, I'm not going to rule anything out. But I damn sure know I want to fuck that sweet ass of yours again, whatever happens." Here he began to caress that aforementioned body part and to finger my hole. "When's the last time you had a prick in here, and who was the lucky guy? C'mon, let's get another drink, and tell me all about it ... I want to know." He gave me a quick kiss and got up, headed for the kitchen.

In the kitchen we refreshed our drinks and stood there, naked, with our arms around each other. Mike began to sink to his knees, and his hands cupped my buttocks as he took my cock into his mouth and began to suck. I held his head in my hands and fucked his mouth gently. "My God, that feels good."

He stopped sucking, and looked up at me. "Feels good to me, too ... In fact, this is hot as hell." He deep-throated me, and sucked fiercely for quite a bit, then stopped again. "Man, I have to admit, this really is a great sensation – I can see why you like sucking dick. I'm gonna give you a blowjob as good as those fantastic ones you've been giving me. Okay?"

I leaned over and kissed him. "I can't wait." He returned to his sucking for several minutes, then stood up and kissed me. I sucked his tongue as if it were a cock. His "Mmmmmmmm!!" and the grinding of his pelvis seemed to indicate he enjoyed it! I whispered, "Man, Mike Sharp has sucked my cock, how about that?"

"Trust me ... he's gonna suck it a lot more. Okay, that was just a sample. Back in the bed. And I want hear about the last guy who fucked that hot little ass of yours."

I led him to the bed, and cuddled with him as I said, "I can't tell you who the last guy who fucked me was, because you know him, and I'm sure he doesn't want anybody to know we had sex ... but I can tell you it was great, and he's very, very handsome, he's really got a great body and a nice cock, and he's hot as hell, too."

31

"Is his cock as big as mine?"

"Nobody else I know around here now has as big a cock as this beauty of yours, Mike. Richard, my lover a year or so ago was huge, too, but it's been over a year since he fucked my ass."

"But I'll bet he fucked you good, didn't he?"

"For the couple of months we were together, he fucked me at least once a night … usually more … and I hadn't been that satisfied in years."

"If I fucked you at least once a night, would you be happy again?"

"Shit, Mike, I'm happy now … just fuck me when you can, as often as you can, and yeah, as close to every night as you can … or every single night, or more than once every night, okay?" I kissed him deeply. "I'd like you to fill my ass with that huge hot prick of yours all the time."

"I'd like to fuck it every night … shit, I'd love to … but we both know I can't. But I'm sure as hell gonna fuck it a couple more times tonight before you take me back in the morning, and there's also gonna be a helluva lot of Mike Sharp cock in your future. Anyway, if you won't tell me who it was that fucked you last, tell me all about what he did."

I recounted the recent night and morning with Cary; Mike was horny as hell as I described Cary exploding in me, followed almost without pause by my frantic ride on his cock as he sat in the chair and came in me again. I knelt on all fours next to Mike, and lubricated my ass. "He started out with me just like this. Want to refresh my memory?" Mike grinned, positioned himself behind me, and put his hands on my waist and the tip of his prick at my asshole. "Then he shoved it in," I said, "and fucked me like a demon."

Mike's huge cock entered me slowly, penetrating to a wonderful depth – it seemed to never stop going in, and it felt absolutely stupendous. He whispered, almost reverently, "Jesus, you feel so fucking good. I can't tell you how I love the way it feels holding my prick inside you like this."

"I can't tell you how honored I feel to have you inside me like this. Just stay like that for a few minutes." He was completely inside me, and his stomach pressed up against my buttocks. I held him tightly with my sphincter muscle, and I moved forward so that I drew my sphincter all the way along his cock, almost to the end, keeping the muscle tight, and all but allowing his huge prick-head to slip out, then I pressed myself back forcefully, and rammed my ass against his stomach again.

I continued to work Mike's cock this way as he moaned in ecstasy. "You can't imagine how good that feels."

I assured him I knew – after all, I'd had a number of hot young men treat my own cock to the same thrill. Slowly, he began to fuck me in counter-rhythm to my working him. His moans almost turned into whimpers as he panted his appreciation of the wonderful feeling, and I must admit I was groaning and panting with utmost passion myself. We continued for a long time, until I put my hands behind and pulled him down to the bed on top of me, where

I lay flat on my stomach as he kept fucking, and I continued my own exercise for his invading shaft. He was kissing my neck and ears feverishly. "God, John, I love you when I'm fucking you."

"Fuck me, Mike, love me. I love you ... I love it!"

After another protracted, delirious spell of his fucking me while I lay on my stomach, his tempo began to increase markedly. "Get on your knees again, I'm getting close." I rose on all fours as his fucking grew so fast – and wonderfully so, without losing any of the depth of his stroke – that I could no longer work my ass for him. Finally, he fell over me, clasped his arms around my waist, drove his cock as deep inside me as he could, and left it there while his hot load shot forcefully into me in massive, palpable, multiple gushes. He almost shouted, "Take it, John. You wanted my love? This is it ... this is my love inside you." After his huge orgasm had ended, he pulled us on our sides, and his still-huge prick remained buried deep in me. He kissed my neck and whispered in my ear, "Jesus, John, I'd rather fuck your ass than do anything I know of."

"That's really nice, because I can't think of anything I'd rather do than get fucked by you." Mike pulled out, and we faced each other, kissed gently and lovingly, and held each other tightly for a deliciously long time. No words were really necessary at that point. It was probably 2:00 in the morning, and we drifted off to sleep.

Waking in the morning, we both used the bathroom and brushed our teeth. I had told Mike on awakening that he hadn't finished what he said he was going to do, and as he got back in the bed after I had already finished, he held me in his arms and kissed me. "Still want that blowjob?"

I rolled him on his back and knelt over his head – my prick only a couple of inches from his mouth. "What do you think?"

"I think I'm gonna suck dick." He opened his mouth and I drove my prick into it. His hands held my ass as I fucked him, and he murmured his satisfaction, servicing my eager shaft as perfectly as if he had been doing it for years, with his nose pressing deep into my pubic hair when he deep-throated me.

Breaking for a moment, Mike smiled and said, "Please blow me while I'm sucking you ... that would really be hot." I reversed my body and lay on my back. He knelt over me, and his huge prick hung down directly into my face as I gazed up at the beautiful twin orbs beneath it and his mouth again took my cock into it. I first sucked Mike's balls, and then began to tongue-fuck his ass. He groaned in ecstasy, but never slackened his attentions to my prick. His finger fucked my ass savagely as he sucked. Soon his cock was deep in my throat, and we each fucked the other's mouth as deeply and hard as we could.

I murmured around the mouthful of dick I was servicing, "I'm gonna shoot my load."

Mike murmured around my cock, "Give it to me, and get ready for mine."

Soon each of us was shooting deep into an adoring mouth. Mike swallowed every drop of my emission, as I did with his, and our tongues continued to lick and caress each other's cocks long after orgasm.

We realigned our bodies so we could hold each other and kiss. Mike grinned at me, "Hey, I've just given my first blowjob ... and it was incredible."

"You suck like a fuckin' pro ... I have to give you an A+!"

"Thank you, professor. Your own blowjob, if I may be permitted to say so, was off the scale."

"Jesus, Mike, you are the champion lover of all time."

"You inspire me, John! I can't believe what's happened with us here, and I can't believe how much I've enjoyed it." He looked very seriously at me. "Thank you for being such a wonderful friend and such a fantastic lover."

"Mike, thank you for giving yourself to me like you have. I can't think how you could have been better."

He laughed. "Hey, I could let you fuck me, like I said you maybe could."

"You know I want to Mike ... but when you're ready. I know you'll love it."

"I'm ready now ... and I'm pretty sure I'm gonna love it ... but we both have to get to school." He kissed me and then smiled at me for a long time. "Out of the bed ... we're gonna get dressed. But next time I really want to try taking you up my butt, okay?"

"As long as you'll give me plenty of time with you in mine, okay?"

"You're terrific, John."

"Still the greatest piece of ass you've ever had?"

"More so now than ever." He slapped my ass. "Up!"

We had to dress and get about the day's business, but I had seldom faced a morning in a better frame of mind, or ended an encounter with a greater sense of accomplishment – or something like that.

When I had picked Mike up at the dorm the night before, I had expected him to allow me only the administration of a series of blow jobs to his magnificent prick, but when I dropped him off there the next morning, I had, in addition to having thrilled to the anticipated sucking of his exciting and extremely satisfying cock, also: (1) necked with him at length; (2) had his super dick shoot several loads deep inside my adoring ass while he fucked it like an absolute master; (3) had my ass eaten by him – as I had, of course eaten his; (4) had him suck my cock and swallow my load; and (5) got him to promise to let me fuck his tight little ass. The question now was, when would accomplishment (5) become a reality? I eagerly anticipated its resolution soon and began to think that something pretty serious might be developing with the handsome, monster-dicked fuckmaster, Mike.

4. FULL FRUITION
WITH TWO YOUNG STUDS

It was only a few days later that I encountered Mike as I was walking across campus. We chatted for a while, and I told him I hoped to get together with him again soon. He grinned, "Yeah, we've got some unfinished business, don't we?"

"Well, yeah ... and it would be nice to repeat the business we did finish."

He laughed. "I think nice is way too mild a word. It would be great ... and it'll be in the next few days, okay? I want in that hot ass of yours again in the worst way. I'll call you one night soon."

I also sighted my gorgeous "Danny" a time or two – and he looked better and even more tempting, but, alas, just as apparently unreachable. As the weather was now considerably colder, he had stopped wearing shorts, and his pants now provided a better idea of what his butt looked like – and it promised to be the rounded, boyish bubble butt I dreamed of for him. I was truly dying for an opportunity to meet him and find some justification for an acquaintance. His face was the most strikingly beautiful I had seen since I had come to Dowd; handsome just didn't seem strong enough.

Speaking of someone whose beauty pushed the limits of the word handsome, I sighted Cary walking along the outer reaches of Main Street in town one afternoon shortly after Mike's promise of "soon," and offered him a ride. He seemed grateful, since it was cold, and rain was threatening.

"Man, you came along at just the right time."

"Glad I spotted you ... been hoping to have a chance to talk with you for a while now."

"I know. I've been meaning to get you aside to talk, but I really have been busy. But that doesn't mean I don't remember what I promised you. I get horny every time I think of that night we jacked off together over the telephone." His hands were fondling his crotch as he said this.

"You remember you promised me you'd give me all the cock I want?"

"I remember it well. And I remember how great it felt fucking you up in Knoxville! Shit ... feel this." He spread his legs, and moved forward in the seat. My right hand sought the plentiful bulge he had been stroking, and it was abundantly clear his cock was fully erect. "How does that feel to you?"

"Feels like you're glad to see me. Can we do something about it? Needless to say, I'm in the same condition."

His hand sought my cock and he began to rub it. "Mmmm, feels like you are ready." He unbuttoned his Levi's, pulled his prick out, and guided my hand to it. It felt wonderful, and it throbbed as I stroked it. He said, "Why don't we take this to your house and service it right now? I've got a couple of hours ... do you have time?"

I squeezed his cock. "I've always got time for this beauty." I pulled over to the side of the road and stopped momentarily, leaning over him and taking his prick in my mouth. His hands seized my head and held me tightly as he humped into me.

"God, John ... let's get on the road. I want to get naked so you can do that properly."

"My bed awaits. My mouth awaits ... my butt awaits."

"My cock can hardly wait. Let's get to your bed."

When we pulled up in my driveway, I took Cary in my arms and kissed him, long and passionately. Our tongues intertwined feverishly, and I sucked on his while he drove it in, as if he were fucking my mouth with it. He stopped and grinned at me, "That's what I'm gonna do to you with my cock ... in every hole you'll let me in."

"Cary, you're more than welcome in all my holes! I've got a couple I really need you to fill, okay?"

"Let's get in there so you can give 'em to me."

We lost no time whatever in getting naked and within minutes were tangled together on the bed, necking exuberantly, and grinding our naked cocks against each other. Cary lay on his back, and I began to kiss him all over. He looked perfectly beautiful, and his muscular body was unbearably sexy. He moaned in passion as I sucked his nipples, licked his stomach and navel, licked up and down his hard cock, and took his balls in my mouth for a long, hard suck. My hands were all over him also: I fondled his ass, tantalized his asshole with a fingertip, stroked his cock as I sucked his balls – even licked and kissed his legs and feet, ending up with a series of licks and kisses along the inner surface of his legs. By the time I had worked my way back up to his cock, he was urging me so enthusiastically to suck it that he finally simply grabbed my head and forced my mouth down violently over his rigid shaft.

I sucked as hard as I could and he fucked my mouth savagely. "Eat my fucking cock, John ... take me down your throat ... let me fuck that cocksuckin' mouth until I shoot it full of cum!" My hands had come up beneath him, and I cupped his muscular buttocks as they writhed beneath me. His prick felt huge and wonderful as it drove so deep into my mouth it was all I could do to avoid gagging. He was incredibly hot.

He released my head and rolled over, so I could kiss and lick his other side. I did as he obviously wanted, beginning with the velvety smooth cheeks of his rounded ass – up to his neck, and back down until my face was buried in the crevice of his ass. He raised his butt, exposing his asshole to my adoring mouth, and I tongue-fucked it eagerly as he humped. I pulled his cock between his legs, and sucked it, with his balls beneath my nose and his hot asshole pressed against my forehead. He panted, "Jesus that feels good."

Cary used his hands to spread his asscheeks wide, and urged me to eat his asshole again, so I licked and sucked and tongued that pulsating orifice in

36

abject worship. With a fingertip, I began to palpate his ass ring. He moaned in pleasure, and I was surprised when he reached behind, took my finger in his hand, and began to insert it into his asshole. I was surprised, but I was glad to see he was perhaps interested in taking something more than just my tongue in his ass.

He held my hand tightly, and used my finger to fuck his own asshole. He moaned and murmured in obvious delight then he released my hand and rolled on his back. "Get some Vaseline," he said, spreading his legs and raising them high. There was a large jar of Vaseline on the nightstand next to my bed, and he had obviously seen it. His beautiful ass was open before me, and I generously applied the lubricant to his opening. "Just use your finger at first ... and go slow, okay?"

I carefully inserted my forefinger all the way into Cary, and he began to squirm. The sphincter muscle gripped my finger tightly as I began to move it in and out. Cary moaned in passion, and I gradually insinuated another finger as well. I leaned over him and kissed him; he kissed back frantically. "Can I fuck you, Cary?"

"I don't know if I can take it, but I want to try. Just be very easy, okay? Give me your prick, but go slow."

I removed my fingers and positioned my cock for entrance. Very gradually I began to penetrate his tight orifice. I urged him to relax his asshole as much as he could, and he tried very hard to do so – spreading his raised legs as far apart as he could. His hands held my arms as my cock moved inexorably inside him. "Ow, that hurts."

"Oh baby, please don't make me stop. It'll only hurt for a little while."

"Just go slow. It hurts, but it feels great, too." His own cock had completely lost its erection. Finally, I was all the way inside him. "Oh Jesus, John, that feels incredible. Fuck me slow ... be careful, please."

"Cary, your ass is so beautiful and so hot and tight ... my God I've been dreaming of fucking you." I was, in fact, fucking him by then – slowly and carefully, to be sure, but my prick was completely buried in his burning-hot ass.

"Fuck me, John ... give me your prick, God I see now why you enjoy getting fucked. Your dick feels wonderful inside me. Ohhhhhhh ... just fuck my hot ass!"

His legs locked around my waist as I increased the tempo and ferocity of my fucking, and Cary responded with increased vocal exclamations and humping of his ass. His prick was now hard again, and he began stroking it. I took over for him and masturbated it fiercely as his ass was driving down on my cock to meet every thrust I made into it. We continued that way for some time, and as I obviously neared orgasm, Cary urged me to cum in him. As I erupted, he cried out, "Oh God, I can feel you shooting ... that feels wonderful. Oh God ... here I come!" His big orgasm was an explosion of cum, shooting violently from his prick, and spraying all over our faces, our chests, and his hair. After quite a number of these wild bursts of cum had shot from him, his emission continued to bubble up around the tight sleeve of my fist. Cary's eyes were closed, and his face was a study in absolute rapture. His legs relaxed and slipped from my waist, but I kept my prick inside him.

His eyes opened, and he smiled at me. "Incredible!" I smiled back and slowly licked his cum from my hand as he watched. I carefully removed my cock from him, and his whole body went limp. I licked every drop of cum from his chest and face, and sank my cum-covered tongue deep in his mouth. He sucked my tongue and murmured approval. "What a fantastic fuck."

I held him in my arms. "Fantastic for sure. God, Cary ... how can I thank you? You are so incredibly beautiful and I've wanted you so much ... and to think that you actually let me fuck you. And Jesus Christ, what a fuck! God, it was wonderful. I got your cherry, didn't I?" He grinned, and nodded. "I really feel honored."

He held me tight and kissed me. "It was wonderful, wasn't it? I just wanted you in my ass. Jesus, John, I'm the one to thank you ... you're a wonderful lover."

After a brief break, during which I cleaned my cock, we lay together, kissing and snuggling for a very long time without saying anything. Eventually we were both hard again, and Cary rolled me over on my stomach and lubricated my ass. Without saying a word, he lay on top and put his cock into me. He began to fuck gently, and I began to move with him – but within a few minutes he was fucking me savagely, and I was working his cock as much as I could. He nibbled my ears and grunted in passion as he fucked fiercely for a long time, finally shooting another massive load into me. He continued to fuck long after his emission, and only gradually subsided, as his body grew totally limp, still lying on top of me. "God, I loved that," he said, very quietly and peacefully.

Cary rose up a bit, so I could turn my body over, and he still lay on top of me. "I loved it even more," I said. "Your pretty dick feels so good in me, and I love to feel your cum shooting in me. Your prick belongs inside me, Cary." We kissed for a very long time – my hard cock between his legs, under his balls.

He smiled down at me. "I guess you were surprised when I asked you to fuck me."

"To say the least. Thrilled, but surprised, yeah."

"You'll be more surprised to learn that I decided I wanted you to about a week ago. Thinking about what we'd done in Knoxville, and knowing how much I enjoyed fucking you ... and seeing how much you obviously enjoyed getting it ... I wanted to know what it was like."

"And?"

"And it's even better than I could have hoped. I think I liked getting fucked even more than I did fucking you. I loved the feel of your cock in me ... and the surprises aren't over." He kissed me, and then began to move his head down, kissing my chest and stomach, and was soon nibbling at the head of my cock. "You want me to?"

I gently held his head. "Oh God, yes, Cary ... take me in your mouth!"

He opened his mouth and went all the way down on me. I fucked gently, he sucked and slurped and groaned in delight, and his tight lips rode up and down the length of my cock endlessly – wonderfully. He stopped and again kissed me. "You want to blow your load in my mouth?"

I reversed my body so that his prick hung down over my mouth as he poised his mouth over mine. "Now I want to," I said as I began to suck his cock while he returned mine to his mouth and continued the masterful blowjob he had begun earlier. We had each shot our loads fairly recently, so it took a long time before we neared orgasm. As mine approached, I told him, speaking around his fat prick, "I'm about to get it ... take it if you want it."

He sucked all the harder, and soon I was discharging into him. He murmured "Mmmmmmmm!" as he continued to suck gently, long after I had finished my orgasm. He did not need to warn me of his impending orgasm. I knew it was due when he began to pant heavily around my cock, and his beautiful ass drove his prick wildly into my throat with fierce, deep jabs – culminating in another fountain of white hot cum delivered to my worshipping mouth.

We rolled on our sides, and each kept the other's prick in his mouth as we cuddled together for a long time, arms around asses. At last we broke, and hugged and kissed for ten or fifteen loving, satisfied minutes. Finally, Cary said he had to get back to school, so we showered and had no more than begun to dress when Cary hugged me from behind, greased me up, bent me over, and fucked me again while I stood there. His hands held my waist as he drove himself into me savagely for a delirious, miraculously long time. I did my best to work his prick as he fucked, and eventually he grunted a feral cry and shot another load of cum in me. He put his arms tightly around my waist and pulled me close to him – his still-throbbing prick planted deep inside me yet. He nibbled my ear and kissed my neck. "I told you I was gonna give you all the cock you want."

My hands reached behind us and pressed his ass tightly against me. "I'll never get enough of your cock. But don't stop trying."

He turned me around. "I won't ... if you'll keep feeding me yours."

I laughed. "Oh, you can bet your beautiful hot ass I'll keep feeding you mine. But Cary, what about ... well, you said ..."

"Look we've sucked each other off, we've fucked each other, we want to keep doing it, right?"

"Absolutely! But ..."

"No 'buts.' Just please be here for me when we can get together to fuck, okay? I love having sex with you more than I even want to think about. Deal?"

"Deal, Cary. I love sex with you ... well, it's so incredible to find that you're just as hot as you are beautiful, and that you're willing to share that with me."

"Believe it!" He gave me a quick kiss. "Look, I've gotta get you to take me back to campus, but we'll get together for a whole night soon, okay? And you'll fuck my brains out, and I'll fuck your brains out, and we'll have a helluva time."

"I can hardly wait!" He sat very close to me on the way back in, his hand resting on my crotch, and mine on his. As I let him out, he kissed me for a long time. "Thanks ... you're wonderful, Cary!"

"So are you. Save it up for me. Soon, okay?"

"You got it."

Wow! The very beautiful Cary and the very hung Mike – both fucking me, both sucking me, both willing and eager to share passionate kisses. I had now even experienced the wonder of plumbing Cary's rounded, muscular ass, and although I had yet to plant myself deep inside Mike's no-doubt tight asshole, even that seemed right around the corner. Given that both these ultimately desirable young men had implied that our sexual relationships were going to be ongoing, I had an unbelievable amount to be thankful for as Thanksgiving approached that year. Now was learning who "Danny" was and developing a relationship with that unbelievably beautiful man too much to ask for? Yes, probably so, but both Cary and Mike had seemed too much to hope for until very recently.

Before Thanksgiving actually arrived, I had succeeded in cementing relationships with my two hot young lovers. Cary called for me to pick him up only about a week after our first all-out, full-blown adventure, and it was as hot as could be imagined. We pretty well went over the same ground, but with plenty of embellishment.

The vision of the golden beauty's muscular body bouncing up and down as his tight ass-ring grasped my cock when he rode me was thrilling beyond belief, for instance. He looked heart-breakingly handsome as he rode – his face absolutely angelic, fucking himself on my cock with complete abandon, with his eyes closed and his mouth open in abject ecstasy. My hands held his waist as his tempo grew frenzied, and the length of his riding increased to absolute maximum, He had been masturbating as he rode, and as I thrust upward and delivered my orgasm into him he shot a huge load of his own cum all over my chest and face. I hope I looked and felt even a fraction as good to him when I returned the favor and rode his delicious cock a bit later. Cary also knelt on all fours and had me fuck him from behind that night, but he seemed to especially enjoy the "missionary position" fucks we gave each other a bit later – as, in a way I did, since it allowed us to kiss as we penetrated each other, and Cary was as accomplished a kisser as he was a fucker.

That pre-Thanksgiving night, an entire, delirious night, included his blowing his load in my butt twice and delivering three massive ones in my mouth – five hot, generous orgasms given me by Adonis in one night. He seemed especially eager to get fucked, so I obliged him with two loads up his ass that night. I shot another load inside his mouth – but I also, at Cary's request, jacked off on his face and shot most of another load into his open mouth. The entire night had been one of complete sexual sharing, and it seemed unbelievable to me that Cary was anything but a fully committed homosexual, given the scope and passion of his performance that night. That had been Sunday night before Thanksgiving.

Only two days later, Mike came out and spent the entire night with me, and, as with Cary, we pretty well recreated our most recent hot coupling. The real highlight with Mike, however, came when he finally yielded up his virgin ass to me.

I was lying on top of him, between his wide-spread legs. We had been double-sucking only a few minutes earlier, but had stopped without orgasm and begun a protracted session of passionate kissing. He whispered into my ear, "Do you want to try fucking me?" He raised his legs and circled my waist with them My prick was pressing against his ass.

"More than anything I know, Mike."

"Get the Vaseline and do it."

I liberally lubricated both my prick and his asshole and very slowly and gently inserted myself inside his ass. He grunted, but did not seem to be in much pain as I penetrated him, and as I gradually entered deeper and deeper, he murmured in pleasure. I was all the way inside him before he actually said anything: "That's the greatest feeling I've ever had. Your dick feels huge inside me, but it feels wonderful ... I feel hot all over, and just full of ... I don't know, full of ..." He grinned up at me. "Full of your love maybe? Just leave it there for a while before you fuck me ... you feel so good inside me." I tried to comply, but was unable to keep from beginning to hump, and soon Mike's ass was meeting my thrusts in counter-rhythm. I fucked slow and deep for a long time, Mike and I both murmuring our delight and exchanging both very sweet and extremely passionate kisses.

"Stay inside me if you can, and turn me over where I can get on my knees." He basically rotated his body on my prick. It was a bit tricky, but we accomplished it, and soon I thrilled at the exciting view of Mike's beautiful ass and muscular body, writhing and humping as my cock was penetrating him – both stimulating and satisfying beyond belief. We each stepped up the pace of our movements, and I was soon fucking him quite fast, and very hard. He gasped, "Oh God, yes, fuck my ass!" He began to buck and drive his ass back onto my cock in absolute frenzy, and we continued thus for some time, each of us crying out frequently in rapture until I told him I was going to shoot. "Fill me up with your cum, John ... fill my fuckin' ass full ... I want your load shooting inside me!" I held his waist very tightly and discharged violently and copiously inside his still bucking ass. "Oh shit, that feels so hot! Keep cumming ... give it to me!"

Finally we both collapsed and Mike asked me to stay inside him. "You feel just right inside me. No wonder you love getting fucked so much."

"Yeah, and just think how fuckin' huge that beautiful prick of yours is. When you're fucking me with that, it really feels right."

Eventually he rolled over, and we kissed and cuddled for almost an hour of sheer, sweet bliss, before the urgings of his huge, throbbing cock took over, and he returned the favor I had just given him.

Our night together found Mike fucking my ass three times, as Cary had done earlier in the week, although he was too sore from his virtuoso maiden effort as a bottom to take me up the ass again. He did, though, suck a couple of loads out of my adoring cock, and I swallowed a couple of his; it only seemed polite.

As with Cary only two nights before, it seemed impossible to believe that a young man capable of such accomplished, masterful love-making of the kind we had experienced could be anything but a dedicated homosexual. I didn't care if Cary and Mike were gay or straight; however, they were both magnificent lovers, and I was an incredibly lucky man to be the recipient of their sublime sexual favors.

I could not help wondering if my two hot young sex partners were not also having sex with other boys or men. Both had recently regarded themselves as strictly straight, but were now regularly enjoying all-out gay sex with such joyous abandon that they must surely be considered at least bisexual – if not, in fact, homosexuals who had finally realized their true nature. I never asked them, since to question them would have seemed jealous and petty, considering that they both knew I was fucking with at least one other student. And they never volunteered the information. Selfishly, I wanted for myself everything they could give, sexually – and there was the danger they would find younger, better looking guys with great bodies, monster cocks, and sexual technique more persuasive than mine. Had I felt altruistic about our relationships, I might have thought it a great shame if Cary and Mike were not sharing their sexual precocity and mastery with others who would appreciate it; but I didn't. Fuck that, I thought; no one could have appreciated their beauty and their talents more than I did. To be honest, I also hoped, in any case, that they were no longer having heterosexual relations; to my mind, it would have been such a total waste of their glorious sexuality.

5. A NEAR MISS, AND CONTEMPLATION OF COMMUNITY

I finally got a break in the "who is Danny" sweepstakes shortly after Thanksgiving. Walking across campus, I encountered one of my saxophone players in conversation with that vision of ultimate beauty I had nicknamed Danny. The conversation had apparently just ended, and Danny walked away just as I arrived. I greeted Ron, the sax player, and we engaged in a mindless conversation for a while, until I asked him casually, "Who is that you were talking to? He really looks familiar, but I can't place him."

"He's in my chemistry class, but I don't know his name. I'll bet you've seen him at soccer games. He's on the team, I know."

I had never been to a soccer game at Dowd, but I said, "Sure, that must be it."

So, a soccer player. A start, at any rate, toward discovering his elusive identity. Unfortunately, the soccer season was over. At that time, virtually every student got photographed for the yearbook, and I had already determined I would probably find his name and his picture in it when it came out at the end of the school year. But with this new information, I might be able to pursue an earlier course of action. Unfortunately, although I had no trouble finding a team membership list for the current soccer team, I could find no pictures. I assumed I would have to wait until the spring exhibition games.

And so I did. It was a long time before spring soccer, but I could wait. There was no urgency about discovering the elusive beauty's name, after all; I was only curious, and only sort of "hoping against hope" that I could meet him anyway. It was unlikely to an unthinkable degree that I would get to seduce him. Quite honestly, his beauty was so exquisite, that I held out virtually no hope for that; surely I'd be lucky if I could just get to talk with him. On the other hand, Cary was inordinately beautiful, and I marveled at what had happened with him. One could always dream, after all. I remembered well that when I was an undergraduate back in Texas, the two most astonishingly beautiful men on campus turned out to be gay, and I wound up having sex with one of them a number of times – the legendary Hal of the ten-inch prick – and joined both of them, along with my roommate, for four-way sex once. Mike was handsome – certainly well-built and marvelously well-hung – but he was not really beautiful, yet he seemed to grow more attractive every time we got together to make love. Furthermore, Mike had taken to wearing contact lenses, so his glasses no longer detracted from his good looks – if they ever had.

So, although I had to wait to even learn Danny's name, I had both Cary and Mike providing me with wonderful, fully satisfying sex. Except for the Christmas vacation, I probably managed a session with each of them an average of something slightly in excess of once a week. I was getting happily, deliriously, wonderfully fucked about three times a week, and fucking hot young butt with equal frequency.

Amazingly, my two hot lovers never crossed paths. The fact that neither of them had a car on campus helped, since I invariably had to pick them up to bring them out to my house, and I could control their coming and going to a certain extent (and I may as well state the obvious – I especially loved controlling their cumming). Both knew I was having sex with someone else as well, and while it did not bother them at all initially, as our respective relationships developed, they seemed to display a bit of jealousy, although both denied it made any difference to them. And, although each knew that my other partner was someone he was acquainted with, I don't think either one had an inkling as to the identity of "the other man."

On only one occasion did they almost overlap. Mike had been out to see me one afternoon, and we had spent a wonderful several hours making uncharacteristically quiet and leisurely love. It was a very cold day, and he built a fire in the freestanding fireplace in my living room. We grabbed a blanket from the bed, so we could make love on the floor, in front of the fire. Mike had stretched out on his stomach, studying the fire – nude, of course – and his ass was irresistibly beautiful in the flickering light. I began a slow worship of his ass with my hands, lips and tongue, which soon turned into a very general adoration of his whole body – ending, not surprisingly, with his huge prick buried deep in my throat.

We lay on our sides, and Mike took my prick into his mouth, saying, "Let's just cuddle for a while ... plenty of time to cum later." So we lay in a languorous sixty-nine for a long time, fondling and caressing each other's asses and bodies, licking and very gently sucking each other's cocks, and simply enjoying one another. Eventually, of course, we both got quite excited and the sucking got serious – ending in the predictable showers of cum lovingly consumed. Mike also fucked my ass – nothing languorous about the way he did that – and left a massive load in me. After I had saluted his beautiful butt with the same treatment and we were preparing to get him back to the dorm, he pulled my pants down, bent me over a table, saying "I need one for the road," and fucked my more-than-willing ass again as I stood in the living room. His final explosion of cum seemed as generous as his first, and my happy ass was awash with his juice as I took him back to campus.

About a half-hour after returning home, Cary showed up in his roommate's car, apologizing for not having called to say he wanted to come out. "I just took a chance ... hoping to find you here. I'm horny as shit, and I sure hope you'll take care of me."

As Cary came into the living room, he could not help but notice that the blanket was still spread out on the floor in front of the fire, and several towels and a jar of Vaseline were in evidence. "Were you expecting someone, or did I miss someone?"

I grinned sheepishly, "You just missed someone."

He seemed more than a little put out. "So, are you fucked out, or what? Do you want me?"

I took him in my arms and kissed him tenderly. He resisted at first, but his arms did finally encircle me, and he returned my kisses. I took his face in my hands, and studied it. "Jesus, Cary, you are so fucking handsome. You're the most beautiful man I know." This wasn't completely true – a vision of the stunning Danny flashed across my mind – but Cary was, indeed enormously beautiful, as gorgeous and golden as Mike was dark and dangerous-dicked. "You know I want you ... I always want you; I could never be too fucked out to make love with you. Please don't be angry."

"Oh, I'm not. It's just that, well ... I don't know. No ... it's fine, really." He brightened up and kissed me, then grinned slyly. "It's nice that you think I'm handsome."

"Beautiful!"

"Okay, for the sake of argument ... beautiful. Anyway, thanks. I'm glad you see me that way. Is ... well, whoever you were just with ... do you think he's beautiful too?"

"He's very handsome, but not in your league." I began unbuttoning his pants. "Nobody's in your league, Cary." (Danny was in my mind again, though.)

Cary began unbuttoning his shirt and kicking off his shoes. "Has he got a big dick?"

I laughed. "He has an enormous dick. You wouldn't believe how big."

Cary took me in his arms. "Hmmmmmm. Did he fuck you?"

"My ass is still filled with his load ... with a couple of loads, actually. You want to get in there and add to them?"

"More than you can imagine. You know, it really makes me hot to think of doing that."

"Not as hot as it makes me to think of you doing that." I began to strip, and Cary finished undressing.

We stood and embraced, fondling each other in front of the fire. Cary knelt and took my cock in his mouth. I held his head and fucked happily for several minutes. Cary drove his finger in and out of my asshole as he sucked, and then he pulled me down to the floor. "Get on your knees and let me fuck you ... I can feel how hot and wet you are. I'm not going to need any Vaseline tonight." I knelt on all fours. Cary positioned himself behind me and drove his cock roughly all the way into me in one thrilling thrust. "Here's another big prick for you."

"Oh yeah, fuck me baby. That feels so fucking good."

I was driving my ass backward to meet each violent forward thrust Cary was giving me. He moaned in ecstasy, "God damn, your ass is juicy with all that hot cum in there. This is so fuckin' hot ... my prick is swimming in someone's cum, and I don't even know whose it is. Jesus, this is incredible ... it feels wonderful." He fucked savagely for a long time, holding my waist very

45

tightly, and I did my best to grasp his prick with my sphincter and work it as vociferously as he was fucking me. Working together, we brought him to a huge climax. His cum seemed to shoot endlessly into me. As soon as he had finished discharging his exceptional load, his arms went around me tightly, and we collapsed on the floor, his cock still inside me.

We lay on our sides, and my hands were behind me, holding his pretty ass. "God, Cary, what an exciting fuck."

"Was I as good as ... whoever he is?"

"You're better than anybody I know. Jesus I love it when you fuck me."

He kissed my ear and whispered, "Can you fuck me? I'd really love to feel your cock shooting in me ... that's what I really was looking forward to when I decided to come out here this afternoon."

I turned around, and Cary's prick slipped out of me. "I wouldn't dream of disappointing you ... especially when I can slip my dick into the most beautiful ass I know."

Cary rolled on his stomach, presenting his magnificent ass for my delectation – velvet, golden, two perfectly rounded globes of muscular flesh with heaven between them. I took his buttocks lovingly in my hands and fondled them as I buried my face between them. He raised himself slightly and pressed back against my tongue as it slipped into the tight ring of his asshole. "Mmmmmm ... that feels so damned good. Eat me out good before you fuck it."

I tongue-fucked him as eagerly as I could, and he writhed and humped, moaning with pleasure. His sphincter muscle seized my tongue and pulled on it, and the tip of my tongue danced around and licked inside him. His hands were behind him, pressing my head into his ass, and we were both experiencing total rapture. Finally his hands left my head and pulled his cheeks far apart. "I can't stand it any more, shove your cock in me and fuck me as hard as you can."

I rose up and quickly lubricated my cock before pressing the head to his asshole. "Shove," he gasped, "Fuck me hard!" I drove myself in with one fierce jab. "Aaaaaaaahhh! That's wonderful! Fuck me, John ... fuck my hot ass as hard as you can." His ass humped backwards to meet my thrusts, and since I had not very long before blown a load into Mike's mouth and another into his ass, it took me quite a while to reach orgasm, which seemed to delight Cary especially. "This is so great. Keep fucking me ... fuck me forever!"

As I neared orgasm, I held back, wanting to prolong this fuck, since Cary was enjoying it so much. Finally, I could hold back no longer. "I've gotta give it to you, Cary."

"Give it to me ... fill me up." I discharged, with an enormous amount of heaving and panting, which Cary matched with heaving and humping. "Man, that feels so good ... God I love to get fucked." His ass worked my cock long after I had stopped cumming. I rolled off him, and lay on my back. He got over me and kissed me lovingly. "What a man! What we're doing may be queer, but there's no question you're a man when you fuck me like that."

"Cary, only a real man could take me like you do ... or could fuck me as wonderfully as you do."

"Do I fuck you as good as the guy who just left ... the one with the huge cock?"

"You fuck as good as anyone I've ever known," I replied – the kind of fib that hurts no one.

"Do you think I could take his cock up my ass?"

"I know you could ... it would probably hurt a little at first but you'd love it."

"And you won't tell me who it is?"

"Cary, I can't. Look, he knows I'm fucking with someone else, too. Would you want me to tell him who you are?"

"No ... well, I guess ... no ... no, I wouldn't. Okay, I'll quit asking, but he really does sound hot."

"He really is hot ... almost as hot as you ... and it makes me hotter than you can imagine to think that your prick was coated with his big load while you fucked me." We kissed and held each other tight for quite some time before getting in the shower, where we played for another long period, and where I sucked Cary almost to the point of orgasm again, at which time he bent me over and shoved his cock into my ass and fucked until I had yet another load of hot cum up my ass.

He laughed as he pulled out and I straightened up. "You're gonna be sloshing you're so full of cum." He knelt in front of me. "Let me see if I can drain a little out." And he sucked me passionately, and so expertly that, although I was really pretty thoroughly exhausted, he managed to coax another load out of my prick and into his hungry throat. I raised him to his feet and knelt in front of him, and although he had cum in my ass only ten minutes or so earlier, I worshipped his dick so long and so passionately that he filled my throat with another load.

As he kissed me when he was leaving, he said, "I sure would like to know who the big-dicked wonder is who helped me fill you up today. Don't you think it would be fun to be with both of us at the same time?"

"Cary, do you want me to tell him who you are?"

"No ... I guess I don't. If I knew who he was, it might be okay, but ..."

"Let me think about it, okay? It would be hot as hell to have your dick and his dick in my mouth or in my hands at the same time, though."

"We could take turns fucking you ... how'd you like that?"

"How would you like it?"

He laughed. "I think I'd love it! I've gotta get back ... don't worry about the three of us getting together. I'm happy as hell having you to myself when I can. Well, gotta fly." He kissed me quickly. "Love you, John!"

47

"Love you, baby!" And I watched his adorable ass head toward the car. He hadn't said, seriously, "I love you," nor had I, but we had both used The L Word, nonetheless, and I felt very warm inside. I guess part of the reason I felt so warm inside, though, was that I had taken four hot loads of cum up my ass, and two more down my throat, all put there ecstatically and expertly by two different hot young men.

I did begin to consider the possibility of introducing Cary and Mike to each other as my lovers. They knew each other well, of course – they sat almost next to each other in band rehearsals and lived on the same dormitory hall – but apparently neither suspected the other's identity as a "rival lover" of sorts. What purpose would it serve, however? Might they not get together and cut me out? Of course they might, but either one of them would surely find a different partner sometime anyway. The idea of them taking turns fucking me, or of my being able to watch them fuck and suck each other – or, indeed, almost any of the myriad other sexual possibilities and permutations the situation might present – seemed very exciting to contemplate.

I well remembered two series of incredible threesomes I had participated in ten or eleven years earlier, in Texas. One series had involved my roommate, Jim, and the aforementioned, incredibly beautiful and sexy Hal of the ten-inch cock; the other involved my eighteen-year-old lover Billy and his high-school football teammate, Phil. The memory of getting double-fucked by both Billy's and Phil's cocks on one of those occasions would always be vivid. Both series had been capped by a one-time, but unforgettable three-way with the sweet and beautiful Billy and the monster-hung and gorgeous Hal. I thought that if a threesome with Cary and Mike could prove as rewarding and thrilling as those had been, I should seriously make a plan to bring it about. My first step, of course, would be to sound out both Mike and Cary on the subject of a threesome. As it turned out, I didn't have to make the suggestion to Mike.

Several days later, Mike was lying in my arms. Already that evening his beautiful body had accepted a couple of my loads, and three of his had been discharged into me in his usual masterful fashion. I told him that "the other guy I'm seeing" had appeared at the house right after I returned from taking him to campus last time, and he had found the towels and Vaseline sitting on the blanket in front of the fire. "You guys almost crossed paths."

"Was he upset?"

"Not really ... well, maybe a little bit, yeah. Would you have been?"

He snickered, "Not unless you wouldn't let me screw you."

"Oh, that wouldn't happen, I promise you." I kissed him then continued. "I had two of loads of cum up my ass when he got here, and I had two more in there when he left. And he really enjoyed the feel of all your cum bathing his prick when he fucked me."

"I would have, too. Sounds hot as hell. But you must have been just about filled up by the time he was through."

"Filled up and happy as hell."

"I can understand that. I sure feel like I'm filled with your love right now, and you've got a lot of mine in you ... and I feel happy as a clam."

"I feel a lot of love when we're together, Mike ... and I'd be lying if I said that didn't mean a lot more to me than just having sex. I honestly feel we're making love when we fuck, and I think you feel something like that also ... or am I reading something into this relationship that isn't there?"

He kissed me very seriously. "I feel a lot of love when I'm with you, you know that. But mostly I feel we love each other as friends, and as friends we also enjoy fucking each other and sucking each other's cocks. But yeah ..." He grinned and kissed me again, "There's real love there, too."

"That says it as well as it needs to be said. But anyway, my seeing someone else is not a problem with you?"

"Nah. Like I said, just keep fucking me, and letting me fuck you, and we're fine." Nonetheless, there was something in his voice when he asked, after a slight pause, "Is this other guy really hot?"

"He's hot, Mike, and he's really beautiful. But he's certainly not any hotter than you are, and he sure doesn't have a dick like that hot fuckin' ass-reamer of yours."

"Would I be attracted to him, do you think?"

"Yeah, I'm sure you would. You couldn't help but think he was handsome, and he's got a great muscular body. And you know him, as I've told you, and I know you like him as a friend. You know, it's funny you should ask ... he was wondering if he could take your big dick up his ass."

"He knows who I am?"

"No, of course not, but I told him about your dick."

"Did he say he's like to get fucked by it?"

"Of course he did. He's not a fool."

Mike grinned crookedly. "Well, did he think he could take it?"

"He didn't know. I promised him he could, but you'd probably have to go slow at first. But once you had that fantastic tool inside him, he'd love it ... and you'd love fucking him. I can assure you he's a great fucker, too, and you'd enjoy his cock up your butt as much as I do."

"Man, he sounds great. I wish I knew who he was, but I understand you can't tell me unless he says it's okay. Look, will you ask him if it's okay? And maybe ... maybe the three of us could get together. That would be hot as hell, wouldn't it?"

"Let me think about it, Mike, and I'll sound him out when the time seems appropriate, okay?"

"Fair enough. Look, my dick is getting a little cold; don't you think we could find a place to warm it up?"

We did – and I got another dose of Mike's liquid love to warm me up as well. And after I dropped him off back at his dorm that night I realized he had

Heels over Head in Love

used the L word, too! Valentine's Day was coming up, and love was "sweeping the country" as the Gershwins had observed in song.

6. A SHARING AND A PAIRING

An opportunity presented itself for a possible confluence of Mike, Cary and me shortly after the spring semester began. The University of Florida was playing host to a Southeastern all-college band in late January, and Dowd College was allotted four seats in the band – to be filled by students I recommended and brought with me to the campus for the four-day-long rehearsal period and culminating concert. I chose my first-chair clarinetist and my first-chair flutist, both young ladies, and two trumpet players. The trumpet players were both male, and I doubt seriously the reader will be surprised to learn that they were Cary Adams and Mike Sharp. This was not entirely dictated by sexual considerations; Mike and Cary were both superb performers. It would, however, be less than honest to say that I was not seriously considering, and even cultivating, the possibility of bringing about the threesome we were all contemplating.

I made the motel arrangements carefully, with the possible threesome in mind: Judy and Nancy would be housed in one room with two beds, and Mike and Cary would be housed in another with two beds. It was clearly stipulated that my single room would adjoin Mike and Cary's, and that there would be a usable door between the two rooms.

On checking into the motel the afternoon of the first rehearsal, scheduled for that evening, Mike and Cary both thought the adjoining-room arrangement ideal. They expressed their opinion of the latter feature to me separately and privately, however. Mike grinned as he slipped into my room through the adjoining door while Cary was unloading the car. "Be sure you leave this door at least unlocked ... you're sure as hell gonna have a horny visitor tonight."

"I welcome all horny visitors to my bed. The hornier they are, the more welcome they are."

"Then I'm going to be as welcome as it's possible to be." He took my hand and guided it to his crotch. "You can see that I already qualify as welcome." He did indeed!

Cary ducked into my room while Mike was taking a shower, and basically relayed the same message. "Keep this door unlocked, and you may find a cock up your butt tonight."

I grinned, and groped him. "If I find one there, I'll sure as hell know what to do with it." He grinned also and groped right back. There was no doubt that if we had been alone, we both would have been ready for a quick pre-rehearsal fuck right at that moment.

Following that evening's rehearsal, all four students gathered for a while in my room, and we enjoyed visiting, telling stories, and discussing the upcoming rehearsals and concert. The girls left for their room about 11:00. I broke out the bourbon and talked and drank for another hour or so with my two hot young lovers – each unaware of the other's role in my life. Around midnight, we all turned in. Needless to say, when I poked my head in Mike and Cary's room and told them to get a good rest because tomorrow was going to be a demanding day, I was sure to leave the adjoining room ajar. "G'night Dr. Harrison!" from one; "See you in the morning, Dr. H!" from the other. Which one was going to be in to see me first? Would the other wait and come in later? It was going to be interesting.

As it turned out, about twenty minutes or so after I turned out the light, Cary crawled in bed with me, put his arms around me and pressed his naked body and erect cock against mine. He whispered, "Mike's asleep." We kissed passionately for quite a while and soon were locked in sixty-nine, where we sucked each other's cocks for another considerable period. What little talking we did was in whispers, of course; we didn't want to wake Mike up. (We didn't? I sure as hell did).

After a long and delightful double-suck, I asked Cary to kneel at the edge of the bed, so I could stand behind him and fuck his luscious ass. He knelt there, his toes over the side of the bed, and although there was not a great deal of light in the room, I could see well enough to thrill at the beauty of his fine body and ass. I tongue-fucked him for quite a while, as he murmured ecstatic encouragement, and then lovingly licked and sucked his balls from behind, and pulled his cock back through his legs to suck and worship. He whispered passionately, "Shit, that feels great. Shove your cock in me and fuck me hard."

I stood, and had to crouch just the least bit to line my cock up perfectly with Cary's lovely, waiting, tongue-primed butthole. I lubed us up, plunged myself into him, and began a committed, vigorous fuck, which he was obviously adoring, given the enthusiasm with which he drove his ass backward to meet every thrust I gave him. I guess I sensed Mike behind me, since I wasn't at all surprised when I felt his cock pushing in between my legs, and his hands reaching around to play with my nipples. He knelt behind me and buried his face in my driving ass. His tongue darted in and out of my asshole as I fucked Cary; he had made no sound whatever, so Cary was probably not aware that we were now, in fact, a threesome.

Mike quit eating my ass, stood, walked to the other side of the bed and climbed on, kneeling in front of Cary as I fucked. Cary gasped in surprise when he felt Mike join us on the bed, "Damn, Mike, you scared the shit out of me!" Cary never stopped backing up on my cock to meet my forward thrusts as I continued to plow him, however.

Mike held his enormous hard cock in front of Cary's face and said, "Come on, Cary, suck my dick for me." Mike was practically forcing his cock into Cary's mouth. "Suck me while John fucks your butt ... you'll love it."

Cary took Mike's cock in his hand and began to kiss it. "Jesus, Mike ... this is the biggest fuckin' cock I've ever seen!"

"Suck it, Cary, take it down your throat."

"Hell yes ... give it to me," he gasped. "Fuck me hard John; it looks like I'm gonna get it at both ends." He took the proffered monster prick in his mouth, while Mike grasped his head and fucked him vigorously.

Mike leaned over Cary's back and kissed me as we both serviced Cary, who was moaning in delight. "So it was Cary all along, huh? Jesus ... this couldn't be better. Come on Cary, deep-throat my big cock."

Cary stopped sucking long enough to praise our efforts. "Fuck me, both of you guys; this is the hottest thing I've ever felt." And he returned to sucking Mike and driving his ass back against my thrusting shaft.

"Mike, why don't you take over for me back here. I don't think Cary's gonna know what hot really is until he takes your monster up his butt."

As Mike got off the bed and joined me behind the kneeling blond, Cary said, "Go easy, will you, Mike? I really want you to fuck me, but your cock is so fuckin' big, I don't know if I can take it."

I turned on the lights, so I could enjoy the full beauty of these two hot studs, and knelt in front of Cary on the bed; he raised himself, and we put our arms around each other. "I'll hold you Cary ... hang on tight; it may hurt a little at first, but it's worth it. Nothing feels quite like Mike inside you ... believe me, I know."

"God I'm glad your other lover was Mike," he turned and said over his shoulder to Mike, who was lubricating both Cary and himself very liberally. "I've seen your cock in the showers so many times, Mike, and lately I've really been thinking about it a lot. This is almost too good to be true."

"You'll see how true it is in a minute. I'm gonna make love to your ass like it's never been loved before."

I added, "And Mike's going to want you to fuck his ass, too, Cary. He loves getting fucked as much as we do. Right, Mike?"

"Hell, yes. You better plan on giving me at least one good load up my ass, Cary. I know John's gonna give me one or two."

"Fuck me, Mike ... I want you inside me," Cary said as he wriggled his pretty ass. I held him as Mike began to insert his huge prick into his willing, but – for a cock this size – very tight hole. "Oh God, that hurts ... . ooohhh ... Ouch! ... No, don't stop, keep going, but slow." Finally, Mike was completely buried inside Cary's rounded, muscular, beautiful, and now magnificently filled ass. "Christ, Mike, you're huge!"

"Too big for you Cary?"

"God no. I love how it feels. Just go slow at first, but fuck me deep, Mike. Make love to me with that wonderful dick."

Cary held me very tightly, obviously in a bit of pain as Mike began his assault, but he soon relaxed and started to hump backward to meet the magnificently long thrusts entering his ass. He kissed me and mumbled how wonderful Mike felt as he fucked. Finally he fell to all fours and encouraged Mike even more eagerly to fuck him. I lay on my back on the bed, put my head under Cary, and took his prick into my mouth and sucked eagerly. "Jesus, John, I'm gonna cum if you keep that up." Needless to say, I didn't stop.

Soon Mike was ready. "I'm gonna shoot my load in you, Cary, Take it, baby, here it is ... Aaaaaaaaaahhh!"

"God that feels so good Mike. Fill my ass with that big load. Shit, I'm gonna cum, too ... eat my cum, John." And as he said that, his prick shot into my throat – an enormous load, delivered with maximum force in seven or eight copious spurts.

We all froze for several minutes, Cary's cock softening in my mouth as I savored – but did not yet swallow – his cum. Mike's cock was still buried to the hilt in Cary's fine ass, and Cary was panting his appreciation for our efforts. I pulled out from under Cary and moved to stand behind Mike as he stood there pressing his ass against the beautiful young stud he had just fucked so thoroughly and expertly. I spit out Cary's huge load on Mike's back, and directed it down into the crack of his ass. "Watch this Cary, I'm gonna fuck Mike's ass and use your load to get him ready." I used my fingers to lubricate my cock and Mike's asshole. Cary pulled away from Mike's invading cock, and turned to watch. Mike fell face down on the bed, and both studs encouraged me as I sank my prick inside Mike and fucked savagely. Mike moaned in passion, and Cary played with my ass and kissed me while I fucked. Very soon, I erupted inside the youthful, wonderful hot ass that continued to grip me and exercise my prick for some time afterward.

We all collapsed and engaged in gentle, loving three-way kisses, hugs and gropes. Cary and Mike both talked about how incredibly happy they were that each had been "the other man" with me. I reveled in their happy talk. "God, I love you guys."

Cary and Mike looked at each other, grinned, and put their arms around me. "This is great, John ... love you, too," from Cary. "God, yeah ... that goes double for me," from my other hot man.

Cary and Mike were absolutely fascinated by each other and spent what I inevitably had to consider a frustrating amount of time exploring each other, kissing endlessly, embracing and fondling. The sight of these two perfect specimens making love was stimulating beyond belief, of course, but I also felt somewhat left out. They both tried to include me in their attention to each other, but couldn't get away from the fact that each had just discovered the ass, cock, body, and kisses of the other, and were fascinated. After all, they had been familiar with what I had to offer for some time now. So, I observed them with mixed feelings of paternalism, pride, love, strong sexual attraction to each of them and to their unbearably sexy coupling, and (I must admit) some confusing jealousy. I sublimated my jealousy by licking, kissing, sucking, or poking any body parts not actually being enjoyed by either at the moment.

Cary was anxious to fuck Mike's ass, of course (Who wouldn't be?), and, since Mike seemed equally anxious get fucked by the adorable blond, he was soon getting drilled savagely by a panting, writhing, humping, joyous Cary. While Cary was driving his cock deep into Mike's hole, Mike evinced the same kind of ecstasy that possessed Cary.

As he kissed me while fucking Mike, Cary praised the wonder of making love to this hot stud's butt, and he assured me that he enjoyed it even more since the sublime orifice he was plugging was hot and slippery with my cum. Soon Cary added a load to the one I had given Mike earlier, and judging by the grunt that apparently accompanied each spurt of his cum, his load rivaled the copiousness of the one he had spurted in my throat earlier. Mike cried out in ecstasy at the feel of Cary's hot, generous discharge – accompanied by even louder cries of rapture from his gorgeous blond fucker.

Later, I was mesmerized and thrilled to watch these two young demigods engage in sixty-nine. Their two perfect bodies were locked together in writhing, undulating passion, with their cocks buried deep in each other's throats. Their exploring hands fondled the delectable, velvety, golden asses, and those sublime, perfect pairs of rounded, muscular globes of beauty humped sinuously as they drove their delicious pricks enthusiastically. Their heads drove up and down over the perfect, engorged tubes of young flesh, and their tightly clasped lips rode the smooth, exciting shafts, while the play of their cheeks revealed the enormous suction each brought to the task of serving the other's pleasure – an erotic picture as fascinating and stimulating as anything I had ever watched. Cary's cock was completely concealed by Mike's adoring mouth. Cary wasn't able to take all of Mike's gigantic shaft in his mouth, so about an inch at the base of it was still visible as the two double-sucked like twin gods of beauty and passion, each worshipping at the other's altar. It wouldn't be long before Cary was able to deep-throat and fully service a cock as big as Mike's, however.

I masturbated as I watched them, and when their breathing and movements indicated they approached orgasm, I brought myself near my own discharge. When it became obvious they were filling each other's hungry mouths with their hot emissions of passionate love, my cum shot out onto their two bodies. Spent, I lay across them as they continued to hold each other's bodies in their arms, and their beautiful cocks in their adoring mouths.

It was getting quite late, and they both had a full day of rehearsals ahead of them. I suggested we call it a night, and plan on renewal of our lovemaking the next night. They agreed.

Cary apologized for his and Mike having spent so much time focused on each other, and excluding me to some extent. "Hell, you haven't even got fucked yet, have you?" I admitted I had not. "Mike, I think we need to do something about that."

Cary told me to get on all fours, and he directed Mike to lubricate my ass. "We're both gonna fill your hot ass with cum before we quit for the night." He drove himself into me for a long time, grunting and panting with passion – I backed up on his thrusting big cock, and my ass-ring held it tightly as I countered the plunging shaft invading me so thrillingly and – since Cary had blown a load so recently – endlessly. Finally, with loud cries of joy he spurted palpably into my body, and he continued to fuck, although with somewhat abated passion, long after his orgasm. Then he said, "You ready to take over, Mike?"

Mike was, and Cary pulled his cock from me as Mike shoved his monster deep into me, in one fierce plunge. As wonderful as Cary's prick had felt, Mike's much larger weapon increased my pleasure exponentially. He, too, fucked long and very hard, and I was almost exhausted when his shouts finally signaled the approach of his orgasm, which was unmistakable as I felt him explode deep inside me.

My ass had just been treated to something like twenty-five minutes of straight pounding by two of the sexiest young men imaginable, and I was in absolute bliss as those same two Adonises now kissed me and cuddled with me for the remainder of the night.

We awoke and snuggled the next morning, each getting up to pee, but returning to the bed to cuddle and play. I told them it was about time to get up and get ready for the day's activities, but Mike wanted a slight deferment. "We've got time for one round of fucks, don't we?"

Cary put his arms around Mike's hips and kissed his prick. "God, I want this monster again, Mike. If we have to, we'll make time for me to take it up my ass at least once this morning." I enthusiastically agreed, saying I was eager to watch the operation closely.

Cary knelt on the side of the bed; Mike stood behind him and lubricated his ass. Then, with my face only inches away, I watched as Mike's huge prick penetrated that heaven between Cary's beautiful cheeks. Cary squirmed and humped, and Mike fucked like there was no tomorrow – driving his enormous cock as far as it could go, and then almost pulling out with each backstroke. The lubricant made his fat, luscious shaft glisten as he plunged it in and out, and the ring of Cary's sphincter muscle followed the driving monster as it went in and out. It was a beautiful, exciting, and totally hypnotizing thing to watch. "Look good?" Cary asked me. I kissed him and assured him it looked so good I needed to take Mike's place when he finished. "You're next in line to fill my ass with cum this morning," Cary promised. I kissed him again, and returned to my study.

Soon Mike was unable to control himself, and pressed as hard against Cary as he could. I watched his buttocks quiver while he delivered short little strokes and his load erupted into the beautiful blond's perfectly formed golden ass – which twitched along with his invader's. As Mike finally subsided, he turned and grinned at me. "Your turn, baby."

Mike pulled his still enormous cock out and I immediately stepped behind Cary to replace Mike's prick with mine. Having been on the receiving end of a relay-team fuck like this only a few hours before, I knew how wonderful Cary must have been feeling at that moment. Mike played with my ass as I fucked Cary vigorously. "Feel my cum in there?" he whispered into my ear as he nibbled on it.

"Jesus, Mike, it's plenty hot and slippery; you really filled him up. I didn't think it was possible to improve on how Cary's ass feels when I fuck him, but you've done it! Cary, you're absolutely crammed full of Mike's love ... God, you feel incredible."

"Yeah, fuck me, John ... put your load in there with Mike's."

Mike got on the bed and lay on his back, his head between Cary's legs, looking up at his ass as my prick was driving in and out. "Man that looks hot ... and I can see my cum all over your cock."

"Suck my balls, Mike," Cary gasped. Mike cheerfully honored the request, and I felt my own balls rubbing against Mike's forehead as he sucked Cary's dick.

Soon I was ready to supplement Cary's morning cum intake, and with a cry I began to shoot inside him. He backed all the way against my cock and wriggled his ass. "God that feels good. Just fuckin' fill me up!" I did my best.

At long last I pulled out of Cary, who turned and said, "I've got a helluva load I want to put in somebody. Who's gonna suck it or take it up the butt?"

Cary sat on the edge of the bed, and Mike knelt before him, saying, "We'll both suck you off, how's that?" Cary agreed that sounded fine, took Mike's head in his hands, and with a lunge drove his prick deep into his mouth. He fucked Mike wildly as I knelt next to him, and in a few minutes took his cock from Mike's mouth and drove it into mine. Mike's head and mine were side-by-side, Cary holding them in his two hands, and he now began to alternate fucking our eager mouths, all the time urging us to suck hard and get ready for his load. Our eager lips clasped him tightly as they rode up and down his hard, but velvety shaft while it plunged in and out of our mouths.

Considering he had not cum yet that morning, Cary went a very long time before his orgasm loomed. Finally, he stepped back a pace and said, "I'm gonna shoot on both of you ... open your mouths for it." Mike and I were kneeling shoulder-to-shoulder, and we put our mouths next to each other. Cary seized his prick, masturbated savagely, and soon was spraying a huge of load of cum into our mouths and all over our faces. His prick looked absolutely beautiful as his scalding hot, white cum exploded out of the end with enormous force. He flopped it around after he finished discharging, and the final few drops spattered our adoring mouths. Mike and I turned to each other and licked Cary's cum off each other's faces, then kissed passionately as Cary pressed us to him. Cary knelt and put his face between ours. "You guys are great. I've never had this much fun in my life."

We all agreed we were having a helluva good time, but duty awaited. We also determined that we needed to take it easy during the day and evening, so that tonight could be as hot as last night had been. We took a three-way shower that was as much fun as it was inefficient – lots of kissing and sucking and caressing – but we were finally ready to face the day.

The next two nights were fully as hot as the first, actually – all three of us fucked each other to orgasm at least once and sucked at least one load out of the other two cocks each of those two nights. The kissing, caressing, hugging and snuggling were unbounded and wonderful.

Mike and Cary were totally captivated with each other, and I loved to watch their very tender kissing and caressing almost as much as I adored seeing them fuck and suck each other like sex-crazed savages. I was, thank God, very much a party to their lovemaking, though. They were obviously falling in love with each other, but they were also apparently conscientious about the fact that we were here together, and that I had been the agency that brought about their confluence. They shared their wondrous cocks and beautiful asses with me. Their kisses and caresses favored me as much as they did each other. They eagerly welcomed me into their mouths and asses and accepted my emissions with as much eagerness as they consumed each other's. Each of them fucked me with as much passion and joy as he did the other. By the time we were ready to return home, I felt like one half of a pair of lovers – beautiful, blond Cary and dark, exciting Mike together made up the other half. And it had been lovemaking of the highest and most rewarding order on all sides.

There was little about our second and third nights of frenzied lovemaking that was significantly different from our first. One milestone was achieved, however, when Cary at long last rimmed me. I had, of course, eaten his ass frequently, and his ass-ring always gripped my tongue tightly when I did so, but he had apparently not yet been moved to reciprocate. On our second night as a threesome, however, we all began eating ass and tongue-fucking. After Mike and I had spent some time sharing Cary by alternating one sucking his cock and the other eating his ass at the same time, Cary was so excited he pressed his face first into Mike's ass and munched noisily and happily before according me the same honor. Mike got so horny watching Cary eat my butt at one point that he jacked off, and his cum shot all over my asshole and Cary's mouth while I was getting tongue-fucked by my young blond stud. Cary happily made sure none of the precious juice was wasted, and was so excited he asked Mike to eat my ass while he jacked off on us. Mike was happy to comply, and I was certainly not averse to taking part in the exercise, either.

At another point we were showering together, and instead of permitting Mike to get out and pee, we insisted he pee on us, which he did, and which started a round of very stimulating play in streams of piss shooting from all our cocks onto our chests, our asses, and even onto our upturned faces. Very, very hot! I had been taught by my high-school lover, Bob, how very exciting it is to begin a blow job by starting to suck a cock just as your partner stops peeing, and

I was glad to experience it with Cary and Mike, and to introduce them to the sensation.

Our lovemaking in that motel was wonderful – committed, varied, incredibly stimulating, totally and magnificently passionate, and yet very often as sweet and tender as it was frenzied and savage. During the space of our three nights of sex, each of us surely took a total of around fifteen loads of cum in his mouth or up his ass, although I suspect Cary and I did even better, since Mike – characteristically – was an incredible cum machine feeding both of us. All those hot loads that had graced my mouth and butt had been delivered with astonishing style by two of the hottest, most beautiful young men I have ever been to bed with – and yet at the same time, we enjoyed a sweet sharing of our complete selves with each other, and a joyous camaraderie

The final sex we shared before preparing to check out was actually a ritual, which I suggested to the two young studs: "I want us to do something special to mark how wonderful it's been sharing this bed. I want us to drink a toast in cum from all three of us to our friendship, and to ..."

"To our love?" Cary said.

Mike kissed Cary, then me. "Yeah ... to our love."

"Okay. One of us can jack off in his hand and keep his cum there while the others shoot off in his mouth, and he saves it. Then he can take his own cum in his mouth with the two loads he's got there, and we'll all share it. How's that?"

"Sounds like a good plan. Who's the lucky guy that gets to collect loads?"

Mike laughed. "Hell, John, it's your idea ... I think Cary and I ought to start getting ready to fill up your mouth."

We all masturbated, and soon I shot my load into my cupped palm as Mike and Cary beat their beautiful cocks frantically, almost under my nose. Cary noted he was getting close, and shoved his prick into my mouth and fucked for only a few strokes before delivering a massive amount of hot cum. Mike was not far behind, and soon I had his cock inside my mouth to receive his offering. I looked up at both of them as they smiled down at me, and took my own load from my hand into my mouth. I swished the mouthful of cum around in my mouth to mix it thoroughly. We three knelt together, head-to-head, and I leaned over and kissed Cary, giving him a part of the mouthful of cum I had for us to celebrate. Then I kissed Mike and gave him another portion. We looked at each other solemnly, I nodded, and we all swallowed. Then, after a minute, we broke out into huge grins and laughs, and hugged tightly.

In our last few minutes together in my motel room, where my bed had been an altar of sensual adoration of a magnificent order for three nights, we kissed and held each other, and – yes – used the L word a lot. It wasn't just, "Love ya!" either. Cary and Mike each looked into my eyes as they held me, and very seriously said, "I love you, John." I said the same to them, and with equal honesty and fervor. But as I watched them say "I love you" to each other, with total dedication and seriousness, followed by their sharing very long and tender kisses, I felt I was seeing a meaningful love develop between them. I also felt joy in sensing I would be included as at least a part of their love and an almost paternal pride in knowing I had helped bring it about. It was only intuition at that point, but it soon crystallized exactly as I sensed it would.

On the drive back to Dowd, the girls occupied the back seat of the car, and were unable to see, as I could, that Mike and Cary held hands for almost the entire trip.

7. HOUSEHOLD GROWTH AND TELEPHONE ENCOUNTERS

The sexual activity I enjoyed with Mike and Cary individually before our trip to Florida changed surprisingly little afterwards. It seemed clear to me the two were falling in love, but it might also have been simply fascination for the plain out-and-out lust they had shared. Time would tell, of course, but I felt sure they were going to be seeing a great deal of each other in the future. Who could blame them, of course? Mike was as hung as Cary was beautiful – and if Mike wasn't as gorgeous as his blond admirer, he was extremely attractive, and if Cary's prick wasn't as large as his dark devotee's, it was certainly of a generous size and was as beautiful and juicy as could be wished. They were both trim and muscular – beautiful bodies by any standards. Most importantly, they were both extremely nice young men as well as extremely horny ones, and they admired those qualities in each other. I certainly admired all these qualities in both Mike and Cary and feared they might become so taken with each other that I might no longer be included as a part of their sexual diets.

It was no surprise, then, when Mike called me a couple of days following our return from Florida and said he and Cary wanted to have a talk with me. "We can come out to your house, if you want to pick us up. We really want to talk, but if you want, we can fool around afterwards. Sound good?"

"Sounds great. Pick you guys up at the dorm at eight?" That was agreed upon. I was afraid they were going to tell me this was a "goodbye fuck," or something – that they had decided they were going to fuck only each other in the future. Certainly the way they had held and kissed each other toward the end of our Florida visit and the way they had held hands like young lovebirds on the way home suggested something like that might be in the wind.

They piled into my car boisterously at 8:00 and sat together on the front seat, again holding hands. I was pleased to note, though, that Cary played with my leg all the way out to my house. Our conversation on the way was strictly trivial and stayed so until I had made them drinks and we all sat down in the living room – I on a chair, and Cary and Mike next to each other on the sofa, opposite me.

I opened the discussion. "So, unless I'm blind, you're going to tell me you're in love with each other, right?"

They exchanged grins then Mike transferred his to me. "Jesus, is it that obvious?"

I laughed. "No, of course, not, but I'm not blind, either." They moved even closer to each other and linked hands. "I don't blame either one of you. In fact, you'd both be stupid not to fall in love. You're not only the nicest and hottest guys I know, you're both beautiful. Shit, I love you both."

Cary stood and came to me. Taking my face in his hands he kissed me sweetly. "We both love you, too, John ... but the way we feel about each other, well it's ..."

"Cary, I know the difference between loving someone and being in love with him. I love both of you guys, but I'm not in love with either of you." It was my turn to grin. "It's a good thing, too, since I can see you are both totally, understandably and ... I think ... wonderfully in love."

Cary returned and sat next to Mike again, who kissed him and put his arm around him. "You're not mad, or jealous, or something like that?"

"Mad? Not at all. Jealous? Well, certainly a little envious, but I honestly am pleased to see what you guys feel for each other. It's a wonderful thing, being really bit by the love-bug the first time."

They both agreed they had thought themselves in love before – with girls, of all things – but it had been nothing like what they had just begun to feel toward each other. Cary said, almost defiantly, "So I guess that means we're both gay, but it's the way we feel."

"Cary ... Mike ... you're in love with each other, and I think that's great. Practically everyone you know would condemn you as queer if they knew ... there's absolutely no sense in beating yourselves up over it. Needless to say, you can't flaunt it, but you can't deny it, either, can you? Not to each other."

"We talked a long time about this," Mike said, "and we both know we're in love ... queer or not."

"So be in love, just keep it your little secret."

"That's almost exactly what we hoped you'd tell us, and it's also what we've already decided we need to do."

"Good. You guys will be fine. You'll probably have to date a few girls once in a while, to keep up appearances, but there's no reason anyone should suspect you're anything but best friends. I certainly never suspected either one of you was remotely gay."

"Cary and I have talked about this so much in the last few days ... almost nonstop ... and neither one of us had really thought we were anything but straight, either."

"Neither of you has ever been attracted to guys?"

Mike grinned sheepishly. "Well, yeah ... I guess deep down it's been in my mind all along, but I really just thought it was a normal way to feel."

Cary added, "Me, too."

"Guys, it is a normal way to feel; don't let anyone ever convince you otherwise. I know when I first approached you, Mike ... uh, have you guys talked about that?"

"Sure ... I told Cary about our first experience, and he told me about the first time he did anything with you." He grinned hugely. "You're a horny guy, John."

"Well, when I started sucking your cock in that hotel room in Atlanta, Mike, and that night you pulled your cock out in my car and let me blow you, Cary, I had no idea either one of you would ever let me do anything like it again." They both laughed and agreed we had all gone quite a bit past that. "But

I sure am glad you did ... and I have enjoyed sex with both of you guys so much, and the sex we all three shared was incredible. But, unless I miss my guess you're basically here tonight to tell me it's coming to an end, right?"

"Get over here and sit between us," Mike said. I did as he asked. "John, you're going to be happy to know that you miss your guess completely."

"You mean you both still want to ... well ..."

"Yeah! We both still want to do all those wonderful things we've been doing with you ... it's just that there's gonna be a lot of the time when we're alone together, and really making love to each other. But that won't bother you if we can still have sex with you like we have been, will it?"

"Of course not ... in fact, it sounds perfect."

"Great, then it's set."

"So, are we talking about regular threesomes, or what?"

Cary said, "There are gonna be plenty of times when I'm horny and Mike is busy, and if it's okay with you, I'm gonna come over and give you the same kind of fucking I have been."

"And if Cary's busy or out-of-town or something, and I'm horny," – Mike snickered – "like I almost always am, you better expect to take care of my big cock for me."

Cary added. "The thing is we both love sex with you, and we feel that you're really a part of our being together, so we don't want to cut you out, no matter how much Mike and I want to be together. And there'll be plenty of times when we want to share our love with you ... three ways, just like we did in Florida."

"Jesus, I love you guys."

Mike stood and began to unbutton his Levi's. "And we love you ... and we're about to fuck your brains out."

Cary stood and followed suit. "We, on the other hand, don't have any brains left ... we fucked each other's brains out practically all day yesterday, but we want you to fuck us both anyway."

Mike was already displaying a magnificent, huge hard-on, Cary's beauty was soon bared, and I lost no time in getting naked. Within minutes we were in bed together, repeating the incredible sexual antics we had explored only a few nights earlier – and although both Cary and Mike professed to be near exhaustion from their previous day's marathon sex, they both delivered wonderful hot loads to all asses and mouths in attendance and eagerly took everything I was moved to give them – which was all I could.

It proved difficult for the two young lovers to find a safe location for their lovemaking, especially when they practiced it as assiduously as they did. They explored the possibility of exchanging roommates, but that didn't prove feasible, so they asked if it were possible, providing Mike could bring one of the family cars to campus, for them to live unofficially in my spare bedroom at the lake. I agreed, and subsequently I often fell asleep to the sound of their lovemaking in the next room. It didn't bother me too much, since the arrangement afforded me easy opportunity to make love with one when the other was gone or otherwise busy – which happened often, thank God – and it made it much easier for them to call for me to join the two of them on threesome nights. The most fun, though, was when the two of them appeared naked and erect at my bed for a thrilling three-way love feast.

I had been having sex with Mike and Cary an average of at least once a week with each before they became partners, and I was thrilled to find that we pretty well maintained that schedule now, but added the thrilling, at-least-weekly threesome to the arrangement.

Living in a house on a very secluded part of a large lake, with a private dock and a ski-boat, proved to be very attractive for my new roommates as well, and we soon formed something of a household. It was only the second time I had enjoyed a sex life with a live-in lover – the first having been the unforgettable Richard Austin, with whom I had fallen deeply in love, and who for a summer had shared my bed, and whose beautiful face, wonderful body, and "Mike-size" cock had been the most important things in my life. The affair had ended rather abruptly and painfully, but I still held warm regard for Richard and treasured memories of his magnificent lovemaking.

Now, even with two hot live-in lovers – admittedly in love with each other, but magnanimously and gloriously sharing their love with me – I still fantasized about the gorgeous and elusive "Danny"; each time I saw him on campus, he looked more appealing. I really felt he was the most beautiful boy I had seen since I had spent my freshman year in high school drooling over a magnificent boy named Alan. Alan had permitted license on only one occasion – and then he only allowed me to suck his cock in a bathroom stall, after which he blew his load on the wall and told me never to bother him again. I was hoping for much more with "Danny," but had no reason to expect it; just because I thought he was beautiful did not mean anything would ever happen between us. Given that reasoning, I would have been going to bed regularly with Tab Hunter, the movie actor who, at that point, I probably regarded as the most beautiful human being alive. Hope, on the other hand, doesn't cost a thing – so I continued. The intramural spring soccer matches were coming up soon, and I hoped at least to learn his name; where it would go from there, if anywhere, remained to be decided.

I was of course on hand for the first soccer exhibition game in the spring, and there on the field was my beautiful idol sporting the number 11 on his jersey and shorts. The program revealed that number 11 was Alan M. Hagood. So, my high school Adonis and this latest demigod I worshipped coincidentally shared the same first name

I had never, I think, sat through a soccer game, but suddenly I was an avid fan, and if I learned little about the game from watching, it was because I never took my eyes off the trim figure wearing number 11. He looked absolutely magnificent, running around with his perfect, long legs disappearing into the shorts that also revealed what I had hoped to see – a beautifully rounded ass that was particularly attractive. His loose jersey did nothing to hide his broad shoulders and narrow waist, and when he was sweaty, it would cling to his chest, clearly showing his nipples. I sat in the front row, near the bench, and observed him as closely and as often as I could, my sexual fantasies not distracted by his teammates – most of whom were foreign students from Africa and the Middle East. Only one of them – according to the program, John R. Farrar – struck me as attractive, a tall, blond, very handsome guy. Had Alan (no longer "Danny") not been on the field, young Mr. Farrar would have struck me as very, very attractive indeed.

Knowing his name at last, I had no trouble learning more about the fabulously beautiful Alan Hagood. He was from Pennsylvania, a freshman, almost nineteen years old. He was a solid B+ student – major undeclared as far as I could tell – and he lived in the athletic dormitory. I also learned his telephone number and finally decided that calling him was probably the only way I was ever going to be able to talk with him and – hopefully – get to know him. Since I had absolutely no other reason to telephone him, I decided simple frankness was the best approach: I would just tell him up front how beautiful I thought he was and how much I enjoyed looking at him. Needless to say, I did not plan to tell him who I was – certainly not initially, and not even later unless some reason for me to let him know my identity crystallized. If he was offended, and hung up on me, I was no worse off than before, after all. It was certainly worth a try.

This was long before telephone equipment allowed someone to see the number of the person calling. Caller ID has dealt a serious blow to the obscene telephone caller's game.

Finally determining that I had to talk to Alan, at least, I called him one Sunday evening. "Could I speak to Alan Hagood, please?"

"This is Mark Hagood ... Alan is my first name, but I go by Mark."

"Oh, I'm sorry. Mark, then. Look, this is going to be a very strange call, I guess. I really hope I won't offend you."

"Offend me?" A little laugh. "Well, I hope you won't either. What can I do for you?"

"Mark, I can't say who this is, for reasons that will become obvious, but let me tell you that I'm not some kind of nut or something. I'm a professor here, and I've been seeing you around campus a lot. In fact, I first noticed you at freshman orientation in the fall."

"What's this all about?"

"I'll be frank, Mark. I just ... I wanted to call and tell you how very, very much I admire you."

A rather awkward pause, then: "Admire me? Do I know you? Your voice doesn't sound familiar, and I'm pretty good with voices."

"No, you don't know me, and I don't know you either, so when I say I admire you, obviously I'm talking about physical appearance here. What I mean to say is that I think you're probably the most handsome guy I've ever seen in my life. And I just want to tell you how really attractive I think you are."

"Well, gosh ... I don't know quite what to say. I mean, it's nice that you think I'm attractive. I ... well, thanks."

"I know what that probably makes me in your eyes, telling you I think you're attractive, but it really doesn't make any difference, I guess. That's basically it, anyway; I am an expert on good-looking guys, Mark, and I think you are the best looking one I've ever seen! I guess that's it."

"Wow... I really don't know what to say, except to thank you again. Yeah, it's really nice of you to feel that way about me. I'm flattered."

"I don't really mean to flatter you so much as I want to be able to tell you what I've felt about you for a long time now. Do you mind if I use a little stronger word?"

Another laugh from Mark. "No, I don't mind ... I'm a big boy."

"Yes. You are a big boy, except man is a lot better word in your case. Well anyway, the word I think of when I think of you ... and I think of you a lot, Mark ... is beautiful. I think you are a truly beautiful man."

"That really is nice of you to feel that way, and it's nice of you to want to say it to me ... even if it does embarrass me a little bit. So, can I ask you a question?"

"Sure."

"Where does this lead? Are you asking to meet me, or something? I mean, do you want something from me, or did you just want to tell me you think I'm ..."

"Beautiful is the word. Really."

"Okay ... sounds weird to me, but okay, beautiful. So is there something else?"

"Mark, I'd be lying if I said I didn't want to meet you and a lot more. Obviously, if I feel as I do about you, I'm gay, and I have no idea how you feel about that."

"No, no, that doesn't bother me at all, but look, I've got to tell you that I'm not ..."

"No, don't even say it, that's beside the point. It doesn't matter whether you're gay or straight. I'm not asking you to do anything with me. I just wanted to speak with you at last, and to tell you that someone finds you unbelievably handsome and attractive. I wish I did know you because just talking with you now, I'm pretty sure you're a nice guy, too ... but ... Oh hell, that's it, Mark. A couple of times I've almost stopped you on campus to tell you, but I had no idea how you'd react, so I decided I'd take the cowardly way and call you, in case you got pissed off. Anyway, I feel good having told you, and feel even better having talked with you."

"Well, thanks again ... that really is nice of you. And I wouldn't have been pissed off, really; I'm not that kind of guy."

"Do you mind if I call you again some time?"

"No ... that would be fine. Call me. It's nice to talk to someone that admires you. No one's ever told me I was beautiful before."

"Now, I'll bet your mother has!"

He laughed again. "Well, sure, but ... well, you know what I mean. It makes me feel really good to be told I'm that good-looking, and I can tell you're a nice guy, too. So, call me again, okay?"

"I will, and I promise not to call too often, and be a pest. And I'm John, by the way."

"Fair enough. Well, thanks again ... John. And we'll talk later."

"Great. Thanks for being so nice, Mark. You really are unbelievably beautiful. Maybe gorgeous is a better word, though."

He laughed. "You've got great taste, John. First handsome, then beautiful, and now gorgeous. You keep upping the stakes." Another laugh. "Hey, I'd better go. Bye now."

My heart was pounding as I hung up. He was really nice as well as beautiful. He seemed intelligent, and I loved his voice – soft and sexy! Most important, he hadn't been offended, and I really felt he was pleased for me to tell him how gorgeous he was. When I encountered him walking across campus, as I seemed to do frequently, he now looked even better. Mark. Nice name – solid and masculine and sexy, better than Alan, even given the resonance of that name in my memory. And the equally resonant Danny sobriquet was quickly forgotten, of course.

I thought about the beautiful Mark more and more in my fantasies. I often breathed his name as I masturbated, envisioning him in my arms or in some place even more intimate. I frequently listened to the sound of Mike and Cary fucking each other in the next room as I pretended Mark was with me, and I must confess the thought of Mark even crossed my mind occasionally when it was really Mike or Cary I was sucking or fucking, or who was actually the one plowing or draining me.

I called Mark about every other week. With each call he got friendlier, and he recognized my voice the second time I called him. Each conversation yielded a bit more familiarity, and he was soon telling me about how his class work was going, details of his family life he felt he just wanted to talk about, and he even revealed, when we talked about his situation regarding a love interest in his life, that although he was "seeing someone," he didn't think it was going anywhere special.

"That must be your choice. Hell, she'd be crazy not to want to pursue a relationship with you."

"You know, John, not everyone thinks I'm as attractive as you do."

67

"Mark, nobody thinks you're as attractive as I do ... even though I'll bet practically everyone else thinks you're plenty attractive."

"Well, this ... this person says I'm attractive, but its more me that's really attracted to ... well, I don't think I should use the name. Let's just say it's not as two-sided as I'd like for it to be."

"She's crazy! God, if I thought you found me attractive, I'd be falling all over myself to get to you. But, hey, I know that's not even a remote possibility; still, I wish you ... oh, never mind."

"Now how would I know if you're attractive? But you know, one of these days, we are going to meet ... I have a feeling. And I'll bet you are a very attractive guy. I can tell you're a nice person."

"Thanks. Nice to hear. But you know what I mean; I couldn't be attractive to you in the way that you're attractive to me."

"You mean sexually attractive, right?"

"Right. There's a lot working against me, after all. I'm older, I'm not beautiful like you, and you may have noticed by my voice and my name, I'm the wrong sex."

"You're not that old (I had told him my age), and I'll bet you're a lot more handsome than you care to think ... and you're just naturally assuming I couldn't be physically attracted to another guy."

My heart beat a bit faster. "Mark ... have you ever made it with another guy?"

"You haven't really told me you have, although I assume you have, since you told me you were gay. Before I answer your question, you answer mine. Have you ever had sex with another guy?"

"You'd be better off asking me if I've ever had sex with a woman."

"Okay," he chuckled, "have you ever had sex with a woman?"

"Once ... and I didn't think it was any fun at all. But guys? Yeah ... lotsa guys, I'm afraid."

"Was it fun? Never mind, don't answer. Stupid question. Now, answer this: Do you want to have sex with me?"

"I'll be completely frank with you, Mark. I want to have sex with you more than anything I can think of. Plain enough?"

"Plain enough. I don't know, John. I can't encourage you, but I enjoy talking with you, and I don't know where this will all lead. I'm not going to tell you flat out that it can never happen. I'm an open minded kind of guy, after all."

"Jesus, Mark, that's the most ... well, okay, I'm not going to push it. I want to get to know you, and maybe someday you'll ... well, you know."

"I know."

"And you haven't answered my question yet. Have you ever had sex with another guy?"

"John, someday we're going to meet, and we'll talk all about that then, and about anything else you want. Let's just leave it there, okay? Look, I've got to study. Call me again soon?"

"I will. I think you encouraged me a little bit, Mark. Thanks."

A laugh. "I don't know if I meant to or not. I didn't discourage you, though, okay? Talk to you soon, babe!" He hung up.

Babe? Sounded pretty chummy! And – he hadn't said he'd never had sex with a guy, or that he would categorically refuse to consider it with me; there might be hope, after all. However, the school year was about to end, and I knew Mark would be in Pennsylvania for the summer. So – if anything were going to develop, it appeared it would have to wait for the fall.

My last call to Mark before he left for the summer yielded nothing particularly new. He did, however, suggest we finally get together and meet in person when he got back for the fall. "I really feel I know you now – and I want to meet you in person. Surely you know there's no need to keep anonymous any more. You should know I respect your confidence, like I respect your right to feel about me the way you do. Hell, you haven't been offensive about it at all. I feel really flattered by your feelings, and I also feel that you respect me and my feelings."

"I do, Mark ... and I'm going to miss talking to you this summer, but we'll talk when you get back, and if you still want, we'll get together then and have a beer and really get to know each other."

"Great, babe ... have a good summer.

8. DEAN

As both Mike and Cary were going to their respective homes for the summer, it seemed that the hot season promised to be a very dry one as well, and it would have proven to be just that had it not been for two unexpected situations: the re-entry into my sex life of my big-dicked, studly ex-lover Richard, and the appearance of the super-stud, Dean.

Had it not been for the success of my getting acquainted with Mark by telephone, however limited that had been at that point, Dean would probably not have been anything in my life except a fleeting, albeit gorgeous and unbelievably sexy, will-o'-the wisp.

I first encountered him at the local high school, where I was meeting the school band director, who planned to ride with me to a nearby town to see his band perform at a spring exhibition football game. He asked if it were all right if a couple of the high school boys rode with us, since they otherwise had no transportation. Sight unseen, I agreed that the boys were welcome, and when they appeared I rejoiced that I had. Although one of them was ordinary enough, the other was a real gem – Dean Williamson. He was tall, over six feet, and well built, though not unduly muscular, with the kind of long legs that really turn me on. He had fairly short, golden-blond hair and was extremely handsome. Not only was he extremely attractive physically, he had a very knowing air about him, exuding an almost palpable cockiness and manly sexiness I found captivating. In fact, he was considerably more cocky and sexy than he was pleasant and friendly – which was fine with me, of course.

The thing that really switched my libido to "ready," though, was his clothing, and what it revealed. He wore a very tight tee shirt, which emphasized his washboard stomach and nicely developed chest. That was sexy and very appealing, but those adjectives are totally insufficient to describe the revelation of his pants. He wore Levi's so tight I wondered how he got into them. They delineated his legs beautifully and also acted as a perfect medium to display a rounded, and – for one with a basically lean frame – ample and succulent ass. But it was where the legs joined in front that the real thrill was manifest. It was easy to see there the outline of his obviously huge prick nestling along his left leg, and the considerable bulge at the groin seemed to promise balls of a magnitude I had not seen in ten years or so. At that time, my high-school-aged lover, Billy, and I had nursed on the massive testicular endowment of Phil, a classmate of Billy's and our sometime fuck partner. In short, Dean seemed to be as well-endowed as he was attractive.

Naturally, I made it a point to sit next to him at the game and engage him in conversation. Though he was fairly sullen and uncommunicative, I did learn a few things. He was eighteen, and although he was a high-school senior, this was his first year in Dowd. His father was a physician who had just set up a practice here; prior to this, Dean and his family – which included four older brothers – had lived in Athens, Georgia, where his father had been on the medical staff of the University of Georgia. To date, apparently, Dean had found little to like about living in his new hometown. He seemed restless and bored.

When he decided he had to go pee, I accompanied him, and stood next to him at the urinal trough in the stadium bathroom. He had to completely unbutton his Levi's and lower them a bit in order to release his cock – it was that big, and his pants were that tight. He was wearing no underwear, which turned me on even further, and I got very excited indeed as I surreptitiously watched him reach down into his left pants leg to free the undoubtedly magnificent thing that had been bulging so temptingly there. He pulled it out with his right hand, and flopped it noisily into his left as he started to piss. His cock, as he revealed it to my gaze – unwittingly, I assumed – was astonishing. It was circumcised, smooth and white, and though flaccid, was about eight inches in length, and of extremely large girth; how big it might grow when erect was glorious to consider. Instead of encircling it with his fist as he peed, in the normal way, he let it lie flat across the open palm of his left hand – an extremely fat shaft of throbbing, exciting young cock lying there in all its magnificence, shooting a forceful stream of piss from the large, beautiful, light purple head. I stood to his right and was therefore afforded a full view of the tempting and extremely exciting sight. I couldn't really see his balls fully, but they promised to be as ample as his bulging basket had promised they would. He looked neither right nor left, but I had the feeling he sensed my examining him and was presenting his luscious monster cock for me to appreciate. I imagined he might actually hear my salivary glands working overtime as I fantasized about sinking to my knees in front of him to worship the thrilling equipment he displayed so alluringly and feasting on it. When he finished peeing, he slapped his prick loudly against his left palm a few times and then shook it for some time before returning it to his pants. I had as much trouble getting my prick back in my pants as he did – mine, because it was so hard, his because it was so large and his sexy pants so tight. To say that I was intrigued by Dean is an understatement of cosmic dimension.

There was no excuse for me seeing him again. As I had with Mark, I decided to telephone him and see if we could get together. Dean was so uncommonly sexy that I really felt a direct approach might be best – simply call him and ask if he would be willing to consider having sex with me.

I tried any number of times to call Dean, but someone else always seemed to answer the telephone. Needless to say, I never left a message. Finally, one evening in late May I called, and he answered the phone himself.

"Look, you don't know me, but I met you a while back, and I just wanted to tell you how hot and sexy you are."

"Who the hell is this?"

"I can't tell you that right now, but I was just wondering if there's any way you'd be interested in meeting with me for a while."

"Is this a joke?"

"No, I'm dead serious. I think you're the hottest guy I've ever seen, and I'd really like to get together with you."

"Get together with me for what?"

"Dean, you know damn well what I mean."

"Yeah, I do, but what makes you think I'd want to do anything with you? I don't even know who you are."

"Well, is there anything I could offer you to convince you?"

"What did you have in mind?"

I swallowed, and jumped in. "Well, for openers, how about a good blow job?"

"I can get one of those any time I want. Anything else, or are we just wasting our time here?"

"What about cash?"

He laughed. "Well, it took you long enough to get around to it. Twenty bucks. You get one hour, and you can ..." There was a click on the line, and I could hear a radio playing in the background. Dean said, "Okay, who's on the phone? Get off, this is personal." There was a snicker on the line, but the radio continued to play. "Look, I'm gonna hang up ... maybe another time." He broke the connection.

I was crushed; it had looked like he was going to come through for me. Twenty dollars was a lot of money for me at that time, but Dean Williamson was a lot of hot man, too. True, I had Mike and Cary, but they were both about to leave for the summer, and an occasional liaison with a stud such as this one promised to be would easily be worth a twenty-dollar investment. I tried to call Dean again and again, but as before, I always got someone else.

One evening shortly after the summer vacation began, I was driving home around 7:00, heading for the lake. I saw someone hitchhiking, and he looked attractive. As I slowed down to look better, I saw that it was Dean, dressed as sexily as before. Of course, I stopped and offered him a ride. "Where are you headed?"

"Out to the lake. Gonna go swimming off the bridge."

"Be glad to take you there. You're Dean Williamson, right?"

"Right. I don't know you, do I? But you do look familiar." I reminded him that he had gone to the spring football exhibition in my car. "Oh yeah, I remember. So, where are you headed?"

"I live out on the lake, a few miles from here. I can drop you at the bridge, or if you want, you can go swimming at my dock, or there's a swimming pool next door and no one home."

"You got a beer?"

"Sure."

"Sounds good. Let's go."

My heart began to beat considerably faster. On the way out to my house I asked him if he liked it around here any better yet, and he said he still hated it. Nothing to do – no excitement. "There was plenty of action where we lived before, but this place is dead."

"What kind of action?"

He smiled – the first time I remembered seeing him smile. "Oh, messin' around ... you know. I could always find something to do or someone to mess around with there." I intended to pursue this subject. "By the way, if I go out to your place, will you bring me back to town?"

"Sure, I'll drop you at your house if you want. How much time do you have?"

"I don't have to be anywhere tonight ... just whenever I get home is okay. My folks don't mind. Shit, they don't know what I do most of the time, anyway."

At my house I told Dean I'd get us a beer. He had seen the array of whiskey bottles on the bar, and asked if he could have a real drink. "A little bourbon would sure go down good right now!"

"Well ... okay. You're only, what, nineteen?" I knew he couldn't be more than eighteen – if that – but I wasn't in a mood to enforce the drinking laws at that moment. He nodded, and I added, "But what the hell ... you didn't get it here, right?"

"Right! And I may be only nineteen, but I'm a big boy now." He put his hand on my shoulder and squeezed. The first time he touched me, and it felt electric.

I looked down at his feet, and up to the top of his head, where he towered about three inches over me. "You're definitely big, Dean ... but I wouldn't call you a boy." I dropped my gaze to the massive bulge of his groin and along his left leg for a moment then looked back up at him. "No, definitely a man."

He cupped the back of my neck with his hand and laughed. "Damn right I'm a man." He looked down at his bulging crotch and looked back up, grinning. "A pretty big man, too."

I grinned back and looked down again pointedly. "Looks damned big to me." I was getting very excited and wasn't absolutely sure where this was going, so I changed the direction of the conversation. "So, bourbon and ...?"

"Coke, if you got it." I shuddered inwardly, but filled his request – and if it was just a touch strong, well maybe I felt that might loosen some inhibitions.

He took a sip. "Wow, that's great. So, lake or swimming pool?"

"Strictly up to you ... still too light out for skinny-dipping in the lake, but clothes are strictly optional in the pool."

"Let's go in the lake for a while ... then maybe we can hit the pool."

I went in to my room and put on my bathing suit; Dean had stripped down to his by the time I returned. He wore a very tight, tiny red Speedo bathing suit, and the bulge that I found so fascinating in his pants was really impressive now – and the ass stretching the material in the back was tempting beyond belief. His body looked really great, also. He was well tanned, his legs were muscular, long, and smooth, and the well-defined chest and stomach muscles his tee shirt had displayed looked even more luscious bare. Given his facial beauty and ultra-sexy demeanor, Dean Williamson was "the stuff which dreams are made of" – wet dreams and sexual fantasies, to be sure.

We went down to the dock and swam for quite a while – Dean was a very strong swimmer – breaking only to go back up to the bar and refill our drinks. Given the lateness of the hour, I did not suggest we go water-skiing, but held out the promise of that for another visit. As it was beginning to get dark, we again went back to refill our drinks, and this time headed next door to the swimming pool. Once there, Dean asked, "You're sure it's okay to get naked?"

"Absolutely ... I'm going to." And with that I stepped out of my trunks. I made absolutely no attempt to hide the fact that I was about three-quarters erect. Dean turned away and stripped off his suit. As he bent over to pick it up, I was treated to the sight of his lovely, rounded ass, and when he turned to face me, I was thrilled. I had seen his dick in the stadium bathroom, of course, and so I knew it was big and beautiful, but as I viewed it hanging down in front of his incredibly perfect body, I almost gasped at its size and beauty. Hanging there, his cock was flaccid, but it would have been a large, tempting tool if that were its size with a raging erection. Considering that it obviously had a lot of room to grow, it was magnificent. I couldn't help but stare. "Wow!"

Dean grinned crookedly, "I've got a big dick, all right."

"Jesus, Dean ... big isn't the word for it. I can only imagine what it looks like hard."

He began to stroke it. "Hell, you don't need to use your imagination, I'll show you." He began working on it, pulling it up so that his balls were exposed as well – and the luscious, low-hanging sac with his huge nuts clearly outlined as he stroked his cock let me know that the promise of his Levi's had been real. As his fist massaged it, his large cock became gigantic. He grinned proudly, "You're lookin' at ten full inches of meat."

My own prick was now impossibly hard as I stared. "My god, Dean. You are a real stud."

He flopped his prick around a bit. It was fully erect now, and as he let go of it, it bobbed in front of him, almost parallel to the ground. "Yeah, I get told that a lot." He went over to take a sip from his drink, and with his monster cock still pointing toward the horizon, he dove into the pool. He had not commented on the obvious fact that I had been turned on by his cock; it seemed to indicate to me that I should not rush things – if I should rush at all. His having stroked himself to erection was quite possibly just for the purpose of displaying his full endowment to me, not to suggest he was going to offer it to me. Probably he was merely proud to display it; God knows he had plenty to be proud of. To calm down, I joined him in the cool water.

He played around in the water like a seal, and I spent more time watching him than I did swimming. Eventually we left the pool and flopped down on the patio furniture. Dean lay on a chaise longue with his big cock resting on his stomach, pointing at his chin, and his massive balls hanging down between his spread legs. I wanted to dive into his crotch as I had the pool, but offered instead to refill our drinks.

We had drunk several fairly strong cocktails, and Dean was getting much friendlier and more relaxed than he had been. As I stood there looking at his delectable body, my erection was unmistakable. He grinned at me, "You sure do stay hard a lot of the time."

I walked over and stood next to him. "Maybe you just turn me on."

He began to stroke his cock and looked at me, still grinning, "I turn on a lot of guys, I guess." He looked down and watched his hand bringing his cock to full attention. "Does this look good to you?"

"Yeah, Dean, it does."

He stood up slowly, allowing his prick to stand straight out, and put his hands on his hips and rotated them so his cock weaved and bobbed in front of him. "Now what are we gonna do about that?"

"That's up to you, I guess. What do you want to do about it?"

He walked up to me, grabbed a handful my hair in his hand, and forced me to my knees. "I wanna get it sucked." He held his cock with one hand and pulled my head in to it. "Open that fuckin' mouth and chow down on this big dick." I opened wide, and he drove himself rudely into me and began to fuck. He now grasped my head with both hands and drove it up and down his huge shaft. I gagged, and he eased up somewhat, so I could accommodate him. "I don't wanna gag you, I wanna get this hot cock sucked off ... I've got a big load I need to blow." My lips grasped his shaft tightly, and I exerted as much suction as I could. My hands held his driving buttocks and pulled him in to me. "God damn, that's hot," he gasped. "Suck my big fuckin' cock for me." I sucked greedily, and he mouth-fucked happily for some time, until he pushed my mouth away from him, knelt in front of me, and looked closely into my eyes. "Do you like that?"

"Yeah, Dean, I like that a lot."

"I don't usually fuck face on the first date," he laughed and rumpled my hair, "but I'm makin' an exception for you. You want me to put a big load down your throat?"

I smiled at him very slowly. "I want you to give me the biggest fuckin' load you ever shot in there."

He stood and dragged me to my feet. "Come on ... you're gonna get your wish." He took my hand and began to lead me next door. I realized then that he was more than a little drunk. We left our clothes at the pool and walked next door, totally naked, hard cocks wagging. He led me directly to my bed and forced me down onto it, on my back. He looked down at me. "I'm gonna fuckin' drown you in my cum."

I knew I could say anything I wanted – he wasn't going to remember it. "Yeah, put that huge fuckin' cock down my throat and fill me up with your hot, creamy load. I want to eat every drop of cum you've got in those huge, gorgeous balls."

"Fuckin' right ... we're gonna drain my balls." He knelt over my face, jammed his cock into my mouth, and began fucking savagely. "Gonna fuck your hot mouth. Come on and eat my big fuckin' cock ... suck a load out of it for me." I sucked as hard as I could, holding his wonderful driving ass, and fingering his asshole as he plunged into me. I opened my throat as much as possible, but was still unable to take all of his prick, but I did manage to avoid gagging.

Years before, I had learned to deep-throat Hal Weltmann's stupendous prick – a lip-stretcher perhaps even bigger than the one Dean was ramming in me – so I knew I could manage all of Dean's with a bit more effort. I exerted the necessary effort, and in a minute had all of his monster prick inside my mouth.

He grabbed my head and cradled it in both arms, and began to face-fuck me with very fast, shallow strokes. "You ready to take my load?" I nodded and sucked like a demon. Soon he drove in as far as he could and froze as I felt his cum shooting into the back of my throat with incredible force. Dean actually shouted, "Oh, Man. Eat my fuckin' load ... take all that hot cum. God I love fuckin' your hot mouth." He was heaving with passion, but re-commenced his shallow fuck as he urged me. "Take it all ... suck me dry." I relaxed my throat even further, and every bit of his delicious monster was now inside me. The cum drained from his cock into my throat as I feasted – worshipping his stupendous tool, completely thrilled.

He eventually calmed down, pulled his cock out of my mouth, and still holding my head firmly in his hands, planted a huge, passionate kiss on my lips. His tongue drove in and out of my mouth wildly, and I sucked it as I had his cock. He stopped kissing and looked into my eyes. "I can taste my cum in your mouth. Tastes great, doesn't it?"

"It's fantastic, Dean. Best and biggest load I ever ate."

He grinned crookedly, "I can tell you've eaten a lot of 'em. Well, there's plenty more where that came from."

"Yeah, it all came out of those monster balls of yours."

"And they're just achin' for you to suck them." He dropped my head and straddled it, his balls hanging over my mouth. I licked them and played with his still fairly hard cock. He groaned in delight, and I was able to take both balls into my mouth only by stretching it open as far as I could. I licked and sucked eagerly, while Dean murmured his satisfaction. Keeping his balls in my mouth, he worked his body around so that he was facing my feet. I looked up at his exciting ass as I continued to nurse on his balls.

He lowered himself so that he lay on my stomach and began fucking my ass with a finger. "How does that feel? You like that?" A muffled groan of pleasure from me spurred him on to deeper and faster fingering. I released his balls, used my hands to spread his cheeks, plunged my tongue deep into his asshole, and tongue-fucked him as feverishly as I was able. He continued finger-fucking me, but suddenly his mouth took my entire prick inside and he began to suck passionately – driving his head up and down the entire shaft, his lips tightly locked around it.

The complete abandon of my rimming and Dean's cocksucking continued for a long time. Soon I was near orgasm, and had to stop eating his ass to tell him. "Dean, I'm gonna get my load." But he only sucked harder, and soon I was spurting into his hungry mouth. He swallowed and continued to suck as if nothing had happened. I had to make him stop after a while, pulled out from under him, and knelt before him. I took his still very hard cock in one hand and held the back of his neck with the other, pulled him toward me, and kissed him before saying, "Are you gonna fuck my ass?"

He grinned rather drunkenly. "Fuckin' right I'm gonna fuck your ass. I'm gonna fill your fuckin' ass with my cum, just the way I filled your mouth."

I reached for the Vaseline, which I always had handy, and liberally coated his cock and my ass before I turned and knelt on all fours so that my ass was the obvious target for his monster. "Give it to me ... fill me up with that fuckin' dick."

"Can you take all of it? A lotta guys can't take this much meat up their butts."

"I want it in so deep it's coming out of my mouth. Come on, Dean, give it to me Fuck me!" He seized my waist and began to penetrate me. His prick was enormous, but it felt absolutely thrilling as he drove it in inexorably, muttering about my hot ass, his big prick, and all the cum he was going to put in there. I loved it, and soon his stomach was pressed against my buttocks – his entire prick buried amazingly deep inside me. "Just fuck me as hard as you can ... fast and deep, Dean ... and give me another big load."

My ass-ring held his prick tightly, and he began to thrust himself in and out with the very long, thrilling strokes only a cock of his length could manage. I backed against his cock with each thrust, and we worked in perfect counterpoint while this magnificent stud fucked me as savagely as he could – and he was obviously capable of masterful sexual ferocity. It was hard to believe a high-school student was such an accomplished fuckmaster, but I wasn't arguing. I relished his mastery and domination, and we both encouraged each other to even greater heights of passion with loud, extremely erotic talk.

Dean took quite a while to deliver his load – after all he had given me a massive one not long before – but when it finally came, it was thrilling. Again, I felt it shoot strongly into me, and it kept shooting – another enormous emission for my appreciative consumption. Jesus, what a stud!

But that was it for the night for Dean. He collapsed on top of me and muttered he was "fucked out."

"That's maybe the greatest fuck I've ever had, Dean ... you are incredible."

He rolled off me, onto his side and grinned, "I can really fuck, can't I?"

"Best ever. Look, we'd better get you sobered up some before I take you home."

"Fuck goin' home! I wanna sleep right here and fuck you again in the morning. Okay?"

"Can you?"

"Can I stay here? Up to you. Can I fuck you again in the morning? You just tell me where to put this big ol' prick, 'n I'll fuck you silly!"

"Sounds wonderful. Do you need to call and say you're staying out?" He did, and he talked to one of his brothers, telling him only he "got lucky," and wouldn't be home that night. He got up and peed while I locked up the house and turned out lights. Our clothes were still strewn around the pool next door, but we could worry about that in the morning.

He was lying on the bed when I got back in the bedroom. "Turn out the lights and get in here." I did as I was told, and we kissed and held each other tightly. Then Dean turned my body around, so that I was lying on my side facing away from him. "Here's the way I wanna sleep," he said, as he gradually put his cock deep into my ass again. "Man, you're full of my cum. That feels good ... just hold me like that." He drifted off to sleep very quickly, and was soon snoring.

I was completely thrilled with Dean's powerful and assertive lovemaking. I couldn't remember having been so excitingly dominated in years, if ever. I also sensed he would not remember – or, if he did, certainly not admit – he had kissed me or sucked me off. I reached behind him as I lay there impaled on his huge, but fairly flaccid cock, and played with his ass. After a while he grunted, pulled out, and turned over, lying on his stomach. I knelt over him and studied his magnificent body and ass in the moonlight coming through the window. I kissed and licked him all over, then spread his legs, put my face into his ass, and administered another worshipful tongue-fuck, which he acknowledged only with a very slight "Mmmmm." He was decidedly "out" for the night. I reached for the Vaseline and lubricated his asshole, which I began to fuck gently with a finger – no reaction from Dean. Eventually, after having two – and then three – fingers pretty seriously fucking him, I put his legs back together, and plunged my prick into his tight asshole. I fucked hard and deep for a long time, and Dean slept on – giving him something else to not remember in the morning. Eventually, totally enraptured by the feel and smell of this young satyr's body, and the heat and tightness of the perfect ass I was invading, I delivered my load into him and continued to fuck and pump long after I had finished – adoring the sensation, and wishing he were sufficiently conscious to enjoy this as much as I. I lay on top of him for some time before I rolled us on our sides, and with my cock still in him, I joined him in sleep.

The next morning decidedly did not begin as the celebration of sex Dean had promised the night before. He was rather seriously hung over, and sat in the kitchen drinking coffee for some time. "Where are my clothes?"

"They're still over by the pool. I'll go get them"

"No, let's both go. A swim really sounds good."

So, we took our coffee over by the pool, and spent a quiet hour or so, floating and enjoying the morning sun. Finally, Dean asked, as he was lying on a float in the pool, "Our clothes were over here. Did we fuck last night?"

"You don't remember?"

"I remember you had a hard-on, and I remember I wanted to get a blowjob."

"Believe me, you got a blowjob ... and a lot else. I hope you're not mad."

He raised his head and grinned at me. "Mad? Shit, I wish I could remember. I guess I had a good time. Did you?"

"I had the best time I can remember."

"Did I suck you off?"

I grinned back at him, "Well ..."

He laughed, "Guess I did. I usually do. Is your butt sore?"

"It feels like a train went through it."

He laughed. "Now I know I'm sorry I don't remember. You wanna give me a 'good morning' blowjob before I have to go home?"

"You want me to?"

"Oh yeah. Get over here and show me what I got last night."

I began as he lay on the float, standing in the shallow water, but he got off the float and went to the side of the pool, where he lay on his back with his legs in the water. I stood between his legs and sucked his enormous cock, doing most of the work until the last few minutes, as he neared orgasm. Finally, he was bucking and snorting and driving his cock upward into my mouth as he shot his apparently characteristic huge and high-velocity load into me. He clamped my head down on his prick and urged me to swallow every drop – which I had planned to do anyway. "Was that as good as last night?"

"Every bit as good. You know, both times I took your load last night you shot with as much force as I've ever encountered. I'd love to see you just shoot it one time, to see how far it goes."

He grinned lazily. "We'll do that next time ... if you want a next time."

"Oh yeah, I want a next time."

"Next time, don't get me drunk, so I can remember how much fun we have. Look, don't call me, though, okay? You wouldn't believe the weird calls I get some time, and my brothers are always on the phone anyway, so I'll just get in touch with you, okay?"

I gave him my name and phone number as I took him home, realizing that he probably didn't even know my name, unless he had remembered it from when we had first met – which seemed unlikely. As we rode, he told me he had enjoyed the evening a lot. "Damned near the first thing I've really enjoyed this whole year. Back in Athens, I used to go out and fuck two or three nights a week before we moved here. There was a railing in front of the bus station – the 'meat rack,' they called it – and I could stand out there, and somebody'd always come around wanting to have good time. But there's nothing like that here."

"Sounds hot; I wish there was something like that here."

"Yeah, I used to make a lot of money at the 'meat rack,' too. A lot of guys paid me well to let 'em blow me or fuck 'em up the ass. If I really needed money, I could line up three or four a night." He grinned, "Hell, even here I manage to sell my cock to some guys anxious to have it. Why do you think I wear my jeans so tight? It pays to advertise, you know."

"Dean, do you want me to pay you?"

"No, I don't think so ... no, it was fun, let's just do it for fun."

"Well, I'll be glad to give you some money from time to time."

"Okay, but that's not gonna be for screwin', alright? If you just wanna give me a present once in a while, fine ... but you don't have to. We'll go water-skiing, and use the pool, and if you want to blow me or get fucked, we'll have a ball, okay? It'll be fun."

"Sounds perfect!" Following his directions, I dropped him off near – but, as instructed, not at – his house.

As he got out of the car he smiled. "You know, my butt's sore this morning, like maybe somebody fucked me. That couldn't have happened, could it?"

"Dean ..."

He laughed and got out of the car. "I'll be in touch."

I didn't have long to wait before Dean made a return visit. I had hoped he would call right away, but after a few days I decided it could be a long time. I was, of course, strictly subject to his whim. I was seriously missing the expert sexual ministrations of Mike and Cary, and Dean's rampant sexuality had seemed to promise something as good or better, so I was very anxious. However, as I arrived at my house a day or so short of a week following my first sexual encounter with Dean, I found him stretched out on the porch – his Levi's as tight as ever, and his cock and balls still thrillingly outlined by them.

I was happy to see him there, but I had arrived happy – the second unexpected encounter of the summer had just materialized: I had that afternoon received a call from ex-lover Richard Austin, saying he was at loose ends for the summer, and wanted to come up in the next few days, and stay with me for a month or two. He made it quite clear that he wanted to share my bed as well as my house.

The season that Richard and I had shared as live-together lovers had been one of the happiest times I had ever experienced, although the ending was painful. A couple of months of getting fucked by Richard's magnificent cock at least nightly – and often twice in a single night, with additional, impassioned "good morning" fucks not at all unusual – plus added oral draining of that same fabulous organ almost as frequently, was not something likely to be forgotten. We had greeted every morning in our relationship with a mutual blowjob – even when Richard had awakened me during the night to fuck me, as he not infrequently did. His attentions to my sexual gratification were not as diligent as mine were to his. Of course, he gratified me immeasurably as he drove his wonderful shaft into my mouth or ass, erupting copiously inside me, and he regularly sucked me off with a masterful technique, but he never let me fuck him up the ass, insisting he just wasn't a bottom. I fucked his ass with my tongue a great deal, and even had a finger or two up it now and then, but never more than just part of the head of my cock had entered him there. Still, he was a memorable, stunning lover, and I was thrilled to think that we might resume our relationship in some form.

But I was also wary about Richard's return. The relationship had ended abruptly. I had begun to suspect he was fucking with other guys, although he denied it, saying he was only interested in me. Then, during a very minor argument about something totally inconsequential, he told me had been seeing someone else for some time and was leaving me. That night he was gone, and I was bereft – still very much in love with him – and very hurt by what I viewed as his cruelty. I later tried several times to see him and heal the wounds, but he was apparently not interested in either getting together again, or even admitting he had treated me badly. He moved to Atlanta, and I had not heard from him for six months or so before he called the day I found Dean on my porch; his call was as unexpected as it was exciting.

Although I still loved Richard, I knew he didn't love me, and I wondered what his motives might be in reappearing in my life. I will admit, though, the prospect of again enjoying his masterful lovemaking overrode, but did not erase, my reservations about the permanence or sincerity of a renewed relationship with him. I could, after all, enjoy the all-consuming rapture of his fat, long cock driving in and out of me, or the joy of shooting my load deep into his throat, and still realize this might not be long-lasting, true love on his part.

So, I had been anticipating a renewal of hot sex with the beautiful stud as I drove up to my house that afternoon, and had found the prospect of hot sex with the fascinating high-school fuckmaster awaiting me then and there. As I got out of my car, Dean got to his feet and came to meet me.

"I took a chance on coming out. Caught a ride, and only had to walk a little way. I hope you're not busy – hoped we could do some water skiing."

I greeted the prospect with enthusiasm, and we spent a couple of very enjoyable hours on the lake. I was a capable skier, but Dean was extremely good, and was obviously having a ball (I was hoping to have two balls soon – extra-large ones.). The only reference to sex or to our earlier meeting had been brief, but encouraging: I had provided Dean with a bathing suit, and as he stripped to change into it, he fondled and displayed his luscious prick, smiling and asking, "Look good?" When I eagerly declared it looked good enough to eat, his smile turned into a grin. "Ski first, and picnic afterward, okay?"

Finally tiring, we tied up the boat and went over to the pool to swim. Dean declined anything to drink stronger than Coke. "I'll take the hard stuff later."

"I'll be glad to get some hard stuff later myself ... and I'm not talking about drinks."

He laughed, "Oh you're gonna get something plenty hard ... and I know where I want to stuff it, too."

He was lying on a chaise longue as he said this, and he looked unbelievably good. I said, "You know, Dean, when I first saw you, I thought you were one of the best-looking and sexiest guys I'd ever seen." He smiled. "But after I saw with you clothes off and your cock hard, I decided you've gotta be *the* best-looking and sexiest guy I've ever seen."

His smile became a near smirk. "Right now I'm the horniest guy you've ever seen." He raised his hips and slipped his bathing trunks down to his knees. "Get over here and let me show you." By the time I shed my bathing suit and knelt at his side, his prick was already hard in his hand – gigantic and mouth-watering. "Meet your best friend!" I began to lick the huge shaft as he raised his feet, slipped his trunks off completely, and spread his legs wide. "That's right, make love to this big dick." I cupped his huge balls in my hand as I kissed and licked his big cock-head, then opened my mouth and very slowly began to take him inside. I relaxed my throat as much as possible and managed to take every throbbing inch of fat cock this stud offered me. My lips and nose nestled in his pubic hair, and he caressed my head. "That feels so fuckin' good. Man, you are a champion cocksucker ... I love it."

Soon my sucking and his humping got pretty frantic. He pulled my head off his dick and said, "You wanted to see how far I could shoot? Let's do it." He stood and had me kneel in front of him as he fucked my mouth wildly, and I sucked as hard as I could, taking his entire cock down my throat while I held his beautiful, driving ass cupped in my hands. Soon he was ready. Again he pulled me off his cock. "Watch this." He seized his huge cock, and in a few strokes brought it to orgasm; I watched a couple of huge spurts shoot out of his incredible cock, and then I quickly took it in my mouth again so I could receive the rest into my throat – and there was still plenty of force and plenty of cum for my mouth. After he finished, he giggled, "Wow ... look where it landed."

I reluctantly stopped sucking and looked to see how far he had shot. A big white gob of his cum lay on the cement, at least ten feet from where he stood. I stood and put my arms on his shoulders. "God, what a man you are."

"You're fuckin' right I am." He put his arms around me, drew me close, and kissed me, driving his tongue into my mouth and exchanging frantic passionate kisses with me as we ground out pelvises into each other.

He had kissed me the first time we had been together, but only after he got drunk. "You really surprise me, Dean. I didn't think you'd kiss!"

"Look, around my friends I talk about girls and all that shit, and we make jokes about faggots, but the only thing that turns me on more than getting my cock sucked or fucking a hot guy up the butt, is taking a load from a big cock down my throat, or feeling a cock shoot a load inside my ass. And if I kiss you, it's because I like you, and you fuckin' well turn me on."

"I would never have suspected ..."

"You know how many guys I've told that to, and I've let fuck me? Maybe a dozen or so out of the hundreds and hundreds of guys who've blown me, or who I fucked. But I can tell you're okay, and you're not some queen or something ... that really turns me off ... and I know you're not gonna tell anyone." He grinned. "Not if you want me to fuck you again."

I held him tight. "I want you to fuck me again, believe me."

We kissed and hugged for a while, and then Dean sank to his knees and took my cock in his mouth. He moaned in pleasure, and sucked voraciously for a long time while I fucked his throat as hard and as deeply as I was able. Soon I was ready; "You wanna take my load?" His "Mmmmmm Hmmmm," and his continued sucking seemed to indicate assent, so I drove myself all the way into him and discharged into his greedy throat. He held my hips in his arms as he sucked every drop from me before standing and kissing me again.

"God damn, that was good ... John. It's John, right?" We'd each fucked each other and blown each other twice, and this was the first time he had even thought to use my name! At any rate, I told him he had the name right. "Man, John, I love to suck cock." We kissed some more. "And you obviously love to suck cock, too ... so let's go get on your bed for a hot sixty-nine!"

This time we took our clothes with us when we went over to my house, although we were totally naked as we walked there. (Living in isolation has certain advantages.) Dean flopped on his back on my bed and smiled up at me. "Climb on top of me, man, give me that cock," I knelt over his head, facing his feet. He immediately took my cock in his mouth, deep throated it, and began sucking fiercely as I opened my own mouth eagerly to accept his awesome endowment, and drove my mouth all the way down to the base of it, beginning a fantastic mutual blow job that was especially gratifying in that it was as prolonged as it was exciting – we had, after all, both shot our loads only recently. We finally reached mutual orgasm as we lay on our sides with cocks deep in each other's mouths and hands frantically fondling our asses. Dean's orgasm again was copious and extremely intense – shooting into the back of my throat with a force I had seldom encountered, even when taking a long-delayed, forceful "first load of the evening" from a partner. My own orgasm, while not as vehemently propelled as his, was surely as large. We each discharged into the other's mouth in a long series of loving spurts, and neither of us removed his prick from the other's mouth as we lay there in the satisfying afterglow of two thrilling orgasms, respectively delivered to, and received in, appreciative receptacles. The salty taste of Dean's cum and the bulky wonder of his shaft were incredibly toothsome. His murmurs of contentment, and the way his tongue licked and wrapped around my cock inside his mouth, led me to believe he felt the same way about what I had lovingly offered him.

Eventually our bodies meshed, and we lay in gentle embrace, kissing and enjoying quiet talk, which led to a drink, which led to Dean's admonition to "Get on your knees, I'm gonna fuck your ass!"

He made good on his promise as I knelt willingly before him and thrilled to his savage penetration, although by the time his monster cock delivered another explosive, huge load into my body, he had thrown me on my back, was cradling my upper body in his arms, and kissing me passionately while his wonderful shaft plunged rapidly and deeply into me to deliver its precious fluid. His cock had barely stopped shooting its burden before he was urging me to repay him in kind. He raised up slightly, swiped his hand across my ass, and transferred lubricant to my cock. Then he positioned his asshole at the tip of my prick and sank down on it with a cry of delight as his ass met my stomach. "Give it to me."

Dean bounced up and down on my cock as if possessed, and I met his downward plunges with my upward thrusts while I held his hips and watched his hand masturbating his huge prick, still steely hard, and shiny wet with his cum. It took little time before I gave him as good as he had given me.

We made sandwiches and had another drink as I told Dean about the return of Richard to my life. I described Richard's physical endowments and beauty, as well as his sexual prowess, and Dean was fascinated. "He really sounds hot. If I come around, can we both fuck with him?"

I explained that while I felt sure Richard would be glad to fuck him and suck him, and accept a friendly blowjob, he wouldn't take Dean up the ass. Dean laughed. "You wanna bet? Just let me at him for a while. I bet you he'll beg me to shove my big ol' dick up his butt before I'm through with him."

"Look, I'm still in love with him, but I sure as hell wouldn't mind sharing him with you ... if he's willing."

"You told me you thought I was the sexiest, best-lookin' guy you ever saw. Right?" I nodded. "So, do you think this Richard is gonna feel something like that?"

"He'd be a fool if he didn't ... and he's no fool."

"Just leave it to me. And you sure as hell will be sharing; I promise you, you'll be involved. I really wanna get fucked by a big cock like you say he's got, but ... well, let's just see how it goes. You be sure to tell him all about me, and get him interested in sinking that big cock in me. Leave it to me, we'll have a fuckin' ball."

Before taking Dean home that evening, he lay on his back and I rode his cock to another thrilling eruption, after which he raised his legs while I knelt between them and fucked him – cuddling and kissing him at the same time, as he had earlier done to me. We firmly agreed to a threesome with Richard in the near future, if the latter was agreeable.

Knowing how Richard would probably react to the prospect of sex with an incredibly gorgeous stud like Dean, I felt sure he would be anxious, at the very least, to avail himself of the opportunity

9. A PICNIC IN THE PROMISED LAND

Richard arrived a few days later, and our reunion was both joyous and passionate. One would never have thought that our affair had broken off so rancorously. We had not been together fifteen minutes before we were both naked, and I knelt before him while he held my head tightly and fucked my mouth fiercely. His beautiful prick was just as perfectly formed as I remembered it, and if it wasn't quite as big as Dean's, it didn't miss it much – it was a magnificent mouthful of cock, soon to become a thrilling assful of cock.

I sucked for a long time as Richard's prick plunged deep into my throat and was rewarded with a mammoth load of his hot semen, which I savored lovingly, and swallowed only after bathing his prick in it for a long time – holding my lips tightly over the head of it and massaging it with my tongue. Richard's eyes were closed in rapture and he murmured his delight as I worshipped this rod that had given me so much pleasure. Then he pulled me to my feet, kissed me deeply – remarking on the exciting taste of cum in my mouth – and knelt before me to accept the ecstatic mouth-fuck and ensuing orgasm I offered him. Just before I came, he pulled his mouth away from my cock, held his mouth wide open a few inches from it, and we both watched as my cock discharged into his throat, after which he again took me inside and sucked the last drops from me.

Still kneeling, licking my prick and looking up at me, he grinned. "I needed that ... and I need to fuck your ass just as much."

"You know how hot my ass is for your cock."

He laughed as he stood and took me into his arms. "Only too well."

We caught up on each other's lives for a while, and shared a few drinks before going to bed. Once there, Richard was an absolutely maniacal fuck machine that first night back. I never had a chance to suck another load from his magnificent cock, as he had it buried up my butt most of the time – which was a more-than-satisfactory arrangement, as far as I was concerned. Richard not only had a very large, fat prick, he employed it skillfully and with savage abandon. Once fucked by Richard, one knew he had been fucked!

He fucked, as he always did, hard and fast, with strokes of enormous length. He seemed to have an instinctive knowledge of exactly how far he could pull back without actually slipping out, and then his inward thrust was – again, typical of this magnificently hung and beautiful fuckmaster – hard-driving, going as deep as he could possibly go, which was very deep, thrillingly deep. At the same time, he cried loudly in passion and his ecstatic words ("Take this big prick," "Take my love in your ass," "Gonna fill your hot ass with cum," etc.) were interspersed with rapturous animal moans, while all the time he held my body tightly. The first orgasm I took from him anally that night was prolonged, and probably better than any I had ever known with him. He started by kneeling behind me and fucking me "doggie style" at great length, but he eventually forced my body down to a prone position, and he lay on top of it while our asses worked together in a frantic effort to bring his monster cock to a generous explosion – which was triply welcome, since it took a very long time to arrive. When he actually began to climax, he put his arms around my waist and lifted my body up, while his ass drove his cock in very rapid, short strokes and I reveled in the palpable sensation of his cum discharging deep inside me. When he collapsed over me at that point, I felt as well-fucked as I ever had, and remembered only too well why I had fallen in love with this gorgeous, divinely endowed Satyr.

He fucked me in the missionary position later and had me ride his prick to climax the next morning. And Richard had not neglected my needs, although he still would not let me fuck his ass, as I so wanted. He sucked me off again that night, and the next morning, after I took my wonderful, productive ride on his prick, he raised his legs high so I could eat and tongue-fuck his ass. He urged me to shoot my load on his asshole – alas, not in it, where I so wanted to deliver it as he put his knees up to his shoulders and presented it to me. After I coated his asshole with my discharge, he played in it, and actually massaged most of it into himself with his finger. "This way I can take your hot cum into my ass, John."

A long session of cuddling followed, culminating in our traditional mutual blowjob, and by the time we got out of bed to face the next day I was rapturous.

For a week I lived in sexual heaven with Richard, his body and cock thrilling me as they had when I first met him and fell in love. He fucked me several times a day, we sucked each other off a couple times each day, and we lay wrapped in each other's arms, kissing and caressing endlessly. True, in recent months I had been served regularly and wonderfully by the beautiful Cary, the hung and passionate Mike, and the stunningly sexy Dean, but with Richard – wow! He was as beautiful as Cary, his cock was at least as big as Mike's, and if he wasn't quite the insatiable stud that Dean was – who was, after all? – I loved him (was actually in love with him), and that more than made him equal to that high school master-sensualist.

Intellectually, I knew it was unwise to trust my love to Richard, based on past experience, but emotionally, I had no choice. Within only a few days after our reunion, I again thought of him as my lover.

Perhaps sensing that I needed some time to "catch up" with Richard sexually, Dean did not call for more than a week after our last session together. He asked if I had approached Richard about fucking with him, and I had to admit I had not yet done so. "Look, I'm so fuckin' horny I can't stand it," he said, "so I'm coming out to your house tomorrow, and I'm gonna cram my dick down your throat and up your butt, okay? And you tell your lover that I'm bringing my big fat cock and my hot ass out there to service you, and he's invited to share 'em with you."

"I'll tell him. I'm pretty sure he's gonna be excited, and once he gets a look at you, he'll be ready to share everything you've got."

"Has he let you fuck him?"

"No, I told you ..."

"Twenty bucks says I shove my cock all the way up his ass and he loves every inch of it." I accepted the bet happily. It would easily be worth twenty dollars to see Richard getting fucked, and perhaps it would finally open the door to my – well, we'd see.

That night I told Richard all about Dean, describing his beauty and his sexual power. He was fascinated, and agreed that he would do a lot more than just watch when we three got together. As he fucked me that night, he fantasized aloud about sinking his shaft into the beautiful, sexy Dean's hot ass the next day, and as I was cumming in his mouth I described the force of emission he could expect when he sucked Dean off. The next morning we abstained from sex, even the mutual blowjob we normally celebrated just before getting out of bed each day we were together, agreeing we would hold off in order to be extra horny for Dean later that day.

Richard stayed home while I went to pick up Dean, shortly after he called around 7:00 that night to say that he was ready. Wearing Levi's that were so tight they almost seemed painted on, and which clearly outlined his massive tool and huge balls, Dean looked irresistible. We speculated about Richard's receptivity to his charms, and the likelihood of his playing bottom to the insatiable high-school stud's persuasive top. Like Dean, I thought Richard would probably be thrilled to take his hot cock up the butt, and I was looking forward to losing our bet.

I had told Richard about Dean's revealing Levi's, and was amused to note that Richard had changed to very tight pants himself, which – like Dean's – left little to the imagination, clearly displaying his ample endowment as well. I introduced them, and they obviously "sized each other up," each clearly impressed with the tantalizing equipment displayed by the bulges in their respective jeans. Although Dean was a couple of years younger than Richard, he took charge of the encounter. He stepped up and groped Richard's crotch. "John wasn't kidding when he said you were hot."

Richard smiled sexily and returned the caress, rubbing his hand along the considerable length of Dean's clearly visible cock. "He told me you were hung, too, but this feels even better than he described ... and it sounded stupendous when he described it."

Dean began to unbutton his Levi's. "I'll bet it tastes better than he told you, too." He had to reach down into his extremely tight left pants leg to pull his fairly erect cock from it – he was wearing no underwear – and he held it out for Richard to see. "Why don't you find out?"

Richard knelt and took Dean in his mouth, and sucked for a few minutes. Dean pulled him to his feet and kissed him hard. "Let me see what you've got to give me." He knelt, unbuttoned Richard's Levi's, and pulled them down; Richard had decided to go without underwear as well – tight Levi's like theirs displayed huge cocks much more enticingly without underwear. Richard's prick sprang to full attention as it cleared his jeans. Dean studied it and kissed it. "Man, that's really beautiful." He opened his mouth and Richard fucked it for some time, both of them murmuring their delight.

As Dean sucked him, Richard kicked off his shoes and removed his shirt. "Get your clothes off, too, John ... this is gonna be hot as hell." Dean stood and began to strip as well. Soon the three of us stood together naked, and as Dean and Richard moved in to kiss, I somehow managed to take the heads of their two gigantic dicks into my mouth at the same time, and licked and sucked them lovingly.

We moved to the bedroom, where the two studs fell on the bed in a frantic, noisy sixty-nine, their two beautiful asses driving their fine cocks deep into each other's mouths. They were such a magnificent pair that I felt more inclined to watch and masturbate rather than participate, as they began their serious sex play. Their sucking, fondling, and kissing was extremely passionate, and each obviously regarded the other with enormous desire. Dean knelt over Richard as he lay face down on the bed, and buried his face between the cheeks of his ass. Richard raised his ass somewhat, and I could clearly see Dean's tongue darting in and out of Richard's asshole as he kissed and sucked it. Judging by his moans and gasps, Richard was in heaven. Then Dean spread Richard's legs, put his arms around his waist, and raised him to a kneeling position. He began to apply Vaseline to his cock as he almost snarled, "Gonna fuck that hot ass of yours."

I had expected a show of reluctance on Richard's part when Dean proposed to fuck him, if not an outright refusal. Instead, Richard cried out, "Oh yeah! Bury that monster cock of yours in my ass," and Dean complied!

Although Richard had always assured me he did not take it up the butt, it became obvious this was far from the first time he'd been fucked – and when he took Dean's colossal meat without any apparent pain, it was obvious there had been at least one really huge prick up his sweet ass before – and frequently!

I watched in awe as Dean steadily sank his monster shaft all the way into my lover's writhing ass. He began to plunge in and out savagely as Richard urged him, "Oh yes! Oh God, that big cock feels so good, Fuck me hard!" And as he held Richard's waist and fucked his ass with profound strokes, Dean turned to me, grinned, and winked very broadly.

Why had Richard always denied me access to his ass? Who knew? It was now obvious he had welcomed others inside, and had probably done so even when we were together as lovers and swearing our devotion to each other. Given the just-demonstrated strength of his appetite to get fucked, I guessed there had even been many of them while he was protesting that he never bottomed. He had admitted to me when we broke up that he had gone to bed with quite a few others while were living together.

90

I was still in love with him and I again thought of him as my lover, but I knew I couldn't trust him. My affair with Richard had been marred – and subsequently destroyed – by his inability to be honest with me, and his unwillingness to practice the monogamy I had pledged to him, and which he had sworn to maintain for me. Obviously, I was not nearly as sexy, or young, or attractive, or hung as the magnificent Dean, so I could readily understand how Richard yielded favorably to Dean's declaration he was going to fuck him. Having seen his utter joy as Dean fucked him, I was absolutely certain that if I had ten inches of fat, hard cock, like Dean, Richard would have opened his legs for me the first time we went to bed together.

Of course, any boy or man, even an inexperienced or virgin bottom, who would refuse to let a glorious, sexy fuckmaster like Dean pound his ass would be as foolish as one who might similarly deny giving up his ass to the gorgeous stud, Richard. I had not for a split second considered not getting fucked by either of the two sexy Adonises when I first began to make love with each of them. I knew the moment I saw Richard's colossal cock or Dean's gargantuan tool that I was going to have it inside my ass as soon, and as often, as possible. I would probably have felt that way had either of them been only moderately attractive in other respects, but the fact is that they were both as stunningly handsome as they were gloriously endowed.

Dean flipped Richard over and began to fuck him missionary style. Richard's legs rested on Dean's shoulders, and Dean's ass looked unbelievably sexy as he drove himself frantically into the voracious hole I had so long sought to fill. He motioned me near as he told Richard, "I want to watch John fuck you for a while. That'll really be hot. And then I want to cum inside your ass." And with that, he pulled out of Richard and moved aside, motioning me to take his place. Richard transferred his legs to my shoulders.

Richard was completely rapturous, almost feverish from the sensation of Dean's masterly lovemaking. "Both of you cum inside me," he cried. I was fully erect, of course, and Richard was sufficiently lubricated and opened up by Dean's titanic shaft that I was easily able to drive myself in without any preparation. As I entered him, Richard cried out again, "Yeah, John, fuck me hard. I want to feel you blowing your load inside me."

As I started to fuck Richard, I stared into his eyes and panted, "At last! I've been wanting to fuck you since the day I first saw a picture of you."

Richard's eyes were glazed over with the delirium of lust, and he rolled his head from side to side as he gasped his reply, "I've always wanted your dick up my ass, John." Yet another lie from my gorgeous lover, a big one – as big as the monster prick he was stroking while I fucked him – but I was so thrilled with what I was doing, I could have forgiven any lie at that point.

I fucked Richard's ass as though I had been saving up for years to do it – as, in fact, I had. We both moaned in passion while Dean knelt over Richard's head, facing me. "Suck my balls and eat my ass while John fucks you," he told

Richard. Then he wrapped me in his arms and pulled me in to him. We held each other and kissed while I fucked Richard's ass and – judging by the muffled sound of Richard's cries, and Dean's ecstatic whimpers – Richard ate Dean's. The sensation of Dean's hot tongue fucking my mouth, the ecstatic encouragement of Richard, and the incomparable feeling of my lover's ass clamping my cock as I drove it in and out of him soon brought me to orgasm.

As I cried, "I'm getting ready to shoot," Dean backed away, and Richard extended his arms to me as he panted, "Oh God, fill me with cum." I reached down and took my lover in my arms, and we kissed as finally I shot my load into this beautiful man I had loved and desired for so long. By then, Dean was kneeling behind me, kissing my neck, and fucking me with a finger as he whispered into my ear, "Best twenty bucks you ever spent," reminding me of the bet he had made – and won without any resistance of any kind.

After I had calmed down and pulled out of Richard, Dean leaned over his cock. "Gonna get you in the mood." He sucked fiercely, and Richard thrust upward into Dean's mouth as the younger stud feasted. Dean told me to kneel next to Richard and lubricate my asshole, instructing Richard, "I want to see your cock inside John's butt, and I'm gonna finish fucking you that way, okay?" I was ready, and Richard was obviously eager, as he knelt behind me and drove his big prick all the way into me in one smooth movement – which felt wonderful! He fell over my body and urged Dean to take him again; I could tell by Richard's cries of delight that the young fuckmaster was re-entering heaven, and Dean's delighted, "Oh man, you are so wet with John's cum!" confirmed he was in place. I could feel the violence of the fucking Dean administered to Richard's lucky ass, transmitted to me by Richard's body and his deep-plunging prick. Richard fucked me while he was being fucked, but the strength and ferocity of Dean's ass-pounding made it almost impossible for Richard to coordinate his thrusts properly with Dean's. Richard's cock felt marvelous inside me, and was really acting as an instrument for Dean to fuck me indirectly while he slammed his prick savagely into Richard. I considered I was being fucked simultaneously by two mega-hung studs, and simply wallowed in ecstasy.

This delightful double-fuck-of-sorts lasted a wonderfully long time, but eventually, with huge cries of joy, Dean exploded inside Richard, who encouraged him, "God, Dean, give me that hot cum. Jesus, I've never felt a load shooting that hard in me. Keep it coming ... fill me up."

As urged, Dean apparently kept it coming for some time. "You are filled up now," he gasped. "You like those two big loads inside you?" Richard acknowledged that he certainly did. "Now I'm staying in you," Dean said, "and I want you to keep fucking John, and shoot your load in him."

"Okay," Richard said, "but you're gonna let me fuck your ass, too, aren't you?"

I could feel Dean start to fuck Richard again as he replied, "Believe me, you're not gettin' out of this room until you've filled my butt with a load of your hot cum. But right now I wanna feel your ass gripping me while you fuck John." Richard raised himself to his knees, and pulled my body upward so that I was on all fours. He seized my waist as he fucked savagely, and in just a few minutes he cried out, "Here I come." I felt an entire series of his spurts shooting inside me.

When Richard had finished his orgasm, and had ceased voluntarily driving his dick into me, I could feel Dean start to fuck him again, so that Richard, in effect, continued to fuck me.

Dean stopped fucking. "Okay, Richard, out of the way while I fill John's ass, too." Richard moved aside and Dean pushed me down onto my stomach as he fell on top of my body, driving his cock up into me, replacing the magnificent one I had been enjoying with an even more generous one. "And your hole is all full of Richard's cum ... damn, this is hot!" Dean had cum just a few minutes earlier, so the fuck he gave me was wonderfully, deliriously lengthy, but it was magnificent and culminated in another palpable discharge of his cum. I could not see, but from part of what Dean said while he was fucking me, I knew that Richard was eating his ass most of that time.

We all lay in exhaustion for a while, until Dean said, "Well, both of you guys have two loads in you ... that means you've gotta give me one apiece." Both Richard and I pleaded temporary exhaustion, so we had a drink and relaxed for an hour or so before Dean decided it was his time to get filled up. He lay on his back, spread his legs and raised them high. "Who gets first crack at this hungry ass?"

I held Richard and kissed him. "You go first. I want to feel your cum inside there when I fuck him."

Richard knelt between Dean's legs and raised them to his shoulders. "This is what I've been waiting for all night." He lubricated his cock, slipped it easily into Dean's ass, and began to fuck him savagely. "God damn but your ass is hot. How does this feel?"

Dean grinned happily. "It feels great. I sure love to get fucked by a big prick like yours, Richard ... give it to me as hard and as deep as you can." Richard put one hand down on either side of Dean's head, Dean held his legs high, and Richard's beautiful ass drove his massive meat deep down into the beautiful stud who had so recently plowed him. This was the first time I had ever watched Richard's ass as he fucked (I later got to see it a number of times in the several porno movies he subsequently made), and it was unbelievably exciting to me. At the same time, I could study his fat cock plunging into Dean – shining with lubricant as it stretched the tight hole, and inspiring ecstatic cries of appreciation for the masterful technique my lover wielded (how well I knew that!). I had long known that Richard was one of the most impassioned and expert fuckers I had ever encountered, and it was an exciting change to watch him exercising his art – and it was art of the highest order.

Dean told me to straddle his head and fuck his mouth while Richard serviced his ass. I was happy to comply, and he held my hips and sucked feverishly as Richard approached orgasm. Soon Dean shouted with pleasure as he felt Richard's orgasm erupt inside him, and Richard moaned in rapture at the same time. I got out of the way, so the two magnificent studs could kiss each other to celebrate the moment – Dean's body still playing host to Richard's splendid shaft. In a few minutes, Dean stopped kissing and told me, "Get in there, John ... he's got my ass ready for you."

I needed no lubricant to enter Dean; he was still somewhat distended from the bulk of Richard's cock, and his passage was hot and slick with the load my lover had left there only minutes earlier. Richard declared he was going to clean up and come back to fuck Dean's mouth as I had done. He returned shortly to kneel over Dean's head, and I watched his ass humping his cock into Dean's throat. It was so exciting, I put my face into Richard's ass and began to tongue-fuck him as I ass-fucked Dean.

Richard reveled in having his ass and his cock eaten at the same time; Dean evidenced great joy in both getting fucked and eating a big, throbbing cock while he did so; and I was in heaven as I fucked the hottest guy I knew while I rimmed the man I loved. It was a wonderful circumstance, and although we continued thus for some time, it was over far too soon – but by then each of us was happily filled with two big loads.

Another rest led to an impassioned sixty-nine between Dean and Richard, during which each came in the other's throat almost simultaneously. I amused myself during their lovemaking by eating first one driving ass and then the other, and then – at his request – jacking off into Dean's open mouth.

Dean had to go home, so I drove, and he and Richard groped and kissed all the way back into town. Dean promised to see us again soon, and when I called him back to the car as he started walking up his parents' driveway, he grinned and winked as I slipped a twenty-dollar bill in his hand. "Worth it?" he asked?

"Oh yeah!"

Richard was very loving that night – no sex, of course, we were both exhausted – but we celebrated our usual getting-out-of-bed mutual blowjob the next morning. He never mentioned having freely opened his ass to Dean and then, finally, to me, but acted as if I had been fucking him that way all along. I didn't care, really, as long as he would now let me make love to him the same way he did me – and from that point on, he always did.

Sport-fucking with the hottest stud I knew, lovemaking with my finally-returned beautiful lover, the pair of lovers Cary and Mike waiting for me "in the wings" for individual and three-way fucking: I surely should have been sexually satisfied to the point of not even thinking of anyone else, but the vision of the breathtaking Mark Hagood would not leave my mind.

10. MANY, MANY HAPPY RETURNS

The beautiful Mark was not even due back until mid-August, so although I thought about him a lot, thinking was all I could do – and I still had no reason to believe it would ever go past the thinking stage. The summer was proving to be absolutely wonderful, sexually, and its apex was achieved on July 14, when I both celebrated my thirty-fourth birthday and achieved the highest point of passion I had ever known. Observance of that birthday was far more than just a celebration – it was a feast.

Mike and Cary had come to visit around the beginning of July – and had kept the spare bedroom steaming for several hours after they first arrived. It was the first time they had been together in almost a month, and they had a lot of catching up to do. Richard knew all about them, of course, and had been eager to meet them. He was obviously smitten with Cary's beauty when they did meet, and dropped innumerable hints about going to bed with him, or with Mike. He hadn't seen Mike's cock yet, but he'd heard about it, and obviously was eager to sample its delights – or perhaps a threesome with them both or even a foursome, involving me as well.

Both Cary and Mike knew about Richard, and while they both commented on how good-looking he was, neither expressed to me any particular interest in having sex with him. They were, after all, very much in love with each other, although they somehow – because of our history – thought of sex with me as one facet of their relationship. It seemed fairly clear to Richard that sex with either Cary or Mike was probably not going to happen, and this was frustrating to him, I think, because he was very much used to having whomever he wanted. He was really a bit put out when, around midnight of the first day they visited, Cary came into our bedroom – naked, and looking like a blond god – and asked Richard if he minded if I joined him and Mike in bed for a while. I feel sure Richard didn't mind if I had sex with Mike and Cary, but he was obviously unhappy that he hadn't been asked. Nonetheless, he was gracious, and I went into the spare room with Mike and Cary, and enjoyed an extremely loving threesome – more loving than hot, since they were both exhausted from having just fucked each other's brains out. I was reasonably satisfied at the moment also, since Richard had become so aroused listening to the sound of Mike and Cary's passion, he had thrown a savage fuck into me – after which he had sucked me off, and was still so horny he jacked off on my face, shooting another big load into my open mouth.

The next morning, Richard came into the guest room, where Mike and Cary and I were snuggling, to announce that he had made coffee. He was naked, and his beautiful, big cock was fully erect – lumbering out in front of him as he walked, and looking particularly delicious. Mike got out of bed and went to pee, and his monster prick was not just erect – like Richard's, it protruded and bounced, parallel to the floor. Richard began to salivate as he watched it – and so did I. Cary seemed unaware of Richard's admiring gaze – although "admiring" is far too weak a word – as he got out of bed and stretched, showing his physical beauty and muscular body to best advantage. I must admit that Richard behaved with commendable restraint, given the temptations of Mike's huge cock and Cary's matchless beauty, which he had just been exposed to.

While we all drank our coffee outside on the porch, Mike and Cary played around with each other, and Richard was noticeably disturbed. He stroked his still-erect cock as he said, "Jesus, you guys are making me so horny I can't stand it."

Mike grinned. "I guess we haven't been very attentive to our hosts, have we, Cary?"

"No, I guess we haven't. So, Richard, what could we do that would make up for that?"

Richard looked at him for a long time before replying. "You could let me fuck both of you." He looked at me, and smiled crookedly as he added, "Or you could both fuck me."

Mike and Cary exchanged looks then Mike nodded, and it was Cary's turn to grin. "You think I'm attractive, Richard."

"I think you're one of the most beautiful guys I've ever seen, and I've hardly been able to take my eyes off you or your hot ass ever since you got here."

"Well, take your eyes off my ass and put your cock in it, if you want." And with that, Cary turned around, leaned over the table, and spread his asscheeks. Richard knelt behind him and buried his face between the two perfect golden mounds Cary offered him. Cary wiggled his ass and moaned, "Oh God, that is so good. Eat my ass, Richard, get it good and wet."

Mike approached me and put his arms around me. After a long, passionate kiss, he said, "That sure looks like fun, doesn't it?" After I agreed, Mike turned around, stood next to Cary, leaned over, and spread his asscheeks. Soon I was kneeling alongside my lover as we both ate ass. In a few minutes, Mike sank to his knees while I continued to tongue-fuck him, and Cary followed suit. Richard and I soon had our dicks plunging in and out of the two beautiful young studs. Mike – and Cary, I assumed – needed no lubrication; it was clear he had been fucked very recently, and was still well greased with lubricant and cum. Cary and Mike exchanged kisses, and encouraged us both to fuck harder, faster, and deeper. Richard and I were able to exchange kisses as we fucked the kissing lovers, and, following the injunction of the two hot studs, we fucked harder, faster and – insofar as possible – deeper.

Richard's arms went around Cary as he neared orgasm. "Can I cum in your ass?"

"Oh yeah, give me your big load ... I want to feel that huge cock filling me up." In only a few more strokes Richard erupted inside the beautiful blond, who cried out with passion. "Yes! I can feel you shooting inside me. Give me all of that big load." I didn't have to ask Mike if he wanted my load, so I simply delivered it to him, and he reacted with the same kind of enthusiasm his lover had registered. All four of us fell to the deck and lay there for a while.

Richard kissed Cary. "My God, you are so fucking beautiful, and your ass is absolutely perfect. I can't tell you how much I loved fucking it."

Cary smiled, and put his arms around Richard. "Your cock felt wonderful ... mmmmm, so hard and big!" Cary's kisses and Richard's response were torrid! Cary continued, "I'll bet Mike would like that huge dick in his ass. Are you up to it?"

Mike was more than willing, and I was not at all surprised when Richard proved he was up to it – and performed magnificently again. Cary and I watched them fuck as he backed up to me, and I had Richard's cum to ease the way for my cock to penetrate that entrance to heaven between the perfect golden globes of Cary's gorgeous, endlessly succulent ass. I was getting near orgasm again when Cary told me to hold off. "Mike and I decided before we got out of bed this morning that we wanted to fuck Richard ... why not give him three loads?" I agreed it was a good idea, as did Richard, who had just deposited another big load in Mike.

Richard lay on his back, and raised his legs high. "Here's a fuck target for all three of you; John and Cary fuck me first, and give me your loads ... then you can drive the first two loads even farther in, Mike." So, I fucked Richard as Mike and Cary alternated sitting on his face. Cary's rapt expression seemed to indicate that Richard was doing an unusually good job of eating his ass. Once my load was safely in place, Cary replaced me and fucked Richard unmercifully for a long time, as both fucker and fuck-ee shouted their exuberance. Once Cary had delivered what Richard affirmed was a huge load, explosively deposited, Mike slammed his monster deep into Richard's cum-filled ass with one furious lunge, and fucked him with very rapid, extremely deep thrusts – surprisingly maintained during the entire term of his very long, brutal fuck. Cary and I watched closely and cheered Mike on. Following his eruption, Mike fell over Richard, and the two kissed rapturously while Cary and I did the same.

It was, needless to say, a good way to start a day. Mike and Cary had not planned to welcome Richard into their lovemaking, but since Richard and I were lovers, they apparently felt it was somehow natural. Needless to say, Richard's huge prick and his extreme beauty were no doubt an additional factor.

Mike and Cary had to go back to their respective homes early the next morning, and they asked if Richard and I would be offended if they kept to themselves that night. "We'll try to get back soon, and we can all fool around again then."

We all agreed that was a good plan and spent the day skiing and swimming – no sex, but a lot of happy intramural groping. By the time Richard and I went to bed in our bedroom that night, he was so horny he immediately rolled my to my stomach, and continually panted and grunted like a savage all the while he fucked me the first time. I fucked him just as eagerly, and as we lay together later, with my cock still in his ass, Richard mused about how beautiful Cary was, and how big Mike's cock was. "Do you suppose they'd come back for our birthdays? That'd really be a nice present."

Our birthdays were only one day apart; mine was July 14, and Richard's was July 15. I was quite a bit more than one day older than he, however – thirteen years and one day, to be exact. We agreed to ask Mike and Cary to return for our joint birthday observation if they could. Both were enthusiastic about the prospect and promised to be back by my birthday.

In the interim, Dean called to come out, and it happened that Richard had gone to Atlanta to visit friends, so I welcomed the magnificent high school stud to my bed all by myself. By the next morning we were both exhausted from a whole night of wild and wonderful fucking and sucking. While Dean admitted he really would have loved getting fucked by Richard's eminently satisfying big prick, it was nice for us to be together alone – and besides, we both knew that in no time my lover would be plumbing the depths of Dean's hot, appreciative ass again, and no doubt frequently.

Over coffee the next morning, I told Dean about our recent foursome with Mike and Cary, and about our plans to celebrate the upcoming joint birthday. He asked if he could join in. I assured him that Richard and I would be thrilled, and thought that once Mike and Cary got a look at his prick, they'd be more than agreeable. Richard, when informed, was eager about the prospect of Dean's hot sexual power joining forces with Mike and Cary to salute us. I telephoned Mike and Cary separately to get their reactions and both agreed that for this special occasion, the proposed fivesome would be somewhere between "interesting" and "fantastic"! My ass was almost constantly wet, just thinking about the impending confluence of the matchless huge cocks of Dean, Richard and Mike, and the stunning beauty of Cary – all making love with me at the same time.

And so it was all set, but on July 13, Dean called. "There's this guy, Eddie Bliss that I used to fuck with all the time back in Athens. He's in the Army, and he's home on leave, and he wants to come up and get together with me. He really means a lot to me, and I wonder if I could bring him along."

"Would he have a good time?"

He snorted, "Oh yeah, he'd have a good time. And believe me, John, you would have as good a time with Eddie as you can imagine ... and you'd see why he means so much to me, too."

"What do you mean?"

"Hey, my prick is big, right?"

"No, your prick is way past big. Your prick is enormous, and it's the biggest I've ever had." Certainly no one could have denied that Dean's cock was enormous, but the latter assertion was not quite the truth – the most stupendous prick I'd ever had belonged to the magnificent Hal Weltmann, but Dean was a very close second (however, no point in telling him that).

"Well, Eddie's is about an inch longer, and fatter, and ... well, he's got the biggest cock I've ever seen."

"Wow! Sounds great. No ... scratch that. Sounds fantastic. Were you guys in school together?"

"No. Eddie's about three years older than me. He picked me up one night at the 'meat rack' back home, and we had such an unbelievably hot time that we got together a lot until he went in the Army and I moved up here."

"And you were how old when all this happened?"

Dean laughed. Well, I was almost sixteen the first time we fucked, but I didn't tell him how old I was until that gigantic prick of his had already buried a couple of loads way up my ass. Well anyway, you can see why I think he might be a hit at the birthday party."

"I don't know how Mike and Cary will feel, but I'm positive Richard will welcome the biggest prick you've ever seen, and I know I will. So, yeah ... get him to join us if he will.'

"Look, he's coming in this afternoon, and I'll bring him out to meet you guys. After that I know we'll want to be alone together for the night, but I haven't figured out where we can go yet. It's liable to be a little noisy, if you know what I mean."

I laughed. "I know what you mean. So, are you really asking if you and your friend can stay in the guest room and fuck all night?"

"Well, now that you mention it ... yeah, I was hoping we could."

"Of course you can. And if he's agreeable, tomorrow could be the hottest day of the summer."

Eddie was agreeable, and Dean brought him out late that evening. He was nice looking – although not terribly handsome – and tall, with a lanky frame. He had a big, goofy grin, and seemed to be unassuming, and even a bit shy. My impression was that he was a friendly, easy-going kind of guy. I liked him immediately. He and Dean were obviously anxious to get into bed together, if the fact that they couldn't keep their hands off each other was any indication.

Richard and I were getting ready for bed a few minutes later. He observed that if Eddie had the kind of cock Dean said he did, it looked like a fantastic birthday party was in store for us. We had just turned the lights off, when Dean came into our room and asked if he could show us something. I switched the lamp back on.

Dean was standing there naked, stroking his huge, and very hard, cock. With a big grin he said, "Eddie thought you might like a little preview." And with that a naked Eddie came into the room and put his arm around Dean's waist.

Dean had not exaggerated at all: Eddie's prick was gigantic. It was longer even than the legendary (to me) Hal's, and was – as best I could judge – even fatter. It was unquestionably at least eleven inches long, and probably something like seven inches in circumference. I had never seen – and, except for films of the likes of John C. Holmes, Ken Ryker, Kevin Dean, or Rick Donovan – have yet to see a more impressive prick than Eddie Bliss's. And it was as beautiful as it was big: white and smooth, with a massive, pale purple head crowning the gargantuan shaft. His balls were a perfect match, too – they were enormous and hung and swung deliciously below the titanic meat of his bobbing and throbbing prick – an incredibly appetizing set of balls to complement an incomparably toothsome cock.

Eddie grinned hugely, "Y'all gonna be able to take this?"

Richard and I agreed that, come hell or high water, we were somehow going to take every fabulous inch up our butts the next night. Dean laughed as he fondled Eddie's huge, rock-hard prick, "It took some practice for me, I gotta admit."

Eddie turned around and kissed Dean – displaying a small, but very cute ass – and then moved behind him, holding his arms around Dean's waist and smiling at us over his shoulder. Dean opened his legs a bit, allowing Eddie's prick to pop up between them, just under Dean's balls. "But we practiced a lot, didn't we, baby?"

Eddie's wide, infectious gin appeared. "We could let Richard and John watch us practice some more right now, if they wanna."

Eddie pushed Dean up to the bed and forced his upper body down. "I think we oughta give 'em a real preview of what they're gonna get tomorrow." He took a finger full of Vaseline from the open jar on the nightstand and began to lubricate Dean's ass. Dean murmured, "Oh yeah," as he spread his legs to receive Eddie. Eddie lubricated his prick, and Richard and I moved in for a close look as Eddie pressed his monster cock slowly into Dean. It seemed to take forever going in, and Dean was moaning in ecstasy by the time the huge sac of Eddie's balls pressed against his ass. Then Eddie began to fuck very slowly and deeply as Dean's ass moved backward to meet his forward thrusts. Their fucking gained speed and force and was nothing short of epic. It seemed to take forever before Eddie seemed ready to shoot his load deep inside Dean, who was moaning loudly in ecstasy. I learned later that it was taking so long because they had gone off into the woods and fucked each other for most of the afternoon.

Eddie was pounding Dean's ass like a pile driver as he said to Richard and me, "You two jack off and shoot your loads on my dick and on Dean's ass. That'll be so fuckin' hot ... right, Dean?"

Dean panted, "Yeah, and you can pack it up in my ass with yours, baby!"

Richard and I masturbated furiously, and in a moment, Richard declared he was ready to cum. Only a minute or so after Richard had bathed Dean's asshole and Eddie's cock with his discharge, I was ready, and added mine. When Eddie finally got his load, very soon thereafter, his cock was awash with cum, and Dean's ass was squishing audibly while Eddie continued to plunge his cock in and out.

Dean declared he was about to cum, so Eddie pulled out as Dean stood and turned to face him; Eddie knelt with his mouth open, and Richard and I were treated to the sight of Dean's massive spurts of white cum bathing Eddie's adoring face, and shooting deep into his throat. Dean licked his own cum from Eddie's face, and we went to our separate beds. Richard and I both agreed, after they left, that we were far more than just eager to take Eddie up the ass the next day, and so stimulated that we sixty-nined and ate each other's loads, even though we had ejaculated only recently on Eddie and Dean.

Our joint birthday party the next night was unbelievably hot – a group sex encounter that foreshadowed a number of orgies that will be detailed later in this memoir.

When they arrived that afternoon, Mike and Cary readily agreed that Eddie should be a part of the festivities, and when Dean and Eddie drove up around 6:00 they found four very excited guys waiting for them.

All participants, not just the birthday boys, quickly got into their birthday suits, and although we sat around and drank and cooked hamburgers before starting the festivities, there was a lot of casual groping and kissing. Dean's huge cock and Eddie's even more impressive monster were the object of much attention and favorable comment by both Cary and Mike, who were viewing these wonderful natural resources for the first time. Richard was practically, if not literally, drooling with anticipation as he studied Eddie's stupendous endowment. Before we finished eating, everyone had also had at least three or four different guys – if not, in fact all of them – kneeling before him and having a brief deep-throat taste of what was to cum. Eddie's unbelievable equipment had been "saluted" orally by everyone several times, and each of us had speculated if he would be able to take him up the butt – except for Dean, who proudly admitted he had experienced that unforgettable honor countless times.

After Dean demonstrated that he could take every inch of Eddie's cock into his throat, we all tried. Cary and Mike were not quite able to achieve this feat – although they tried hard and came close – nor was I, although I came closer. But Richard simply opened his throat and gobbled the stupendous organ down – which earned him a huge grin and passionate kiss from Eddie and a big round of applause from everyone else.

We also ate food. And after we had finished eating that less exciting fare, Cary announced, "Time to get started giving birthday presents." All applauded and agreed, and from that point on, Cary took over, and directed the festivities, and although he was the smallest among us, and – like me – not impressively hung, everyone seemed to think it natural.

"First," he said, "exactly what do the birthday boys want? John?"

"I want every one of you hot guys to fuck me and shoot a huge load as far into me as you can. Just line up and gang-bang my ass."

"Fair enough. Sounds reasonable and sounds like a great way to start! Richard?"

"Well, at the risk of not seeming original, I want the same thing. I want so much cum up my butt it's gonna be leaking out."

"Great, but I think we ought to start with Richard and John exchanging birthday presents ... up their butts. I sure as hell want to watch."

Everyone agreed it was a good way to begin, so Richard lay on his back on an air mattress we had placed on the patio. He held out his hands to me, and raised his legs. "Fuck me slow and sweet, baby ... I really want it from you." I knelt, greased him up, and drove my prick into his ass. Verbal encouragement all around accompanied the onset of my fuck. Mike knelt over Richard's head, and I watched his pretty ass undulate while he fucked Richard's mouth. At the same time, Dean stood astride Richard, facing me, and fucked my mouth with his huge cock while I fucked Richard's ass. Soon, Eddie pushed Dean aside and his astonishing prick again was inches from my adoring gaze and my eager mouth.

I opened my mouth very wide to admit Eddie, who held my head and humped slowly into it. I relaxed my throat as much as possible, and again managed to take most of his monster into me. It was an incomparably exciting thing to feel such a huge organ driving into my mouth, and I was anticipating how wonderful it was going to feel in my ass. Eddie was very complimentary. "Jesus Christ, John, that's really good cocksuckin'. Lookit how much of my cock he's takin'." Another round of approbation, and Cary knelt over Richard to suck his shaft while I continued my assault on his ass.

Soon I said I was ready to cum, and all stepped away to watch. With a shout I erupted into Richard, who expressed his joy at feeling my orgasm, and I leaned over, and we kissed passionately while I continued to fuck until every possible drop of my cum was in my lover's hot body. I pulled out and lay on my back, telling Richard to do the same for me. Without hesitation, he lubed me up and drove his huge cock deep into me with one fierce thrust, which brought a cheer from the watchers, and a gasp of delight from me. He fucked me like a wild man – wonderfully, as he always had – and accompanied it with a litany of hot talk – "Wanna fill your ass with my cum! Take my big cock! Gonna fuck your hot ass," and the like. The onlookers all added their comments, and I watched Eddie's ass as he stood over me and drove his prick into Richard's mouth, until my view was cut off by Cary kneeling over my face and fucking my mouth. Then Cary moved forward to sit on my face, and humped up and down while I tongue-fucked him. Someone wiped my cock off and began to suck it. Then Dean's cock replaced Cary's ass in my mouth, and I sucked it happily until Richard declared he was ready to shoot. He drove himself all the way into me and froze there while I felt tremendously strong spurts of cum shooting into me. Again, all had stood aside to watch "the moment of truth," so to speak.

Richard still had his cock buried in me as he looked around the circle and grinned. "Who's next?"

As Richard withdrew, Cary knelt between my legs and smiled down on me as he announced, "John's got four more loads coming, and I think you guys should just watch now while we fill him up."

I agreed. "Yeah, I want to watch each of you while you fuck me."

Cary needed no lubrication to enter me – I was soaking with Richard's huge load. He continued to smile as he fucked me long and hard and expertly, and I gloried in the sight of his beautiful face transformed with rapture. I fondled Cary's glorious tits, and pinched his nipples while he fucked. No one said much of anything, watching the interaction between the beautiful young blond honoring my hot ass with his throbbing cock, and his appreciative honoree. After a long and thrilling fuck, Cary cried out that he was cumming, and I felt another sizable load erupt in me. The formerly silent group cheered him on.

Cary fell over me and kissed me. Then, as he pulled out, Mike knelt between my legs, and like Richard, he thrust his monster shaft all the way into me in one movement He fucked me wildly, his head was thrown back and his eyes closed tightly as he held my legs high and pounded my ass with his balls. His fuck was so wild and exuberant that the other guys began to urge him on even before he neared orgasm. Just as he was ready to cum, he pulled his cock out and shot two large spurts on my asshole before driving it back in and finishing inside me. This drew a cheer from everybody – including myself. He kissed me and whispered into my ear, "My cum's on you and in you, John ... right where it belongs. Happy birthday!"

Mike pulled out, and Dean stood over me. "You want me next? Get you ready for Eddie?"

"God yes, Dean ... ream me out so I can take Eddie's monster." He knelt and pushed his huge cock into me gradually.

"Wow, you are really full of cum! This feels so fuckin' good. Oh man, Eddie, you're not gonna believe how hot this feels."

Eddie knelt next to me to watch, and told Dean, "And it's gonna be even better with your big load in there, too."

Dean pushed my legs up over my shoulders and did push-ups over my raised ass, driving his magnificent shaft straight down into me. He fucked me this way for a very long time, kissing me as he did so. He fucked my mouth with his tongue as his load shot palpably into me. After the initial burst of his orgasm, he stopped kissing me and raised his head. I studied his face – his eyes closed, with a look of absolute ecstasy suffusing his beautiful features. Finally he finished cumming, and with his cock still in me, he looked down into my eyes and smiled warmly. "You ready for the big one?" I agreed I was, and Eddie took Dean's place between my legs.

Eddie's prick looked unthinkably large as he grinned at me. "I'm gonna shove every inch of this thing all the way up your hot butt, and you're gonna

103

love it, ain'tcha?" I agreed I was. Then Eddie turned to Richard. "Hold his head in your lap while I fuck him. Watch what you're gonna get a little bit later!"

Richard cradled my head – and his hard prick pressed against my neck. He looked up at Eddie. "Show me what you're gonna do to me!"

Eddie raised my legs and began to put his prick into me. I had expected to have great difficulty accommodating this gargantuan cock, but it pretty well slipped in without trouble. It was, after all, the fifth prick to enter me in the space of an hour. I was well lubricated with four apparently copious loads of cum, and Mike and Richard's huge cocks had opened me up for Dean's monster, which left me sufficiently dilated to accept one of the biggest shafts I had ever felt. Eddie grinned, leaned over me, and then kissed me passionately as he slowly penetrated me, and I thrilled to the enormous bulk invading me. Finally it stopped going in, and Eddie's belly was pressed against my ass as his goofy grin shone on me. "I'm all the way in you. Ya like it?"

"God, Eddie, I can't believe how big you are, or how wonderful you feel. Just fuck me long, and slow, and hard with that amazing meat."

He raised my legs and began to fuck me in earnest. He was not only incredibly hung, he proved to be a masterful lover as well. On almost every stroke he drove himself all the way in, wiggled his hips, then slowly pulled almost all the way out before thrusting himself back in fiercely – cycling like a huge, hot piston. "God I love ta fuck butt," he chuckled as he grinned at everyone watching. "And John, yours is so fulla cum, my dick is swimmin' in it ... grip my cock with that hot ass-pussy while I fuck you hard as you ever got it!"

While Eddie fucked me, he and Richard often kissed, and Richard kept telling him how he was looking forward to the same thing. Eddie looked into Richard's face for a minute and said, "And I've been checkin' out that big meat o' yours, and I wanna get it up my ass before the night's over. Deal?" Then he looked down at me. "And I want you ta fuck me too, okay?" Richard and I both enthusiastically promised to honor his wishes.

Eddie fucked me for what seemed an unbelievably long, deliriously satisfying time. My ass and back were more than a bit sore, but this was the most exciting thing that had ever happened to me, and I was enjoying it as I had never enjoyed anything before. Finally, Eddie was obviously about to cum. "Watch this," he cried, and he quickly pulled his prick from me. He shot three fierce spurts of cum on my belly before shoving his cock savagely all the way back into me, and even though I was awash with the cum of four other hot men, I could still feel the force of his orgasm inside me – deep inside me, probably as deep as anyone had ever blown one. It was truly thrilling!

Eddie put his arms under me, lifted me, and turned so that he could lie flat on his back, with me still impaled on his huge prick. "Ride that cock, birthday boy." I bounced up and down for a long time, until Eddie said, "I'd like ta have ya keep ridin' me until I give ya another load, but I've gotta service

Richard's hot ass, too." So, what may have been the most profound fuck of my life to that point ended at last. When I finally stood, and Eddie's cock slipped out of me, a flow of cum came out of my ass and coursed down my leg – which drew whistles and applause from those whose semen was now leaking from me.

Cary asked Richard if he was ready to get gang-banged, but Eddie said, "Look, I'm the new guy here, and botha the birthday boys promised to fuck me, so, since we all need to rest a few minutes anyway, I'd like ta get 'em to do it before we start up again. Anybody got a problem with that?" Everyone agreed it would be fun – especially the birthday boys.

Eddie knelt on all fours, and I knelt behind him to give him the hardest fucking I was capable of – and he was as fine a bottom as he was a top. His ass was tight, and gripped my cock and rode back and forth on it while I fucked. He didn't say anything, because Richard had positioned himself on his back under Eddie, and the two were kissing almost constantly – Richard's arms tightly clasped around the super-hung stud's neck, and his legs around his waist. I could see there was a real connection developing between my lover and this Army fuckmaster.

As I shot my load into Eddie, he and Richard stopped kissing, and he looked over his shoulder to smile and wink at me, "Great load, man!" Then Richard quickly took my place behind the kneeling Eddie's eager ass, and Eddie cried out in rapture as Richard's much larger cock plumbed his asshole in one deep, fierce thrust – Richard's typical opening gambit. As he fucked the obviously appreciative stud, Richard was wilder and more passionate than I had ever seen him, and Eddie obviously enjoyed it equally. Richard was kissing Eddie's neck and back with unbelievable excitement as his hands feverishly fondled him all over, while Eddie's hands reached behind to pull Richard's ass tightly into him as he countered his manic deep thrusts with equal ferocity – and the two were groaning in a kind of ecstasy that could only be described as rapture. They were so completely lost in lust and wrapped up in each other that the rest of us watched in amazement. As he was nearing orgasm, Richard rolled Eddie onto his back and drove himself back in, missionary style, and they began passionate kissing that continued as Richard's driving ass and panting indicated he was shooting inside Eddie.

They lay together for a long time, arms wrapped around each other, still kissing with unflagging ardor and Richard's cock still buried in Eddie's ass. We were all a little embarrassed, I think. Finally they broke and Eddie smiled up at Richard. "That was incredible."

Richard realized that everyone had been somewhat dumbstruck by their naked display of mutual passion, and laughed. "Well, now it's my turn to get gang-banged, right?" That broke the tension, and we all laughed nervously. He lay on his back, raised his legs, and extended his hands to Cary. "C'mon, Cary, still plenty of John's cum in me for you to slide that beautiful prick inside me easily. Come on and fuck me like you've never fucked before."

I knew exactly what my calculating lover was doing in asking Cary to fuck him first. As nicely endowed as Cary was, his cock didn't compare to the behemoth Eddie employed when he fucked – and Mike and Dean's pricks, respectively, were steps along the way from Cary to Eddie. I knew Richard wanted to finish up with the biggest available – which he would regard, I knew, as the best (and I would be hard pressed to disagree with his thinking).

Cary first lay on top of Richard, and the two kissed sweetly for a very long time. Richard raised his legs and Cary inserted himself into the eager hot ass, then – as enjoined by Richard – fucked like a demon. He and Richard both encouraged each other with impassioned cries. When Cary neared orgasm, they re-commenced kissing. Cary's cute ass plunged his cock in and out of Richard in very quick, very short strokes before he finally drove himself extra deep and raised up with a loud cry, "Take my load!"

Richard's "Yes! Give it to me ... I can feel your cock filling me up!" was almost drowned out by the eager vocal approval we all gave Cary's masterly fuck.

Cary smiled at Richard – his prick still inside him – as he asked, "You ready for Mike's big prick now? He'll fuck you like a pro, believe me. You want him to show you how he makes love to my ass? I guarantee you, he's the best." Cary looked up at his lover. "I love getting fucked by Mike more than anything in the world."

Richard played with Cary's succulent tits as he grinned and said, "I want him, now."

Mike knelt next to Cary and took him in his arms. "I'm gonna fuck Richard now, but you can bet this cock of mine is gonna be inside you before the night's over. I Love you, Cary!"

Cary kissed Mike. "I love you, too, baby. Now fuck Richard's hot ass while we watch ... my cum's already in there for you." He pulled out, and Mike moved into place. Positioning the very tip of his big prick at Richard's asshole, he asked, "You want me, Richard?"

Richard raised his legs higher. "God yes, Mike ... fill my hole and fuck me hard." With one sudden thrust – Richard style – Mike drove the entire length of his massive prick all the way in, and his balls pressed up against Richard's ass. "God damn that feels good. Now fuck me as hard as you can." And Mike fucked him as hard as anyone could possibly have wanted. His attention was on Richard, but he cried out, "Your cum is so hot in here, Cary ... it feels wonderful." His ass pumped fast and hard, and his strokes were so long that his big prick often slipped out, but he invariably plunged it all the way back in without losing a stroke. It was a masterful example of "piston fucking," and Richard seemed almost drugged with extreme passion as he repeatedly cried, "God that feels good." Mike's orgasm was apparently forceful and copious, if his and Richard's cries were any indication. They both froze *en tableau* while

Mike unloaded in Richard's eager ass, his head thrown back and his eyes closed in ecstasy.

Dean knelt next to Mike. "Got it hot for me?" Mike agreed the asshole Dean was about to enter was hotter than hell, and all primed for his huge shaft. And Dean proceeded to fuck Richard in the same way Mike had – deep, savage strokes, and with animal cries of delight from both participants.

"Your prick is so fucking big, Dean," Richards gasped. "I love it!"

"Your ass is so hot, Richard ... and full of cum. God, I love fucking it." He looked around and grinned as he continued to fuck wildly, "You guys did a great job of getting it ready for me."

Dean's fuck was so intense and masterful, we all watched in silence, appreciative of his sexual mastery. When Dean and Richard were not grunting in passion, you could hear the squish of all the cum inside Richard as Dean's monster cock drove in and out. That same wonderful lotion so coated Dean's thrusting prick that it was clearly visible on his lengthy back strokes, and some even leaked out around the invading shaft. As his orgasm arrived, Dean did for Richard what Eddie and Mike had done for me – he pulled completely out and shot several huge spurts of cum on him before savagely shoving his throbbing, exploding prick back in to finish. It was a magnificent sight, and we all expressed our approval loudly.

Dean pulled out and kissed Richard, who thanked him for a wonderful fuck and extended a hand to Eddie. "Now I want that unbelievable prick of yours."

Eddie stood, came over to Richard, and knelt over his face. "Suck it first."

Richard again demonstrated his virtuosic ability to take every inch of the mammoth shaft in his mouth, and he gobbled hungrily and noisily as Eddie fucked his mouth energetically, his balls slapping against Richard's chin. Richard took Eddie's monster balls in his mouth, and licked and sucked them eagerly. Eddie was ecstatic. "Those balls are fulla cum for ya." He pulled back and fell over Richard, their arms went around each other, and they began kissing at first sweetly, and then wildly. Their kissing went on for a very long time as their hands fervently explored each other. Finally, Eddie looked at Richard closely and murmured quietly, "Gonna fuck that sweet ass o' yours now." He positioned himself between Richard's legs and raised them to his shoulders. "You want it gentle or hard?"

Again, Richard seemed drugged with sheer animal lust. As if crying out in a fever, he gasped in a hoarse voice, "Hard! Fuck me as hard as you can!" And when Eddie's unbelievable organ penetrated him in one savage thrust, Richard's cry was almost a scream of ecstasy: "God I've never had a prick like that in me. I want you to fuck me forever!"

And Eddie did seem to fuck Richard forever. After a long time, he neared orgasm, but continued his fierce thrusting as he cried out, "Take this big load, baby, I wanna give it to ya."

Richard's face was a study in total bliss as he encouraged Eddie Bliss to give it to him. Eddie's ass tightened as he clearly planted his cock as deep inside Richard as he could and kept it there while his load exploded.

Richard moaned, feverishly, "I can feel your cum shooting in me, Eddie. Keep fucking ... don't stop ... keep fucking me with that wonderful cock."

And an impressive thing happened then. Eddie had obviously shot a huge load into Richard's ass, but he never stopped fucking. He continued the wild assault as requested. His ass continued to drive his cock deep into the seemingly delirious Richard, whose moans of passion only increased, accompanied by Eddie's grunts and gasps. His huge prick was shining with its coating of cum as it emerged from Richard's ass, and that same cum was dripping from it as its magnificent length and bulk was revealed, and then continued to plunge back in – deep, hard, fast, in and out, over and over repeatedly, accompanied by animal cries of excitement from both Richard and Eddie. I think we were all excited to realize that it was all the hot loads of cum that we had already deposited in Richard's ass – mine, Cary's, Mike's, Dean's, and now even Eddie's, too – that served to lubricate this magnificent organ in its savage and wonderful assault on the lucky man receiving this wild and epic fuck. Richard's legs were on Eddie's shoulders, and his ass was far off the mat, driving backwards to meet the fierce, profound thrusts. The two were so completely insane with ecstasy, we all watched in awe. After a good ten or fifteen minutes of this unbelievable assault, Eddie shot another load into Richard. Two consecutive, separate fucks, each delivering a load – huge ones, both of them, if Richard's cries were true – without losing a stroke.

Eddie was truly an incredible fucking machine, and Richard showed himself to be an almost insatiable bottom. He lay before me, having been fucked consecutively by five different guys, and with six loads of cum inside him – the last two from the biggest prick I had ever watched in action. The memory of his telling me even recently that he could not take a cock up his ass was not only ironic – it was more than a little irritating.

After his second orgasm, Eddie pulled out of Richard, the two wrapped their arms around each other, and they began kissing again, almost as if they had forgotten we were all watching – and in fact, I think they were both so euphoric that they had forgotten they had an audience. Eventually they broke off, and laughed nervously about their having gotten completely caught up in the fuck.

We took a break to refresh drinks. Eddie and Richard sat off to one side and talked as Dean approached me. "It looks to me like we may have both lost a lover. Eddie's not really my lover, but something like that. I'm sorry, John ... this is my fault."

I put my arms around Dean and kissed him. "I think you called it. Look, it's not your fault, and I'm not really surprised. Richard dumped me before, and I can see why he might want to again: Eddie is incredible. But why Eddie Bliss would even think of giving up this incredible thing called Dean Williamson even for something as sexy and beautiful as Richard Austin, is past my understanding."

"You're sweet John ... and we may have to console each other for a while."

I grinned at him. "If I need consoling ... and I do think I will ... there's no one I'd rather have comfort me."

It was his turn to grin. "My cock and my butt are at your service. I'll lend consolation about nine inches up your butt any time you want it." He kissed me sweetly. "Deal?"

"Deal!" I looked over at the mat where Richard and I had both been gang-banged so unforgettably. Mike and Cary lay on their sides, locked together in sixty-nine, sucking each other's cocks avidly. I grinned at Dean. "I see somebody got horny. Let's join 'em." We went over and Dean ate Mike's ass while I provided the same sort of salute to Cary's. Then we decided to emulate their example and we double-sucked for a long, wonderful time, concluding with each taking a load from the other. By the time we had finished, Mike and Cary had slaked their own thirst, and we four lay there and talked for quite a while. It was then we noticed that Eddie and Richard had gone off somewhere. Mike and Cary offered their condolences over the obvious infatuation that had developed between my lover and the monster-cocked Eddie. They, like Dean, offered to keep me supplied with all the cock I wanted.

At any rate, the hour was late, and the birthday party was obviously over. We went into the house, where Cary and Mike went to their room, and Dean and I found Eddie and Richard sucking each other's cocks in my bed. We opened the sofa bed in the living room and spent the night together there, locked in each other's arms.

We were awakened the next morning by Richard and Eddie, both naked and with erect cocks. Richard kissed me, and as if nothing had happened the night before, asked "You gonna take your regular morning load?" He knelt over my head and I began to suck. Eddie offered the same service to Dean, who also availed himself of such a splendid opportunity.

Eddie was still fucking Dean's mouth eagerly after Richard had discharged a large offering into my throat. We both urged them on, but Dean pulled away. "John didn't get to suck you off last night, Eddie ... let him have your load. I'll get another one soon." Eddie transferred his monster shaft to my mouth, and I thrilled at its bulk, and at its owner's mastery of mouth-fucking. Soon he was ready, and the eruption of cum in my mouth was as copious as I could have wished. My swallowing was unable to keep pace with Eddie's discharge, and his cum was frothing at the corners of my mouth, and oozing out onto my chin. Dean licked the cum from my chin as I savored and swallowed the remaining precious nectar.

Richard kissed me deeply, as soon as Dean had licked my chin clean. "Mmmmm! Eddie's cum tastes good, doesn't it?" I agreed it was indeed delicious. He knelt between my legs. "Am I gonna get a load from you to start my birthday?"

I stood on the bed, and watched as Richard licked my balls and my prick, murmuring his enjoyment. His blowjob was exciting and expert – and the apparent love and dedication he brought to the task seemed to belie what Dean and I – and, I was sure, Mike and Cary – had thought the night before as we watched him and Eddie make love – that the two had been struck with a mutual love – or, certainly, lust – at first sight.

Standing there with my dick in Richard's throat, I looked down at Dean, who was lying on his back, his perfect face wreathed in ecstasy as Eddie rode eagerly up and down, impaled on the magnificent shaft that had come to mean so much to me since that night I first saw it, lying fat and tempting in the palm of his hand when he pissed in that football field men's room. Eddie's unbelievable prick – still hard, even after the load he had delivered into my mouth – flopped up and down as he rode, with eyes closed, head back, looking as ecstatic as his partner. I wondered, as I admired this largest, most enticing cock I had ever experienced, if I would ever feel it in my body again.

Actually, I was to feel the bliss of Eddie Bliss' gigantic tool in my body once more – about two hours later, as Eddie and I went next door to the pool to clean up. While there, I complimented him on the perfection of his cock and of his fucking technique, and he acknowledged my compliment in the very best way he could: he bent me over a table, drove his throbbing, monstrous prick all the way into my ass, and fucked me long and hard while I stood there and enjoyed the thrill of this accomplished young fuckmaster-soldier shooting another forceful, copious load of his precious cum into me. He had blown a huge load in my mouth a very short time before, so it took him a heavenly long time to fuck me to climax – and a truly unforgettable fuck it was. I could well understand Richard's adoration of this epic prick. I was not to experience a cock of anything like that astonishing dimension again for three or four years – and, coincidentally, it was again to be Dean who brought it to me and shared it with me. Much to my regret, I never saw Eddie again after that morning.

As I gazed down lovingly at Richard's Adonis-beautiful face, enraptured by his delight in exercising one of his favorite things in the entire world – sucking cock – I thrilled to watch my prick entering and leaving his mouth, honored to be fucking such an incomparably beautiful man. I reveled in the feel of his hands pulling my ass in to him, his lips tightly grasping the shaft of my cock as they moved up and down its entire length, the enormous suction he employed on me, and the sensation of his busy tongue licking and playing with the head of my cock. I blew a load into Richard's ravenous mouth, and he savored it and bathed my cock in it for a long time before swallowing it and lying folded in my arms.

In spite of the usual wonderful morning sex we had just shared, I still sensed the imminent collapse – again – of my relationship with Richard. Holding him there, I wondered if I would ever experience his magnificent prick in my body again. Every single time I had sex with this beloved, magnificent, hung, beautiful, stud was ecstasy. Every time we kissed, or I felt his wonderful big cock explode inside my ass, or thrilled at the blast and flow of his cum in my throat I was in heaven. Rapture and thrills of this kind with Richard were not yet over for me – as, after that morning, the thrill of feeling, or even seeing, Eddie's gargantuan endowment was – but they proved to be, as I suspected, almost over.

11. EXIT ONE, STAGE LEFT – ENTER ONE, STAGE RIGHT

Eddie went home to Athens that day after our fabulous birthday celebration, and Dean accompanied him for the few days remaining before he had to fly to San Francisco and report in at The Presidio, his new duty station. I drove down to pick Dean up and bring him home after Eddie's departure, and on the way back to Dowd we had a long discussion about the obvious fascination Eddie and Richard had displayed towards each other.

"Man, Eddie couldn't seem to stop mentioning what a nice guy he thought Richard was. He said he had enjoyed the party more than anything, but had enjoyed meeting Richard especially."

"Yeah, except he probably meant meating Richard ... m-e-a-ting ... instead of m-e-e-ting him."

Dean laughed. "Well, it was pretty obvious he enjoyed getting Richard's meat inside him. And just as obvious Richard loved Eddie's big meat."

"Well, shit, Dean, I loved Eddie's big meat ... who wouldn't?"

"I can't argue ... that's the biggest and best meat I've ever had, and I love the hell out of it." He laughed, "Eddie has told me about all sorts of straight guys who have been so fascinated by his dick that they asked to feel it, and then wound up playing with it, and most of 'em wound up sucking it. He says there were even quite a few who wound up taking it up the ass."

"Funny, Mike told me almost the same story. Well, I can't blame any of 'em for being fascinated with Eddie's dick, but I wonder how many of them were really straight."

He snorted, "You mean before getting Eddie's cock up the butt or after?"

"Yeah, I'll bet he brought a lotta guy out of the closet with that monster. How many times did you guys fuck each other in the last few days?"

He grinned and gave me a quick kiss on the neck. "You wouldn't believe me if I told you. My asshole is as fucked out as it's ever been ... and I about wore my prick out shovin' it in Eddie. But it was great."

"I was kinda hoping you'd want to shove it in me this afternoon. And I'm sure Richard would be happy to share the wealth."

"Hey, give me a day or so to recuperate. I'll be back better than ever, and I'll fuck you both silly."

"That sounds great. Promise?" He assented. "By the way, I want to give you some money ..."

"No! The way I've come to feel about you ... well, I really feel you're a good friend now. I don't really care about those guys I fuck for money. And you know how much I enjoy making love with you."

"Making love?"

"Okay, fucking with you! I ... no, John, I really do mean making love with you. I'm not in love with you, or anything like that, but I do love you, and it's not just sex anymore. So ... I guess it's making love, right?"

"It sure is with me. And I'm not really in love with you either, but I really do love you, too. I am in love with Richard, but I have this feeling he's getting ready to bail out. He hasn't said anything ... in fact, he won't talk about it ... but I think he's so hot for Eddie he's going to dump me again."

"Again?"

"Yeah. Do I look like I ever learn?"

He laughed. "Hell, Richard is beautiful, he's hot, he's hung ... I can't blame you. And you can't really blame Eddie, either. It's just one of those things, I guess. Anyway, if he does dump you, there'll be someone else to love."

"I could fall in love with you in a heartbeat, if I let myself."

"Well don't let yourself, okay? I love you, you love me, and I can't see any reason why we can't go on screwing around with each other as long as we want, but I'm not ready to tie myself down."

"Why Dean Williamson, do you mean to say you'd fuck with someone else?"

His grin was so adorable I wanted to eat him up. "If he was cute, built, hot, hung ... whatever ... I'd have my dick up his butt at the first opportunity. But maybe I'd bring him by so we could share, okay?"

"Fair enough, my friend." I stopped the car and we put our arms around each other as we shared a long, sweet kiss. "Thanks for being such a good friend, Dean. And thanks for sharing that beautiful big prick and hot body with me; I really love having sex with you."

"That goes double for me, John."

A letter for Richard arrived from San Francisco around the first of August. There was no return address, but I suspected it was from Eddie. I gave it to Richard without comment, and he offered none; it seemed significant that he didn't open it in front of me. He later did mention it was from Eddie, who, he said, "just wanted to say hello." Richard hid the letter, but I found it the next day in the bottom of one of his dresser drawers. I normally did not pry into Richard's affairs, but if this affair was to become an "affair," I wanted to know about it in advance, and be prepared for him to dump me this time; the first time he had done so had caught me completely by surprise. I copied the letter, correcting some obvious spelling mistakes as I did so:

"Dear Richard:

"I was so happy when you said you would come out to San Francisco to be with me! Like I told you, the second I saw you I knew I wanted to be with you – you're so beautiful, and I love your cock so much! When you fucked me, it was the best thing ever happened to me, and when I shoved my prick in your ass, I thought I was in heaven! I know we were meant for each other, like you said,

and we'll work things out somehow where we can be together all the time out here. I can get an off-base living allowance, so we can get an apartment, and we can fuck each other every night (maybe we'll just suck each other off every morning, huh? Like you said you and John do. Man – I sure would enjoy that!) Wouldn't you like to be fucking me right now? And think about my big prick shooting a big load all the way up your butt when you read this, and jack your big, beautiful cock off until you shoot a big load (and I sure wish I was there to get that load – I'm so horny I'm jacking off while I write this letter).

"Come to me as soon as you can – I told you I love you, and I know it's awful sudden, but I know I do! And when you told me you loved me, too, it made me the happiest guy in the world! I'm dying to hold your beautiful body in my arms again, and feel your wonderful lips kissing me and sucking my cock (which I'm going to take a minute before I finish this letter to jack off!! I'm so fucking horny thinking about you it will only take a minute or so, too) (ha ha)!.

"Well, it's a few minutes later and I'm back, and I shot a really huge load of cum, and I closed my eyes and I could see your hot ass, and I pretended it was shooting inside there. Why aren't you here to take it in your mouth or up your ass again? Come and be with me soon! I love you!! Don't forget to go and jack off and think of me when your big prick is shooting all that hot cum! I love you. Come to me as soon as you can!!!! You told me my prick is the biggest one that has ever fucked you – your ass is the hottest one I have ever fucked, and your prick is really big, too, and except for Dean, maybe the biggest one I have ever taken. Come out here and give it to me soon and often!!!!

"Love,

"Eddie

"P.S. The next page is all wrinkled up because I shot my cum all over it when I was thinking about you and jacking off. I let it dry, so you can suck on this paper when you get this letter and taste my cum and pretend it is shooting inside your hot mouth or your even hotter ass! While you're doing that, shoot a big load on a piece of paper and let it dry and send it to me so I can taste your cum again!! And then get your pretty ass out here to California and give it to me in person! I want it NOW!! More love!"

In truth, I was not surprised, but I was still hurt. At dinner that night I steered the conversation around to Eddie. "Did Eddie say he had a good time when he came to our birthday party?"

"Yeah, he said it was really fun."

"I could tell you guys really had fun together."

"Well, we did, what's wrong with that? We had fun with everybody."

"Richard, come on. You guys were all over each other like you were the only two people in the world. Everybody could tell there was something special when he was fucking you, or you were fucking him – and when you were holding each other and kissing, it looked really serious."

115

"John, I ... okay, it was serious. I'm in love with Eddie, and he's in love with me."

"A couple of weeks ago you said you were in love with me."

"I was ... I am, John. I love you, but I love Eddie now, too, and I ..."

"Are you going to him?"

He kept his eyes on his plate for what seemed like a long time. Then he looked up at me and said, simply, "Yes."

I should have blown up, I suppose, but any anger I felt was muted by the fact that this was not unexpected, that he had done this to me before. But most especially I could not get angry because huge tears welled up in his eyes and began spilling down his cheeks. "I still love you, John. I'll always love you. Please don't stop loving me because I go to Eddie. I want to be with him so bad that I have to go."

We both stood, and he sobbed on my shoulder as I folded him in my arms. "My baby. I love you, too, you know that, and I'll always love you. Go to him if you have to, Richard. I hope it works out for both of you. You know how much I'm going to miss making love with you, sleeping with you, waking up with you, skiing, swimming ..." I began to cry also. "I just wish you didn't want to leave."

"I don't want to leave, John, but I have to. When I made love with Eddie, it was ... magic. I've never felt what I felt with him before."

I pulled myself together and tried a small laugh. "Well, I've never felt anything as big as what I felt with him before, I know that."

"Oh, you know that's not the only thing!"

"No, but it's a big thing isn't it? A really big thing?"

He laughed, "Yeah, okay ... it's a big thing. I've never taken such a big prick in my life, and I loved it, and it was exciting ... but you felt the same way, I know."

"Absolutely guilty! Eddie's cock is one of the Wonders of the World, and he's a fantastic fucker."

"But that isn't the only thing, please believe me. I really fell in love with Eddie. I know, it was all in one night, but I know I'm in love with him. I just know! Please don't be angry with me, and let me go to him and still be your friend."

"You'll never be my friend, Richard." He began to say something, but I put my hand over his mouth. "You will always be my lover. I will always love you and want you. Go to Eddie if you have to, but go on loving me, please."

"I will, John. Come to bed right now, and show me how much you love me, and I'll show you that I really do love you, too." We went to bed, and had probably the most exciting sustained sex since the first time we had spent an entire night together, but I felt his mind was really on Eddie while he fucked.

The next day, Richard made plane reservations to go to California, and in the four days remaining before he left, we hardly stopped kissing and fucking.

116

He assured me he would always love me, and would be back often to bury his prick in me, and to take mine in him. We agreed that no matter what happened, no matter whom we might meet or be with in the future, we would always find a way to make love to each other when we could. I know I was sincere, anyway.

I took him to the airport and wished him well, after which I went home and cried.

Dean was a great comfort to me in the period following Richard's departure. He was sweet, he was solicitous, but most importantly, he was horny and hot, and his huge cock and busy ass kept my mind off my loss. We spent far more time together in the couple of weeks before school began for the fall than we ever had before. He slept with me almost every night, and his brothers somehow seemed to cover for him with his parents. We fucked each other at least once every night, and most nights I went to sleep with his magnificent shaft buried in my ass. He knew of Richard's and my tradition of enjoying a mutual blowjob to start each day, and he made sure he was there to keep it alive.

Mike and Cary did not move back into my guest room, since they had rented an apartment together in town for the upcoming school year, but they came out to visit often. I helped them move into their new apartment a few days before fall registration, and we had a housewarming threesome that was truly memorable. They both had been so taken with Dean's beauty and his sexual power, that they eagerly sought a foursome, including him. Strangely, they only wanted to go to bed with Dean when I was with him. They seemed to feel that it was really having sex with me – the only one they agreed they would continue to share sex with – but by this time they viewed Dean as my partner, so naturally he could be party to the festivities. They were probably rationalizing, so they could fuck with the incomparable high-school fuckmaster, but it was sort of true; by that time, Dean and I almost did seem to be partners.

Dean was beginning his senior year at the local high school, so he had less free time, having to get home at a reasonable hour during the week, so our all-night fucks were going to be limited to Fridays and Saturdays, but the super-hung stud promised a lot of those – and he certainly didn't rule out some mid-week fucks at reasonable hours. As a senior, Dean was now allowed almost free use of one of the family cars, so he often dropped in to suck and be sucked, fuck and be fucked, and was so attentive to my sexual needs and desires, and so solicitous about my mood following Richard's departure that I almost felt like he was a protective older partner – nothing protective about the ferocity with which he regularly sank his monster prick into me and filled me with his hot cum, however.

The day before classes at the college began for the fall semester, I picked up my class rolls, and was excited to discover a familiar name appearing there for one of my sections of Music Appreciation: Alan M. Hagood – Mark, of course.

I had planned to call Mark, of course, and pursue our telephone friendship, but was going to give him a week or so to settle in before pushing the possible meeting he had suggested the last time we talked. Now I was excited to learn that I was going to get to see him and to speak with him face-to-face in a day or so, even though it was only going to be a perfunctory professor-student exchange.

The first time I met the Music Appreciation class in which Mark was enrolled, I was nervous as a cat – unbelievably eager to see this paradigm of masculine beauty, and hoping desperately that something meaningful might come of our meeting. In spite of his beauty, it seems strange that I was so smitten with Mark. After all, I was not just seeing two incredibly handsome, beautiful men, I was fucking them and they were fucking me with some regularity, along with a third who was almost as handsome, and was a well-built, super-hung stud into the bargain. Yet, I really ached to get to know this perfect Mark Hagood, and to explore a sexual relationship with him.

Mark was seated toward the front of the classroom when I met his class the first day, and as I called the names on the roll, I asked each student to verify his presence by telling me the name he preferred to be addressed by. When I got to Mark, I called him Alan Hagood. He surprised me not at all, of course, when he responded by saying he was called Mark. Before I went on to the next name I asked Mark, "You're a soccer player, right?" He said he was, and I told him I thought I had seen him somewhere ("Mr. Disingenuous," that's me!), and went on to the next name.

During the lecture that followed – mostly an open discussion of exactly what we meant by "music," and what we mean by "good" or "bad" music, etc. – I noticed that Mark was an extremely attentive listener, although he did not volunteer to take part in the class discussion. I tried not to look at him too often, but whenever I did, I found his eyes fixed on me. When the bell rang to end the period, he filed out along with everyone else.

Late that afternoon, Mark came by my office with a form to drop my class. I was really disappointed, but I signed it, and told him I was sorry he wasn't going to continue in my section. "Is the time bad for you, Mark?"

"No, it's just that ... well, I'll be honest, Dr. Harrison. I recognized your voice. I told you I was pretty good with voices ... John. I guess it's okay to call you 'John' in person, isn't it?"

"I really don't know what to say. I'm a little embarrassed, and ... no, I'm more than a little embarrassed, but I'm glad to finally speak to you in person. But I also wish you didn't feel you needed to drop my class."

"There's nothing to be embarrassed about, but I feel I do need to drop your class. It would be awkward for you and for me, under the circumstances."

"I guess you're right, Mark, but I was so excited to find that you were going to be in my class. I was really hoping to get to know you."

He grinned at me – a totally engaging, huge grin. "I don't know why you can't get to know me. It would be awkward for me to be in your class, but why can't we get to know each other outside of class? I've been curious to meet you, too, you know."

"Wow! Does that mean you'll ... that you'd be willing ..."

"Do you want to take me out to dinner and a show, John? Get to know me? A date? You want to call it that? Just ask me."

I looked into his eyes – his beautiful, sexy eyes – for a minute before I said, "Mark, would you go out on a date with me?"

"Why would you want to take me out on a date?" He grinned again. "Do you ... find me attractive or something like that?"

I grinned back at him. "You're the most beautiful man I've ever seen, and I want very much to get to know you and to be with you. Will you go out with me?"

"I'd be honored. And I think you're a very handsome man. I've been wanting to meet you, and to get to know you, too."

"I'm really pleased, Mark. Okay, how about Friday night?"

"Friday night is perfect. Pick me up in front of the Athletic Dorm at 6:00, and we'll have an honest-to-God date. It seems strange to me, but ... what the heck, a real date, okay?"

"I'll be there! You'll recognize me ... I'll be the one with the happy grin on his face."

"I'll be the one grinning back at you. I'm glad we finally met, John."

"Me too, Mark, and I can hardly wait until Friday."

That evening, Dean came out to the house, and we had hot, wonderful, stupendous sex. Shortly before he had to leave, I lay there on my side, with his huge prick deep inside my ass and his cum filling that same appreciative orifice. "Dean, I don't know what you had planned, but we can't get together Friday night."

"That's no problem ... what's happening?"

"Would you be angry if I said I had a date with another guy?"

"John, of course not. I just hope it's somebody terrific. Hell, Richard's gone ... probably fucking my Eddie right this very minute ... you need to find someone else to really love. That doesn't mean we won't still be friends, and still fuck each other, right?" I agreed that nothing was going to stop that. "You two gonna fuck each other's brains out? Just promise me you'll give me all the hot details. Maybe you need help fucking him? If you do, this prick would be at your service." At that point, he shoved the prick in question even farther into me.

I laughed, "No, nothing like that ... not yet, anyway." I described Mark to him, told him a little about our telephone relationship, and showed him his picture in the annual.

119

"He really is cute, isn't he? Man, I'd like to look down at that pretty face and see my hard cock going in and out of those lips. I'll bet he puts out for you right away."

"I think at best this is going to move slowly. I know I'm going to have a nice time meeting him, but I don't think anything major is going to happen this first time we go out. And I bet I'll be horny as a snake when I come home afterward."

"Leave the door unlocked. When you come home, I'm gonna be here. If this guy is with you, tell him I'm just a friend who is using your house to study, but will have to leave in a few minutes ... and I will. If you're alone, I want to know all about it. And if you're horny, I want you to take it out on my butt, okay?"

"Can I take a little bit of it out on your butt right now?" He pulled his cock out of me and rolled on his stomach; he used his hands to spread his cheeks as he put his beautiful ass high in the air and told me to "do my stuff." I did!

12. FIRST DATE JITTERS AND BEYOND

I was so excited about my date with Mark, that I washed my car, took forever getting ready – including three changes of clothes – but was still all set to go a full hour early. I had made reservations at the best restaurant in town, and did everything except buy him a corsage. I felt like a high-school student going to the prom with the prettiest girl in school. Of course, I was taking out the prettiest guy in town.

I drove up to the athletic dormitory about 5:45, and then had to drive around to kill time, but still arrived back five minutes early. Mark was waiting for me, and he looked heart-stoppingly beautiful. He was dressed simply, in khaki slacks and a dark green polo shirt, with penny loafers. His shirt wasn't tight, but it was clear that although he was fairly lean, he had good upper-body musculature, a narrow waist, and well-muscled arms as well. His trousers were not tight either, but the fine rounded shape of his ass was unmistakable. His short brown hair and lean, triangular face framed dimples, high cheek bones, dazzling white teeth, and a smile that lit up his angelically beautiful face as he bestowed it on me. My heart was pounding when he opened the car door and got in.

After the usual "Hi" and "How are you?" kind of greetings, I told him, "I haven't really had anything like a regular date in so long, Mark. I almost feel I should have brought a corsage."

He laughed. "It's really funny, isn't it? I couldn't believe I asked you if you wanted to date me, but I guess it's the right word. I guess it's no big surprise that I've never dated a guy! I've always dated girls, of course, and I've been the one bringing the corsage, and worrying about cutting myself shaving, and changing clothes three times before picking up my date. You know what I mean?"

"Would you believe I changed clothes three times before coming into town to meet you? And would you believe I'm nervous as hell right now – wanting to make a really good impression and feeling like a total klutz?"

"John, you look great, and you're certainly not a klutz. I don't know exactly what a klutz is, but I know it's something awkward. And you're not awkward ... and you made a good first impression on me the very first time you called me. After we talked that first night, I thought a lot about it, and I was really flattered, and felt good about your admiring me the way you said you did. And every time we talked after that, I felt closer to you. I really had been wondering who you were, and wanting to meet you, so, I'm glad we're having a date."

"I said it the first time we talked, and I guess I said it every time: I think you're the most attractive guy I've ever seen. Hell, I wanted to say it in class the other day, and I want to say it again now. You are truly a beautiful guy, Mark. I find you very, very attractive, and I feel really happy and honored that you're willing to go out with me. If it never goes past that, it never goes past that ... but I'm very pleased to be with you, in any case."

"Thanks, John you really flatter me ... way too much ... but it's nice. So, where are we going to eat?" I mentioned the local steak house where I had made reservations, and Mark was pleased to be going there.

Dinner was mostly small talk, learning about his family back in Pennsylvania – father a military man, mother a housewife, one brother, Steve, eight years older than he, married, and with a two-year old son. Steve was, in actuality, an adoptive brother, but Mark thought of him as his real brother. Mark's mother had been told she could not bear children, and a year or so after adopting Steve she got pregnant with Mark. I told Mark about my background, of course, and he seemed genuinely interested. I made no bones about being gay, and it didn't seem to bother him at all.

After dinner, I suggested we go to see the movie, *Who's Afraid of Virginia Woolf*, which had recently opened and was very controversial.

"I know I mentioned a show when I asked if you wanted a date, but if you don't mind, I'd really rather just go somewhere and sit and talk."

"That would be even better. I want to get to know you better ... and I'd be able to look at you more, and just enjoy seeing your beauty."

Mark laughed. "There you go with the flattery again. Let's just get a six-pack and go out to the park and sit by the lake. I want to get to know you better, too ... and I'm going to enjoy watching you watching me, okay?"

"Great. And you promise you'll tell me if I start drooling?"

He laughed, "I promise."

We got some beer and drove out in the country, finding a comfortable place on a bluff overlooking the lake. I got a blanket from my trunk to spread on the ground. "Mark, you promised that someday we'd talk about you and ... well, about you being with other guys, remember?"

"Sure. You want to talk about my sex life, right?"

"If you don't think I'm prying, I do. I'm interested in getting to know you, and I find you extremely sexy, so if you don't mind telling me, I'd like to know everything about 'The Sex Life of Mark Hagood.'"

He laughed again. "Okay, but it's not very exciting. What do you want to know first?"

"Are you dating a lot of girls? Do you have one in particular?"

"Well, I date several girls ... not an awful lot ... and there's not any one of them I'm serious about, or even have any really special feeling for."

"Sex life, Mark!"

"Right. No, I'm not screwing any girls, if that's the question. I have, of course, but not right now."

"You said you were seeing someone but didn't know where that was going. Who is she, then? If you don't mind my asking."

He smiled and propped himself up on one elbow. "You're assuming it's a girl. I never said that. In fact, it's a teammate of mine on the soccer team."

"Wow. So you have had sex with another guy."

122

"I didn't say that, either. To be frank, though, I'm pretty sure I want to have sex with this teammate of mine. He's really handsome, and it turns me on just to look at him."

"Is it ... what's his name, Farrar? John Farrar. Is that who it is?"

"How did you know that?"

"It's just that he's the only other guy on the soccer team I think is attractive ... and he really is damned attractive. I could see why you'd be interested in him. But ... you mean, you want to have sex with him, but he's not for it?"

"Well, something like that. Johnny really gets me excited, but we've never done anything, really. He's let me hold his hand when we're alone, and once in a while he'll even start it. A couple of times he's let me hug him and kiss him, and he'll hold me, but he doesn't much kiss back ... just kind of let's me kiss him. He says he really likes me, but doesn't think he wants us to be anything but good friends."

"He looks more intelligent than that."

Mark grinned. "Well, anyway, I'm attracted to Johnny ... more than I am to any girl, I guess ... but we haven't really done anything about it, so I don't know if that makes me gay, or what. To finally answer your question ... no, I've never really had sex with a guy. Naturally I experimented a little bit when I was a kid, with some of my buddies, but nothing really happened ... we just sort of played with each other. I've always known I was attracted to boys, but I didn't think there was anything unusual about it. Shoot, I found a bunch of pictures of naked guys in my brother Steve's dresser one time, and I thought he must be attracted to guys, too. But Steve's married, so if he is attracted to guys, he's attracted to girls, too. He may be gay, I don't know. It doesn't make any difference. Anyway, I know when I think about Johnny, I have to admit I really want to do something more with him."

"What do you do when you think about Johnny, and about sex?"

He blushed a little then laughed nervously. "What do you think? I do the same thing I'll bet you do when you think about someone who turns you on."

"I know what I do when I think about you, Mark. I beat off."

We were face-to-face as we lay on the blanket, each propped up on an elbow. Mark smiled at me and put a hand on my shoulder. "I'm flattered, John, and I have to admit that a couple of times after I've talked with you on the phone, I thought about what might happen when we met, and I've got horny and beat off."

"Why didn't you say something?"

"John, I'm still not sure where I'm going sexually, much less where we're going. I will tell you this ... if you're really serious, I think I could be interested in making love with you." I began to speak, but he stopped me. "But I don't know. I'm frustrated about the way Johnny is not interested, and I've

123

never done anything. Look, I'm a virgin, okay? I've never had sex with anyone, really, not even a girl ... I just said that a little while ago because it seemed like I should have been more experienced. When it happens, I want it to mean something, especially the first time. Do you understand?"

"Of course, I understand, and if it's okay with you, I'll be hoping that something will happen with you and me."

"Good. Keep hoping, and please ... be patient, okay? It's just going to take time for me to sort things out. Don't try to move too fast, and don't be angry or give up on me because it does take time, please. I don't think anything is going to happen with Johnny, but I think I might like something to happen with you, okay? Be patient?"

I put my hand at the back of his neck. "I'll be as patient as I need to be with you, Mark. I'm really hoping."

He gave me a very warm smile and put his hand at the back of my neck and drew my lips to his. We shared a long, very sweet kiss – no tongues or passion, but enormously exciting, nonetheless. After that chaste and unforgettable kiss, we looked into each other's eyes for a long time. I finally broke the moment. "Thank you, Mark, I can't tell you how wonderful that was. I think you're incredibly beautiful and attractive, and that was maybe the sweetest kiss I ever experienced."

"I enjoyed it, too, John. Remember: patience." He kissed me again quickly, and we broke.

He asked me about my sexual experience and present situation. I told him freely about my past, and even the present – Cary, Mike, Richard, Dean, even Eddie. He was more than a little astonished, and I considered I had perhaps admitted to too much, that he might think me obsessed with sex – which I probably was – and already too occupied with other guys to pay any attention to him (Never!). He was not judgmental; however, and I admitted I still loved Richard – even though he was apparently out of my life again – and was still in love with everyone I had ever loved, for that matter. However, I stressed that although I was involved in some sexual situations, I was not involved in a loving relationship, and that was what I really sought. "I'd like to have sex with you, Mark ... I think that would be wonderful ... but I also want to see you, to have dates and see if anything further develops. In spite of how it might look, I'm not just hoping to make Mark Hagood another notch on my gun."

"Frankly, John, we're not going to have sex together unless some meaningful relationship develops. When I finally go to bed with someone, it's going to mean something. I don't know, my attitude may change later on, but the first time has got to be special. Do you understand?"

"I understand, and I respect that, Mark. I really hope when you decide you do want to make love with someone, it's going to be me. And I'll keep trying and hoping unless you tell me to stop."

He stood and smiled down at me. "At this point, John, just keep trying and hoping, okay?" I stood and took him in my arms and we hugged and kissed for a long time before driving back into town.

We went to a restaurant and drank coffee as we talked a lot further. He expressed interest in seeing my house, and said he wanted to come out for swimming and skiing soon. I was quick to invite him; "I'll cook you dinner, too. Candlelight, soft music, all that, if you want."

"Sounds like you're asking for another date."

"I sure am. Will you accept?"

"With the greatest pleasure. I look forward to it." We set the following Tuesday evening, and I dropped him off at his dormitory. He held my hand all the way from the restaurant, and when we pulled up in front of his dorm, he looked to see if anyone was around (no one was), leaned over to take me in his arms, and we embraced and kissed very tenderly. Driving home I was in seventh heaven, still acting like a teenager on a first date with his dreamboat.

As promised, Dean was at the house when I got home, watching television in my bedroom. "So, how was the big date? I assume you didn't fuck each other: you're home too early."

"It was really fun. He is so cute, and a really nice guy, too ... and no, we didn't fuck each other. In fact, we kissed a couple of times and held hands, and that was it."

He stood up, took me in his arms, and ginned hugely. "I'll bet you're really horny, then, aren't you?" He kissed me and began unbuttoning his shirt. "Take your clothes off." I hesitated. "Now! Get naked for me ... let me see that prick of yours." By the time I had my shirt off, he was completely nude, stroking his massive cock to erection. I was soon naked, and the sight of his beautiful prick had already aroused me. We again embraced, our hard cocks pressing against each other, and our tongues intertwining in passionate kisses. Dean pulled back and looked down at me (he was three or four inches taller than I) and smiled. "Do you want to pretend I'm Mark? Just pretend I'm him, and you can do anything you want to him, and he'll do anything you want to you."

I looked up at him. "Dean, when you're in my arms, and I feel that big prick of your pressing against me, and feel these huge, cum-filled balls," which I squeezed at that point, "and know how wonderful and sweet you are, and when I see how incredibly beautiful and sexy you are, too, I don't even want to pretend you're someone else. I'm as eager to make love with Dean Williamson right now as I would be with anyone in the world."

"Good answer. But I will be glad to pretend I'm Mark, though, any time you want. But right now it's just Dean and John, and I want to do more than fuck and suck with you."

"More? What did you have in mind?"

"I want to make love to you, and I want you to make love to me. Okay?" He kissed me very, very sweetly, and we spent the next two hours in the slow, sweet, wonderful bliss of mutual worship with our mouths, our hands, our bodies, our cocks, our asses, and our several, copious emissions. I was still high from my date with the beautiful Mark, and I had great hopes for making love to him some day, but the lovemaking Dean and I shared that night was as satisfying as anyone could possibly have desired. Although he had planned to go home that evening, he called one of his brothers and got him to cover for him, and we spent the whole wonderful night locked in embrace.

As he left the next morning, I told Dean how much I loved him. "I could easily forget everyone else and be happy being only with you, Dean. You're a wonderful guy, and as tender a lover as you are a hot stud. I'll forget even trying to get to know Mark better if you'll be my lover. I know you love me, too. What about it?"

He kissed me tenderly. "You know I love you, and we'll make love many, many times, as often as you want, like we did last night ... and we can do just as much of the really wild kind of fucking we've done in the past ... but you also know I'm not ready to settle down. Christ, I'm still in high school. I'm not even nineteen yet. Get to know Mark, and make love with him if you can, but be sure you save time to make love with me, too. I want us always to be the closest kind of friends: not lovers, but friends who are so close we even make love with each other. Okay?"

"Of course. I love you, Dean."

"I love you too, John. And next time's gonna be wild ... I'm gonna fuck you so hard you'll walk bowlegged, if you promise to do the same for me."

"You got a date."

He kissed me and winked. I reveled in the sight of his beautiful long legs and cute, rounded ass moving within his skin-tight Levi's as he walked to his car. He turned and waved before getting in, and the sight of his huge cock and balls clearly defined by his jeans was as exciting to me as it had been the first day I met him.

Mark came by my office Monday morning to tell me again how much he had enjoyed our date. He agreed to come out to my house the next day for an afternoon of skiing and swimming, followed by a quiet – hopefully romantic – dinner for two. As he prepared to leave, I walked him to the door, and I was especially pleased to note that he briefly put an arm around my waist and hugged me as he said "See you tomorrow."

Tuesday with Mark began around 3:00 in the afternoon, and we spent several delightful hours on the water. He wore loose-fitting swim trunks, not very sexy, but showing his thin, muscular body and long legs to perfection. At the spring soccer game I had studied his body carefully, but he had always worn a shirt. I was now able to admire his broad chest and narrow waist as well. He also smiled a great deal, and was absolutely as charming as he was handsome – which meant he was charming to an unbelievable degree. I cooked steaks for us, and we had a candlelight dinner on the porch overlooking the lake. We toasted

126

each other, and even held hands frequently – and he looked stunning in the candle light. Following dinner, we sat on the couch and watched television. Mark put his head in my lap as he watched, and I stroked his hair, occasionally leaning down to kiss him. Later, we cradled each other and necked for a long time, without any passionate embracing.

It was a delightful evening, and so innocent, that I never sought to do more than caress or kiss Mark, or to hold his hands. As we held each other tightly and kissed goodnight, I did fondle his cute ass, and he giggled a bit, without remonstrating, but I knew that I should not go further than that yet. Although I really wanted to make love with him, I was so happy sharing his sweetness and innocence that I felt little frustration. I was not even horny when he left, although if Dean had showed up about then, I know erection and subsequent ejaculatory exercises would have followed immediately.

13. MAKING MY MARK

A number of innocent "dates" ensued with Mark – dinner, movies, and the like. Throughout, I was careful not to push him into sexual action he was not yet ready for. This would have been frustrating under normal circumstances, but Dean was wonderful about making love with me and listening to me hymn the praises of the beautiful Mark, and while sex with Mike and Cary had become relatively rare, it had not stopped. Dean and I had, for instance, been invited to a sort of housewarming dinner for Mike and Cary's new apartment, and the dessert was predictable, Mike and Cary a la mode, and we were all filled with cream by the time the party was over.

It was probably the third or fourth time Mark had come out to the house for dinner and TV when he began to show some interest in advancing the sexual status of our relationship. We were sitting out on the dock having a drink – it was a warm, moonlit night, and we were still in our bathing suits – when he told me he had gone out with Johnny Farrar several times, and had finally simply come out and asked him if they had any future as lovers, or if he was interested in at least going past the simple kisses and hand-holding that had so far been the sexual high-water mark of their relationship. Johnny had admitted he was attracted to Mark, but only as a friend. He said he really wasn't interested in anything past that, and he felt he had somehow allowed things to go too far by permitting Mark to kiss him. Mark bore the disappointment well. "If he doesn't want me, then I just have to move on to someone who does." He put his hand over mine as we sat there. "Do you know someone who does want me?"

I brought his hand to my lips and kissed it. "I've wanted you from the first time I saw you, Mark – at freshman orientation a year ago. I thought then you were the most attractive guy I'd ever seen, and now that we've become close, I feel it even more strongly."

His arms went around my neck and he kissed me. "I know I'm strongly attracted to you, too, John. Be patient with me, and let's allow this thing to develop naturally. Okay?"

"More than okay, Mark. Please be patient with me if I seem impatient. I have a feeling something very good is going to develop between us."

"I feel the same thing."

We had finished our drinks, and I offered to go up and make new ones. Mark said he would stay down on the dock to enjoy the moonlight and the balmy air. "Back in a minute," I called as I went up the hill from the lake. I refreshed our drinks and headed back to the dock. As I arrived, I could see Mark standing there, clearly visible in the bright moonlight, He had shed his clothes, and was waiting for me there, totally naked.

I stepped onto the dock and could clearly see him smile. "I thought you'd like to see me. I know I want to see you. Take your trunks off." I set our drinks down, and removed my bathing suit.

We stood about ten feet apart and looked at each other without a word being spoken for some time. Finally, I said, "You are truly beautiful, Mark. I've wanted to see you this way for a very long time ... and it was worth the wait."

He approached me and took my hands in his. "I've wanted to see you, too, and I like what I see very much."

I knelt, and my face was only inches from his cock, which was not erect, but stood out at about a thirty-degree angle from his body. It was circumcised, and good-sized, but not especially large. The moonlight was sufficiently bright that I could clearly see how perfectly formed and breathtakingly beautiful it was. Mark put his hands on my head and kept me from taking him in my mouth. "Not yet, John ... please. I really want to move slowly, all right?" He knelt. "I know I'm going to want you to suck me, and I know I want to suck you, too ... and do everything with you ... but I'm still nervous and I'm even a little bit scared. Just be patient with me, and let's not rush." He was still holding my head in his hands, and he now moved in, our arms went around each other, and we hugged and kissed for a very long time as we knelt there.

We stood, and I turned Mark so that he was facing the moonlight. "Let me just drink you in and enjoy your beautiful body." My hands gently caressed his shoulders and his arms, moving down to explore the muscular chest and flat stomach. His skin was warm and like velvet, his flesh was firm, and his muscles very well defined. He murmured in pleasure as I knelt again, and ran my hands lovingly up and down his legs. His pretty cock was still not fully erect, but it was decidedly moving in that direction. I turned his body around and admired the beauty of the perfectly rounded twin globes of his ass. My hands softly brushed over those beautiful bulging cheeks, and I again stood as I caressed his sides and back. Then I began to kiss the nape of his neck and reversed the circuit I had manually made of his body, this time kissing and licking. I licked down his back, and kissed all over his buttocks. He purred with pleasure, and I was so bold as to kiss and lick into the crevice of his ass, including a lengthy and chaste kiss on his asshole. I licked down his legs, and then licked back up the inside of them. As I again reached his asshole, I turned his body around, and very gently kissed the tip of his cock, now fully erect, and considerably larger. I licked gently down the shaft, kissing and licking around and under his very ample balls, before I began kissing his navel, his stomach, and his nipples as I gradually rose. As I worked my way up to his neck he was breathing heavily. "Oh God, John, that feels so wonderful." He took me in his arms, and we kissed and caressed again. Our cocks were both fully erect, and pressed against each other's stomachs, but I refrained from grinding into him just yet.

Then he used his hands to push me back, and he began an exploration of my body – almost identical to mine of his. He did not go so far as to kiss my asshole, but he did carefully kiss and lick my cock and balls. When he had finished, and we were again standing together in each other's arms, our kisses

130

were more heated than before, and for the first time he opened his lips, and our tongues entwined together and explored each other's mouths. He pulled away and smiled as he looked into my eyes. "Let me watch you jack off." He stepped back three or four paces and knelt to watch.

Seeing this beautiful man kneeling before me, remembering the wonder of the feel of his body, and still tasting his sweet mouth, it took very little time for me to reach orgasm. "I'm cumming, Mark, I'm cumming. Oh God, you are so beautiful, Mark ... this is for you!"

"Yeah, John ... let me see you shoot your load." And with that my emission began shooting wildly onto the dock as Mark stood and murmured, "Oh god, what a big load." And, in fact, it was an enormous load. He continued to encourage me as I milked every drop from my cock.

I fell to my knees in front of him. "Please, let me just kiss the end of your prick again, Mark." I moved in, and he took my hands in his. Just as I began to plant a kiss on his prick, his hands tightened on mine, he drew his breath in very sharply, and panted, "Oh, John," and at that moment he began spewing hot cum all over me, in a long series of violent spurts. I quickly opened my mouth and managed to take a good bit of it inside, but much of it bathed my forehead, my hair, my entire face. His hands were clutching mine so tightly it almost hurt. "Oh John, I'm sorry ... I didn't mean to do that, but I couldn't stop. You got me so excited!"

I stood, savored and swallowed that portion of his orgasm I had managed to get in my mouth, and faced him, with his cum dripping down my face. "God, Mark, don't apologize ... that was wonderful. I feel so honored having you shoot on me."

"That was the first time I ever shot my load with someone else, John. Watching you cum got me so ... I can't believe how excited it got me. I just had to cum, too." He held me tightly and kissed me, ignoring his cum on my face and mouth. "I'm really glad this happened with you."

"I really am honored by you Mark."

He kissed me again, and once more our kissing was extremely passionate. "Next time, I want to cum in you ... and I want you to cum in me."

"Mark, you don't have to do that, I understand how ..."

He put his hand over my mouth. "No, I really want to. When I watched you cumming a few minutes ago, I knew I wanted to be taking it from you. Will you give it to me next time, please? And will you take my cum, too?"

"Believe me, there is nothing, absolutely nothing in the world I would rather do." He pulled me down to the dock with him, and we lay together and snuggled for a very long time – saying little, but enjoying each other enormously.

As I dropped him off at his dormitory late that night, he kissed me before getting out of the car. "I had such a good time, John. I want to really make love with you, I know that now."

"And I with you Mark. And we will next time, if that's okay."

He grinned. "Next date is the all the way date."

I grinned back. "I'm horny already."

"Hey, me, too!" He took my hand and put it on his bulging crotch, where I could feel his fierce erection. "This ain't a pickle in my pocket, you know."

And the next date was the "all the way" kind of date with Mark I had been hoping for for over a year. I picked him up at his dorm around 7:30, and we drove directly to my house. On the way, he let his hand rest on my leg, and soon my right hand was cupping his crotch. He began to get hard, and as he did so, his hand moved up my leg and began to stroke my own hard cock. "This really feels good, John."

I squeezed his fully hard erection. "Not half as good as yours does. Jesus, Mark, I've wanted to hold you like this for such a long time now."

"Well, you can hold it all you want tonight ... it's all yours. And I've wanted to share it with someone for a long time, too, but it's never seemed right before. I wanted to with Johnny, like I told you, but he wasn't interested, so it wasn't right, I guess. And now I'm with you, and I know after the other night on the dock that it's going to be more than right with you."

"I just find it so hard to believe that anyone as beautiful and as sexy as you hasn't had sex before. I would think you would have had to fight guys and girls off."

"Well, not many girls have bothered me because I didn't really encourage them; I think I always knew I was more interested in guys. Still I've always had a lot of dates with girls, but nothing ever happened, because I never really wanted it to, I guess. And there have been a few guys that came on to me, but none that I was interested in." He leaned over and kissed my neck. "I'm pretty sure I'm interested in the last guy who came on to me though."

"A horny guy who found you naked on his dock the other night?"

He snuggled up next to me and put his hand in my shirt. "That's the one."

When we arrived at my house, Mark asked that we take our time. "Believe it or not, I'm still nervous, and I'm still scared." He put his arms around me and kissed me gently. "This is a very big step for me."

I kissed him back. "I know it is, Mark. And the prospect of being with you at long last is a very big step for me, too. Look, we've got all the time you need ... all the time in the world. I don't want to rush it either, you know. Making love with Mark Hagood is something I've dreamed of for so long I can enjoy the anticipation even more now, knowing that it is going to happen."

"It's going to happen John. I want it to happen as much as you do."

We made drinks and snuggled together on the sofa – no television necessary as an excuse. We actually said little, just kissed and caressed at length, and this time we both felt free to explore each other fully as we fondled. We both had erections, of course, but there seemed to be no urgency to get to sex. After at least an hour of this sweet foreplay, Mark stood, and pulled me to my feet. He began to kick off his shoes and unbutton his shirt as he looked dead into my eyes. "I want you, John."

I undressed also, and soon we were facing one another, completely naked. Mark came to me, and we embraced, our very hard pricks grinding against each other. After a very passionate kiss, Mark slipped to his knees and took my cock in his hand. He stroked it and licked it as he cupped my balls and I murmured my delight. "I've wanted to do this to another guy for a long time, but it's never seemed right; now it does." And with that he opened his mouth and took me into it.

I held his head firmly as he began to suck and move his tightly clasped lips back and forth along my shaft. "My God, Mark, this is so wonderful. I've never felt so honored in my life." His hands pulled my buttocks in toward him, and I humped his mouth gently, but with long strokes, driving my cock slowly into it. Looking down at him, with his eyes closed and his beautiful face bathed in innocent ecstasy, I was in heaven. He took my prick all the way into his throat. His lips nestled in my pubic hair while his busy tongue licked the head and shaft of my cock and his hands played over my ass.

He released my cock and looked up at me. "Fuck my mouth, John ... fuck me hard with your beautiful dick." He again took me inside and began to suck frantically this time. I held his head tightly and fucked him fast and hard.

I was not too far from orgasm. "I'm near cumming, Mark." He stopped sucking and stood. His arms went around me and he whispered in my ear, "Not yet ... I want this to last forever. But I do want you to cum in my mouth ... and I want to cum in yours if you'll let me."

I was fondling his very hard and now quite large prick as I replied, "Of course! My God, this cock feels so wonderful Mark ... I want to suck every drop of cum out of it. I want us to fill each other up with love."

I fell to my knees and without ceremony began to suck Mark, who cradled my head in his hands and almost whimpered with delight. "Nothing has ever felt this exciting. Suck my prick, John. Oh God, I love you so much!" I sucked happily and energetically until Mark made me stop, took my hand, and led me back into my bedroom.

We lay down on the bed and kissed and caressed for some time, saying nothing, but murmuring in delight. Finally, with Mark poised over me and looking down into my face, I asked him, "Did I hear you say you loved me?"

"I know it's too soon, but I do, John." A moment of silence, and a very serious look on his face. "I love you." He kissed me very slowly and very sweetly on the lips before pulling back and looking down at me again. His gold-flecked brown eyes glowed with love, and his perfect face, with its triangular shape, high cheekbones, thin chin, and wonderfully white, even teeth looked like that of an angel. He smiled and his entire face glowed with youth and love. "I love you, John."

"It's not too soon, Mark. I love you, too. I think I fell a little in love with you the first time I ever laid eyes on you, and that feeling has grown every time I've seen you over the last year ... and I've seen you a lot more than you realize. To hear you say you love me, and to hold you in my arms, and to know that we are finally going to make love together tonight makes me happier than I've ever been."

Again, not strictly a true statement. I had enjoyed some moments of supreme rapture before that, from the first time the godlike Latino-Indian Danny held my head and drove his cock down my young throat, finally giving me the longed-for chance to suck dick and give me my first taste of someone else's cum, until the delirious joy, almost twenty years later, of lying on my back with my legs in the air while five hot men lined up and fucked me in sequence – filling my ass with five huge, hot loads of cum to celebrate my birthday. Nonetheless, that moment with Mark was certainly one of the happiest I have ever known.

"I'm so happy now that I've never made love with anyone else, John. I'm really glad you're the first."

"I can't deny I've been to bed with a lot of other guys, Mark, and I've loved other guys ... you know that. But believe me when I say it ... I love you. And there is no one in the world I would rather make love with than you." I grinned at him. "And you know what I'm really thankful for?"

He grinned back. "What's that?"

"That Johnny Farrar is such a moron." Mark laughed, as I added, "You might be with him right now if he wasn't"

"I'm right where I want to be, John."

"You're right where you belong, Mark ... in my arms, and in my bed."

He kissed me, at first sweetly, and then passionately. He moved his head downward. "I want to suck you off. I want you to fuck my mouth and give me your load." He took my cock in his mouth and drove his lips up and down zealously. As he did so, I reversed my body and took his prick into my mouth – both of us lying on our sides. Our sucking grew feverish, and we were each driving our cocks deep and hard into each other. Finally, Mark stopped sucking me long enough to say, "I'm not too far from cumming, but I want you to cum first. Keep me in your mouth, but don't make me cum; I want to concentrate on your cumming in me. Okay?" I murmured my assent, and he began sucking very intensely. His lips held my cock tightly as he drove his head up and down the entire length of my shaft. As my orgasm approached, I began to fuck more rapidly, and his driving mouth countered my thrusts perfectly, until at last I wrapped my arms around his waist tightly, and pulled him toward me as I planted my prick deep in his throat and began to explode a massive load into it.

He murmured delightedly, and sucked avidly while I continued to discharge. His tongue lapped my cock, and he swallowed as his arms held my body tightly.

After a few moments, he began fucking my mouth, apparently signaling that he was ready for me to take his load. I sucked hard, and he fucked me rapidly and very deeply, and in a few minutes he panted around my cock, "Here it comes, John. Take my love!" And once again I thrilled to the taste of his wonderful cum, but this time the excitement of feeling it erupt deep in my throat and the bulk of his big shaft driving deep into my mouth as he shot increased the wonder and excitement by an infinite factor. His load was copious, and he delivered it to my eager mouth in eight or ten huge spurts, accompanied by whimpers of excitement, deep thrusts of his prick into my throat, and eager humping of the beautiful ass I held clutched in my hands. It was a matchless moment, increased in its wonder by the fact that he still continued to suck and fondle me.

We lay together for a very long time, neither of us wanting to let the other's cock leave his mouth. Finally, without a word, Mark disengaged, reversed his body, took me in his arms and kissed me very tenderly. "I have never experienced anything so absolutely wonderful in my entire life. I can't begin to tell you how much it meant to me, or how much I love you. I love sucking your beautiful dick. And your cum tastes wonderful ... better than anything I've ever tasted. Oh man, I have finally sucked a guy off, and I'm in love with the guy I sucked off."

"The guy you sucked off loved sucking you off, and loves you ... and I could drink your wonderful cum all night. It tasted incredible the other night when you shot all over me, but tonight, with your big fat cock shooting it all the way down my throat ... God, it was terrific. I love your cum, I love your prick, I love you ... I am so glad you love me, Mark."

"I've never been so happy. I should get back to the dorm, but I can't leave you. Turn out the lights and just lie with me and hold me."

We kissed and snuggled and played with each other. We told of our love for each other, and eventually went to sleep. Sometime during the night I was awakened by Mark sucking my prick again. I held his head with my hands and fucked as he sucked – and without a word, he took another load in his throat, which he swallowed. Then at my bidding he knelt over my face and fucked my mouth until he shot another load into me while my hands kneaded his beautiful, driving ass. We still said nothing as we snuggled and caressed and fell asleep again.

Waking before him, quite early in the morning, I went out and started coffee. Walking back to the bedroom, I found Mark wide awake, smiling at me, with his hard prick standing straight up. I crawled on top of him, in sixty-nine position, and took him in my mouth as he took me in his. We sucked this way for a long time, fell on our sides and sucked quite a while longer. We wound up with Mark on top as I drove my cock upward into his eager mouth, while his

135

prick thrust downward into mine and I gazed at the sight of his balls swinging free, with his matchless ass driving his cock into me. Finally we both exploded again, and after taking every drop of cum from his prick, I moved my mouth upward and sucked his balls for some time before burying my face in the wonderland between his rounded cheeks, and tongue-fucking him gently.

"Oh God, John ... what a feeling. I can't believe you're doing that to me, and I sure can't believe how wonderful it feels."

I reversed my body and took him in my arms. "There's a lot of territory for us to explore. I'm going to love loving you in every possible way."

"And I you ... and I love you ... and we have to get up, and I couldn't cum again now if I had to. But do you know what day this is?"

"What day is it, Mark?"

"This is our first full day as lovers, isn't it? Aren't we lovers, John?"

"We are lovers, and this is our first full day, and I love you very, very much, Mark. I'm as proud as I am happy to be your lover."

Before finally getting out of bed and getting on with this miraculous day, we kissed and snuggled for a long time. And although neither of us came again that morning, we still spent a good bit of time − no, a wonderful bit of time − locked in sixty-nine, adoring each other's cocks and asses. I now knew that Mark's cock and ass were as beautiful as the rest of him, and the generous size of his stunning prick looked like it was going to be a perfectly wonderful, eminently satisfying assful. It wasn't in the same league as Mike or Richard's, and nowhere near the same class as Dean or Eddie's, but it was Mark's, and that put it in a class by itself. I looked forward to the time, hopefully soon, when I could gauge the wonder of his cock filling my butt, and also when I could watch my own cock driving into the paradise that lay between those two perfectly rounded globes of his beautiful ass. Of my lover's beautiful ass!

Mark was like a kid with a new toy. He had discovered the wonder of sex, and could not leave it alone − nor did I want him to, of course. The afternoon of that first full day as lovers he came to my office and, once the door was closed, kissed me warmly, declaring he couldn't wait until we could make love again, but he was crushed that he had soccer practice that afternoon, and wouldn't be able to meet me until around 7:00. I had been merely hoping we could somehow get together that night for a while, and I was eager to be with him again soon, but he was even more eager than I. We did get together that night, and almost every night for the next several weeks at least. This kid really learned how to play with his new toy.

I picked him up at his dorm promptly at seven, and we drove directly to my house, were in each other's arms before we got out of the driveway, and in bed naked within five minutes after that. That sounds a bit like sheer rapacity, but actually we were unstoppably impatient just to be in each other's arms, not yet necessarily sucking or fucking − although the latter activities were never far from our minds. Lying in a loved man's arms nude, kissing and caressing was new to Mark, but not to me, and yet I was as eager as he, and I'm sure I enjoyed it just as much. His beauty of face and body seemed even more awesome than it had the night before, and his impassioned declarations of love for me seemed even more miraculous now than they had then. Looking at his adorable face, kissing his full lips, feeling the velvet of his skin and the muscular curves of his upper body and rounded buttocks, feeling the bulk of his hard prick pressing into me, and smelling the fresh, clean wonder of his youth made me realize what incredible luck had come my way, especially as I received his eager, darting tongue in my mouth and felt his hands caressing me passionately.

Our early lovemaking that night was again oral. Mark knelt before me to take my first load, He said he had loved seeing me cum on the dock in the moonlight a few nights earlier, but now he wanted to see me cum up close, and in full light. After sucking me almost to the point of orgasm, he held his mouth open wide as he finished me off with his hand, and he watched my cum shooting into him, after which he took me inside again and sucked until every drop had been given to him. I took his first load as I lay on my back on the bed and he knelt over my head and fucked downward into my mouth – his big cock probing the depths of my eager throat and delivering an explosion of his love into it.

We spent a great deal of time in a gentle and sweet sixty-nine, sucking lovingly on each other's cocks and balls, and I managed to roll under Mark again, so I could tongue-fuck him once more as he sucked me – and even his asshole was a thing of great beauty. He loved the sensation of my tongue in his ass, and knelt on all fours on the bed, so I could kneel behind him and hold his cheeks far apart to sink my tongue as deeply into him as possible. At the same time, I pulled his cock back between his legs and took time to feast on his cock and balls from behind.

"God, John, your tongue feels so incredibly hot in me like that. I want you to put your cock in there soon. I can hardly wait to get fucked by my lover's big prick."

"Are you sure, Mark? I want to fuck your ass, of course, but not until you're ready. It hurts, right at first."

"I don't care if it hurts; I want to get fucked like a real man. Use your fingers and tongue tonight – maybe we'll have to wait a few days for your cock, but at least start getting me ready for you."

I reached for the Vaseline and lubed his ass and my forefinger, and slowly began to penetrate him. He squirmed and said it hurt, but insisted I continue. Soon I had my entire finger in him, and fucked gently.

He lay down on his stomach, but held my hand in place. "Keep your finger in me for a while; it does hurt, but it feels wonderful, too. It makes me really hot. I know your big prick is going to be hard to take, but I want it ... I really do. You remember I told you I found a bunch of pictures of naked guys in my brother's dresser?" I said I did. "Well, they were more than just naked. They were sucking each other, and fucking each other in some of them, and one of the guys in the pictures was Steve, I think. I couldn't tell for sure, but I'm almost positive it was him."

"What was he doing?"

"Everything. He was sucking and getting fucked, and getting sucked and fucking ... and in a couple of them two guys in the background were sucking each other off while the guy who I think was Steve was getting fucked in the mouth and the ass at the same time ... and the two guys fucking him had incredibly big pricks ... at least they looked huge to me. I don't know how he was taking it, but it sure looked like they were all having a heckuva good time!"

I laughed. "If it was him in the pictures, I think your brother's bisexual at the very least. Hell, even having the pictures probably means he's at least that."

"Well, he's been married about four years, and they seem real happy. He's crazy about his wife, Sandy, and they're both nuts about Randy, my nephew. He may like guys, too. I don't know, but he sure never even hinted anything to me about it. If I hadn't found those pictures, I wouldn't suspect him at all. But, you know, I've always hoped he'd come on to me. I know it sounds crazy, but I'd love to have sex with my brother."

"I don't see anything wrong with that. You're not gonna make each other pregnant and have retarded kids, or anything. And besides, Steve is only your adopted brother. Is he cute?"

"He's absolutely gorgeous. You'd go crazy over him. I used to listen to him jacking off in his bed, when he thought I was asleep, and the next morning I'd get his shorts our of the laundry in our bedroom ... or the towel, or whatever he'd shot his load in ... and ... well, hell, might as well be honest ... I'd smell it and suck it where his cum was drying, and I'd jack off and mix my load with his and pretend I was one of those guys in the pictures with him."

"Mark, you know being married doesn't mean anything. Steve probably likes guys."

"Well, that's okay, I like guys! And I hope he finds as great a guy to make love with, like I have. And keep fucking me with your finger ... it feels better all the time." He was now humping his ass down onto my probing finger, obviously beginning to enjoy the sensation.

I rolled him on his side, and as I continued to service his writhing ass with my finger, I began to suck him again. We kept this up for some time until his breathing grew heavy and he was soon discharging another load into my mouth as his ass now drove itself wildly down on my finger and he cried loudly, "Fuck me, John! God, I want to feel your big prick in there soon, fucking me in the ass."

After his orgasm, he made me stop my manual love making, saying he was tender, but he would try his best to take my prick in there the next night. He lay on his back as I lay over him, and we hugged and kissed. Finally I rose up and positioned my asshole over his still-hard prick. "I want you to fuck me, Mark. I want to ride your beautiful prick."

"Oh God, yes! I want to be inside you."

"I want you inside me more than anything in the world." I greased up his cock and my ass, and began to take his prick into me, but before I was settled all the way, he was fucking savagely up into my body and moaning in ecstasy. I rode his driving prick with complete rapture and abandon, and the considerable bulk of his shaft invaded me magnificently – heating my entire body and making me feel as filled with love as I was filled with hard-driving cock. He had cum only shortly before this, so we were able to continue this perfect ride for a very long time, my body driving down as hard and as far as it would go, and his beautiful cock driving upward into me as forcefully as he could – and to a very satisfying depth. Mark's cock was long, but not as long as Dean's monster or Eddie's super-monster, but it still seemed to satisfy me as much as anything ever had. The sensation of a big hard cock driving into your ass is about as wonderful as anything imaginable, but when that shaft is being wielded by someone you love, it is the most sublime sensation. And how I loved this beautiful young man, and how wonderfully he was filling me with his love – and this was the very first time he had ever fucked anyone. What incredible experiences surely lay ahead!

Finally, I could hold off no longer, and began to masturbate my flopping cock. Mark took over from me, and raised his head as he beat me off. "Shoot in my face. Show me what you're gonna put up my ass tomorrow. Give it to me!" As he said this, my prick began to erupt all over his face and chest, but Mark continued to fuck and buck under me, and in a minute or so, I felt his load exploding inside me as he cried out, "Take it, John. God, I love you."

We rolled to our sides, and his dick slipped out of my ass. We cuddled as I licked my cum off his face, and he sucked it off my tongue. "I've dreamed of fucking a guy ever since I saw those pictures in Steve's dresser, and it's even better than I ever thought it could be. And I'm so very, very glad the first guy I ever fucked was you, John. I love to fuck you, I love you, and I know I'm going to love getting fucked by you even more." I fingered his ass again as we lay there, and he murmured his excitement about the prospect of taking my load the way I had just taken his. I was pretty excited about it myself.

Again, Mark spent the night, and the next morning we had little time for play, but before I got into the shower he knelt before me and sucked a load from me. Then, in the shower, he bent me over and fucked me wildly. His hands held my waist in a fierce grip as he drove his prick deep into me, almost shouting his excitement as he froze, buried as deep inside me as he could go, and erupted in a fountain of wonderful, hot cum. After he calmed down, he pulled out, spun me around and held me very tightly as he kissed me with utmost passion. "I adored that and I love you, and I can hardly wait until I feel you all the way inside me, filling me up that way."

139

"Mark, you're the sweetest, most exciting lover in the world ... and I'm so eager to sink my cock in this wonderful, beautiful, hot ass of yours I can't wait."

He grinned, "You won't have to wait long, I promise." And, in fact, I didn't have to wait long ... within twelve hours of his having told me that, my cock was buried inside his perfect ass, delivering a load of cum to it.

Mark had come out to the house immediately after soccer practice again, arriving in his roommate's car, and we kissed and snuggled just inside the door. We didn't even make it to the bedroom before we were naked, lying on the living room floor, locked in sixty-nine and each driving his cock down the other's eager throat. We stopped short of cumming, and Mark stood, took my hand, and led me to the bedroom. Following him, I commented, "Really cute ass!" – and God knows, it was incredibly cute.

He turned and smiled at me. "It's yours, John. Do anything you want with it. I hope you're gonna fuck it, like I want to fuck yours again."

I kissed him. "I want to fuck it, Mark, believe me, and I can't wait to feel your big prick inside me again."

We lay on the bed and kissed and caressed for a long time. Finally, I had Mark roll on his side as I lay behind him, and greased my cock and his asshole thoroughly. "Relax and let me in slowly, Mark. It's going to hurt some, but I'll be as gentle as I can. Once it's inside, it will feel better than anything you've ever felt ... believe me."

He put his hand back to guide my cock to his asshole. "I believe you, and I don't care if it hurts or not ... I want you inside me. If I feel as good to you as you felt to me last night, you're in for a thrill." He backed up to my cock, and I gradually began to enter him. He grunted and gasped a bit with pain, but was surprisingly receptive. My cock slid all the way into him in five or six slight penetrations. Once I was all the way inside, Mark almost exploded in ecstasy. "Oh Jesus, John ... your prick feels so good in me ... God, I want you to fuck me and shoot your load inside me ... I love you so much ... Give me your big cock and your big load." His ass was humping backwards onto my prick, eagerly countering every forward thrust I made. He continued to moan in rapture and encourage me to fuck, although I certainly needed no encouragement. He was unbelievably tight, and the feel of his hot ass-ring clamped over my cock and riding it up and down was stimulating beyond belief.

He rolled on his stomach, and then got to his knees with me continuing to fuck all the time. I held his waist with my hands, and looked adoringly at his thin but muscular torso and the rounded globes of his perfect, velvety ass. The sight of my prick driving into his asshole as he pushed it back to me was almost as stimulating as the feeling of his tight grip on it. He turned his face and smiled back at me. "My ass feel good?"

"You've got the hottest, most beautiful ass I've ever seen, Mark. I love fucking it."

"Fuck it hard and deep ... and I want to feel your cum filling me up. But please take your time, this feels so wonderful, I don't want to even think of your stopping."

I did my best to make the fuck last, but eventually I could hold back no longer, and with a final lunge I planted my cock as deeply into my beautiful young lover as I could, and discharged. He cried out as I did so. "Oh John, I can actually feel you cumming in me. God, I love you so much ... just fill my ass up with your load."

I held him closely and panted how much I loved him and how wonderful his ass felt. He collapsed onto his stomach, and I fell on top, still inside him. I kissed his neck as his hands felt behind and caressed me, and his tight asshole continued to work my cock for a very long time.

"I want to stay in you forever," I whispered, "but I need to pull out so you can fuck me. I've been dreaming all day about how wonderful your big prick felt inside me last night, and looking forward to riding you again." I pulled my cock out of him slowly, and he turned around so that we could hold each other and kiss.

"Last night and this morning was the most wonderful thing that ever happened to me, until now," Mark said. "This morning I thought fucking you was the greatest thing that could happen, but now I know that your fucking me is even better. I love it, and I love you, John."

"My sweet baby, I just know that my cock belongs inside you ... it feels exactly right ... and your cock inside me feels just as perfect. Please fuck me, Mark, put that beautiful, big, hot cock deep inside me and show me how much you love me."

"Lie on your back, John, so I can kiss you while I fuck you." I lay as requested and put my legs on his shoulders as he knelt between them and put his prick inside me. Our arms held each other, and we kissed gently and sweetly as he fucked me similarly, with very slow and very deep thrusts. Eventually his thrusting became impassioned, his breathing grew heavy, and his tongue was fucking my mouth almost as hard as his cock was by then fucking my ass. With a final cry of "I love you," he threw his head back, with his eyes closed in rapture, and he shot an enormous load into me, continuing to fuck long after his discharge. Then as his prick finally stopped moving in me, he beamed a huge grin down at me, "God, I love you."

I reached up and pulled him down onto me. "And I love you, Mark. You're as much a stud as you are an Adonis. You are undoubtedly the most perfectly beautiful man, and the hottest fucker I can imagine."

He giggled. "Did I give you a big enough load?"

I laughed, "I am fucking awash with your cum. Jesus, you really did fill me up, baby."

We kissed and cuddled, cleaned up, and sucked each other off. Before leaving, Mark fucked me again as I knelt on all fours in front of him, and he

141

declared that that might be his favorite way to fuck me, since he could watch as his cock penetrated me; I knew what he meant, having so recently thrilled to the sight of his magnificent ass taking my love that way. I tried to fuck him once more, but he was tender, so he had me shoot on his face and into his open mouth again, but promised he'd be ready to give his asshole to me again the next night.

And he did, and so, within a week of my first having seen Mark's beautiful naked body that night on the dock, we were completely dedicated lovers – kissing and fondling, fucking and sucking, and worshipping and adoring each other almost nightly.

14. EXPANDING MARK'S FRONTIERS

Dean telephoned a couple of times during that wonderful first week of my sexual relationship with Mark. He seemed pleased that Mark and I were in love and was kind enough to refrain from pointing out how very, very quickly that love had developed. He was fascinated by all the details of our lovemaking – this was Dean, after all – and he wanted, and got, a complete rundown of all we had done. One afternoon he called me in the early afternoon. "Are you gonna let me meet Mark? He sounds terrific."

"Do you want to meet him, or is it that you want to go to bed with him? Or with us together?"

"I know I want to go to bed with you and soon. I'm horny as hell, and you've been neglecting my big ol' prick, you know. You're not gonna stop going to bed with me, are you? Remember we made love last time, and I promised I'd give you a really wild fuck next time, you know."

"Believe me, I remember, and there's no way I want to stop fucking with you, Dean. I'm going to explain to Mark that you and I are friends and we fuck; I don't know how he'll react to that. I hope I can convince him that loving you as a friend and having fun with you sexually doesn't mean I can't be his lover. I'll bet if he gets a good look at that incredible cock of yours he's going to want to join the fun."

"Hey, he'd be a fool not to, right?"

"Right. And I know when you get a look at him, you're gonna want in."

"John, I've seen his picture, remember? I know I want in. But how about this afternoon? You're probably going to see Mark tonight, but I hoped maybe I could come by, and we could get in an afternoon fuck. I've got the car."

"Come out. I'll be waiting for you wearing nothing but a smile and a hard-on."

He arrived fifteen minutes later, and he was wearing one of the things I had promised to have on – although with clothing. He shed the clothing as soon as he was through the door and we fell on each other like animals, He hadn't fucked in about a week, and I had been missing the ferocity of his lovemaking and the huge beautiful cock that had come to mean so much to me. The wild fuck he had promised me materialized wonderfully. We sucked each other for a long, hot time before he fucked my ass savagely – and fucked it twice, shooting a huge load in me each time. I fucked him, but he agreed he'd be content with my giving him only one load, since I needed to save something for Mark. As he got ready to leave I agreed to talk to Mark that night about their meeting.

"I'm going to come out tomorrow night, okay?"

"Sure, that's great."

"But just to visit."

"Yeah, right ... just to visit. Sure."

"Right." He raised three fingers, as for the Boy Scout oath, "And the check is in the mail."

"Right. And you promise to stop if it hurts," I replied, citing another traditionally bogus promise.

"Right. And I promise I won't cum in your mouth." He giggled. "No, I won't promise that."

"I assure you I wouldn't want you to keep that promise. Just be sure to wear the tightest pants you've got, without underwear, and if he's not interested when he sees that huge basket of yours, I'll be very surprised."

He kissed me and laughed. "Hell, I'll even be sure to have at least a partial hard-on when I first come in, so it ought to really impress him."

"I just hope I can keep my hands off you until Mark agrees to fool around."

"I just hope neither one of you can keep your hands off me ... or your dicks out of me." He pulled his cock out; it was, not surprisingly, hard again. "How about a blow job to hold me over?"

I knelt and he fucked my mouth wildly until he shot another big load, deep into my eager throat. As he adjusted his Levi's and got ready to go he kissed me deep – a real tongue-fuck. "God, my cum tastes good in your mouth. I really hope I'm gonna be tasting both yours and Mark's tomorrow night."

"I hope so, too. Just don't get so carried away by Mark you forget me, okay? I want to be sure to get that beautiful monster of yours inside me. I'm in love with Mark, but I love you, too, you know."

"John, you know I love you, too, and I'll always have a load for you. But I'll bet Mark wants a few loads from me tomorrow night."

I laughed. "I'm not betting with you. I remember the twenty bucks I lost when you sank that big cock in Richard's ass the first time you saw him."

"Yeah, but that was twenty bucks well spent, right? Come on. Twenty bucks says Mark wants me to fuck him tomorrow night."

"It's a deal. And it's another bet I hope to lose. Just be sure to give me a good hard fuck to console my loss."

He winked and grinned. "You'll lose. And I'll fuck the hell out of you, but you've gotta fuck my ass, too, and let Mark watch, okay?"

"And why do I have the feeling your butt's gonna be full of Mark's cum when I fuck it?"

"Maybe because I'm gonna do my best to be sure it is." He grinned again and headed up the driveway.

That evening I broached the subject of Dean with Mark. He had, of course, seen pictures of "the cute high school guy with the huge cock," as he referred to Dean, and when I told him he was coming out for a drink and an introduction to him the next evening, he seemed pleased. "Gosh yes, I want to meet him; he looks like a really interesting guy." I felt sure Mark was probably finding Dean interesting in the same way I initially had – meaning cute as hell and sexy as the devil. Still, I looked forward to an accommodation between my lover and my fuck-buddy that would at least allow for harmony between the

144

three of us, and also open the way to some exciting three-way sex. During the course of our lovemaking that night, Mark referred to Dean several times. I felt sure tomorrow night was going to prove exciting.

I picked Mark up around 7:30 the next evening, and we had been home only a few minutes when Dean drove into the driveway. He didn't bother to knock or ring the doorbell, but came right in the living room where Mark and I were seated on the sofa. He was indeed wearing the tightest imaginable Levi's, and the outline of his enormous – even though not, as promised, hard – prick was clearly seen along his left leg, and the bulk of his massive balls was as easily discernible on the right side of his crotch. And he looked wonderful, generally. It was clear that both he and Mark had dressed and groomed themselves carefully to make the very best impression on each other.

Mark stood when I introduced them and offered his hand. Dean shook it and expressed his pleasure in meeting him. "And believe me, I've heard a lot about you ... all of it good." He took Mark's waist in both hands and looked into his face. "You know, I've seen your picture, and I've seen you on the soccer field, but Jesus, up close ... my God, John, you said he was handsome, but Mark, you're breathtaking, if you don't mind my saying so."

Mark ducked his head in embarrassment. "No, no ... it's nice of you to say that. I'm really flattered." Mark had been completely disarmed by the younger man's flattery and seeming command of the situation, but he now clearly asserted his own confidence. He put his hands on Dean's waist. "I've heard a lot about you, and seen your picture, too, and I must say you're even more impressive than I imagined you would be. And I figured you were going to be very impressive."

Dean looked down very obviously at his bulging crotch before he grinned crookedly at Mark. "I tried to dress as impressively as I could, anyway."

Mark laughed, stepped back a pace and also looked down at Dean's obvious endowment. "Believe me, I'm impressed." Then he ran a finger under Dean's chin as he gazed into his eyes. "Very impressed." He sat back down on the sofa, Dean sat on a chair opposite, and I went to the kitchen to mix us all drinks.

When I returned, Dean and Mark were chattering like old friends about their respective school work and home towns, and for the next half-hour or so we all had an extremely pleasant, friendly visit – eventually getting to the subject of sex, of course. As Mark began talking about discovering his true sexuality in my bed, Dean began caressing the magnificent shaft he barely concealed in his tight Levi's, and it began to grow noticeably. He grinned at Mark and me, and began to pull his tee shirt out of his Levi's. "Do you guys mind if I get comfortable?"

I looked at Mark, and he nodded to me. I looked back at Dean. "Get as comfortable as you want; it looks like if you don't let something out of those pants pretty soon, you're going to be extremely uncomfortable."

Dean stroked his bulging erection – now obviously throbbing for release. "It does seem to need a little air." He pulled his shirt over his head and kicked off his shoes. He stood, walked over to Mark, and slowly began to unbutton his Levi's. He grinned at Mark, and asked, "You want to help me?"

Mark looked up at him and smiled as his hands sought Dean's fly. "I'd love to help you." With one hand he worked on the buttons, while his other stroked the bulge of Dean's prick. "And I'd love to help myself to some of this."

"Help yourself to all of it you want. There's plenty there for you and for John, too."

Mark knelt in front of Dean and finished unbuttoning his fly. He and Dean worked together to drag the Levi's down – they were that tight, and Dean's cock was crowding them that much. The massive balls and the base of the enormous prick were soon visible, and Mark began to murmur his admiration. As Dean's cock was at last fully released, it gradually rose to meet Mark's awe-struck gaze – nine or ten stunning inches of fat, juicy cock throbbing tantalizingly in front of my lover's face. "My God, Dean, that's the biggest cock I've ever seen."

Dean took Mark's head gently in his hands. "Do you like it, Mark? Does it look good enough to eat?"

Marks hands rose, and one gently circled the magnificent shaft while the other cupped the massive, low-hanging ball-sac. "It's beautiful. It's incredibly beautiful, like a wonderful birthday cake ... too beautiful to eat."

Dean pressed himself in toward Mark. "But birthday cakes are meant to be eaten. Go on, take a few nibbles."

Mark began to kiss the end of Dean's cock and to lick the shaft. Soon Dean was murmuring his enjoyment, and when Mark finally opened his mouth all the way and began to drive his tightly-held lips up and down the big shaft, Dean's hips began to undulate, and his meat was gently, but unmistakably fucking the adoring mouth. "That feels wonderful, Mark. Eat it for me. Open up your throat and take me all the way inside that pretty mouth."

Mark's hands cupped and caressed Dean's driving buttocks as they began to sink almost all of the enormous cock into his throat. I stood and took Dean's head in my hands and we kissed passionately.

"He's beautiful, John."

"You're beautiful too, Dean. And I want to watch you fuck him, and I want him to watch you fuck me, okay?"

"For sure! But don't forget you fuck me when I've got an ass full of his cum, right?" I agreed eagerly, and Dean added, "And I think you owe me twenty bucks again."

"Thank God!"

Mark was still sucking eagerly and loudly when Dean raised him to his feet. They embraced and kissed for some time, their bodies grinding together, one nude, one still clothed. Dean fell to his knees in front of Mark and began to

146

unbutton his pants. "When do I get to see your cock? I'll bet you've got a beauty for me." Mark began to remove his shirt, and by the time he had it off, his pants were around his ankles, with Dean feasting on his prick – his nose completely buried in pubic hair as he nursed. Mark seized Dean's head and began to fuck the worshipping mouth while both murmured their delight.

I watched, fascinated, as I stripped my clothes off and stood behind Mark, pressing my cock against his ass and kissing his neck. "You are so sexy, my baby ... I want to see you have a really good time tonight. I want Dean to know why I'm so proud to be your lover."

Dean stood and took Mark in his arms again. "Every inch of you is beautiful, Mark. Come to bed and let me make love to every inch of you."

Mark looked at me; again I nodded. He kissed Dean. "And let me make love to every inch of your beautiful cock."

"That's a lotta inches."

"And I want every one of them deep inside me."

Dean kissed Mark and smiled at him. "I'm gonna fill you with cock, I'm gonna fill you with love ... man, I'm gonna fill you with hot cum."

"Fill me, Dean, the hotter the better."

As Mark stepped out of his pants, Dean took both of us by the hand and led us toward the bedroom, where he quickly stripped the cover off the bed and lay on his back. He held out his hands. "Make love to me, Mark." He spread his legs and Mark positioned himself between them, lying on top of the tall, beautifully proportioned young stud. Their groins pressed together and Dean's legs circled Mark's golden body. The two began to kiss, and Mark's bubble butt writhed gently as he ground his cock against Dean's ass.

I lay on the bed next to them and studied the two handsome faces locked together in obvious passion. "You two look so great together."

Dean broke the kiss and turned his face to me. "I'm going to fuck your lover's ass, John. I'm gonna stick my cock up his ass and fill him with cum. Is that okay with you, Mark?" Mark grinned and murmured his eagerness, and Dean smiled at me. "Is that okay with you, too?"

I kissed both of them. "Just be sure you save some cum for me ... both of you."

They returned to their passionate embracing, and soon had reversed their bodies so that they lay on their sides and sucked each other's cocks in a very heated sixty-nine. I watched their marvelously beautiful asses humping and driving their cocks deep into each other's throats as they moaned in ecstasy, and I put my face into that heaven between the wondrously rounded cheeks of Mark's ass, and tongue-fucked him as deeply as I could. As I was happily eating ass, Mark stopped sucking long enough to urge me, "Get my hole ready for Dean's big cock." I provided this delightful service to my lover for some time then turned my oral attentions to his suck partner. After I had eaten Dean's ass for some time, he encouraged me, "Put something bigger in there." I greased up his hole and sank my eager cock into it, and as I eagerly fucked the driving ass, Mark's hands came around and pulled me in tightly. Mark's mouth and my cock were servicing Dean only a few inches apart, and the savage humping motion of his ass served to stimulate us both to greater heights of worship, driving his cock deeper into Mark's throat, and my cock deeper into his hungry asshole – where I soon shot the first load of cum to be produced that evening.

After my orgasm, I pulled out of Dean, who rolled to his back, pulling Mark's mouth off his prick. At the same time, he abandoned Mark's cock, and said, "Ride me, Mark. Sit down on my big cock and let me show you what heaven is like."

I hurried to lubricate Dean's cock and Mark's asshole, and Mark poised himself over Dean. The tip of Dean's huge prick was pressing against the pink target it sought, while Mark began to rotate his hips and gradually settle down over the massive shaft challenging him. I sat back and watched in awe as Dean's beautiful cock began to slowly enter the undulating asshole of my lover.

Mark cried out, "Oh God, Dean, you're so fucking big."

"I don't want to hurt you, Mark!"

"No, don't stop. I want your beautiful big prick all the way inside me. Fuck me, Dean ... fuck me!"

Then, with one savage lunge, Dean's ass rose from the bed and drove his cock all the way into Mark's ass. Mark threw back his head and cried "Aaaaaaaahhhh!" as his prick – with no one even touching it – began to shoot thick, white cum all over Dean's chest and face. Dean and I watched this impressive shower of seven or eight huge spurts, and we both added our cries of excitement and admiration to Mark's cry of rapture. I could not help but think of the way this same beautiful shaft had in the same way discharged a similarly copious load all over me that night on the dock, the first time I had gently kissed it.

All three of us were totally thrilled with the display, but Mark began a fevered ride up and down the considerable length of Dean's probing monster. "Fuck me, Dean, fill me up with that huge prick. God, I love it."

Dean held Mark's waist in his hands as he fucked upward into the eager receptacle he was filling so expertly, and I licked Mark's cum from Dean's chest and face, then shared the bounty with Dean in a wonderful, long kiss. I licked the few drops of cum still threading out of Mark's prick as it bobbed up and down in front of him while he thrilled to his ride. I, too, straddled Dean, facing Mark, and took my young lover in my arms as he continued his feverish ride. His kiss was utter passion, and to my question, "Do you like it, baby?" he replied breathlessly, "God this is the best of both worlds ... you in my arms and this fabulous cock up my ass." Soon I was able to share Mark's thrill as I held him in my arms, for Dean pulled my body backward and also began to fuck me, but with the darting muscle of his driving tongue. I eventually dismounted, so I could watch at close hand the wonder of Dean's huge shaft plunging violently in and out of Mark's beautiful ass, the ass-ring clinging tightly to the huge, glistening shaft as it disappeared and re-appeared into its hungry sheath. This ride of ecstasy continued for some time, until Dean called out, "Take my load, baby!"

Mark sat down heavily on Dean, but Dean's ass twitched and drove upward as he discharged his love. He cried out loudly, but Mark's simultaneous cry of "God, I can feel your cum shooting in me so hard ... give it all to me" fairly drowned him out. They both froze for a few minutes, and Mark fell forward onto Dean's chest – the monster cock still firmly planted in him – and they began to kiss breathlessly, seemingly trying to eat each other's mouths with incredible passion. Finally, they calmed down and spent a long time caressing and assuring each other it was the greatest sex ever. I had to admit it had been great to watch, and although I had recently shot my load in Dean, I was incredibly horny again.

I straddled Dean's legs, positioning myself behind the kneeling Mark, and began to play with his ass. Mark raised his head, and although he was still plugged by Dean's cock, he told me he wanted me to fuck him while Dean's cum was still hot inside him. He raised his body so that Dean slipped out, and I entered him easily without lubrication. Dean's obviously huge load was wonderfully still present in the tight, throbbing chamber I now began to explore. The extreme passion I had just witnessed, the vocal encouragement the two hot men gave me as I sank my cock into Mark, the slimy wonder of Dean's hot and generous emission easing my way, the beauty of the hot young body kneeling to receive my thrusts, and the feel of my beautiful Mark's tight ass-ring riding my cock as I drove it in, all combined to bring me to orgasm very quickly, after which we all collapsed for a long time in a delightful sort of sexual afterglow.

My afterglow was perhaps a little more dim than my partners – I had cum twice, while Dean and Mark each had only one orgasm. They soon made up for lost time, however.

After a brief respite for refreshing drinks and using the bathroom, we renewed our assaults. Dean knelt on the bed and encouraged Mark to fuck him from behind, which Mark did with enthusiasm and obvious effectiveness, this time depositing his second load deep inside, rather than all over, the hot high-school stud. Wishing to be fair, Mark had me kneel and he fucked me for some time, but since he had just blown his load, he finally turned his work over to Dean, and I soon felt the thrill of that matchless forceful discharge of his, warming me deep inside.

Dean collapsed on top of me and whispered in my ear, "Remember you were going to fuck me when my butt was full of Mark's cum? Now's the time." I was really not ready to deliver a third load, but the feel of Mark's cum in Dean's hot ass was so stimulating that, although it took me some time to do so, I joyfully fulfilled my promise.

The three of us lay together in sweet embrace, kissing and hugging and giggling about the wonderful sex we had just enjoyed. After a while our cocks had all returned to full erection, and Mark suggested daisy-chain cocksucking. We lay in a triangle on the bed as Mark took Dean's throbbing, driving monster into his throat; at the same time I began to worship Mark's cock while he fucked my mouth eagerly, and I thrilled to the feeling of Dean's lips driving up and down my prick as he exerted wonderful suction on it. It took quite a while before we were ready to cum, but eventually Dean's sucking stopped for a minute, and he muttered around my cock, "Eat my load, Mark," as he obviously shot a wad into my lover's throat. Mark murmured delight and renewed the intensity of his drive into my mouth, and I was shortly rewarded with a violent, copious discharge into my hungry throat. As I swallowed it, Dean renewed his efforts, and I was soon delivering my cum to the young stud, who sucked all the harder as I shot into him.

We lay for a long time with our softening pricks still lovingly encased in mouths, and eager, appreciative hands and fingers exploring hot ass-cheeks, and assholes still wet with cum. Eventually, we clasped together in a loving embrace and managed some very hot three-way kissing. As we were doing so, Dean remarked, "You know what I'd really love to see?"

"I can't imagine it could beat what I've seen tonight, but what?"

"I'd really like to see Mark making love with Cary. That would be a match of two unbelievably beautiful guys, wouldn't it?"

Mark knew who Cary was and had seen pictures of him. He said, "I'd like to see somebody make love with Cary. I don't think I'm beautiful, but he sure is, and I'll bet his body is great. Has he got a big cock like yours, Dean?"

I laughed before Dean could reply. "Nobody except Eddie's got a cock like Dean, and he's no longer around, so Dean is the monster prick in residence. Cary's cock is maybe only a bit bigger than average, but it's pretty, and he uses it like a pro."

From Dean: "He sure does, and his body is as perfect as his face ... muscles and tits to die for. He's got a cute little rounded butt that anyone in his right mind would love to fuck and eat. I know John and I both do, and Mike – Cary's lover – gets to do it all the time.

"And Mark, Mike's cock is almost as big as Dean's," I added. "It would really be fun for the three of us to get together with Mike and Cary, both, and I think we'd all love watching you and Cary together. It really would be a pairing of two incredibly beautiful, hot guys."

"I'm not beautiful," he pooh-poohed Dean's and my insistence to the contrary here – "but I sure am hot, and I'd love to get it on with Cary. Do you guys think he'd go for it?"

I told him I felt sure Mike and Cary would be especially eager to repeat the foursome they had enjoyed with Dean and me, with the addition of my eager, hot, beautiful Mark. As we prepared to go to sleep, we took time for another three-way blow job, and this time I received Dean's huge cock and forceful load in my throat while Mark took mine and Dean feasted on Mark's. We had each of us blown four or five loads that night, and we were all ready for some rest.

Dean slept with us, and the next morning he insisted on starting the day by fucking Mark and me both as he had us kneel side by side on the bed, and he filled each of us with successive loads. Mark and I each managed only one load each, but we delivered both of them at almost exactly the same time into Dean's eager, open mouth, as we beat ourselves off to achieve the orgasms we had neared while we had alternated fucking his eager, driving ass only minutes before that. Mark's and my cum was mixed on Dean's tongue as we all kissed before he swallowed it.

It was a great way to start a new day, after a particularly gratifying night. Before that new day was out I had called Mike and Cary and they had expressed eagerness to meet Mark. Cary had seen Mark on the soccer field, and had seen pictures of him at my house, so he was eager to make love with him while we all watched – not a difficult assignment to accept.

Mike said he was almost drooling in anticipation of watching Mark making love with his gorgeous Cary. "Just be sure we plan plenty of time for the rest of us to get our rocks off, okay?"

"I can almost promise you that we'll all fuck Mark at some point, and we'll all definitely have plenty of cock and plenty of cum inside us. I personally can't wait to get that beautiful ass-stretcher of yours up my butt again, Mike."

"And I can't wait to get Dean inside me again. God his prick is huge ... and he is really beautiful, isn't he?"

"Wait until you see Mark naked."

"I can't wait."

Cary had been listening to all this on an extension phone. "Wow! Neither can I."

15. ALL IN THE FAMILY

Mark was delighted to hear that Cary was interested in making love with him for Mike's and Dean's and my vicarious enjoyment. Looking at Cary's picture, he said, "He really is gorgeous, isn't he?" I assured my lover Cary was even prettier in person, and breathtakingly beautiful when naked. I was eagerly anticipating seeing my beautiful Mark kneeling behind the equally stunning, muscular Cary with his cock buried deep in that blond Adonis' rounded, succulent ass or that same ass writhing in ecstasy as it drove a loving prick deep inside my lover's own hungry hole. Mark laughed, "But somehow I get the feeling I'm gonna get at least three other cocks shoved into me in at some point." I had to agree that his premonition was probably well founded.

Before we could effect the meeting, however, an interesting offshoot of my love with Mark developed – interesting and fun, and not completely unexpected.

Just a few days later Mark came into my office with the news that his older brother, Steve, the one whom he thought was in the sexy pictures he had found, was coming into town that afternoon – just passing through on a business trip – and could only spend the evening. "He's going to take us out to dinner."

"Us?"

"Well, I told him that we'd become close friends, and he wants to meet you."

"But we're just 'close friends,' as far as he knows, right?"

"Oh, sure. Anyway, if it's okay, we're going to come out and pick you up at 6:30 and go out to dinner." Of course it was all right; in fact, I was anxious to meet Steve – maybe seen in the picture with one big cock down his throat and another bigger one up his ass.

Promptly at 6:30, a car drove into my driveway, and Mark and Steve got out. Steve was about the same height as Mark – perhaps an inch taller – but was more muscular, with very dark, almost coal-black, hair. He didn't much resemble Mark facially, either, but he was very, very handsome. Since he was an adoptive brother, there was no reason to expect a family resemblance, of course. His wide-set gray-blue eyes were a startling contrast to his dark hair, and he had a warm smile, with deep dimples. I liked him at once. No, to be honest, I was hot for him at once.

We had a drink before going out to dinner, and Steve talked about his wife and son, his childhood with Mark, and just about everything except the one subject I nervously expected him to raise – my relationship to his little brother. Steve seemed to evince no curiosity at all about why his younger brother was so very close to a professor fifteen years his senior. I was both relieved and puzzled. There seemed no doubt that Steve was extremely solicitous about Mark's well-being, but he probably sensed that Mark's and my relationship wasn't bad for him, and hence required no explanation. Our pleasant, but innocuous conversation continued at a local steak house.

After dinner, Mark announced that he had to study for a big test the next day, and asked Steve if he would drop him at the dormitory before he took me back home. Steve did as asked, and when we pulled into my driveway, I asked if he wanted to come in for a nightcap. He seemed eager to do so, and we went inside. I started a fire in the fireplace as Steve fixed drinks. He handed me mine then studied the fire for several minutes before he very pointedly raised his eyes to mine. "Fireplaces are so romantic, aren't they?"

I turned to face him. "They always make me feel romantic."

Steve put his drink down, returned to me, and put his hands on my shoulders. "I was really hoping you'd feel that way. I really am feeling very romantic right this minute." He pulled me to him, and his mouth was about one inch from mine as he said, "And I'd really like to kiss you. Is that okay with you?" Still holding my drink, I put one arm around him and drew him close. With the other I pulled his head in to mine, and we kissed for a long time – a kiss that started out sweet and chaste, but finally became extremely passionate. We were virtually fucking each other's mouth with our tongues by the time we came up for air.

Steve's arms were around me, and his hand was exploring my ass as he nibbled at my ear and spoke quietly, but with considerable intensity, interspersing his words with kisses, "I want you to fuck me. I want to get in bed with you and eat your cock, and feel you sucking me off, and if you can take me, I want to plant my prick as deep in your hot ass as it will go. Then I want to feel your cock inside me, shooting a huge, hot load deep in my body." He stepped back and looked into my eyes as he smiled, "How does that sound to you?"

I was trembling with excitement as I whispered, "I can't think of anything that sounds better."

His smile turned into a huge grin. "I began hoping you'd feel that way about fifteen seconds after I walked through that door tonight. Then when I saw how much in love you and Mark are ..." I began to remonstrate, but Steve put his hand over my mouth before I could really speak. "Look, it's fine. I'm not stupid, and I'm only too aware of how attractive my little brother is. Also I know he's never seriously dated, and even though you guys were trying to be casual, I could see how you both felt. How long have you been lovers?"

"Only about two months. But it's been a great two months."

"That's wonderful. Just promise me you'll be good to him, and ... obviously ... don't tell him about this. Check?" I nodded. "So ... you guys do ... you know, everything?" I confirmed that we did. "You know, Mark's my baby brother, but I'm not blind. He's absolutely gorgeous, and if he weren't who he is, I'd be trying to get in his pants regularly, I'd want to do everything with him, just the way you do. I know I've got a wife and a kid, but obviously I like guys, too. I love my family more than I can tell you, and my wife and I have a very good sex life. And since we've got married I never screw around with guys or with anyone when I'm home. But I'm on the road a lot, and when I can, I try to find a hot guy to fuck with. There's no thrill to me like taking a guy's cock up my ass. And Mark is probably the most attractive guy I've ever seen; to be honest, I seriously considered trying to get him in bed many times over the years ... starting about from the time he was sixteen. I really envy you. You know, I'm around him a lot, and I've never seen him like he was tonight. I'll bet you're the first guy he's ever fucked with, aren't you?"

"That's what he tells me."

"And I want to be the next guy you fuck with." He kissed me again, and began to unbutton his shirt. "Let's get naked."

Standing in the light from the fireplace, we watched each other strip, and I thrilled at his muscular, smooth body and flat stomach. When he removed his shorts, he turned around and I was almost struck dumb at the beauty of his really cute, rounded ass. And he didn't just bare it when he turned around and pulled down his shorts, he arched his back and actually presented it to me, smiling back at me over his shoulder, clearly proud of what he was offering. And it was decidedly something to be proud of! I knelt and kissed it as he turned around, and his steely hard prick slapped against my face. It was fully as breathtaking as his ass: no more than average length, but of enormous girth. And it wasn't just fat; it was beautifully shaped and smooth, with a huge pink cock-head, dripping at that moment with pre-cum.

The expressions "bubble butt" and "beer-can cock" were not yet then in use, but for me, they might have been coined at that very moment!

I kissed the end of Steve's cock and licked the pre-cum from his slit. His hands held my head gently as he pulled me toward his fat prick. "Do you think you can take this up your ass? A lot of guys can't."

"I'll take it or die trying." My mouth opened, and I began to suck his throbbing mouth-stretcher; it was all I could do to get my lips around it, but once it was inside, I found I could easily take its entire length, and Steve fucked eagerly, moaning appreciatively.

"If you can take it up your ass the way you're taking it in your mouth, you're gonna make me a really happy guy tonight." He raised me to my feet and kissed me deeply. He reached down and cupped my balls and hard prick. "But this inside my mouth and up my butt is gonna make me even happier." He knelt, took my entire prick inside his mouth with one swoop, and began to suck noisily as the tight ring of his lips gripped me tightly while it traveled all the way up and down my shaft. One hand fondled my balls, and with the other he played with my asshole – fucking it with first one, and then two fingers while he worshipped my prick orally. Then he stood, and our arms went around each other, our hard cocks ground together, our eager hands explored bodies and asses, and we kissed long and hard.

Finally we broke, and Steve grinned, "Let's get into the bed. I may have wanted to fuck with my brother for a long time," and here he laughed, "but I'm sure as hell going to fuck with my brother-in-law."

"Well, your brother-in-law ... or whatever I am ... sure as hell plans to fuck with you. I can't wait to see if I can get that big fat cock in my ass."

"You just let me get it in you, and I promise to give you a fuck you won't forget." He put a hand on my neck and rubbed my nose with his. "I always shoot a really huge load, and I get a lot of force behind it. You're gonna think I exploded in you."

"I can hardly wait."

As I took his hand and led him to my bedroom, he played with my ass. "God this is cute." In the bedroom his arms went around me again. "But it oughta be ... this is a cute guy."

"But you're not cute, Steve."

He seemed flustered. "I ... well, I know, I ..."

"You're gorgeous! And your body, and your ass, and this beautiful fat prick go way beyond that. Mark told me you were handsome, but I had no idea. I sure as hell wasn't prepared for such a perfect body and such a fantastic dick"

"It's all yours, John. I want you to do everything to me that you do to my beautiful baby brother. But I'm not a baby ... I want you to fuck me like a real man."

"Your baby brother's no baby either. He fucks like a real man, and I fuck him the same way ... just like I'm gonna do to you."

He pulled me down on the bed, and we held each other tightly and kissed and fondled for a long time before swapping ends and taking each other's cocks into our mouths for some serious and extremely passionate double cocksucking. I held his cute ass in my hands as it drove his massive prick wildly into my throat, and he murmured his delight and sucked deeply while I fucked his hungry mouth with long, rapid strokes. We were both obviously nearing orgasm when Steve released my prick from his mouth. "You want me to cum in your mouth first?"

"Can you can still give me a load in my ass later?"

"Oh, yeah." He snickered, "Never a problem for me."

"Then give me that hot load." I began to suck even harder, and Steve renewed his efforts, so that in a minute I shot my load before he did – deep into his eager throat. His prolonged "Mmmmmmmmm!" indicated he enjoyed the mouthful of cum, which he bathed my cock with as his tongue continued to lap it inside his mouth. Finally he swallowed and said, "Here it comes, John ... oh God, eat my load!" And with that, as promised, his orgasm exploded violently inside my worshipping mouth. And what a load it was! Eight or ten huge spurts erupted with unbelievable force inside me, as he buried his fat prick as deep as it would go. I almost gagged with the force and volume of his orgasm, but I managed to contain it all, and held it for a long time as I treated his monster cock to the same kind of cum-bath he had shown mine. Finally, I released his prick from my mouth without swallowing, moved upward so I could kiss him, and as our lips met, I returned about half of his load to him. He giggled a bit, but showed his appreciation with a moan of pleasure.

We deep kissed for a long time, with his huge load passing back and forth between us until I finally retained most of it and swallowed. He swallowed the balance before grinning at me. "That's the hottest, the sexiest thing anyone's ever done to me."

"That was the biggest load I ever had in my mouth ... I just had to share it with at least one of the Hagood brothers."

"You know, this is crazy, but I wish the other Hagood brother could have been here to share."

"God knows there was plenty to go around ... and I think Mark would've enjoyed it."

"I would have enjoyed sharing your load with him, I know. Has Mark ... has he ever said anything about how he feels about me ... well, this way?"

"Mark thinks you're beautiful and sexy as hell, and I believe he wants to make love with you. And you really want to make love with him, right?"

"To be honest, yes I do."

"Well, next time you come through town, we can arrange for the three of us to get together if you want."

"Let me think about it. But ... yeah, I'm almost sure I want to do that if he wants to."

"I'll find out for sure. You can always approach him on your own, you know."

"No, I'd rather we sort of buffered it with a third guy. But not just any third guy. Sex with Mark and you together would be just incredible. How do you think he'd feel about sex with two guys at once, though, even forgetting for the moment that I'm his brother?"

"Look Steve, Mark and I had the wildest sex imaginable just a few days ago with another guy, Dean ... a gorgeous high school stud with a prick you wouldn't believe, and an ass to die for. And we finished up the night by deciding to try to arrange a five-way party with the three of us and two other really hot, cute guys that Dean and I have had sex with a lot. Mark enjoyed the three-way as much as any of us did, and he's looking forward to sex with four other guys that are all dying to get their cocks inside him ... and Mark's cock inside them."

"Jesus, I'm learning a lot about my baby brother."

We got up and made drinks. We lay in front of the fire for a while, kissing and hugging gently. Finally, with his finger up my asshole, Steve said, "Let's get back in the bed. I'm ready to give you another big load, and your ass feels like it's gonna be tight as hell and hot as a firecracker."

I grasped his now steely-hard prick in my hand – a truly impressive handful. "Hell, Steve, anyone must seem tight to you. I don't know if I've ever had a cock this fat inside me. But I want it there."

"Well, there's no way you can back out now. I've got to fuck that pretty little ass of yours."

I stood and again led him to the bedroom. "Fuck away Steve, it's all yours."

There was no foreplay now; Steve was eager to fuck. He had me kneel on the side of the bed as he stood next to it and greased up my eager asshole. "God I want to fuck you! Give me the hole you give my beautiful baby brother."

As Steve's massive cock-head began to press against my asshole, I relaxed as much as possible to admit it; I knew it was going to take some real stretching. Steve was gentle, but insistent, and as he cooed his delight in the sensation, I panted my eagerness to take him inside. Although there was a bit of initial pain as he began to penetrate, I was somewhat surprised to find I really had no more trouble taking his cock in my ass ... less, really, than taking it orally. Once inside, it was well worth any pain I might have had to put up with ... my entire body felt warm and sexually stimulated to an almost incredible degree by the all-pervasive feel of the monstrous girth driving into me. "That's wonderful, Steve. Fuck me as hard as you can!"

"I'm so glad you can take it. Your ass is unbelievably hot. Come on John, ride my big prick!" As requested, I began driving my ass backward to meet his forward thrusts, and he all but pulled out as we separated, then drove himself fiercely all the way in each time we forced ourselves together. He fucked for a long time, before he came – a delay largely attributable to several pauses designed to forestall his orgasm and prolong his delicious fucking. Finally, with a wild cry, he shoved his cock as deep as he possibly could, and I felt again the considerable volume of his load, delivered in a number of fiercely powerful spurts. I cried aloud also as he filled my ass with his love, and with his cock still buried in it's adoring sheath, he fell on top of me and kissed my neck passionately while he told me how wonderful I had been.

At my request, Steve kept his prick inside me and continued to fuck long after his orgasm. His prick was softer, of course, but still maintained considerable bulk and rigidity, and felt absolutely wonderful as it "squished" in the huge load of cum inside me. Finally he withdrew, rolled off me and onto his back, raised and spread his legs, and bade me to fuck him. I knelt between his legs and kissed him. "Jesus, I love fucking with Hagood boys."

"Fill me up the way you do Mark. Show me how lucky my baby brother is."

I greased us up, positioned his legs on my shoulders, and situated my cock at Steve's asshole. "Pretend I'm Mark," I cried as I drove myself violently into him and he gasped with pleasure.

"Fuck me deep and hard, John! But I want you fucking me, not Mark ... not right now. Just fill me up with your big prick and give me another hot load. God I love to get fucked!" His hands held my buttocks and pulled me in to him as I drove myself as hard and as deep as I could, and soon – too soon –

discharged violently into my eager partner. "Oh man, I feel your cum shooting in me. That feels wonderful."

After my orgasm, we held each other in our arms and necked languorously, with my cock still in his ass and his legs wrapped around my body. I asked him, "You're sure you don't wish that had been Mark?"

"I'm sure. I just wish Mark was next in line."

The words were hardly out of his mouth before the telephone rang. "God, who can that be?" I asked. "It's damned near midnight."

Steve crawled out of my embrace and began to leave the bed. "I've got to go pee while you answer it." He kissed me briefly as he headed for the bathroom. "Just don't start getting dressed, okay?"

I grinned at his adorable butt as it retreated. "Not a chance." I picked up the phone. "Hello?"

It was Mark. "Don't say anything unless you're alone; just answer my questions. Are you alone?"

"Er ... no, as a matter of fact."

"It's Steve with you, am I right?"

"Yeah, yeah ... right."

"I was getting ready to go to bed, and I'd been calling his motel room off and on for an hour or two, and got no answer. I guessed he might have gone home with you when you dropped me off. I was right, huh?"

"Right."

"Tell me ... and it's perfectly okay if the answer is 'yes,' okay?"

"Okay."

"Have you all been fucking?"

"That's right."

Mark chuckled. "That devil. I figured he'd want to get in your pants. Did he figure it out about you and me?"

"Yes, completely. But it's fine ... not a problem."

"Are you through fucking?"

"I really don't think so."

"I'm tempted to borrow my roommate's car and sneak out there and surprise him. Would he have a heart attack?"

"No, no ... quite the contrary. It would be fine. Maybe even advisable."

"You mean he'd like for me to join you? Is that what you're saying?"

"I'm sure of it. Yeah, right ... I think it would be a great idea."

"This is crazy; you're suggesting I come out there and fuck with my own brother?"

"And me. And only if that's what you want."

"Shit, why not ... I've always wondered, and I may never get this opportunity again. Besides, like I told you he was adopted, so it's not like it would really be incest. Okay, I'm going to park up the road and sneak into the house. Is the door unlocked? And are you in your bedroom?"

"That's 'yes' to both. So ... glad you called, and I'll see you, okay?"

"You'll see me real soon. And I'm coming into that room wearing nothing but a hard-on. Steve is gonna shit."

"Trust me, it won't be a problem for long. 'Bye!" I hung up and turned to face Steve, who was back in bed with me.

"Problems?"

"No, no ... nothing to worry about. Come here and kiss me." I wrapped my arms around him, and we resumed our lovemaking. I intentionally prolonged our hugging and kissing, so that once we returned to sucking and fucking, Mark could catch us at it.

I didn't hear Mark enter the house at all. Steve was lying on his stomach, between my legs, and sucking my prick as I lay propped up against the headboard of my bed, facing the door. I spotted my beautiful young lover standing in the hall, completely naked, stroking his hard cock, and holding his forefinger over his lips to indicate I should say nothing. He entered the room silently, and stood behind his unsuspecting brother.

I took Steve's head in my hands, pulled him away from my cock, and leaned over to kiss him. "Do you wish it was Mark you were sucking?"

"I love sucking your cock. I don't want to be anywhere else."

"But Mark has an absolutely beautiful cock, Steve. It's wonderful the way he fucks my mouth when I suck it. You know you want to suck him!" It was shameless the way I was setting him up.

"I can't tell you how hungry I've been ... and for such a long time ... to get Mark's prick in my mouth and up my butt."

"I'm sure you can have him there if you'll turn around."

Steve whirled around and gasped "Mark!" Mark was standing there with his hands on his hips and his beautiful cock standing straight out and bobbing. He took it in one hand and offered it as he stepped in toward the bed. "You want this, big brother?"

Steve was astonished. His fat prick immediately lost its erection. "Jesus, Mark, you almost gave me heart failure."

Mark continued toward the bed and knelt on it, straddling his brother's legs. "You haven't answered my question, Steve ... do you want your little brother's prick in you or not? I sure want yours in me." Steve's hands came up, took hold of Mark's waist, and drew him in. His head came up and his mouth opened to admit Mark's prick, as he began to suck hungrily. Mark's hands held his brother's head while he fucked his mouth with deep, slow strokes. Mark smiled at me and said, "I guess that answers my question."

I still knelt behind Steve's head. Mark now took my head in his hands and pulled me in to kiss me sweetly. "Thank you, John. I may love my brother, but you're my real lover." He kissed me again, passionately.

"And that make's me happier than you'll ever know," I said. "Do you want me to leave you guys alone?"

"No. I've wanted to do what I'm about to do for years, but now it will be even more fun and more exciting knowing you're with me to watch." He grinned hugely, "And maybe help me do it?"

I kissed him. "I want to help all I can ... just let me know. Make love with your big brother, baby. I'm here, I'm watching, I'm happy for you. Okay?" He kissed me again and drew back, his prick popping out of Steve's mouth.

Mark knelt over Steve, their faces only inches apart. Steve whispered, "I've wanted to do that for years." Mark kissed his lips lightly. "And I've wanted you to do it for years." Then their arms went around each other. Mark stretched out on top of Steve, and they began kissing and fondling each other very, very passionately. I leaned back against the headboard of the bed and watched these two beautiful brothers discover each other.

For the most part I simply observed as they sucked each other's cocks. Mark commented, as he began, "God, how can I get my lips around that monster?"

He managed!

They lay together in sixty-nine as they sucked, ate each other's asses individually and in sixty-nine, sucked each other's nipples and licked each other all over, kissed and fondled endlessly, finger-fucked each other, and fucked each other's asses dog-style, missionary position, and while riding cock. Steve had already that evening deposited two loads in me – perhaps exploded two loads is more accurate – so he wasn't as ready to cum as Mark, but he nonetheless shot a load in Mark's worshipping mouth. Mark almost gagged with the force and volume of the orgasm, as I had, but, like me, he swallowed every drop. Steve blew another up Mark's ass, as he kissed him while fucking him missionary style. Again, like me, Mark had wondered aloud if he could take such a fat cock inside him, but had no difficulty – and, like me, marveled at the force of Steve's orgasm in his hungry and grateful chute.

Mark fed Steve his first load while his gorgeous older brother lay with him in sixty-nine, another one in his ass as he knelt behind him and fucked him, and a third one as he rode Steve's incredibly fat cock. I fully expected to see him blow a load without touching his cock when he lowered himself on Steve – as he had when he sat down on Dean's ass-stretcher, and as he had done when I kissed his prick on the dock that first time I saw him naked – but he actually began to jack himself off as he rode, and then Steve took over and brought him to an explosive climax that deposited creamy gobs of cum all over his own face.

I basically watched this alternating tender and frantic lovemaking, but I frequently caressed either or both of the lovemakers as they played, tongue-fucked the occasional busy, grinding ass, or passionately kissed a beautiful mouth when it was not elsewhere occupied. Mark very often sought my hand and squeezed it, as if to let me know he remembered I was there, and was his lover. At one point, as Steve knelt behind Mark and fucked his ass, Mark had me lie beneath him in sixty-nine, and I sucked his cock while his brother pounded his ass – and he sucked mine, drawing a wonderful load from it while we were so engaged. After Steve had shot his load in Mark's ass while fucking him missionary position, he asked me to fuck his ass while he stayed in Mark. I was happy to oblige.

The two adoring brothers worshipped each other for almost two fuck-and-suck-filled hours. Finally, exhausted, the three of us cuddled, kissed, and caressed for yet another hour or two – with Mark and Steve exclaiming over their delight at finally realizing their secret ambitions vis-a-vis each other. Mark confessed to Steve about accidentally finding the pictures in his dresser. Steve not only forgave him with a laugh, he freely admitted that it was he in the pictures, and the two guys fucking him were, like all the other guys in the set of pictures Mark had found, some sailors he had met in a bar in San Diego, when he was a Marine. One of them had been a navy photographer "with a camera and a lot of Vaseline." Steve said he later got a set of the pictures from the photographer when they met again, and Steve offered his hot ass in trade for it. "The photographer turned out to be an even better fuck than the sailors in the pictures."

I never felt left out as Mark and Steve rejoiced and reminisced, however. Both were quick to express their appreciation to me for finally bringing them together. Steve put his arms around me. "I've finally had my brother's prick inside me, and his cum is deep inside me right now, and that wouldn't have happened without you. And I'm mighty happy for having your cock and your cum inside me, too. Mark is lucky to have you, and I'm lucky my little brother has such a considerate and exciting lover." Mark's arms were around me from behind, and his prick nestled between my legs as he added, "I couldn't have said it better. I echo your sentiments, big brother."

Steve put his hand around me and tousled Mark's hair. "Big-cocked brother!"

"Amen! Big-cocked, beautiful, hot-fucking, wonderful brother!"

We finally dozed off, and in the morning our sex-play was pretty general, with all three of us sharing equally – and the absolute highlight was the finale of the encounter. Mark lay on his back, and Steve was impaled on his hard cock, riding up and down. Steve leaned forward to kiss Mark, giving me a wonderful view of my lover's cock inside his asshole. As I began to insert a finger into Steve's asshole along with Mark's prick, he looked back at me. "Put your whole prick in there with Mark's."

"Can you take it, Steve?"

He grinned back at me. "Believe me, I've been doubled-fucked a lot more than once. Just be sure to grease us up extra well."

In truth, I'd been double-fucked twice myself – both times by the same guys. Ten or eleven years earlier, back in Texas, my eighteen-year-old lover, Billy, shoved his lengthy cock up my ass, to supplement the massive shaft of another high school stud, Phil, as he fucked me – and they each deposited a huge load of cum in me to bathe their probing, wonderful tools. On that occasion – and somewhat later when Billy and Phil again serviced me the same way – I felt I was in heaven. And Phil declared it was pretty heavenly when Billy and I team-fucked his hot ass!

As I began to insinuate my prick into Steve's hole, Mark cried out, "God damn, this is gonna be unbelievably hot." And it was. Steve leaned forward and very gently rode up and down Mark's prick as I gradually entered him. Inside his ass, Mark's cock felt incredibly exciting as it moved next to mine. We fucked in tandem – gently, to avoid pulling out, but with strokes as deep as we could manage – and after a very long time, Mark declared he was ready to shoot his load. I stopped fucking, and Mark fucked very rapidly, rubbing up against my cock, and I was rewarded with the feel of his hot load bathing my prick. Steve was rewarded with the feel of the same hot load, and expressed his appreciation – as he had been almost screaming his appreciation of our dual fuck all along. Once Mark was completely through, he froze in position, and I resumed plunging my cum-coated prick into Steve's ass. Soon Mark and Steve were both welcoming my emission. The sensation of our two cocks together in the hot asshole of a beautiful man, bathed in our joint loads, was as wonderful as I remembered it from the time sweet young Billy and I shared the same thrill inside a happy and satisfied Phil. Remembering the wonder of Billy's and Phil's cocks filling my ass simultaneously, I yearned to take Steve and Mark inside me at the same time, but I knew that the huge girth of Steve's shaft precluded that, so I settled for taking loads from the two brothers' pricks in succession that morning.

Steve, as he left, promised to get back to Dowd soon, and often. He and Mark were thrilled to have finally realized their sexual dreams in this special way, and looked forward to getting together again soon – but again at my house, and involving me as a full partner. And they were as good as their word; many times after that – not chronicled in these pages – Steve and Mark and I shared our cocks, our bodies, and our love in my bed.

They swore they would refrain from sex with each other when they would be together back home in Pennsylvania, where Steve's wife and son would merit his full attention, and that there they would strictly maintain the normal brotherly relationship they had always known. They were to break this vow often, however. They both told me later of many, many occasions where they locked themselves in the room they shared growing up and satisfied their sexual love for each other. Who could possibly blame them?

Rather than detracting in any way from the intimacy of Mark's and my relationship, the opening up to Steve seemed to bring Mark even closer to me. After that, he rarely slept in the dormitory, and the intensity of our sex life and the tenderness of our union diminished not a bit – it grew, if anything, as we spent almost every night sleeping in each other's arms. Each time, following frequent threesomes with the incredible stud Dean, and other multiple-partner sexual escapades we were soon to experience, Mark was invariably as loving and attentive to me as anyone could possibly have wished. Even in the midst of our sexual tangles with Dean, or Cary, or Mike, or any combination of those wonderful, sexy guys, Mark would make it a point to let me know, by touch, or word, or look, that we were a pair of lovers sharing this excitement. We had wonderful sexual fun with others, sharing our bodies and cocks, and although we did feel a special bond with Dean when we made three-way love with him, we saved our really tender affection for each other – and the most satisfying sex was when Mark's beautiful cock drove into me and his wonderful cum flooded my mouth or my ass, or when he proved the devoted receptacle for my own cock and my own cum.

16. DEAN ORCHESTRATES A LOVE-FEAST

Dean came out to my house a few days following Steve's visit, and Mark and I told him all the details of our happy and satisfying encounter with Steve. Dean was especially fascinated by the double-fuck Mark and I had given Steve – as he also was when I told him of my own experiences with Billy and Phil's cocks invading me at the same time.

"I'd really like to try that, I think. It sounds hot as hell."

"You mean double-fucking, or getting two cocks up your ass at the same time?"

"The idea of feeling another cock next to yours while you have it up a guy's ass, rubbing against it and shooting cum on it while you fuck. Man that does sound fantastic. Yeah, I'd love to do that, but I was thinking of getting fucked by two guys at once."

"Well, Mark and I practiced on Steve just a few days ago, we'd be glad to give you a demonstration."

"Great ... then maybe Mark and I can double-fuck you."

I laughed. "I'd love to try it, but I don't know ... just your cock alone is a real assful, Dean."

"Well, we can try!" I agreed we could. He snickered, "Maybe we can get Eddie back here and you can take him and me both at the same time."

"Jesus, wouldn't that be something ... the two biggest cocks I've ever had. You'd split me completely in two."

"I know what you mean. Eddie's cock alone feels as big as two when he fucks you, doesn't it?"

"It sure does, but you don't miss Eddie's size by an awful lot, Dean."

Mark spoke up. "I've only heard about how big Eddie is, but speaking for myself, Dean, your cock is ... like John said ... a real assful."

"Yeah, but you love it, don't you?" Mark agreed Dean's cock in his ass was a real treat. And Dean promised to provide him that very same treat very soon, but first he wanted to try getting double fucked.

Mark and I were more than happy to oblige. I lay on my back as Dean settled down over my cock and began to ride joyfully. He leaned over to kiss me as Mark added his cock to mine in Dean's hot ass. Dean apparently suffered no pain, at all. Rather he expressed huge delight in the feel of Mark's entry. "My God, it feels like I'm getting the biggest prick in the world up my ass ... even Eddie's ass-reamer never felt this good. Jesus, guys, fill me up!"

We happily complied with Dean's request, double-fucking his hungry asshole for a very long time, and shortly after Mark's hot cum boiled out and bathed my cock inside our appreciative host, my own emission erupted, and together we continued to slosh around inside this sexual demigod – this voracious and delicious high school stud – as he moaned in ecstasy and finally raised up to shoot five or six huge spurts of hot cum all over my chest, my face, my pillow, and even the headboard of the bed.

After we had rested, Dean was very eager to try double-fucking me, and as I rode his huge prick, Mark barely managed to squeeze his beautiful shaft in alongside the massive rod that Dean was driving into me so masterfully. It was painful, but when the two magnificent young men fucked me savagely and exploded their precious hot loads in my appreciative receptacle, I was as ecstatic as Dean had been earlier when Mark and I filled his hungry hole with our combined offering.

Although he had cum twice, Dean had not yet fucked Mark as promised, so Mark stood next to the bed, his perfect little ass extended backward, and Dean stood behind him to drive his still hard, stunning cock violently in and out of my lover's writhing ass. As he reveled in the fuck Dean was giving him, Mark asked me to stand on the bed, and he sucked a load from my cock at almost the exact moment Dean erupted inside him.

Following sex, Dean began to think ahead to the pairing of Mark and Cary we were so eager to watch. "Man, I'd love to get them to fuck my ass together. Imagine being fucked simultaneously by the two most beautiful guys you know. Are you game, Mark, if Cary is?"

I laughed. "Look, Dean, why don't you just plan out a whole evening with Cary and Mike and us ... I'm sure you'll come up with great ideas, and I feel confident Cary and Mike will agree. You will, won't you Mark?"

"Absolutely. I'd be happy to do whatever any guy has planned if he looks as good as Dean, has that big a cock, and fucks like he does."

Dean kissed Mark and me and grinned. "Okay! For sure, we're gonna start out watching Cary and Mark kiss and grope and suck each other's cocks. I'll think of a good way to follow it up."

"That's gonna be a hard act to follow, though," I said.

"It sure will, but every act that follows will be a hard act ... meaning everybody's prick's gonna be hard as hell. Mine's hard again just thinking about it." Mark agreed his cock was also hard again thinking about holding the beautiful Cary in his arms, and I agreed my cock was hard again just thinking about the coupling of such a perfect pair.

We were all hard, but since Mark and I had each cum twice that evening, and Dean had shot three huge loads, we went to sleep, and settled for a three-way blow job the next morning before we all had to get to school.

The night we all anticipated, when we could watch Cary and Mark make love as the opening act of Dean's master plan, had to be delayed until after Thanksgiving vacation. For that holiday, Mike, Cary, and Mark went to their respective homes. I learned later that Mike and Cary met in a barn halfway between their home towns for hot sex early Thanksgiving morning, and Mark and Steve fucked each other silly in their childhood room while Steve's wife helped their mother fix Thanksgiving dinner and his son watched television in the family room. Dean was left in town, though, and he and I spent most of the vacation in my bed – for which I was appropriately thankful. Even Thanksgiving morning he found time to come by and give me some special stuffing with his magnificent wishbone.

It was at 6:00 on a Friday evening at the very end of November when Mike and Cary arrived at my house. Oddly, neither Cary nor Mike had met Mark yet, although they had certainly heard a great deal about him. I introduced Mark to them, and we all eagerly discussed the five-way festivities Dean had planned. Dean was already there, having spent the entire afternoon preparing dinner, setting the table with my best crystal and silver, chilling champagne and arranging flowers and candles, etc. For a high-school boy, and a particularly manly one at that, he was doing an extremely capable job. He wouldn't even let Mark and me help; he said this was his evening to plan, and we were going to start it off like complete gentlemen. He grinned as he added, putting one hand on Cary's shoulder, and another on Mark's, "And then we're going to watch the two most gorgeous guys I know make love to each other. Later we're all gonna fuck each other's brains out like complete maniacs."

We all wore suits or sport coats with ties, as Dean had requested, and the conversation at dinner was as civilized as the occasion itself. Dean seemed to be orchestrating our dinner conversation as he had already, I felt sure, orchestrated the orgy that was to follow. I was quite impressed with Dean's ability to stimulate intelligent discussion among five guys who sat there with the full knowledge that they would shortly be fucking and sucking each other in all sorts of interesting ways, according to Dean's master plan – which, he assured me, was inspired.

Following dinner, we retired to the living room, and Dean poured brandy for all. He took the brandy bottle back to the kitchen. When he returned, he was stark naked, and his huge prick hung down half-hard over his magnificent balls. "Would you gentlemen like to get comfortable, too?" he inquired in an ever-so-cultured tone. "Mr. Adams and Mr. Sharp," he referred to Cary and Mike, of course, "You may disrobe in the guest room. Dr. Harrison and Mr. Hagood, you may avail yourselves of the master bedroom." Then he grinned, "And come back with those hot cocks hard and ready, guys." We all went to strip, while Dean spread a couple of blankets on the living room floor, between the lighted fireplace and the sofa. As we returned, Dean welcomed each of us by kneeling and briefly sucking each cock and announcing, variously, "Ah, Dr. Harrison, I taste! Do have a seat!" "Mr. Adams, your cock tastes delightful this evening. Please join Dr. Harrison." Mr. Hagood and Mr. Sharp were greeted in like style.

After we were all seated, Dean extended his hands to Mark and Cary. "Mr. Hagood, Mr. Adams, if you would be so good as to join each other here in front of the fireplace, I will join Dr. Harrison and Mr. Sharp as we sip our brandy." He put one arm around Cary's waist and the other around Mark's, then got serious. "We all want to watch the two most beautiful men we've ever seen make love to each other." He kissed each. "You're on your own. Just enjoy each other and let us share in it by watching. Here's the only part of it I want you to do for the rest of us: When you're ready to cum, I want you to suck each other off and keep the cum in your mouths. Don't swallow it. I've got a bowl here, and we're all going to contribute to it and share our five loads together. Take all the time you want ... the more the better. You two are perfect. Just worship each other."

There was absolutely no frivolity on anyone's part as Cary and Mark made love. The two young men were so beautiful and thrilling together that Dean and Mike and I watched in rapt appreciation of their physical perfection. There was a near religious, ceremonial feeling about the coupling; you could even sense that Mark and Cary were, as Dean had enjoined them, worshipping each other rather than just having sex. As a result, we even kept our hands to ourselves, although each of us was frequently stroking his own cock.

To begin their lovemaking, Cary extended his hands and put them on Mark's shoulders. He drew him in and planted a slow, very chaste kiss on his lips. As he did so, Mark's hands found Cary's waist, and as their kiss grew more impassioned, their arms went around each other, and they pressed their bodies together. They stopped kissing several times to look into each other's eyes. Mark whispered, "Jesus, Cary ... you're beautiful!"

Cary stepped back, still looking into Mark's eyes. "I've never seen anyone I thought was more beautiful than you, Mark." He knelt, and fixed his gaze on Mark's prick, standing straight out and throbbing, looking even bigger than I had ever remembered seeing it. "Give me your cock!" He opened his mouth as Mark looked down, took Cary's head in his hands, and stepped in to slowly drive his cock all the way into the eager mouth awaiting it. Cary's hands came up and held Mark's rounded asscheeks, which began to undulate and drive his prick in a slow, but very deep mouth-fuck. Both expressed their delight with murmurs of ecstasy.

Cary sucked Mark for a long time, while Mark's hands explored the former's head and upper body. Cary also licked Mark's cock slowly and very sensually, then licked his balls and took them in his mouth to suck. He licked Mark's body very nearly everywhere, in fact, spending considerable time sucking his nipples, and then after a particularly impassioned ball-sucking, he ducked between Mark's legs and buried his face between the two golden, rounded globes of my lover's perfect ass. Mark's hands went behind him and pulled Cary's face in to him as he murmured, "Jesus, yes. Fuck my ass with that hot tongue!" As Mark leaned forward, Cary's head burrowed in and rimmed frantically while his hands explored Mark's legs and stomach and chest.

Finally, Mark straightened up and turned around. He raised Cary to his feet and the two again held each other tightly and kissed for a long time. This time, however, the kissing was much more passionate, and their hands feverishly

168

explored each other. With a cry of "Eat my cock!" Cary pushed Mark's head down roughly, and forced his mouth onto his prick. He leaned over and cradled Mark's head in his arms as his perfect ass drove his cock in a savage mouth-fuck. Mark played with Cary's impressive tits and he moaned with passion as Cary's ass undulated wildly. He panted, "Eat it, baby! God, I love fucking your mouth!"

Mark pulled away from Cary's prick, which bobbed and throbbed in front of him. He looked up at Cary and whispered, "I wanna eat your ass." Cary turned around and leaned over, using his hands to spread his asscheeks as far apart as he could; Mark plunged his face in, and his muffled cries of delight seemed to indicate he was enjoying himself as much as the blond Adonis, whose head was thrown back and whose eyes were closed while his perfect face mirrored the rapture his groans of passion evidenced.

Mark finally stopped eating Cary's ass, reversed Cary's body, and took his balls in his mouth, licking and sucking them feverishly. Cary's head was still thrown back in ecstasy, but he eventually looked down at his prick sliding back and forth over Mark's face as Mark continued to suck his balls. He disengaged himself and pushed Mark to the floor, where he fell on top of him, and the two locked themselves in each other's arms, kissing and groping frantically. They were only a few feet from Dean and Mike and me, and we all stroked our cocks more rapidly as we watched the two gorgeous lovemakers explore each other's bodies with eager hands. They continued to kiss as they caressed asses, put their hands between each other's legs to drive their fingers up each other's assholes, wrapped their legs around each other's waists, and all the time moaned in ecstatic passion.

Cary reversed his body, and they rolled on their sides in the sixty-nine position. Each looked lovingly at the other's prick before opening his mouth to suck. They mutually sucked balls, and rolled in an especially tight sixty-nine to tongue-fuck each other's assholes at the same time. They had been mutually sucking cock again for some time when Cary looked up and said, "Dean, you'd better get your bowl ready. I'm gonna blow my load in a minute."

Mark stopped sucking and spoke around Cary's driving prick: "I'm ready, too. Give me your load, Cary!" They sealed their mouths around each other's pricks and the two perfect asses drove in frenzy as their moans signaled the approach of their orgasms. Soon Cary's ass froze with his cock deep in Mark's mouth, and the violence of his moaning indicated he was shooting his load in the adoring receptacle. It was only a moment later that Mark obviously delivered his offering to Cary. They both lay locked in embrace, their asses now slowly and gently continuing to drive their cocks.

Cary and Mark both savored the loads of cum they held in their mouths for some time before Mark rose on one arm and held out a hand to take the small cereal bowl Dean was offering. He let Cary's cum slowly drip from his mouth into the bowl, and then grinned up at all of us. "Quite a load, huh?" We all applauded. Then Cary kissed Mark, obviously transferring Mark's load into his own mouth, after which Mark again leaned over the bowl, and slowly released another generous load into it. Cary grinned as Mark did so, "And that's Mark's load ... and it was a real mouthful, guys." Again we applauded. Cary and Mark stood, grinned at each other, and kissed and hugged happily, like two cute little boys who had just done something terrific. In fact, they had!

Dean had placed a small table off to the side, and on it he had put the small heating unit that kept my coffee warm as I drank it mornings at my desk. He activated the unit, and put the cereal bowl containing Cary's and Mark's cum on it.

We all stood and refreshed our drinks. Mike put his arms around my waist as we stood at the bar, watching Dean mix drinks. His prick was huge and hard as it pressed against my own. "We sure do have a couple of beautiful lovers, don't we?" I agreed with his assessment as I kissed him and played with his tits.

Dean turned and told us, "So, you two are next on the agenda. Mark and Cary are gonna watch their lucky lovers suck each other off and add to the bowl."

"All right, sounds great!" I don't remember whether it was Mike or I who said that, but it doesn't matter. We both felt the same way.

Dean sat between Cary and Mark on the couch, and the three of them played with each other pretty freely as Mike and I performed for them. There was none of the reverence we all had felt watching the stunning beautiful team of Mark and Cary making tender and later highly impassioned love. An atmosphere of high spirits seemed to prevail as Mike and I more-or-less duplicated Cary and Mark's recent performance. Instead of hushed awe, such as had greeted Cary's deep-throating of Mark's beautiful prick, when I began to take Mike's lip-stretcher in my mouth our audience of three whistled and clapped and encouraged me to take it all. "Show us how you can take all of that huge prick down your throat, John." "What a fabulous dick, Mike ... fuck that hot mouth as hard as you can!" "What a lucky bastard you are, John ... I wish that monster cock was fucking my mouth right now." As I finally relaxed my throat enough to take every bit of Mike's mammoth shaft in my mouth, and my lips nestled in the pubic hair at the base of the enormous prick, Mike grabbed my head and fucked for all he was worth, while Dean, Cary and Mark continued their raucous and enthusiastic endorsement.

Mike took every bit of my cock in his mouth in one gulp, and as his tight lips drove frantically up and down my cock – almost pulling away with the back stroke, and sinking into my pubic hair with the forward – his efforts received similar audience approval. Mike and I felt free to indulge our passion by loudly encouraging each other as we had done so many times in private. "Suck my balls!" "Fuck my ass with that hot tongue!" "Stick your fingers all the way in me!" and the like. Once we finally began sucking each other's cocks in a serious, and obviously climax-bound sixty-nine, things got quiet, and when it became clear that I had shot my load into Mike's worshipping mouth, and his very copious emission had filled mine, I heard Dean whisper, "All right!" and either Mark or Cary said "God damn that was hot," in equally hushed tones.

After lying together savoring the huge loads we kept in our mouths, Mike and I stood. Dean extended the bowl containing Mark and Cary's cum to me. Rather than emptying Mike's load into it, I walked over to Cary and kissed him. As he opened his lips, I squirted Mike's cum into his mouth and whispered, "Put your lover's load in the bowl." Mike, seeing what I had done, deposited my load in Mark's mouth and bade him do the same. Together, Cary and Mark let Mike's and my cum drip from their mouths into the bowl, after which they grinned and kissed.

"That was a really great touch guys ... I hadn't thought of that," Dean said. He kissed Cary, and then Mark, very passionately, declaring he could taste cum on both of their tongues; he then did the same with Mike and me, and declared the same delightful taste still lingered in our mouths.

I asked Dean, "So how are we gonna fill this bowl with your big load before we get to share it?"

Dean laughed. "Okay, you four guys kneel right next to each other there, and I'm coming down the line fucking your mouths. Each of you do your best to deep-throat me and suck my cum out when my cock's in you. I don't know who's gonna get it ... this is really a new kind of Russian Roulette. Whoever gets it, save it for the bowl."

Mike was the first to get on his knees, declaring he was going to do his best to be the lucky one, and the rest of us joined him enthusiastically. Our bodies were very close together as Dean started fucking our mouths. He grabbed Mike's head, shoved his huge prick deep into his mouth, and fucked savagely. Mike sucked and moaned as he feasted on Dean's enormous prick. Then, after a few minutes, Dean grabbed my head and transferred his monster to my mouth, and he fucked me wildly for another short time while I sucked as deeply and as hard as I could. Cary got the treatment next, and then Mark, and then he began fucking Mike's mouth again. In all, Dean fucked our mouths through about three entire rotations, and the three of us who were not sucking prick at any given moment were shouting encouragement to both cocksucker and the magnificent cocksuckee.

Finally, as Cary was sucking the huge, magnificent shaft, Dean began to pant and said, "Here it comes!" He drove himself deep into Cary's mouth and the lucky blond beauty gurgled with joy as he received the love offering. In just a few seconds, though, Dean pulled out and rapidly drove his cock into my mouth to finish his orgasm – violently splattering a huge spurt of cum on my face before he got his cock in my mouth – and then exploding another two or three spurts deep in my hungry throat. He finished cumming in my mouth, holding my head tightly and still driving his huge prick, but more slowly now.

He then moved over and put his cock in Mike's mouth. "Help clean it off." As Mike sucked happily, Mark said, "Don't forget me." Dean's cock was softening, but still huge, as he removed it from Mike and moved over to treat Mark with it. "That was fantastic, guys."

I moved on my knees over to Mark, and kissed him, giving him Dean's cum. Cary followed suit, and delivered his portion to Mike. I then stood and told Dean to lick his cum off my face. As he did so, I told Mark and Cary to return all of Dean's cum to him, and let him put it in the bowl with ours. Both Mark and Cary kissed Dean and transferred cum, and finally Dean leaned over the bowl, and all of his enormous load dripped into it, mingling with ours, constituting a considerable deposit of semen for us to share.

Dean got on his knees and asked us to kneel with him in a circle. With his forefinger, he ceremoniously stirred the contents of the bowl, still as warm as it had been when it had originally been produced. "This is the evidence of our love guys, this is for all of us to share, like we share our cocks and our asses and our kisses and our bodies with each other. This is all of us together at once. This is our love, share it with me evenly." He put his face over the bowl, and lapped up enough cum to coat his tongue. He swallowed it and smiled. "God I love this!" He passed the bowl to Mike, who followed suit. Each of us had several laps of our joint orgasm before it was gone, and we all watched as each cum-coated tongue returned to the loving mouth to be cleansed inside as its coating was appreciatively ingested.

Any five-way kiss is bound to be somewhat awkward, but we managed pretty well, nonetheless, with our arms around each other, and our heads pressed together as we shared our mutual love and passion. And so the solemnity of our special sexual communion service came to an end, and what happened after that was the kind of joyous and savage sex we normally practiced.

"Are you still directing this thing, Dean, or are we free to grab anybody's cock we want now?" I asked.

Dean grinned. "Shit no, I've got big plans. First thing, though, we rest for a while. We're gonna need it ... nobody's shot his last load for tonight yet." We all agreed that a rest was in order, and relaxed and chatted about all sorts of things before it became obvious the sap was stirring in our eager cocks again.

Dean stood, with his huge cock standing straight out from his magnificent body, and addressed us. "I guess you notice nobody's got fucked yet, tonight. That's about to change ... in a really different way. We're gonna do something really neat next. Cary, lie down on your back and get that pretty cock standing straight up while I settle down on it." Cary grinned, and lay on his back as instructed. His muscular body looked perfect as with one hand he held his steely hard prick straight up. Dean knelt over Cary's waist, facing him. He leaned down and kissed him and said, "I want you to fuck my hot ass, Cary." He positioned his asshole over the end of Cary's cock, and began to settle down. As the beautiful, muscular blond's prick disappeared into Dean's ass, he began to hump upwards. Dean bounced slowly on the invading prick, grinning and murmuring his appreciation – and Cary was obviously enjoying it as well, holding Dean's waist, and gasping "Take my prick, you fuckin' stud!" As Cary's ass lifted off the floor to meet the undulating and rotating ass he was fucking, Dean looked at us and grinned. "How does it look guys?" We all agreed it looked wonderful.

Dean pressed Cary's humping body to the floor, and seated his ass firmly down on it. He leaned forward, his face only inches from Cary's as he said, over his shoulder, "Mark, get over here."

Mark stood and approached them, laughing, "I was willing to bet I was going to join in about this time." He knelt in front of Dean and kissed him. "And I'll bet I know exactly what you want me to do."

Dean took Mark's head in his hands and planted a very long, very serious kiss on my lover. "Of course you know what to do ... fill me up!" He leaned farther forward, raising his ass enough for us all to see Cary's prick buried in it, and Cary spread his legs wide, while Mark knelt between them, facing Dean's back.

Mark greased his cock generously, lay it alongside Cary's, and began to penetrate Dean's asshole. Cary cried out, "We're both gonna fuck him?"

Dean smiled down at Cary. "You bet you're both gonna fuck me. I want to have two most beautiful guys I know plowing my ass at the same time. Okay with you?"

"You're damned right it's okay with me. Let me feel that fine prick of yours next to me in this hot hole, Mark. We'll fuck him like champs." Mark's cock had been slowly entering, and now he drove it all the way to the hilt, taking Cary's cock with him. The two Adonises had their cocks buried completely in the fabulous Dean.

They began to moan as they worked together, encouraging each other to fuck deep and slow, and telling each other how wonderful their pricks felt together. Dean loudly voiced his delight at the masterful double-fuck he was experiencing, and as his passionate enjoyment of Cary and Mark's efforts increased, he looked over at Mike and me – still sitting on the couch, watching the exciting spectacle with very hard cocks. Mike had been playing with my prick and asking me quietly if Mark and I had done this before with Dean. I assured him we had, and that I'd taken Dean and Mark inside me the same way. Dean grinned at us. "Okay, both of you guys over here. I want two cocks to suck while I get fucked with two other cocks." Mike and I went to stand in front of Dean. Dean reached out and took Mike's balls in one hand and mine in another. "Shove the huge prick of yours in my mouth, Mike, and get your big one in there with it, John. I've never seriously tried to suck two cocks at once, but I'm gonna do my best. I'm gonna have four hot pricks fucking me at the same time!"

Dean's mouth opened very wide, and Mike and I each put one arm around the other's waist, held Dean's head in one hand, and joined our pricks inside Dean's mouth. We got more prick inside than I would have thought possible, and Dean actually did a rather creditable job of providing suction as we moved our pricks together to fuck his adoring mouth. Mike and I kissed a lot; Dean's hands left our balls and went between our legs to finger fuck our asses (I assume he was doing the same thing to Mike he was doing to me). The insatiable stud – who, it seemed hard to believe, was still a high school student – managed to suck and get fucked by all four of us at once.

Mike and I never came really close to cumming – certainly I didn't – before Cary called out, "I'm gonna get my load. Shove your prick all the way in and leave it Mark; I'm gonna drown it in cum!" Cary cried out in passion as he discharged and both Mark and Dean added their cries of delight at the force of his orgasm.

Dean panted around a mouth filled with two dicks, "Fuck, but that was great, Cary. Give me more cum, Mark!" Mark began to fuck violently, holding Dean's waist tightly. With a loud cry he drove his ass up against Dean, as his arms went all the way around. "Here it is … here's my load!" Dean and Cary both marveled at the wonderful feeling as my lover added his offering.

Dean released our cocks from his mouth and grinned up at us. "Guess who's next?"

Mike leaned over and kissed Dean. "I love it! Come on, John, let's get our cocks in there while Cary and Mark's loads are still hot." Dean rose up, and Cary and Mark's cocks slipped out of him. Cary rolled out from under Dean, and I replaced him. Mike replaced Mark, and Dean lowered his asshole over my cock; it felt wonderful: hot as it could possibly be, and filled with wonderful, slimy, red-hot cum, some of which trickled out of his ass and down my prick. Cary and Mark went to clean off their cocks, since Dean told him they were, predictably, going to fuck his mouth while Mike and I serviced his ass.

"Come on in Mike, the cum's fine," I said, and soon I felt his enormous prick beginning to insinuate itself inside Dean, sliding along my own. No lubrication was necessary, between the lube left from Cary and Mark, and the natural lubrication of two hot loads.

Dean cried out as Mike entered him, "God damn your prick is big, Mike!" Mike offered to stop, but Dean assured him he wanted every inch of his monster tool all the way inside him along with my prick. We all three worked together, and by the time Cary and Mark returned to fill Dean's mouth with their cocks, Mike and I were happily fucking Dean's hungry and more-than-willing ass.

Mike and I several times slowed down, and even stopped for a few moments, to prolong the time until orgasm. Eventually, we could hold it back no longer, and we discharged into Dean almost simultaneously. As we continued to penetrate and withdraw from Dean's twitching asshole, cum was dripping down our pricks, and the squishing sound of our fucking was clearly audible.

174

Dean rose up, so Mike and I could slip out, and fell on his back, next to me. I knelt between his legs and raised them high in the air, plunging my face into his ass and putting my tongue deep into his asshole. "This is more exciting than getting it from a cereal bowl!" They all laughed, and Mike, Cary, and Mark all joined me in sampling the plentiful lotion in Dean's ass.

We all sort of sprawled on the floor for a while, resting our heads on each other's bodies, and remarking on how hot our most recent exercise had been. It occurred to me that Dean had – very uncharacteristically – fucked no one yet. "So, Dean ... who's gonna be the lucky one to get your monster cock up his ass? I'm sure you have a plan."

Dean sat up. "Sure I've got a plan, and if it takes me all night, I'm gonna do it."

"We're waiting."

"I'm gonna fuck each one of you, and shoot a load in each ass."

"Four loads?"

I laughed. "If anyone can do it, Dean can. Okay, stud ... just plain fucking, or what?"

"Just plain fucking, But ... the other three guys are gonna be busy while I fuck. Here's the deal: the guy I'm fucking is going to be kneeling over another guy, and they're gonna be sucking each other's cocks while I fuck; another guy is gonna be eating my ass while I fuck; and the last guy is gonna be standing in front of me so I can suck his cock while I fuck."

"Wow, you really do have it planned ... and it sounds fantastic. We all agreed it was a fine plan, and hopefully the gratification Dean was going to be experiencing would inspire him to produce four especially big and hard loads for our four eager butts. "Who gets to do what?"

"You guys can change around, or do it however you want ... I just wanna have my cock up the ass of a guy who's sucking a cock while he gets his own sucked, and I wanna feel a hot tongue fucking my ass, and a hot cock fucking my mouth. Cary kneel down and get ready for my cock up your ass; you get fucked first, because this is gonna be alphabetical ... Adams, Hagood, Harrison, and Sharp get fucked in that order."

"That's the most complicated plan I ever heard in my life," I said.

Dean laughed, "Yeah, but what do you think of it?" We all agreed it was an absolutely flawless, wonderful, irresistible plan ... and we looked forward to following it scrupulously.

"And," Dean added – standing, grinning, and holding his hugely erect prick out for us to admire – "No Russian Roulette this time. I promise each one of you guys is gonna get a full Dean Williamson load of cum up your butt, shot out of this big ol' Dean Williamson monster cock. Satisfaction is guaranteed, gentlemen ... biggest cock around, hottest load you could ask for! I think everybody should salute this baby before it goes to work." He walked over to me, and his cock was in my face. I kissed the head of it, and he shoved it in my mouth and fucked for a few seconds before withdrawing it and moving to Mike, who received the same quick mouth-fuck. Mark's mouth closed over Dean's throbbing monster for a few minutes before the beautiful shaft moved on to lodge in Cary's mouth. As he fucked Cary's mouth, Dean said, "Get on your knees, baby, I want to fill your beautiful ass with my load."

Cary stood and kissed Dean, then knelt on the blanket and wiggled his perfect ass. "I can't wait to take it, Dean. Fuck me as hard as you can."

I quickly moved so that I was lying on my back under Cary, with his prick hanging down into my mouth, and mine standing up to be taken in his. I could see Mark lying on his stomach behind Dean, and burying his face between the cheeks of his ass. Dean panted, "Oh yeah, Mark, eat my ass!" Mike had straddled Cary's body and offered his huge cock for Dean's worship.

Cary was not yet sucking my prick, but was eagerly imploring Dean to shove his prick up his ass. I sucked Cary eagerly, however, as I watched Dean's huge cock. glistening with lubricant, poise at Cary's asshole. Cary began to back up to Dean as Dean moved forward, and soon his monster shaft entered the tight chamber of Cary's perfect ass. I watched Cary's ass-ring ride the stupendous invading prick, back and forth, as Dean began to fuck slowly, but very deeply – his prick almost emerging on the backstroke, and disappearing entirely into Cary on the forward. Cary's cries indicated he was in heaven, until he cut them short when his mouth engulfed my cock and his tight lips began to ride it all the way up and down as he sucked fiercely. I watched in awe as the vast length of Dean's prick entered and left Cary's ass – a sight as beautiful as it was exciting.

I alternated sucking Cary's prick and his balls (as he did with mine), and I frequently licked and sucked Dean's huge balls as he fucked, also licking the massive shaft of his prick as it was presented to my sight and my tongue. The beautiful tool seemed endlessly long as it slowly slid in – and in – and into, and slowly pulled out – and out – and out of the beautiful blond's beautiful ass.

Dean's fucking technique was masterful. He prolonged the thrill of his service to Cary's ass – fucking very fast and hard and deep for a few minutes, then reverting to the slow, sensuous pace that had marked the beginning of his fuck – until Cary was almost screaming with passion. "God damn, Dean, I want your cum ... shove it all the way in and give me your big load. Blow it in me like only you can." His ass was extended as far back as he could put it, and finally Dean drove himself savagely all the way in, his balls swinging back and forth as he delivered very rapid, short strokes. He rotated his hips to stimulate Cary's ass even further, and delivered his load to the frantic beauty he was fucking so perfectly.

"Here it is for you Cary, take it, baby! Aaaaaaaahhh!"

"Oh Jesus, Dean, what a load ... what a fucking man you are! God, you're exploding in me! Oh, man, I love your fuckin' cock!"

Dean fell on top of Cary, "Man, I love your ass, Cary ... you are a great fuck! You're so fuckin' beautiful, and your ass is so fuckin' hot and tight! Jesus, Mike, you're unbelievably lucky to have this ass to fuck every night."

I saw Mike's arms go around Dean, and they apparently kissed before Mike said, "Believe me I know how lucky I am." His hand came into view, and cupped Dean's balls, whose cock was still completely buried in Cary. He squeezed and kneaded them. "And tonight Cary's lucky to get fucked by such a great fucker ... and I'm dying to get you inside me, too."

"Believe me, I'm gonna fill your hot ass just like I did Cary's."

Mark's arms appeared around Dean's waist. "Yeah, but I'm next in the alphabet. I get the next load, and my ass is twitching, just thinking about it."

Dean laughed. "Right. Cary, I really hate to pull out. I'd love to stay right inside and just start fucking you all over again, but Mark's name is on the next load." His cock gradually emerged from Cary's asshole, still huge and hard, and actually dripping with his cum. He stood and stretched – his prick standing straight out, covered with his cum, and looking incredibly hot. He held out his hands to Mark. "If this looks as good to you as your pretty ass looks to me, you're gonna have a fine time."

Mark knelt and looked up at me. "Will you sixty-nine with me while Dean fucks me, too?" He turned his attention to Dean, and gently took hold of the young master-fucker's cock. "I'd really to have my lover's prick in my mouth when I take that beautiful big monster of yours up my ass. Is that okay with everybody?"

Dean smiled. "I'd be happy to keep sucking that huge cock of yours, too, Mike ... it's really terrific! You want to eat out my ass while I fuck Mark, Cary?"

Cary moved in and planted a deep kiss on Dean's lips. "I'd love to do something nice for your ass, after what you just did for mine."

"Great!" Dean knelt behind Mark as I positioned myself under him. He caressed Mark's perfect ass. "Man, this is beautiful." He leaned over and licked Mark's asshole before burying his face in it. He tongue-fucked Mark for a few minutes, and then began to fuck him with first one, then two fingers. "I love fucking this gorgeous baby." Dean was, of course, a couple of years younger than the baby he was admiring, but the incomparable shaft of throbbing cock that protruded from his groin suggested a maturity well beyond his actual age. The masterful way he employed it only added to the effect.

Mark took a gob of Vaseline, greased up his ass, and began fucking himself with his forefinger. "Give it all to me, Dean. Shove it in me as deep as only you can."

"You've got it, Mark," Dean said, as he bent down to kiss Mark's ear. I watched as he put the head of his huge cock against Mark's asshole, and with one fierce thrust, drove himself deep into my lover. "Take every fucking inch of my big prick!" Mark cried out in pain as Dean's cock thrust home, but soon his cries turned to passionate encouragement of the magnificent young stud. His ass drove backwards to meet Dean's thrusts, and his hands went behind him to pull Dean's ass in. Dean's hands feverishly played over the twin globes of Mark's perfect ass as he fucked savagely. I watched from below, my eyes only a few inches away from this truly wondrous sight. Dean's huge balls were slapping against Cary's ass as he drove in, and brushing over my forehead with each stroke.

Mark was almost screaming, "Fuck me, Dean, fuck me!" while Dean cried out "Give me your ass, Mark, your wonderful, hot ass. I wanna blow a huge load in this beautiful ass!"

Their frenzied fuck lasted a long time. Dean had just a few minutes earlier shot a monster load in Cary, of course, so it took him longer than usual to reach climax. But it was a magnificent, awe-inspiring time. His thrusts were deep and fiercely hard. His strokes repeated with almost unbelievable speed, considering that almost the entire length of his epic prick was traveling in and out of Mark's hungry chute. The force of their fucking and their frenzied cries had us all cheering them on. Finally, with a thrust so hard he collapsed Mark's body on top of mine, Dean drove his prick all the way inside Mark, and I could see his ass shudder as he cried, "Take it baby ... take my big fuckin' load!"

Mark's ass 'worked' Dean's cock deeply – his perfect asscheeks pinching in and out around the invading shaft. "God, Dean, what a fucker you are. Your load shot in me like a bullet! Keep cumming, keep loving me!" Dean continued to fuck, and Mark continued to use the muscles of his cheeks to drain the monster prick.

They eventually calmed down. Dean pulled his still-hard prick out of Mark, and rolled him off me and onto his back. Mark spread his legs and raised them to encircle Dean's waist; Dean drove his prick back into Mark's asshole. "I've gotta save my next load for John, but let me fuck your hot ass for just a little bit more." He leaned over and Mark's arms went around him. They kissed with intense passion as Dean continued to fuck gently, but still with very long strokes. Dean's ass, as he fucked, was a truly beautiful sight – driving, revolving, undulating – with his asshole appearing and disappearing as his cheeks separated and met with each penetration of my lover.

By this time Mike and Cary and I were simply kneeling around the pair and watching in awe as they continued their frantic kissing. Dean picked up the pace, and was once again fucking Mark in earnest. Mike whispered, "God, what an incredible stud you are, Dean."

Dean stopped kissing Mark and grinned over his shoulder at Mike. "Wait until I get this prick up your hot ass ... you're gonna think stud!" He turned back and looked down at Mark. "Have a good time, Mark?"

"The fuck of a lifetime, Dean ... I wish it could go on all night."

I laughed. "It seems to me like it is going on all night. Get your cock out of my lover's ass so you can stick it in mine, Dean."

Dean reluctantly drew out of Mark, after kissing him for a very long time. "You're a beautiful man, and an incredibly hot fuck, Mark. Thank you."

Dean rolled off, and flopped on his back, exhausted by the titanic fucking he had just delivered. Mark extended his arms to me. "Come here, and lie on top of me for a minute." I lay on top of my lover, my cock up against his asshole, which was dripping Dean's cum. His legs went around my body as we kissed. Very quietly he said, just for me, "You know, no matter who I fuck with, or how great a fuck it is, it's you I love, and it's your lovemaking that means the most to me."

Dean had overheard this, and propped himself up on an arm. "John, you're next on my fuck list, and I want to fuck you just as hard as I just fucked Mark, so I'm gonna need a little rest. Looks to me like you're right in position to give Mark some of that lovemaking." He snickered, "And God knows he's opened up and ready, and with all my cum inside him, you don't need to lubricate."

Mark smiled up at me. "Please?" He raised his legs, and my cock slid easily into his asshole. Our arms went around each other, and I fucked long and hard, with Mark's ass driving back against my cock with equal passion. Our three observers encouraged us vocally. At one point Dean encouraged me by eating my ass as I fucked; after he had tongue-fucked me for quite a while, he put two or three fingers inside my ass and fucked me with them in counterpoint to my thrusts into Mark. He whispered into my ear as he drove his fingers deep into me, "Gotta get that hot ass ready for the wild fuck I'm gonna give it."

With Dean's fingers deep in my ass, and Mark's legs locked tightly around my waist, I delivered my load into my lover's ass as he worked my cock with it. We both gasped our excitement and love as I did so.

As I lay on top of Mark, my cock still planted inside him, Dean said, "You know, this whole thing started because we wanted to see Cary and Mark make love with each other. Well, we've seen them suck each other off ... and Jesus, guys, that was a beautiful sight it was. But this would be a good time to see them fuck each other. What do you think?"

Mark laughed, "God yes, I'd love to fuck Cary, and have him fuck me. Hell, Mike, you better fuck me, too ... might as well get screwed by every cock here. And you know, Mike, getting screwed by that huge prick of yours is something I really don't want to miss."

Mike put his hand on my shoulder, and knelt next to me. "Okay, John?"

"Sure, Mike. Mark wants it ... understandably ... and we'll all enjoy watching. We can watch Cary and Mark fuck each other as a grand finale."

Dean laughed, "No way ... the grand finale is when I fill John and Mike's asses with cum. This is the intermission ... but I can't think of a better way to end that than watching Cary and Mark screw!"

I moved aside, and Mark's legs went in the air again. The crevice of his ass was coated with cum, and his asshole dripped with it as Mike knelt and Mark raised his ass to accept Mike's monster cock, which entered easily. Mark's arms went around Mike. "Yeah ... fuck me, Mike. I've been dying to get your huge prick in me since I first saw it when you walked out of the bedroom tonight. Jesus, it feels good."

"Your ass is beautiful, Mark ... hell, you're beautiful ... and it's so hot and full of cum. And it really feels tight, too."

"I don't know how it could be tight after Dean slammed that ass-reamer of his in me so long and so hard," Mark said.

Dean broke in, "Fuckin' right it was long and hard!"

"No shit," Mark laughed "And John gave me a great pounding, too. But I'm glad you like my ass, Mike. If it feels tight, it's just because your cock is so big and fat." Mike's ass began to grind and hump as he started to fuck Mark seriously. Mark gasped, "And it's mighty goddamn long, too, Mike. Give it to me as deep and as hard as you can!" And Mike fucked hard indeed.

Mark's legs were wrapped tightly around his fucker's waist, his ass savagely driving backwards to meet Mike's thrusts, their bodies slapping together, their arms tightly around each other as they kissed hungrily. Mike's ass looked magnificent as he fucked between the beautiful parentheses of Mark's legs, and judging by its movement – with the cheeks clamped together on the inward thrust, and spread wide apart as he reached the maximum withdrawal – he was giving Mark the very considerable maximum stroke possible, his prick no doubt driving about nine inches with each stroke. They fucked fiercely, clearly reminiscent of the savage fucking Dean had just given Mark. It seemed like a long time, given the wildness and abandon of their coupling, before Mike approached orgasm. Once he did, he began to fuck even harder, which would almost have seemed impossible. His thrilled cries as his orgasm erupted were matched by Mark's as he felt the explosion inside him. It was obviously a truly joyous moment for both. Dean and Cary and I murmured our encouragement and appreciation.

Cary put his arms around my shoulder. "God damn, we have hot lovers, don't we?" I could not help but agree.

Mark and Mike were locked together silently for some time, still entwined, still kissing, Mike still fucking quietly and Mark's ass still thrusting gently. Finally Mike raised himself and smiled into Mark's face. "Are you ready to fuck my beautiful lover's pretty ass?"

Mark smiled back. "Oh yeah! And I'm still really anxious to get fucked by your beautiful lover's pretty prick! Why doesn't Cary fuck me before I fuck him? I've been fucked by three hot guys in a row ... I might as well go for four." He looked over at Cary and grinned. "You ready to shove that pretty dick inside a one-quart container with about two quarts of cum in it?"

Cary knelt. "I'm dying to fuck your beautiful ass! And fucking it while it's filled with Dean's and John's and Mike's loads is just gonna make it that much more exciting." Mike moved aside and Cary positioned himself between Mark's legs.

Mark's arms went around Cary. "Your prick tasted and felt so good when I sucked you off, and your load felt so wonderful when you shot it in my mouth; I know it's gonna be even better this way."

As Mark raised his legs, Cary rammed his cock into his ass and said, "What's gonna make it even better is knowing I'm gonna have that huge dick of yours up my butt afterward."

As the two began to make love, Dean told them "You guys look so perfect together. Take your time, start slow and gentle, and let us enjoy watching two unbelievably handsome men worship each other."

Mike added, "But when you get near cumming, baby, fuck like a demon ... like you do when you're plowing my ass."

Mike and Dean and I laughed, but Cary and Mark were already completely absorbed in each other. Cary fucked slowly, but deeply. His adorable, muscular bubble-butt looked magnificent as he drove his cock into Mark, and Mark countered his thrusts gently – not just lying there and getting fucked, whatever the tempo. Their lips were only an inch or so apart, but they did not kiss for some time, instead sharing rapt gazes and whispered appreciation of each other's beauty.

The three of us watched in awe and fascination as these gorgeous men enjoyed each other so thoroughly. Cary rolled them, so he was on his back, with Mark riding his cock. As Mark rode, cum trickled out of his ass and down Cary's prick, wetting the nest of golden pubic hair at its base.

Eventually the tempo picked up, of course. Mark bounced ever higher and harder on Cary's cock and Cary's upward thrusts grew frenzied, until he levered his body upward, burying his cock all the way inside Mark and froze as he delivered his load to the Adonis impaled on his prick. "Oh yeah, give it to me, baby," signaled my lover's receipt of the muscular blond beauty's discharge.

They lay locked together for some minutes, kissing, until Mark raised his face above Cary's and smiled broadly. "God you're a wonderful fuck!" he said, and Cary smiled equally and replied, "Nobody could be anything else with such an incredible fucker as you."

Cary stood. "Stand up and worship my body before you make love to it, Mark." He pulled Mark to his feet, who then knelt in front of him and began to caress Cary's ass and legs, and take his still-hard – and still cum-covered – cock deep in his throat while his hands lovingly explored his stomach and chest, and tweaked his nipples. Cary's eyes were closed as he held Mark's head and accepted the body worship his beauty so richly deserved. Mark used his hands to turn Cary's body around, and he buried his face deep between the perfect, rounded buttocks presented to him. From behind, he caressed Cary's stomach and fondled his magnificent tits while he eagerly ate his asshole. Cary answered with moans of ecstasy, as he humped and rotated his ass sensuously – his eyes still closed, his head thrown back, his mouth open, clearly lost in rapturous enjoyment of Mark's ministrations.

After a short while, Mark stood and his hard cock nestled between Cary's legs. "Somebody give me the Vaseline." He was quickly provided with the lubricant, which he applied to Cary's asshole and his own prick. "Are you ready for me, Cary?"

Cary leaned over, used his hands to spread his asscheeks wide and presented his hole. "I want you, Mark. Shove your cock all the way inside me and fuck me as hard as you can, I want you to fill me with hot cum!" He stepped a few paces forward, and leaned over to brace his hands on the arms of a chair. Mark stepped forward, took Cary's hips in his hands, positioned his cock, and savagely drove his prick inside. "That's what I want," Cary gasped. "Fuck me hard!"

Cary was crouching a bit, with his legs spread, and Mark stood between them, his legs also bent, so that as he fucked, he fucked upwards into Cary's ass; as a result of this position, the movement of Mark's ass was especially pronounced, and exciting in the extreme. The quiet awe Dean and Mike and I had displayed as Cary had begun fucking Mark was gone. We applauded and cheered, and urged Mark to fuck harder, and deeper, and faster, while Cary ecstatically urged his beautiful, passionate fucker to do the same. Mark responded with savage thrusts into Cary, and Cary cried loudly and passionately as he drove his ass down to counter the feverish invasion of my lover's driving shaft. Too soon, it was over, and Mark leaned backwards, his cock buried deep in Cary, his hands holding his waist tightly. His impassioned "Take my load, Cary!" overlapped with Cary's "Shoot me full of that hot cum, Mark!"

Mark held his arms tightly around Cary's waist. Cary stood and reached behind to pull the perfect ass in to him, the now gently-driving prick still inside. Mark bit Cary's neck and said he loved fucking with him. Cary turned his head to kiss Mark and express his total appreciation. Cary stepped away so that Mark's cock slipped out of his ass, and he turned around to enfold Mark in his arms. The two embraced and kissed for a long time, their hands lazily, but very sensually, exploring each other's bodies. Finally they turned to face their audience, and grinned.

Dean stepped up and put his arms around both of them. "That was fantastic ... you are the most gorgeous men I've ever seen." Then he turned to me. "And it made me so fucking horny I can't wait for the next guy on my list. Dr. Harrison, on your knees; you are gonna get one wild fuck!"

I stepped in to him, embraced, and kissed him, before taking hold of his very hard, very large prick. "I want you to fuck me as hard as you fucked Mark. I can hardly wait to get this beautiful monster all the way up my butt." I turned to Mike. "Get on your back; I want to suck your cock while Dean plows me, okay?"

Mike agreed happily, and lay down on his back. I knelt over him in sixty-nine position. As I took his prick in my mouth and he took mine in his, I felt Dean lubricating my asshole as he said, "That's right, Cary, eat my ass!" At the same time, Mark straddled me. Dean said, "Change of plan, Mark; turn around and bend over so I can eat your ass while I fuck your lover."

Mark laughed. "Sure! But do you know how much cum is in my ass?"

Dean laughed. "Why do you think I especially want to eat it?" With that he began to insinuate his huge prick in my ass, and we were off. Dean's cock seemed even more gargantuan than usual, and his fucking was as savage as anyone could possibly have wanted – one of the most, if not the most, exciting fucks I ever received. Having cum twice very recently, it took Dean a long time to reach orgasm – which was fine with me, since it did nothing to interfere with the ardor of his fuck, which went on – and on – and wonderfully on! Mike and I sucked each other feverishly, but I often released his cock to express my thrill at Dean's penetration, and Mike often released mine to express his admiration of Dean's expert performance, seen up-close. Having recently watched Dean fucking from exactly that same perspective, I well knew it was a thrilling sight. Still, Mike sucked hard, and before Dean filled me with his cum, I shot a load for Mike, which he kept in his mouth and bathed my cock with as Dean's cries signaled the onset of orgasm. And – not unexpectedly, considering it was Dean – he shot a really huge load into me, delivered with incredible velocity. It would be hard to say whose cries were louder or more impassioned as he discharged his precious offering.

Dean leaned over me. "How many times have I fucked you, John?"

"I don't know. A lot, but not nearly enough. Why?"

"I just want you to know I've enjoyed ... no, I've adored fucking you every time ... but that was the best ever." He pulled out of me and took me in his arms as I got to my knees and turned to him.

I kissed him. "It was certainly one of the greatest fucks of my life, but not the best ever with you."

"No?"

"No. Just the best so far with you. Right?"

Dean laughed. "Right. I promise you plenty of cock if you promise me plenty of ass."

"It's a promise, Dean. Every second your cock has been inside me has been wonderful ... and I look forward to many, many more Dean Williamson fucks."

"And I look forward to John Harrison's prick up my butt and down my throat just as eagerly, and just as often."

Mike spoke up from beneath me. "But right now it's time for some big, hard cock up my butt, Dean! And John, why don't we just change places ... maybe I can do for you what you just did for me while you were getting fucked."

I lay on my back as Mike knelt over me, and his huge prick hung down into my mouth as he and Dean got ready. Soon Dean began sucking Mark's cock as Cary began eating his ass, and I sucked happily on Mike's big prick while I watched Dean's glistening monster driving in and out of his asshole. Again, Dean delivered an astonishingly vigorous and accomplished fuck – hugely enjoyed by Mike – who did manage to shoot a big load into my throat before the fuck was over. Again, I appreciated Dean's technique as a work of art from my unique point of view.

After shooting his fourth load, in Mike's appreciative ass, Dean fell on his back and declared he was exhausted. We all declared he was a stud without compare, and that he had done a perfect job of organizing our orgy. It had been an incredible evening, as the five of us – the gorgeous, muscular blond Cary, his dark, handsome, huge-cocked lover Mike, my unbelievably handsome and hot lover, Mark, "little ol' me," and the incomparably sexy and monstrously hung Dean – came together to form a "critical mass" leading to greater explosions of cum than even our Master-of-Ceremonies for the evening had envisioned.

Although he was the youngest among us, Dean was certainly the most passionate and indefatigable lover in our midst. Only a high-school student, but stunningly handsome, hung with the cock and balls of a giant, and a superb and astonishingly accomplished fuckmaster!

It was quite late when our revels ended, so Mike and Cary went to bed in the guest room, while Dean joined Mark and me in our bed. Before we got to sleep, Mark – whose arms were around me – said, "My God, John, Dean's got his prick up my butt again!"

Dean giggled. "Don't worry, I'm just putting it where it feels good. I couldn't cum again tonight if I had to."

Some time during the night, Dean got up to pee, and when he came back to the bed he made a point of putting his cock in my ass. He sleepily nuzzled me and kissed my neck as he muttered, "Gotta share the wealth, right?" and drifted off to sleep again.

The next morning, as we sat drinking our coffee in the living room, where the blankets were still spread out on the floor, we all marveled at how stupendous the festivities had been, and although we were almost "fucked out," we needed some sort of ceremonial way to end the occasion. Dean suggested, since he had been running things, that we reward his great job of organizing by all shooting one final load in his mouth. It seemed like a wonderful idea, so he lay on his back and we all knelt around his head and jacked off, until one by one we brought ourselves to orgasm. Dean opened his mouth and welcomed the spurts of semen we four aimed at it; most of our cum found its mark, but there was no lack of volunteers to lick off Dean's face and chest where we had missed.

After he had happily swallowed the last of our loads, Dean told us to stand side-by-side as he stood on the sofa and jacked off on us. We did as directed, our arms around each other, presenting a solid wall of eager flesh as Dean's target. He masturbated frantically, and when he shot his load, it was a huge one, and he aimed his copious spurting so that it sprayed all over our faces and chests. We licked each other clean and again achieved some kind of five-way kiss as a final act of shared love.

As he left, I told Dean it had been even hotter than my birthday party. He mused, "Yeah, but think how hot it would have been if we'd had Eddie's cock to make it interesting!"

"Your prick is as interesting as any one I've ever had in me ... even including Eddie's. Thanks, Dean. You're sweet, but you're also an incredible stud! Love you!"

Dean kissed me. "You're more than welcome ... and what a treat it was! Thank you! And I love you, too ... I really do!"

The unforgettable Dean: as already noted a magnificent fuckmaster, but in addition, and surprisingly – given his other qualifications – a sweet young man.

17. DEAN GRADUATES, AND TOGETHER, WE MOUNT A SEXUAL EVEREST OF SORTS – AND GET MOUNTED IN RETURN!

The remainder of that year passed happily, and too quickly. Mark and I slept together almost every night, sucking and fucking each other with love and passion, but lying in sweet embrace much of the time also. We shared our love with our beautiful and magnificently hung high school stud regularly – probably once a week or so – and we often visited with Mike and Cary. Those visits with the two lovers were sometimes just that – Mike and Cary would come out to our house for dinner and visiting, or Mark and I would visit them at their apartment – but often, too, we either had wild, four-way sex, or I would retire alone to one bed with Cary while Mike bedded Mark down. Now and then I would lie with Mike's monster cock buried inside me while Mark and Cary – the incomparable beauties – would be off by themselves, sharing their physical perfection.

The organized passion of the five-way fuck we had celebrated at the end of November was never again achieved, but there were several times when the same five of us got together for astonishingly enjoyable orgies of a more impromptu nature. The most memorable of those orgies occurred one night when Mike and Dean challenged each other to a "fuck-off." This contest came about because Mike, in praising Dean for having shot his load in each of us sequentially that first time we all had sex together, told him he thought he could have done the same. As a result, Mark and Cary and I knelt side by side on the floor that night while first Mike, and then Dean knelt behind each of us and fucked our asses until they shot their loads in each. We each testified to the receipt of the two loads, and after they had both fucked the three of us, Mike knelt while Dean deposited a fourth hot load in his ass, after which Dean knelt and Mike shot his fourth load in his hungry asshole. They declared it a tie – happily, and even expectedly so – and Mark and Cary and I celebrated the outcome by each us of kneeling behind Mike and adding our three loads to the hot deposit Dean had left in him, after which we shot our three loads into Dean's hot ass, still awash with Mike's cum.

Another time Mike and Dean had an oral re-match – a "suck fest," as they called it. Basically we observed the same ritual we had in their "fuck-off," but this time they fucked mouths instead of asses, and Mark and Cary and I finished off by depositing our three loads virtually at once into his open mouth as each lay on the floor. Mike and Dean tied again – as they knew they would, but they certainly did not care. Those contests were simply good excuses to fuck all of us. And we all loved being fucked, whether in our eager mouths, or up our hungry asses, by our two mega-hung studs.

The night of Dean's high school graduation was his night, and in lieu of a graduation present we celebrated it just as he wanted. It was a warm night, and at his request we headed for a park outside of town. There, in a clearing brightly lit by the almost-full moon, we all got naked. Then Dean put his cap and gown – and nothing else – back on, and knelt before each of us in turn while he sucked a load of cum from each of our four pricks; he then opened his gown and lay on his back as each of us knelt between his raised legs and shot our loads into his voracious asshole. Following the final fuck, by Mark, Dean lay there on his back and grinned happily. "Eight big, hot loads in me, from four wonderful, beautiful, sexy friends. What could be a better present?"

Dean stood and took me in his arms. "But I want the last part of my present to be shooting my load in a special way. No ... shooting two loads, like each of you guys gave me. And I want to give them both to John because he's the guy who brought us all together. If he hadn't been such a horny, persistent fucker we might all be sucking and fucking somewhere tonight, but it wouldn't be together. And sucking and fucking together with you guys has made my senior year the best anyone could possibly imagine. I'll never forget being inside you guys, and having you inside me ... I treasure every drop of cum I've ever sucked from your big pricks, or that you've shot into me, and every single thrust those big cocks gave me up my butt. And I'll never forget the feel of your lips on my cock while I fucked your mouths and shot my load into them, or the incredible way your totally hot asses have held my cock and milked it dry while I fucked them. I really love every one of you."

Dean kissed me for a long time then took the other three individually in his arms, and kissed each of them tenderly and lovingly. He expressed his gratitude by asking me to kneel in front of him while he fucked my mouth and gave me a load down my throat. I sucked eagerly, and soon the cum began shooting inside my appreciative mouth. Dean always delivered a big load, but this one was nothing short of spectacular, exploding with such force and volume that I almost gagged at its initial force, and filling my mouth faster than I could swallow, with the result that some of it spilled out from around his shaft, and dripped down my chin. Then he asked me to stand, turn around, and lean over. I braced myself against Cary and Mark and Mike, who stood before me and urged Dean on as he drove his monster cock all the way up my ass and administered a fuck of truly savage force. Having just cum in my mouth, it took him a long, wonderful time to reach orgasm again, but his magnificent fuck ended splendidly with another copious eruption deep inside me.

He continued to fuck me long after his orgasm, and finally he slowed, pulled his cock out, and turned me around to kiss me. "Thanks, John, for bringing us together. Thanks for being a great fuck," here he grinned, "and a great fucker." Another long kiss, then, "And thanks especially for having the good sense ... no, the good taste ... to spot such beauties as Mike and Cary and Mark to hit on."

My arms were around him as I looked into his eyes. Don't forget having the good sense to spot you!"

"Shit, I didn't give you any choice, did I? I remember the first time we met, going to that football game. Remember?"

"Remember? How could I forget? I almost fainted when I saw you, you were so damned hot."

"And you know what? I could tell. I could see you checking out my cock and my balls in my Levi's. That's why I wear 'em tight, you know ... I like to be appreciated."

"Well, I really appreciated you that night."

He laughed. "I knew it, believe me. When you followed me into the men's room and pissed with me, I could see you were interested, and you remember how I let my prick just lay in my hand so you could really get a load of it?"

"I sure do, but I didn't think it was intentional."

"Believe me, I wanted you to see what you obviously were so interested in. It was a little bit hard, 'cause I was thinking about meeting Willie Earl Conn later that night."

"Who's Willie Earl Conn?" I asked.

Dean laughed, "Just the hottest guy in my school. He was on the field playing quarterback that night."

"He may have been the second-hottest guy in your school," I said, kissing him as I did, "but I know who the first-hottest was."

"Well, not in my opinion. Willie and I had been sucking each other off since we were freshmen, and he'd been fucking my ass since we were sophomores, but he had never let me fuck his pretty little ass. That same day I first saw you, Willie had promised to finally give me his ass when we got together after the game, and I couldn't help thinking about it. So, I had a partial hard-on when you first saw it. I thought about beating off in that bathroom, or offering to give you what I knew you were after, but I wanted to save it for Willie. If my Levi's hadn't been so tight, I probably would have played with it a little, anyway, but then I would have had trouble getting it tucked back in."

"You had trouble getting it tucked back in when it was soft. And if you'd played with it and got it hard, I probably would have fainted."

He kissed me again, "Well, Willie damned near fainted with happiness when I planted my cock all the way up his tight little ass that same night. Anyway, I knew right away that you and I were somehow going to wind up in bed together. You seemed like you'd be hot as hell, and I liked the way you obviously got turned on by me ... that really turned me on to you. Then a while later, that afternoon when you picked me up, I recognized you right away, and I knew that the time had come when I was gonna give you this big ol' cock of mine."

We all expressed our appreciation that Dean had sunk his "big ol' cock" in me, and then gone on to plunge it into everyone else – and so deeply, and so hard, and so liquidly, and so frequently.

189

Mark had to return to Pennsylvania for the summer, to work, and Mike and Cary each went to their respective home towns for the summer. After Mark's departure, the frequency with which Dean and I fucked each other stepped up considerably, since that fall he would be a freshman at the University of Georgia, and would be moving to Athens – the same former home town with the infamous "meat rack" in front of the bus station. By the time summer came to an end, Dean was spending at least four or five nights a week in my bed. And what nights they were! He fucked me in every way imaginable, and often, and he insisted I do the same for him. We sucked each other's cocks dry, night after night. Each night, as we prepared to go to sleep, almost always after wild sex, Dean sank his huge prick to the hilt in my ass and we went to sleep that way. If either of us got up during the night, Dean either returned his prick to its perfect resting place, or snuggled his ass up to me and had me plug him as we returned to sleep. I missed Mark, but Dean's magnificent lovemaking was a great consolation; his cock was a huge consolation: a good solid nine or ten inches of it – and the words "good" and "solid" are used conservatively here, since "magnificent" and "steel hard" would be equally applicable.

The night before Dean left for Athens, he had to go to dinner with his family, and arrived at my house late, but he still managed to spend his last night in my bed and in my arms. We had a drink and necked for a long time, remembering the wonderful times we had enjoyed together, and also those we shared with Mark or Mike or Cary or Eddie or Richard, or any of the various combinations of those wonderful studs we had made love with.

Before going in to the bedroom, Dean stood in front of me in the living room and undressed completely – slowly, but not teasingly – gradually and almost reverently revealing his body for me. His body was perfect, his face was that of an angel, and his prick – though not yet hard – hung massively down over his huge balls. "Undress for me John, slowly. Let me enjoy watching you." I undressed as he had, and we faced each other, nude. As we looked at each other, I could see, peripherally, that his huge prick was reaching full erection, and was standing straight out from his body – a stage mine had reached long before his. "This isn't going to be our last time together, by any means, but this is a time of at least some separation, and I want it to be very special." He extended his arms and I walked into them.

Dean enfolded me and kissed me very tenderly. "Kneel for me, and worship me." I knelt very slowly, looking up into his eyes. Once I was on my knees, he said, gently, "Take me in your mouth and let me make love with you. I've fucked you this way so many times, but this time I want to love your mouth while it makes love to my cock." First I kissed his mammoth balls, and opened my mouth very wide to take their unbelievable bulk inside while I sucked and licked them, gently and lovingly. Then I relinquished the delight of his ball sac as I kissed my way from the base of his monster prick to its tip, and opened my lips to admit the glory of his beautiful, throbbing cock head. Dean took my head in his hands very gently, and I slowly moved my lips down his massive shaft and took his huge prick deep inside my mouth, His hands were on either side of my face, and he directed my gaze upward as I sucked. He smiled down, and his prick was driving slowly and deeply into my throat as he said "Love me, John!" I sucked his cock with as much deep and reverent feeling as anyone could have brought to a blowjob. For a very long time, he plumbed the absolute depths of my mouth, and I managed to avoid gagging as his mammoth shaft filled my throat. His hands continued to caress my head lovingly, and my hands reached around to fondle his undulating ass as he used it to drive his wonderful tool into me. The slow and gentle pace enabled us to make love for a heavenly eternity, and even as he neared orgasm, he simply held my head tighter, and drove his prick only a little harder – finally driving it all the way in and pulling my face into his stomach as my lips nestled deep in his pubic hair, and he filled my throat with the huge, violent explosion of his hot cum. "God I love you, baby."

After I had drained every drop of his huge load, and swallowed it, he knelt with me, took me in his arms again, and kissed me very sweetly. "I've never shot a load with as much love as I just gave you, John."

"I've never felt quite so honored by a cock shooting cum into me."

Dean raised me to my feet, so that he now knelt in front of me. "Honor me, John, while I worship you." I loved his mouth with my cock as reverently and fervently as he had mine, and after a long, wondrous time while his hot mouth became one with my prick, my load was delivered into his worshipping throat with equal solemnity. After he had finished swallowing my emission, he removed his lips from around my cock and smiled up at me. I looked down at him, and said, "I love you, Dean."

He stood and kissed me again. "Come to bed with me. There's still more loving and worshipping we have to do." He lay on his back on the bed, I lay on top of him, and we kissed and fondled each other with the same kind of sweet sincerity we had brought to our recent mutual blowjobs. Finally, Dean spread his legs and raised them high. "Enter me John ... don't just fuck me, enter me and fill me with your beautiful prick. Give me another load of cum, John." As my prick began to penetrate him, he whispered, "Fuck me John. My lover. My very special lover."

Our tongues intertwined and danced in our mouths while I slowly fucked his perfect ass as deeply as I could. His asshole gripped and pulled on my adoring cock and his hands pulled my ass in tightly toward him. I had only recently given him my load in his mouth, so it took a long time before my worshipful penetration of this Adonis' tight and feverishly hot sheath yielded the flow of cum he wanted. Dean murmured and cooed his appreciation around my tongue as my orgasm filled him. After I had finished, his legs wrapped around my waist and he held me very tight as he whispered in my ear, "Stay inside me forever, lover."

"I wish I could, Dean. I love you so much ... my very special lover."

I did stay in him for a long time, but finally the pressure of his incredibly hard cock poking my stomach signaled his readiness to service my ass in the same way I had his. I rolled on my back and raised my legs. He raised my legs even higher while he gently began to probe my asshole with his tongue. His saliva lubricated my ass, and, using a quantity of his spit to further lubricate his prick, he slid the enormous shaft slowly and inexorably all the way inside me. As always, It was an absolutely thrilling sensation. His gigantic cock had often been buried to the hilt inside me, often driving fiercely into my ass, but never had the great bulk of his magnificent organ felt more filling and satisfying, nor suffused my entire body with greater warmth. "Fuck me Dean! Fuck me deep and long, and blow your load all the way inside me. Love me, Dean!"

His lovemaking was also protracted, and although he also began slowly and gently, by the time he reached orgasm, he was slamming his monster shaft into me with insane ferocity, and the eruption of his enormous load deep inside me was as thrilling and satisfying as it had been the first time I had experienced the force and copiousness of this incredible stud's sexual power. He lay over me, his softening cock still planted deep inside me, as we kissed and caressed.

We rolled on our sides – still locked together – and Dean smiled at me. "I don't know what's gonna happen when I go away." He laughed. "I'll bet the old 'meat rack' is gonna see my ass a whole helluva lot." Then he turned serious, "but I will always want to make love with you. Whoever is in my life, whoever is in your life. promise me we'll always be able to make love together."

"I promise you, Dean. Mark is really my lover, in the usual sense of the word, and I hope he will be for a very long time, if not always, but even if there's someone else later on, I'll always want to make love with you also. No load will ever taste any better or thrill me any more, no cock will ever feel any hotter or bigger than yours when you fuck me or when I suck you, and no mouth or no ass will ever feel any hotter or tighter than yours when I'm inside you!"

"I couldn't have said any of that better, and I feel exactly the same about you, John."

We spent the night in each other's arms, and the next morning we took our leave following a very slow, incredibly sexy sixty-nine that ended with our shooting our loads into each other's open mouths as we knelt over each other. Dean had said, "I want to see my cum going into you," and he did – seven or eight enormous spurts of hot cum filling my adoring mouth from several inches away – and his aim was unerring that morning. I returned the favor, and he left me for the last time as a high school student. I had thought back in Texas that Phil had to be the hottest high school boy in the world – and perhaps he was at that time – but my wonderful Dean eclipsed even his accomplishments.

Dean – one of the most beautiful human beings I have ever seen; the tightest and sexiest pants I ever saw; one of the most perfect bodies I have ever seen, or held in my arms, or lain over or below; one of the biggest pricks I have ever seen, or touched, or held, or licked, or sucked, or took in my throat or up my ass; and one of the most massive sets of balls I have ever seen, or touched, or licked, or sucked. That thrilling cock and incomparable balls had, in combination, given me some of the largest and most forcefully delivered loads of cum I have ever known. He had one of the cutest, and tightest, and most wildly active asses I have ever seen, or felt, or tongued, or fucked; also one of the sweetest mouths I have ever kissed or felt making love to my cock or my ass; and an unbelievable combination of gentle, sweet man and savage, relentless, and indefatigable fuckmaster! Ironically, he was just barely reaching his chronological maturity as he left me.

Dean will be mentioned further in these pages, and at great length, but it should be noted here that we have kept our long-term promises to each other. Over the years since his high school graduation, whatever relationships we have been in, or commitments we have made, we have regularly lain together – often just the two of us, but just as frequently with our other partners – in sweet and passionate congress, and the thrill of his lovemaking has abated not a whit. And he continues to express his continued appreciation of my sexual devotion to him. Age seems not to have touched him much. He is to this day beautiful, wonderfully built, magnificently hung, and a stallion in bed – but a stallion whose sweetness and tenderness in kissing and cuddling is as memorable as the intensity and ferocity he shows me when he drives his huge prick up my hungry ass or down my eager throat to deliver as explosive, as copious, as hot a load as he filled me with when he was a high school student – the most precocious lover I have ever met.

The following school year, 1967-68, was senior year for both Mike and Cary, since Mike had delayed his academic program, so he could graduate at the same time as Cary. Over the course of the year, they shared their love with me and with Mark, and we continued our mixed pairing and occasional four-way sex. Mike and I especially loved watching the awesome beauty of the incredibly handsome Mark and Cary making love to each other in our presence. While we took turns fucking and sucking each other as we watched. More than once the thrill of observing the orgasm of one of the two beauties triggered a sudden flow of cum from Mike's or my prick. Still, with all the many hours Mike or Cary spent fucking or sucking Mark or me, or both of us together, with an occasional extra playmate added to the mix, or all the hours Mark or I devoted to fucking and sucking Mike or Cary or both – to say nothing of the regular appearances of Dean's huge and thrilling presence in our beds, and up our butts, and down our throats – Mark and I remained devoted lovers. Mike and Cary and Dean were guys we loved and enjoyed sex with, but we were in love with each other.

Steve came to visit only a few times, but he invariably shared his sexual voracity with me and with his adoring adoptive brother, and Mark's visits back to Pennsylvania always found Steve and him managing somehow to fuck with each other. On one occasion Steve's visit to our house coincided with a visit from Dean, and each greatly appreciated what the other had to bring to our bed. Another time Steve and Mark and I visited Mike and Cary in their apartment for a wild evening of sex.

Everyone always adored Steve's unbelievably fat cock driving into his ass and erupting thrillingly inside, and he sucked a load out of every hard cock present, or took it up his ass – often servicing one or all both ways. On many occasions, after fucking, he would tirelessly favor one or more of us with a second load, sucked from his lip-stretching shaft. I can't speak for others, but I know my lips had to stretch to unbelievable lengths to accommodate the huge girth of his cock, but well worth it when they nestled in his pubic hair as he drove his magnificent shaft deep into my throat and flooded it with a load as copious as one could desire.

Dean did, as anticipated, begin to frequent the infamous "meat rack" in Athens, and he regularly regaled us with fantastic and often uproarious tales of his sexual adventures. Academically, he did well at the university, but he always had time for the countless hard cocks and hot asses he found waiting or him at every turn. His tight and obviously well-filled Levi's drew all the attention they merited at the university, and he made a great deal of money from men who picked him up and insisted on rewarding him for his sexual virtuosity.

On one occasion Dean was so impressed by the talent he found at the "meat rack" that he called from his apartment early one Saturday afternoon, wanting to get together with Mark and me to share it. As it happened, Mark was out of town with the soccer team when Dean called, but I very generously offered to share nonetheless. Dean was obviously pleased and excited. The talent in question was a sailor, Tom, whom he had picked up that morning, looking – according to Dean – sexy as hell in a uniform as tight as his own Levi's normally were. The basket defined by Tom's uniform promised a treasure as impressive as Dean's own – enormous cock down the left leg, huge balls outlined at the right. "You remember Eddie, right?"

"Believe me, Dean, I'll never forget Eddie."

"Well, Tom is lying next to me right now, and when you see what he just had up my butt while he filled me with cum, you'll either forget Eddie or think of him as second best."

"My God, his cock is bigger than Eddie's?"

"It's absolutely incredible. I was telling him about you guys ..."

Tom apparently took the phone from Dean. "John? Yeah, this is Tom, and Dean's told me all about you guys, and I sure as hell want to fuck you, too. You and ... uh ..." I heard Dean's voice in the background.

"Mark."

Tom continued, "yeah, Mark. You guys get down here and help Dean service my cock."

"Mark's out of town, but if you're as hot as Dean says, I'm hitting the road in a few minutes. I'd love to service your cock."

Tom laughed. "Great! And you'd better plan on servicing my ass, too. So, come alone then, and I'll fuck you twice as much as I would have if you were both here, okay? And by the way, I am as hot as Dean says. Right, Dean?"

Dean's voice was heard in the background again, this time calling out, "He's even hotter – get down here and help me!"

"Okay John, get your butt down here right away. You know that Dean's cock is a real monster, too, and you should see what he's doing with it right now. He's obviously ready to do to me what I just did to him, so we have to get off the phone and find a place for him to hide that beautiful thing until you get here."

Dean took over the phone. "Hurry, John ... we're gonna have an incredible time. Tom doesn't have to leave until tomorrow night, so bring your toothbrush."

Just before he hung up, I heard Tom saying, "Grease me up, baby, I want that huge dick of yours in ..."

I made the almost-two-hour drive to Dean's apartment in record time, and when Dean answered my ring, dressed only in a very tight pair of boxer shorts that clearly displayed his wonderful endowments, his bedroom door was closed. "I asked Tom to put his uniform on for you, so you can see what almost made me wreck my car this morning. You're gonna flip."

In a few minutes, the bedroom door opened and Tom came out – fully uniformed, except for his shoes. He looked to be in his mid-twenties, was of average height, around five-ten, with dark, crew-cut hair. He was not handsome in a conventional sense. His face was fairly craggy, but quite masculine, and combined with a broad grin and extremely white, even teeth that lit it up like a birthday cake, he was quite attractive. His upper body and upper legs were clearly delineated by his very tight uniform blouse and unbelievably tight thirteen-button pants. He was extremely well-built, without being overly muscular, but his crotch was, as Dean had promised, astonishing. The tight fabric of his trousers clearly outlined what was a prodigious cock snaking down his left leg, and the vast bulge in the upper right pants legs promised a set of balls of Herculean dimensions. Dean grinned and put his hand on my shoulder as he propelled me toward Tom. "John Harrison, meet Tom Fox."

I extended my hand. "Hi, Tom. Seaman First Class Tom Fox, I see from your stripes."

"Right. A Seaman First Class with guaranteed first-class semen for you ... and plenty of it, right Dean?"

Dean eagerly interjected "Amen!" as Tom ignored my hand and enfolded me in his arms instead.

"This is not going to be a meeting where shaking hands will do." With that he threw his hat on a chair, pressed his lips to mine, and drove his tongue hungrily into my mouth as we began a very long and very passionate kiss, while our hands explored each other's backs and asses. Although I hadn't yet seen his ass, it promised to be gorgeous, if my tactile assessment was in any way reliable. As Tom and I kissed, Dean's arms went around my waist from behind, and I could feel his hard cock pressing against my ass. He nibbled my neck and ear and said, "You are not gonna believe how great this guy is."

Tom pulled back and smiled at me. "I'll make a believer out of you. I made one out of Dean, didn't I, baby?" He transferred his gaze to Dean, as he cupped his neck in his hand, and pulled him in for a hot kiss.

When Tom released him, Dean panted, "I'm a believer. I'm a firm believer!" He moved from behind me, now nude, and with his magnificent prick fully erect as he held it in his hand and displayed to us. "See how firm I am?"

Tom grinned at me as he stroked the magnificent shaft Dean was offering. "I love cock, I especially love really big cock, so you can imagine how I've enjoyed Dean so far."

Dean laughed, "God, Tom, if you could fuck yourself you'd be in heaven."

Tom pulled both of us in to him, one arm around each of us, and played with my ass – which I assumed he was also doing with Dean's. "But I like tight asses even better, and if yours is as tight and as hot as Dean's I'll be in heaven anyway. And hey, who says I can't fuck myself? I've got a few tricks I might show you."

I fell to my knees in front of Tom and began to fondle and stroke the huge tube displayed along his pants leg; as I did so, I could feel it growing larger – much larger – until it strained mightily against the prison of his uniform. As I began to unbutton the distinctive thirteen-button flap on his pants, I panted, "I just can't wait any more – I'm dying to see this."

Tom's hands held my head. "I'm dying for you to see it, too – and taste it, and take it down your throat, and all the way up your butt." By this time the flap was unbuttoned, and fell down. Tom was wearing no shorts, and I could see the generous, thatch of black pubic hair above the base of the monster shaft contained so tightly in his pants leg. "Pull it out and feast your eyes on it, John. Yeah, and then you can just feast on it!"

I reached inside and took hold of the incredibly fat, hard shaft, and tried to pull it out, but it was too big and too engorged to allow me to do so. I reached up, unbuttoned the closing over the flap, and pulled his pants down over his hips. As I did so, his cock sprang out slowly, and gradually rose in full erection. It was a sight so magnificent, so beautiful, so awe-inspiring, so absolutely thrilling that I gasped.

Tom used his hands to direct my gaze up toward his face. "Do you like what you see?"

"It's about the most wonderful and exciting thing I've ever seen. Your prick is so ... God, Tom, it's stunning!"

"It's all yours! If you think it looks good, wait until you taste it, or feel it inside you. I know how good it tastes ... and I'll show you later how I can tell how great my lips feel on it. But right now I want to feel your lips on it, going up and down, and your hot mouth all over it. Come on, baby, Dean's got it all warmed up and ready for you."

Dean knelt next to me and put his arm around my body as I continued to stare in awe. He whispered in my ear. "Have you ever seen anything so fabulous? It's the most exciting thing I've ever had in my mouth or up my ass. Go ahead and suck it while I watch."

I was eager to get this astonishing organ in my mouth, but I also wanted to continue visually drinking in the wonder of it for a few more moments. It was so long and fat that it was hard to believe it could stand straight out from Tom's body, but this bobbing, quivering masterpiece of the Creator's art was so steely hard that it actually pointed upward a bit – an absolute triumph of horniness over endowment and gravity combined. Perfectly formed, with a huge, plum-colored head, and a glistening white shaft showing only a few throbbing veins along it's smooth surface, it was not only beautiful, it was also certainly both the longest and the fattest prick I had ever seen – an unbeatable combination. With all due respect to such objects of admiration as the Mona Lisa or the Grand Canyon, this was the single most admirable object I had ever beheld in my life. Dean had been regularly fucking me with one of the biggest and juiciest pricks I had known, but even his truly massive shaft was not quite as stupendous as the gorgeous, unforgettable Hal, who had serviced me so thoroughly back in Texas with a cock that was the biggest I had ever seen until that time. Now an even more imposing, unimaginably impressive shaft of hot, hard, ready prick waited my adoration. Surely at least eleven inches in length, and fully as large in girth as Steve Hagood's, it was the monster tool of every gay man's dreams – an ass-reamer of unparalleled dimension.

Fans of recent gay pornography will understand how magnificent this man's equipment was when I say that Tom Fox's cock was every bit the equal of those legendary pricks of Rick Donovan, Cody James, Ken Ryker, or Kevin Dean. Only the unfortunately unattractive straight porn actor John Holmes was apparently superior in size. Unlike all those incredibly endowed studs of porn, whose enormous pricks seemed to preclude full rigidity (with the exception of the always-hard, unbelievable stallion, Kevin Dean), the fabulous cock filling my view now was actually throbbing with total erection!

And my God, what a set of balls! They were an equally impressive accompaniment to his stupendous prick: low hanging, almost hairless, and each almost a handful by itself. It was only with the very greatest difficulty that I later was able to take both of his nuts in my mouth at the same time – and only then after my mouth had been cruelly – yet delightfully – stretched by his driving supercock. Cupping his balls in my hand as I knelt there, my wonder and excitement grew even greater when I contemplated the load these beauties were going to provide me, delivered through the monster shaft bobbing in front of me.

If possible, I grew even more excited when Tom put his hand over mine and said, "They're full of cum, baby, and I want you to drain 'em dry."

Tom began to pull my head in toward him. "Lick my cock, John ... lick the head of this monster dick." I kissed the tip of his astonishing prick, then kissed my way up and down the enormous length of the glorious shaft before I wrapped my hands around it. I gripped it with both hands side-by-side, and it was so long that the beautiful huge cock-head was still fully revealed to my stupefied gaze. I began seriously licking that perfect head when Dean moved in and began licking and sucking Tom' balls at the same time. Tom's hands tightened on my head, and he began to force his prick into my mouth. "Oh shit, that feels so good! Take me down your throat, John. Suck this baby for all it's worth."

I opened my mouth very wide, and the biggest prick I had ever seen in person – or ever felt, or even dreamed of actually having – began to pass miraculously into my mouth. It was so fat that my lips were automatically tight around it, and as I took my hands from the shaft and he slowly sank it deeper and deeper into my mouth, Tom murmured, "Yeah, suck that big prick, baby. Eat me!"

Dean, who had relinquished Tom's balls when I began to suck cock, whispered into my ear. "Biggest fuckin' dick in the world, John ... worship it!"

Tom's magnificence lodged firmly in my throat, and I began to pay the fervent homage so impressive a man and so stunning an organ deserved. I was delirious with passion as I sucked his prick fiercely, opening my throat to admit passage of more cock into my mouth than I would have ever thought possible, licking as I sucked, pressing my tongue into his piss-slit, and groaning in ecstasy. Several times I released his prick and looked up at Tom to say "God, what a wonderful fucking prick," or "This is the most exciting thing I've ever done in my life," or "What an incredible stud!" or words to that effect. Each time, Tom would smile, lean over, and kiss me deeply before commanding me to continue to make love to his cock.

I sucked for a long time – a divine eternity of total rapture – and Tom sank his prick fast, and deep, and hard as I sucked, really fucking my mouth masterfully. I delighted in the feel of his muscular, rounded ass as it rotated and moved in and out while driving this incomparable monster into me. I had not yet even seen his ass, but if it were to look as marvelous as it felt, it would surely be a prize-winner also. As I sucked, his hands held my head tightly, pulling it violently in toward him each time he drove his monstrous cock savagely into my worshipful mouth. I often gagged, but never stopped sucking – it was too wonderful, and he would always enjoin me to keep eating his cock. He also encouraged me to play with his ass, and I had several fingers up his asshole, fucking it wildly while he was fucking my mouth. As I moaned my pleasure at this masterful lovemaking, so did he. Before I finished this ecstatic blowjob, I was regularly burying my widely stretched lips and my nose in his pubic hair each time his cock drove into my throat. Although I would not have thought it possible, I was somehow taking his entire prick into my mouth, and Tom assured me I was: "That's it baby. I've got it all the way in you now."

Finally, with a grunt, Tom buried his prick completely in me, and it and his undulating ass froze in position, while a hot flood of delicious, salty cum began to fill my throat. I groaned in ecstasy, and Tom panted, "First class semen, John, drink it in, swallow it. Oh God, yeah ... take that big load!" All this while his monster prick continued to spurt his love-juice into my hungry throat.

We both remained motionless for some time – Tom with his head back and his eyes closed in rapture, me looking up in adoration at him, with the enormous bulk of his cock deep inside my mouth, swimming in his copious emission. Finally, I pulled my head back a bit, and began to move my tight lips up and down his prick again, bathing it in the mouthful of hot cum he had given me, and lapping the huge shaft with my tongue as I did so. Tom groaned loudly. "My God that's an incredible feeling. Your tongue and my cum feel so hot on my cock! Oh Christ, keep sucking me, baby!"

Dean knelt next to me. He studied Tom's prick going in and out of my mouth – shiny with the cum that covered it – and then he kissed my ear and said, "Don't swallow all of that ... save some for me."

Above me I heard Tom add, "And give him enough that I can take some from him, and I want some from you too. But don't stop sucking me yet ... shit, I could almost cum again this feels so fucking good!" Eventually I had to swallow, so before I did, I reluctantly let the still driving, still huge, and mostly still erect monster prick slip from my mouth – dripping with cum. Dean moved in and took it in his mouth and licked and sucked until he had cleaned the cum off it, Then he turned to me and whispered "God, that tastes so goddamned wonderful ... give me some more." His mouth sought mine, and as our lips met, our mouths opened, and Dean's tongue played in the mouthful of Tom's liquid treasure. I injected some of it into his mouth, and then stood to kiss Tom. His arms went around me and his mouth opened wide to accept my tongue and his share of the load I was offering. Dean stood, and we all looked at each other, smiling, Tom's delicious, hot cum providing a feast and a mutual communion for all of us. I nodded and swallowed; Tom and Dean did the same.

I kissed Tom again. He grinned at me, "That was maybe the hottest load I ever gave anyone ... you are one helluva fine cocksucker, John."

"If you'll fuck my ass the way you fucked my mouth, this is going to be one of the best days in history."

"Oh, I'll fuck it ... and you'll love it. Dean did, right baby?"

Dean kissed Tom quickly, and then me. "Wait until you get that prick up your butt, John ... Tom gave me the biggest thrill I ever had this morning." I thought this latter statement was probably hyperbole, until I shortly experienced the thrill of Tom's cock invading my ass, and found I could easily believe – and second – Dean's assertion.

Tom began to pull his uniform blouse and T-shirt over his head, exposing his muscular chest with beautiful pecs. He stepped out of his pants and turned around. He leaned over and used his hands to spread the cheeks of his ass – an ass that proved to be every bit as cute and sexy as I had anticipated. As he did so, he grinned back over his shoulder at me. "Dean liked fucking my ass with that gorgeous prick of his as much as I enjoyed taking it. You want to fuck this, John?"

I knelt behind him and buried my face between his asscheeks, kissing him and driving my tongue into his hole – and the muscles of his ass-ring held my probing tongue tightly as I explored. Tom moaned, "Oh, Jesus ... eat my ass, baby!"

I continued to rim for several minutes before standing and putting my arms around his waist, from behind. I kissed his ear as I said, "I'm gonna fuck that hot hole to the very best of my ability; your ass is damned near as exciting as your cock, Tom."

He turned around and smiled at me as he began unbuttoning my shirt. "Come on, get those clothes off ... I want to see the next cock that's going up my ass, and the next ass I'm gonna fuck." I dropped my pants and shorts, and stepped out of them. My prick was fully erect as I finished undressing. Tom knelt in front of me, saying, "Yeah, this is going to do just fine," just before he completely engulfed it in his mouth and began to suck profoundly. I knew that my cock, even though it was nothing to be ashamed of, was nothing like the beauty Dean had been giving him, but I appreciated his attitude. As he sucked me, his hands sought my ass, which he fondled and then began to fuck gently, but deeply, with first one, and then two fingers. He stopped sucking, and used his hands to turn my body around. "Yeah, this ass is going to be just fine, too ... give me a little time and I'll have another load worked up to fill it." He tongue-fucked my asshole as I put my hands behind me to spread my asscheeks.

Dean called, "Time! You guys go in the bedroom. I'm getting dressed and leaving you two alone for a couple of hours."

I was surprised. "Dean ... no! Don't you want to be with us?"

He took me in his arms and kissed me lightly. "John, I want you and Tom to be alone without any distraction for a while. Fucking with him today was completely incredible ... just the hottest sexual experience you can imagine ... and I want you to have him all to yourself for a while, the way I did. Look, you know I love you ... so I just want you to have the same treat I got. But I'll only be gone a while. I'm gonna go do some work in the library for a couple of hours, and the three of us can share plenty of fucking and sucking when I get back, okay?" He kissed me again, this time slowly and very sweetly. "You're going to fuck with the best." He turned to Tom and kissed him. "And so are you, Tom."

While Tom and I lay on Dean's bed, caressing and kissing, and grinding our bodies together, Dean dressed, calling out as he left, "You guys enjoy yourselves ... save some for me, though, I'll be back in around two hours ... and my big cock is gonna be as horny as my ass'll be hungry." And he was gone.

"Incredible guy, isn't he?" Tom asked, "And unbelievably beautiful."

"He's just the best. And he really is beautiful ... but you should see my lover, Mark."

"I wish he had been home, and coulda come with you. Dean said he's maybe the prettiest guy he's ever seen, to say nothing of having fucked with ... and he also told me about some blond muscle boy you guys fuck with who's almost as beautiful as your lover."

"Yeah ... that's Cary. And his lover may not be as beautiful, but he's got a cock nearly as big as Dean's. It's really great; with Dean and them, and Mark around, I get to fuck with some really beautiful guys."

"Sounds like it. I might just have to come up there some time and help share the wealth."

"All right! You won't get away from here without my address. Believe me, we'd all love to make love with you; it would be really exciting to watch Mark's face while he rode that unbelievable prick of yours ... and he's so sweet I know he'd love to watch you fucking me, since he'd know how much I was enjoying it. Anyway, I really am so thankful Dean called me today; like you say, he's a helluva guy."

"And he's got a helluva cock, too. God I love to get fucked almost as much as I love to fuck ... and he's as good as any I've been with."

"I'm afraid my cock's gonna seem pretty puny after Dean's."

He was playing with the object in question as he replied. "Your cock is just great ... and I'm really looking forward to getting it inside me. I did fine sucking Dean's huge prick, but I have to admit he was so big it was at least a little painful when he fucked my ass." He grinned. "But what wonderful pain! He tells me you take all of him up the butt without any trouble."

"Yeah! And as often as I can. Believe me, getting fucked by Dean is anything but trouble."

He snorted, "I know that. But anyway, if you can take all of Dean's prick, you can take mine by opening up just a little more. It may hurt you a little bit, but I want every millimeter of this hard cock buried to the hilt in your ass. Dean wasn't sure he could take all of me, but he sure wanted to try ... and he took it all and smiled every minute and every inch."

"That's a lotta inches."

"He smiled a lot ... and he was grinning by the time I filled that hot little ass of his with my load. There've been a lot of guys who swore they couldn't take it when I began to fuck them, but wound up screaming for more with my balls slapping up against their asses."

"That's how I want it, too. I've never wanted anything as bad as I want this magnificent prick banging my ass."

"Believe me, you're going to have your wish. Give me a little while to build up another load, though. And in the meantime, I want to try to give you as great a blowjob as you gave me. I want a mouthful of your cum." He lay on his back and I knelt with my knees at his armpits; his arms went around my hips as he smiled up at me. "Hold my head in your arms and just fuck me for all you're worth. I want the wildest mouth-fuck you've ever given."

I smiled down at him, and as he opened his mouth to take my prick inside, I said, "Somebody's gotta get the wildest mouth-fuck I've ever given ... I can't think of a hotter guy to get it than you." I held his head tightly in both arms and pressed it to my belly, glorying in the sensation of his tight lips clasping my cock as I started to drive it into him. This magnificent sailor-stud began to moan with pleasure as my prick luxuriated in the hot moistness of his mouth, and he began to suck like the world's most efficient vacuum cleaner, while I began to fuck like the world's greatest pile driver. After ten or fifteen absolutely delirious minutes, including some pauses with my cock buried completely in his throat to allow us to prolong the ecstasy, and with one of his hands playing with my tits while three fingers of his other hand fucked my asshole as wildly as I was fucking his mouth, I drove as deeply into his throat as I could, and held myself there while I literally shot my load into his ravenous mouth. "Take my load, Tom ... oh, god you're hot!" He groaned with passion as I discharged, and then his groans became murmurs of delight when I began to fuck again and he continued to suck expertly ... drawing every drop of cum from me. He lay back and I collapsed over him as he continued to nurse quietly on my prick and I complimented him very sincerely on the virtuosity of his cocksucking.

Finally we disengaged, Tom moved his body down so he lay on top of me, and we kissed and snuggled for some delicious time. He murmured, "Jesus, I love to get my face fucked almost as much as I like getting my ass plowed. Will you do me a favor when you fuck me? You are going to fuck me, you know."

"I know, believe me ... you're not getting away with just my address. You're gonna have at least one more load in you ... as far up that pretty ass as I can shoot it. But yes, I'll do you a favor when I fuck you. What do you want?"

"I want you to wear my uniform blouse and my white hat ... you're about my size; they should fit you."

"Sailors must turn you on as much as they do me. I fucked a lot of them and took a lot of their cocks up my ass and down my mouth when I was in the Navy ... and I especially loved it when they wore their uniforms. The sight of a monstrous hard prick sticking out of the flap of thirteen-button pants has got to be one of the most glorious sights in creation."

"I couldn't agree more; why do you think I joined the Navy?"

"Tom ... if you don't mind, let me ask you something, and it's really none of my business, but I'm curious."

"Okay, shoot."

"First, how old are you. Twenty-four or so?"

He grinned. "Twenty-eight. But thanks for the thought."

"Okay. So, it seems to me that the only way a twenty-eight-year-old sailor could still be only a Seaman First Class, is if he's a screw-up ... and you sure as hell don't seem like that type to me. Also, you are obviously well educated ... most swabbies don't speak anywhere near as well as you ... and as much as I enjoyed seeing them, I can't imagine you'd really wear pants as tight and wonderfully revealing as yours, even on liberty. What's the deal? Or is it strictly none of my business?"

Laughing, Tom first swore me to absolute secrecy, and then confessed. Far from being a Seaman First Class, he was a full Lieutenant – a "two-striper" in Navy parlance – and a graduate of the Naval Academy. Regular Navy. While he had a fake ID card proclaiming him to be Seaman First Class Thomas Steven Fox, attached to the Naval Training Center in San Diego, his real one showed him to be Lt. Thomas Eugene Hunt – at this point the Executive Officer on the destroyer *U.S.S. Stonesifer*, based in the same city. He was now on leave, visiting his family, who lived in a small town nearby.

He adored sex with sailors, as he had said, and went to parties and bars where sailors went to get picked up by gay men. Dressed in his enlisted man's uniform, with the breathtakingly tight pants clearly showing the stupendous endowment he had to offer, he had no trouble being picked up by just about whomever he found attractive – and almost never was turned down by any sailor he approached. He regularly wore sunglasses, both to hide his appearance in case anyone he knew saw him, but also to add to his already prodigious sexiness. He rented a room, with a separate entrance, in a house on Mission Beach, just outside of San Diego, so he would have a place to take sailors he picked up, and to change uniforms. The guy who owned the house, and lived alone there, finally figured out what Tom was doing, and confronted him with it, saying he'd be glad to forget collecting the rent if he could collect some of what Tom was showing off so proudly when he was in his enlisted uniform.

"Since then, Purris and I ... he's the guy who owns the house ... have become something like fuck-buddies, and anything goes with him if I just screw him now and then ... and that's no problem, because he's cute, and is a great fuck."

Apparently only once did he encounter a potentially explosive situation. "Purris was having a big party in the house at Mission Beach, and I was lying on my back on the dining room table, with my legs in the air, and had already been fucked by the first two or three guys in a line waiting to plow my ass, when the next one got between my legs, took my hard prick in his hands and kept staring at it while he shoved his own cock up my ass. When he bent over to kiss me, he gasped and pulled out as soon as he got a look at my face. "Jesus Christ ... Mr. Hunt!" I recognized him as Allen Smith, one of the sailors on my own ship."

"Wow! What did you do?"

"I told him to shut up and shove his cock back in ... we could talk later, but just then I wanted him to fuck me as hard as he could. I pulled his face down and kissed him hard and told him that was an order. He said 'Yes sir, I always follow orders,' and went ahead and performed like the U.S. Navy Fucking Team champion. After he'd shot a huge load in my ass, he took hold of my hard prick and leaned over to kiss me again. 'This will be our secret, Mr. Hunt ... and if you'll do the same thing to me, I'll be so happy I wouldn't ever dream of telling anyone. My lips will be sealed ... especially if you'll let me seal them around that monster prick of yours!' He hung around, waiting, while he watched several other sailors fuck me, and I took him into my room at the back. I threw him down on the bed and when I first hammered my prick up his ass he practically screamed, but pretty soon he was taking every inch of it, and begging me to drive it in as far as I could. We spent the rest of the night together, fucking and sucking each other, and until he got transferred, a year or so later, we were lovers. A can [Navy slang for a destroyer] is pretty small, but we were very creative about finding places on the ship where we could hide to make love to each other. There was a lot of fraternizing between a certain officer and one particular enlisted man on that ship."

"Does much of that go on, as far as you know?"

Tom snorted. "Shit, it goes on all the time. I know two other officers on the *Stonesifer* who have sailors they fuck with regularly, and I know a submarine where every officer except two, from the Captain on down, has an enlisted man he fucks with all the time they're at sea ... and the two officers don't fuck with sailors because they're lovers. Most of them are married, but they're a helluva lot happier at sea, with their sailor-lovers to fuck. I tell you, there's nothing as sexy as a sailor's uniform. Well, anyway, other than that time Allen discovered he was fucking his Executive Officer at that party, no one has ever questioned my being a super-horny enlisted swabbie with a big cock."

"What did you do for sex at Annapolis?"

"The first couple of years I was so afraid someone would find out I liked cock that I hardly even looked at anyone; I must have pumped fifty gallons of my cum down the toilet on my wing of Bancroft Hall [the huge barracks at the Naval Academy]. Maybe once a week or so, some other cadet would waylay me in the head [the bathroom] and suck me off, but I never let on that I was interested in returning the favor ... although I really wanted to. Finally, I met this really handsome, well-built guy on the wrestling team ... Gordy Over ... and flipped for him. He made it pretty clear he was attracted to me and pretty soon we managed to spend a lot of time sucking each other off and riding each other's cocks. One night in Gordy's senior year, the Officer of the Deck walked into a locker room, and there was the wrestling coach lying on a bench with his legs in the air, and one of the wrestlers fucking his ass. Gordy was straddling the coach's head and fucking his mouth while he bent down and was sucking off a different wrestler at the same time."

"Shit!"

"Yeah, needless to say, I was thinking *there but for the grace of God go I* when I heard about it."

"What happened?"

"Gordy and the other two wrestlers got thrown out of the Academy quietly, but the coach wound up in prison. Gordy went back to Idaho and got married to convince his family he wasn't queer, but his best friend from high school ... the first guy he ever fucked with ... is now also his lover, and he travels on business and fucks with guys all over. He and I still see each other once in a while. He's more handsome than ever, and he tells me can't get enough of my cock."

"Now that I can understand."

He smiled and kissed me again. "Anyway, I've been pretty careful, and. I guess, very lucky. And I would say I get to suck and fuck with all the sailors I want, but I don't think I can get enough."

"My God, what a man!" I was fondling his balls and stroking his cock, and his busy finger was again seeking refuge up my asshole. "Well, I'll be more than happy to play sailor for you when I fuck you ... but first, I think it's about time we found out if I can even take all that cock of yours up my ass."

"Would you put my uniform on now, so I can see you in it while I fuck you and when you fuck me?" My answer to that question was predictable.

As Tom watched me putting on his blouse, he said, "I wish I had an extra uniform with me to wear while we fucked. I enjoy my work as an officer, but when I'm having sex, I love pretending to be just a sailor fucking another sailor!" By this time I was dressed in his blouse and cap, and I knelt before him to kiss and gently suck the tip of the gargantuan prick he was fondling. He held my head and murmured "How do you want me to fuck you, John?"

"How about every way possible? Let me ride you first, and then you can kneel behind me to plow my ass. But when you're ready to cum in me, I want to be on my back so I can see you and kiss you while you sink that heavenly fucking cock all the way inside me and give me your load."

Tom stretched out on his back and held out his arms to me. "Grease this big cock up and settle your hot ass over it, baby. Ride it like you would a horse."

I took his huge shaft in both hands and kissed the tip. "I'll ride it like a fucking stallion!" Liberally applying Vaseline to his prick and to my ass before I knelt over him, I positioned the huge, throbbing tip of his cock at my asshole. I wriggled as I began to settle down, and gradually the head passed into me. As the huge shaft began to slide into me, I was suffused with an incredible warmth. Tom told me to stay as I was, and let him drive himself into me. He began to slowly move upward so that a bit more of his magnificent prick entered me then he pulled back and entered just a bit farther. Slowly, gently, but purposefully, he fucked higher and higher, his hands on my hips and his eyes closed in ecstasy. Then, he gave one unstoppable, seemingly endless and breath-taking upward stab, and I was filled with rapture, fully impaled on the biggest prick I have ever known.

He was pressing his stomach against my buttocks as he opened his eyes and grinned at me. "You've got all my prick, now, baby. Fuck yourself on it!" I grinned back and began to ride up and down – increasing the length of my stroke, and riding down harder and faster as he began to thrust upward into me in masterful counterpoint.

"Jesus, Tom, your cock is unbelievable. Fuck me, baby. Fuck me hard!" And he did.

My riding and his fucking grew quite frenzied, but always in sync, and, I think, as gratifying to him as it was to me – if that were possible. After some time, we needed to rest, and I sat heavily all the way down on his cock as he lay for a time with his ass resting on the bed. Even then I wriggled gently and worked his cock with my ass ring. After several resumptions of our frantic fucking and riding brought him close to orgasm, he pulled out and had me kneel in front of him.

With his hands holding my hips tightly, he re-entered me with one long plunge – but it was very, very slow, and from the time the tip of his prick touched my asshole, he never stopped pressing it in until his pubic hair was nestled against my ass. The incomparable length of his cock, and its enormous bulk made the inexorable penetration a thrilling sensation absolutely without compare. By the time he was all the way in, I was delirious with passion, and moaning for him to fuck me like he'd never fucked anyone before. He began screwing me in this position slowly, and deeply, with strokes that must have measured at least nine or ten inches. Then he began a very gradual increase in speed. He too was soon moaning with ecstasy, but he controlled the acceleration of his fucking so that neither of us would reach orgasm yet. Several times he stopped completely and hugged my waist as he rested his body on my back, explaining that he was saving his load. Then he would begin again – finally reaching the point where he was fucking me ferociously, in an absolute frenzy of lust – loud guttural exclamations of "huh!" accompanying every forward thrust, and spurred on by my own savage participation, as I drove my ass back fiercely to meet each thrust of his body and uttered my own wild cries of rapture.

Suddenly, at the height of what was surely the fuck of my life, Tom pulled out abruptly, and rudely grabbed my body and rolled me to my back as he cried loudly, "Spread those fuckin' legs, sailor, and get 'em up in the air!" With one violent, unstoppable, furious lunge, he drove his entire monster all the way back into my asshole and began to fuck like a wild man. "I can't hold back ... I've gotta shoot my load!" he gasped as he slammed himself into me, over and over again, until he threw his head back, squeezed his eyes shut, and buried his immense shaft as far as it could possibly go before screaming "Take it! Oh, god!

Aaaaaaahhh! Oh God ... take my load!" And as he froze in this ultimately satisfying position I was again thrilled by the flood of love-juice his stupendous balls provided to give concrete testimony to his matchless manhood. My own impassioned cries of "Fuck me, Tom, give me your load!" which had threatened to drown out his, died to whimpers of utter bliss as the rigidity of Tom's body very gradually faded, and he melted into my arms, kissing me passionately and murmuring his satisfaction.

We lay in this state of euphoric satisfaction for a long time before Tom raised his head and looked into my eyes as he smiled, "My God, what a fuck. You're an incredible piece of ass."

I smiled back. "What a fuck, indeed!" Speaking very slowly and sincerely, I added, "No one in the history of the human race on this planet has ever been so perfectly, so magnificently, so prodigiously, so ... satisfyingly, fucked! My God but you are an incredible man!"

"You're an incredible guy too, John ... and nobody but another real man could have taken me like you did. Jesus, that was a really epic fuck ... and it takes two really dedicated men to bring off a fuck like that, you know. Look, I'm not bragging when I say I know I'm a great fucker ... too many guys with happy smiles on their faces and my cum dripping out of their asses have told me that for it not to be true. But I can also tell that you're a great fucker, too, even if you were on the bottom just now." He kissed the tip of my nose. "The guy on the bottom is just as much a part of the fuck as the guy on top, if it's a really good one ... otherwise it's not half as exciting. But you really took me and enjoyed me when I fucked you, and I can't tell you how much I'm looking forward to being under you on top of me. And I guarantee I'll be as much a part of the fuck as you were. I loved fucking you, John. It was really the greatest."

Some of this no doubt bordered on – if not centered on – hyperbole and bullshit. After all, Tom and Dean had fucked each other earlier that day. I had fucked with Dean hundreds of times, and knew from experience what an impassioned, appreciative, and virtuoso fucker he was – whether taking a cock inside him or sinking his own magnificent shaft into a hot ass or mouth – and how deeply he would have appreciated the endowment and the talent of this unbelievable fuckmaster who had just plowed my ass so spectacularly. Furthermore, when Tom later told us some of his adventures, I knew he had had probably been serviced by many superior fuckers, and hotter men than I, who had been much better at the art of lovemaking. No matter how well I might have pleased Tom, I suspect his fuck with Dean must surely have been at least equally satisfying, and probably a good bit more, still, it was very nice to hear such high praise from such a master practitioner of the art of lovemaking.

I lay on my back and applied Vaseline liberally to my cock. "Ride me, Tom. I'm just a horny sailor that wants to fuck your pretty ass."

He grinned and straddled my waist. Once he was in position, he sat down hard and my prick was buried to the hilt in him. "Oh shit, sailor, your cock feels so fuckin' good! Give it to me hard!" He began to bounce up and down very energetically, and I fucked upward into him with equal vigor. He threw his head back and voiced a litany of ecstatic cries, "Your cock feels so good ... fuck me hard, sailor ... shove every inch of that throbbing dick in your shipmate's ass ... oh yeah, every single inch of that big prick belongs in my hot ass ... give it me deep … God I love a hard dick up my ass!" Most of his utterances were, however, unintelligible moans of delight – similar to mine!

He rode for a long time, bouncing up and down so violently, that my cock often slipped from his ass, but when it did, he simply sat down that much harder on it and apparently thrilled to the re-entrance even more. He planted my cock all the way up his ass and stayed there as he leaned over and kissed me very passionately for a long time, with his ass-ring clasping my prick tightly while he continued to move up and down. He rolled us on our sides, with his legs wrapped around my waist, and panted in my ear, "I'm getting on my back ... I want to look up at you while you fuck my hole." His legs stayed around my waist as he rolled on his back and raised his ass, while I continued driving my cock as rapidly and as deeply into his ravenous asshole as I could. He was thrusting his ass back violently to meet every forward thrust I gave him, and we fucked in perfect rhythm and with maximum thrust and acceptance for another long while – each continuing to voice hoarse and passionate cries of complete sexual thrill.

I began to near orgasm, and asked Tom if he wanted me to shoot my load now. "No! Wait a few minutes, and let me get on my knees. I want you to fuck me from behind when you fill me with your load ... that's my favorite way to get it."

"Yeah, but you can't see the uniform then."

"No, but in my mind I'll be seeing you in it while I feel your cock blowing in my ass. Pull out and let me get on my knees." He quickly changed his position, and I knelt behind him. I penetrated his ass as far as I possibly could with one long, savage thrust, eliciting a cry of delight from Tom and the immediate start of his shoving backward fiercely to meet every forward thrust I gave him. "Fuck me, sailor! Give me your hot cum up my ass!"

He was so incredibly hot, I couldn't hold back, and dedicated myself so completely to fucking this tight, driving, twitching, unbelievably hot ass that in only about five minutes I screamed, "Take my load, Tom!" and began shooting inside him.

Tom groaned, "Oh yeah, your cum feels so hot in me ... keep fucking me hard in your own cum." He kept humping my cock, and although my natural reaction would have been to bury my prick as far into him as it would go and relax in that wonderful post-orgasm afterglow, I resisted, and continued fucking him profoundly. To my pleasant surprise, I found my cock stayed hard, and I continued to thrill at the grip of his superb asshole – a tribute to the utter sexiness of the super-stud.

I had seen Dean enter the room quietly a few minutes earlier, and we had been smiling at each other as I kept drilling Tom's ass. I watched Dean strip and begin to stroke his already hard monster cock, but Tom only became aware that Dean had returned when he knelt on the bed in front of him and offered his cock to Tom's mouth. Dean grinned hugely at me and winked, "That looks wonderful, guys ... I could almost cum just watching you." Tom took Dean's hips in his hands, and pulled his body in toward him. With Dean's throbbing prick positioned irresistibly at his mouth, Tom said, "Keep fucking my ass, John, and you shove that incredible prick of yours down my throat, Dean." Tom began to suck noisily and worship Dean's magnificent shaft with his mouth, as I resumed plowing his ass.

We both fucked Tom for some time, and he seemed to be in complete heaven. Finally, Dean pulled out, moved behind Tom, and told me to change places with him. I pulled out of Tom and moved aside as I watched Dean's fabulous ass-reamer plunge deep into Tom's twitching hole – well lubricated with Vaseline and my cum. While Tom groaned his added pleasure at the two or three additional inches of cock added by the new invader, Dean looked at me and smiled, "As always, John, fucking an ass full of your cum is a special treat." I stepped into the bathroom and cleaned off my cock before kneeling in front of Tom, who began sucking me fiercely as Dean continued his unrelenting assault behind. Soon Dean's orgasm was announced with his cries of passion, accompanied by Tom's cries of appreciation. Tom held my asscheeks in his hands as he completely engulfed my cock, and the three of us froze for several moments in a tableau of bliss.

Tom fell on his stomach, pulling both Dean's and my prick from him. He turned on his back and grinned up at both of us, playing with his own cock – which was hard as a rock, and truly titanic in size. "Two really hot guys, two incredible fuckers, two boiling hot loads of cum filling up my ass ... man, I'm in heaven."

Dean leaned over and kissed Tom. "You've got heaven in your hand, Tom. Who gets your load now?"

Tom sat up, kissed me then kissed Dean again. "I've got a great idea ... you're both going to get it, but you'll be surprised how."

"I think I can speak for John when I say we both love surprises if we get a load of cum along with 'em."

Tom stood. "Okay. Look, both of you kneel next to each other on the side of the bed, and go along with me. I promise you'll love it. Dean ... put on my hat; that way you'll be two sailors lined up to get fucked."

We knelt as Tom directed, and as he began greasing our asses – and pretty thoroughly probing them at the same time – Dean put Tom's cap on the back of his head, and said, "I like the uniform on you, John ... I think I may have to get a couple of 'sailor suits' for us to play with."

Tom knelt on the bed in front of us. After thoroughly wiping his greasy hands on a damp towel he had brought from the bathroom, he took Dean's chin in his hand and looked into his eyes. "A couple of hours ago I would have sworn you were the best fuck I ever had." Then he took my chin in his other hand, and transferred his gaze, "And then I fucked John, and now I don't know. You guys are both fantastic fucks."

Now, I know that I'm a good fuck. My cock isn't unusually large, my body is fairly ordinary, and I'm no Adonis, like Mark, or Dean or Cary. On the positive side, however, I can stay hard after getting my load, and can keep fucking to produce another one or two – and can recover pretty quickly to fuck some more. If it sounds immodest to say I'm an especially talented cocksucker and am able to provide an exceptionally satisfying experience for a cock servicing my ass, I can only say I am merely telling you what I have been told enthusiastically by hundreds of hot boys and men, a large number of whom had such extensive experience with sex partners that they were particularly well qualified to judge. Moreover, many of those enthusiastic "reviews" were delivered during quiet, post-fuck debriefings, not just gasped out in passion while the reviewer was feverishly driving his prick in and out of my mouth or my ass. In any case, it's always nice to hear your talents praised, and if Tom was merely being polite, it was good to hear.

Then Tom turned to business. "Okay, sailors, get ready to get reamed out royally. Your hot asses are going to get fucked hard and deep. You both told me this is the biggest prick you've ever had, and I know both of you can take every bit of it, so I'm not going to hold back at all, like I sometimes have to do." He stood next to the bed and pressed his stupendous shaft all the way up my ass – slowly, but steadily, then held my waist and fucked me hard for some time before drawing out. I heard Dean's grunt of satisfaction as he received the colossal organ, and I looked over my shoulder to watch Tom holding Dean's waist and administering the same glorious treatment he had accorded me.

Tom fucked us in rotation for a long time, and, as promised, he spared no punches: his fucking was deep and passionate, and each time he returned to fill me with his cock still hot from Dean's asshole, his fucking was faster and wilder, and more wonderful than it had been when he had abandoned my ass for Dean's. Since he took time to change receptacles every few minutes, he was able to sustain his magnificent assault for a very long time, but finally, with his cock driving wildly in and out of my ass, he said, "I'm getting close to cumming. Watch this, sailors."

He pulled out and jumped up on the bed. He cleaned his cock off with the damp towel, and lay on his back in front of us. His cock was throbbing, and unbelievably huge as he threw his legs over his head and bent double, poising the head of his cock at his own lips. "You ever see anyone suck himself off?" With that he raised his head, opened his mouth, and used his hands to pull his body down. The head of his prick and two or three inches of the magnificent, fat shaft were inside his mouth, and he began to suck greedily, his cheeks being pulled inward by the tremendous suction he was obviously exerting. One hand continued to pull on his body, but the other sought his shaft, and he used it to masturbate himself while he sucked. Soon his breathing became very labored, and he released his prick so he could again use both hands to pull his body down. I could see his cock pulsing and throbbing as his load passed through it, to where his hungry mouth worked the end of his prick and drained his own cum from it.

After a few minutes of sucking and moving his lips as far up and down his prick as he could, Tom relaxed, and his legs fell to the bed. As he lay there flat on his back, he turned his head and smiled at us. It was a strange, cramped sort of smile, since it was obvious he had a mouthful of cum he was carefully keeping inside. He held out his arms to Dean, who put his head over Tom's as the latter opened his mouth and Dean's tongue went inside it. They kissed for some time, Tom obviously sharing his cum with Dean. Then Dean sat up and Tom opened his arms to me. I moved in, and as I kissed him, he delivered a considerable portion of his load to me. Then he and I sat up, and the three of us put our arms around each other. Tom looked at both of us and grinned. "I gave it all to you ... I can always get more the same way. If you haven't swallowed yet, do it. Eat my love, guys."

I still had Tom's cum in my mouth, and Dean apparently did as well. We took each other in our arms, looked at each other and swallowed together, grinned, and then began to kiss deeply, sharing what remained of Tom's load on our tongues. Tom joined our hug. "Did you like that?"

I looked into Tom's face. "You've got the biggest prick I've ever seen, and you are undoubtedly the sexiest and hottest guy I've ever fucked with." I laughed, and looked at Dean. "Present company excepted, of course."

Dean also laughed. "No ... I know I'm sexy, and God knows I'm hot ... but I agree with you. Tom, that's the biggest prick I've ever seen, and what could be sexier or hotter than a guy sucking himself off and then sharing his load with his fuck partner?"

"Fuck partners, you mean ... plural," I said. "And how many guys could get such a big load to share? I know you gave me a helluva lot of cum, Tom ... and nothing has ever tasted so good."

We were all relatively exhausted, so we took time to send out for a pizza, and we spent several hours telling stories. Dean and I told Tom about my memorable joint birthday party with Richard, where each of the two birthday boys took, respectively, five and six consecutive loads of cum up his ass. We described the parties with Mark and Mike and Cary, with all sorts of combinations, and described the night that Dean got double-fucked by two guys while he was sucking off two others at the same time – and then repeated the feat with the same guys reversing roles. Dean's told about his graduation party in the woods, taking three different cocks up his butt and down his throat while

211

wearing his cap and gown. Dean seemed to enjoy especially telling about how he had teased me with his huge cock the first time I had seen him, at the football game, how we had first got together, and many other wonderful recollections of our experiences together. It surprised, and gratified me, to realize how Dean had figured so prominently in so many of the hottest sexual experiences of my life in recent years.

Tom had plenty of stories to tell, also. He confessed his true identity to Dean, and told him what he had told me earlier, about the wrestler at the Naval Academy, his lover aboard his own ship, and a variety of other fascinating adventures employing the biggest cock I ever saw.

18. INTERLUDE: A HOLLYWOOD PARTY

By far the most fascinating story Tom told concerned a well-known movie actor who had picked him up one night in a gay bar in Los Angeles, while he was dressed as an enlisted man in the tightest pants imaginable, of course. The actor was Tad Fisher, the very popular heart-throb of the mid-1950s, a devastatingly gorgeous blond with a magnificent jaw line – which especially turns me on – and a wonderful body. I felt in the 1950s, and agree with my taste even now, that he was the sexiest, most attractive man in the movies during those years. Most movie actors of that time, even the ones thought of as hunks, had, at best, so-so physiques by today's standards. But Tad Fisher's body was gym-trained, trim, muscular, and as exciting to look at as his face – to me, at any rate.

The similarity of Tad Fisher's face, physique, and even name, to that other mid-1950s movie star Tab Hunter was not a coincidence. Naturally similar in face and body to the established actor, he was picked out of a line-up of extras looking for work in Hollywood by a producer who lusted after the sexy blond star, but who had been unable to convince that Adonis to go to bed with him. The producer changed the newcomer's name to resemble Tab Hunter's, and even shaped his career to match that of the object of his lust. In short, he created his own Tab Hunter, and, given Tad Fisher's willingness – really, eagerness – to have sex with him, the producer finally managed to enjoy a joyous and completely satisfying sex life with his idol, but by proxy.

Tad's publicity photos regularly pictured him in skimpy swim trunks, usually with a wonderfully bulging crotch, and what made him even sexier to me was that although he was always pictured dating and frolicking with young starlets, the word in the gay community was that he was "one of us," a cocksucker and a butt fucker who loved to offer his cock for sucking and his own butt for fucking. Recent accounts say that at that time his homosexuality was common knowledge in Hollywood, as well as in gay circles, but that a combination of controlled studio publicity management and the reticence of the press in those days to print much about that sort of thing protected his general reputation as a handsome young playboy with normal desires. He had his own sitcom on TV for a season, which was terrible – but I never missed it. The star of *The Tad Fisher Show* was, to me, the prettiest thing on television. He looked good enough to eat, and that's was exactly what I dreamed of doing as I watched his show every week. Even well into the 60s he appeared in the occasional surfer movie, where he was still nearly as handsome as a decade earlier, and with a body I still would have adored finding in my bed. By the time he picked Tom Hunt up, in the mid-sixties, he was beginning to fade from the Hollywood scene, although he continued to make the occasional appearance in films right up to the 90s.

According to Tom, Tad still looked wonderful when he approached him in a bar in Los Angeles and began stroking the magnificent tube snaking down from Tom's crotch and heading south toward his left knee. The actor did not introduce himself, and Tom did not recognize him in the dim light of the bar; it was only later, when Tom had gone with him to his enormous home in the Hollywood Hills ("mansion" was the word Tom used to describe it) and finally saw him in full light, with stills and posters from all of his movies scattered around, that he realized the man was Tad Fisher.

"I should have known even in that dark bar," Tom laughed. "He was always a favorite of mine, and I used to sit in the back row of our local theatre to watch his movies, so I could jack off when he was on screen … God knows how many loads of cum I left drying on the floor of the Orpheum Theatre in Dallas." Tad had got Tom's cock hard and out of his pants while they stood at the bar drinking, and a hundred or so patrons watched as Tad knelt before Tom and sucked his gigantic cock. The crowd applauded as Tad pulled his own cock out and masturbated all over the floor while Tom fucked his mouth. Just as Tom was about to cum, Tad pulled back and opened his mouth wide, so that everyone could see the huge spurts of cum going into his mouth. They actually cheered when Tad swallowed the monster load they had just seen shooting so explosively into his hungry mouth, shot by the sailor stud with the unbelievable prick. Tom went home with him for the promise of a thousand dollars for a weekend visit, and the assurance of "a fuck you won't forget."

Tom Hunt's story – In his own words

Tad Fisher really was hot, and meeting him began a whole series of fucks I didn't forget. He had a live-in lover, a Hispanic guy, Tony Lopez, about ten years younger than he, who was nothing short of gorgeous, and who had at least nine inches of fat, hard meat – probably more – which he shoved in both me and Tad about every way imaginable, and who was just as appreciative of what Tad and I shoved in him. I'll never forget Tony's name, because he and I got together and fucked around a lot later on, especially when I learned he had just got out of the Navy, and looked damned near as good in his uniform as he did naked – and believe me, he looked great naked! But to please me, he always wore his uniform jumper and hat when we fucked. Tad was really beautiful, too – probably in his early thirties, but he still looked as great as he did in his early movies, and he was almost as good at fucking as he was at taking it up the ass. His cock wasn't unusually big, but it was big enough, and he was an absolutely tireless wild man when he was using it – he must have shot five or six loads in me that weekend, to say nothing of what he gave Tony. But between Tony and me he got fifteen or so loads up his butt and down his mouth – including one I sucked out of my own cock and shared with Tony and him, like I did with you guys.

Tad's entire bedroom, ceiling and all, was mirrored, and it was really hot to look in the mirrors while we fucked, to see Tad Fisher – whom I'd thought was so gorgeous for so long, and beat off so many times thinking about – kneeling behind me and plowing my ass, or to see his incredible face as I knelt behind him and gave him every inch of my cock. Or to see Tony's beautiful ass opening and closing while he drove that huge tool into me in incredibly long strokes. Lying on our sides, I looked up at the ceiling and saw this unbelievably lucky sailor fucking Tad Fisher up the butt while a monster-cocked Latin beauty was fucking him at the same time. God, it was heaven!

Tad enjoyed me so much he asked me if I would come and be Guest of Honor at a party around his pool one night, with ten or fifteen of his fuck buddies. He explained that Guest of Honor meant he wanted me to fuck everybody and let everybody fuck me. I told him there was no way I could fuck fifteen people in one evening, but he said I just had to fuck their asses for a while, not shoot my load in everyone, just give them a few minutes of my cock up their butts. He agreed I could blow my load in just those I really wanted to, and felt I could – but he hoped I'd at least be sure he was one of those who got to take a load. He did say that he knew everyone would want to cum in my ass, though, and I had to admit the thought of taking ten or fifteen loads of cum up my butt in one night sounded pretty hot. The party would only last five or six hours, but he wanted me to be there a day early and stay a day after for some private sessions with him, and with some of his best fuckbuddies – including a pair of gorgeous nineteen-year-old identical twins who he said had been Guests of Honor at a party he had thrown a while earlier, when they were only eighteen, and who fucked and got fucked by everyone at the party, just like he wanted me to do. He offered me five thousand dollars, and I figured that if nineteen-year old boys could do it, so could I.

What really made it something I didn't think I could pass up was his agreeing to ask the twins to share a good long private session with me – they really sounded fascinating. He promised me he'd be sure they stayed, but he knew they'd need no convincing at all once they got my dick up their butts. "They love big meat; they've almost worn Tony out a couple of times," he told me. He also promised I'd be offered the opportunity to enjoy the twins' specialty – which both he and Tony always shared when they came to visit. He hadn't said what the twins' specialty was, and when I asked, he just grinned and told me to wait and see. I got Tony aside and he told me about the specialty: the twins loved to double-fuck, and their cocks were fairly thin, so it wasn't too painful taking them, he said, but they were really long, so it made for a wonderful fuck. He said something like, "And as young as they are, they're unbelievably hot – and you can really feel them both shooting their loads in you. Man, they're so young and so cute – it's a real treat to get fucked by them. And if that doesn't sell you on it, they're even hotter when they're getting fucked. I've never seen them fucked by a prick as big as yours, but I've seen one almost as big plugging their cute little butts, and completely buried in their mouths – and they loved it and begged for more." I asked him if the prick that was almost as big as mine had been his, and he grinned and admitted it was.

215

Anyway, the upshot was that I agreed to come to the party – hell I guess I agreed to be the party!

And it was a helluva party, let me tell you.

I got there a day in advance, and warmed up on Tad and Tony. Tad wanted to watch Tony and me make love most of the first night, which was fine with me. Tony was a real typical hot Latin lover type, and combining that temperament with his huge, fat prick, he was a lot of fun to fuck with! I did fuck Tad, but he insisted on my watching some clips from his movies while I plowed his ass, and he had Tony's cock in his hand or his mouth or his ass every time mine was in him somewhere. It was kind of weird, and I didn't know what was happening – something between them I guess. Tony and I each got our load several times, but Tad only shot once – and that was while he was watching Tony and me lie there kissing and cuddling: he jacked off and shot his load all over our lips while we kissed. Like I said, a little strange. I spent most of the night sleeping with my face pressed up against Tony's cock, and his next to mine; later, after the whole thing with Tad was over, we spent a lot of nights like that.

The day of the party we slept really late, and I helped Tony put platforms out around the pool, about two-and-half-feet high, and we draped them all in blankets and sheets. The first was about seven-feet square, and Tony explained that this was where I would lie or kneel while everyone fucked me. The second platform was probably about thirty-feet long, and only about three-feet deep; Tony told me this one would be used first, and he laughed when he said, "You can probably figure out for yourself how it's gonna be used. There'll be twelve other guests here tonight, besides Tad and me, and there'll be fourteen hot naked guys leaning over this platform, with their asses stuck up in the air and hungry to get fucked ... waiting for you to go up and down the row, driving your cock into them. You'll love it ... I sure as hell did!" I asked him if he'd been a Guest of Honor, and he laughed again. "How do you think I got to know Tad? I'd always thought he was as beautiful as any guy in the movies, and he picked me up at a bar and offered me the chance to be the star of the party, if I turned out to be as good in bed as he thought I'd be. I was really excited about fucking with him, and I guess I lived up to his expectations, too, because a couple of weeks later, I was his new Guest of Honor. At the party, I fucked his ass first, and shot a huge load in it, then went down the row sticking my cock into the other ten or so guys, but came back and ended up shooting another load into Tad – I figured he's really be pleased with that, and I wanted to get in really solid with him. I thought he was the hottest guy in the movies then, and I still do. Anyway, he loved it, and when it came time for everyone to fuck me, he went last and shot his load in me then he stayed inside me and just kept fucking and fucking until he gave me another one. He had really flipped for me." I told Tony I could readily understand that. I'd kinda flipped for him myself.

He grabbed me in his arms and we stood there and kissed for about fifteen minutes, then went and hid from Tad while Tony fucked me up the ass; I wanted to fuck him, but I had to save myself for the party that night.

I couldn't believe it when the waiters and caterers and musicians came and started to get ready for the party. They were all young, gorgeous, and really well-built guys – mostly all in their early twenties. Tad had hired them from an agency that specialized in providing hot young studs for gay parties – guys who would do their work, but who would also "cooperate" with guests for extra tips. Even then, Tad handpicked them from the agency's photo album of employees. After they set everything up, and it was about time for the party to begin, they changed into their uniforms – little pouches that barely held only their cock and balls, which were called posing straps back then. Other than that, they were completely naked, their pubic hair showing above those little bulging pouches, which really didn't hide anything. There were pretty, hot asses all over the place, just asking to be eaten or fucked – and believe me, most of them got just that. Several of those pouches had been destroyed by the time they packed up to leave.

Tad was totally naked, but he had me dress in my tightest uniform to meet his guests when they arrived. I guess I had expected older guys – producers and agents, and people like that – but every guy who showed up was hot as hell. It was obvious Tad had fucked with everyone there because as we stood by Tad's front door, and after he had introduced me to each guy, the newcomer stripped naked while he stood there, then put his arms around Tad, and they would kiss and feel each other up. Occasionally one would drop to his knees and suck the other a bit, or eat his ass, but they always watched me as they did – it was obvious they were looking forward to the main event, and it was also pretty obvious they were impressed with the sight of my cock in those tight pants. Apparently only Tony and The Twins had been Guests of Honor at earlier parties, but it was obvious most of his guests had been to a lot of these gatherings.

I actually recognized one of the early arrivals, Davey McCaslin, and he looked fabulous. In case you don't remember, which seems unlikely, Davey was a popular singing star, best known as the baby-faced and gorgeous younger brother on *The Arnie and Jeanette Show*. I'd heard a rumor that he was gay, and it turned out that he and Tad had been lovers for a while when Davey was younger. And judging from the way they greeted each other, a lot of the old love was still alive. I told Davey I'd fantasized about fucking with him for a long time – which seemed to please him a lot, judging by the way he groped me.

The star running back for one of the local Universities – either UCLA or USC, I forget which – showed up, and he was apparently another regular at Tad's parties. I hadn't recognized him, but his name – Boyd Epps – was certainly familiar to college football fans. Like every one of the guests, he was young and cute, had a fantastic body, and the kind of ass that could turn the most confirmed straight man into a rabid, drooling butt fucker. When I was introduced to him, I told him, "I really am looking forward to having you get deep in my end zone!" He grinned, and turned around to display his perfect ass. Then he looked over his shoulder at me and gave me a really sexy smile while he stroked his ass and said, "And I'm looking forward to playing defense to your offense, too. It looks like you're gonna be able to penetrate my defense really deep!"

One other football player was there, too, but he was only a high-school student – unbelievable as that seemed – and one look at his cock let me know how he had become part of Tad's circle of friends. It was very, very long and really fat, too – even bigger than Tony's. Aside from mine, it was one of the biggest tools I'd ever seen. This football player was going to get even deeper in my end zone – quite a bit deeper, I was happy to think – than Boyd Epps. I had the feeling I might both be going into the mass fuck around the pool as a tight end, but was going to be more like a wide receiver by the time I got through.

Tad was the one who fell to his knees when this super-hung high-school stud shed his clothes, and it looked like was trying to eat a whole salami when he saluted the kid's cock the only appropriate way – and the cock he was sucking wasn't even fully hard yet. The kid was a tall blond, raised in the South somewhere – and if he wasn't't really handsome, he looked pretty good, and he had the cockiest and sexiest grin I ever saw. He walked over and shook my hand, looked down at my basket, and stroked my cock through my pants. "I'm Gary Jackson ... Jacks to my friends ... and judgin' by the way this feels, I sure wanna be your friend. I've always got the biggest pecker at these parties, but it looks like I'm gonna have some competition tonight for champion cock." His huge prick got fully hard while he played with mine, and I assured him I'd be happy to share the honors with him any time, and then I took hold of his prick and stroked it a little bit while I told him I hoped we could share everything that night. By this time my own prick was straining at my pants, and Jacks whispered "I can't wait" as he stroked it once more before swaggering out to the pool, his prodigious prick standing straight out, swaying and bobbing with each step.

Two sailors showed up together who seemed to be lovers, – both really hot, with pants almost as tight as mine, and showing plenty of cock inside. They were both dark and kind of short, but both were also extremely handsome. One of them was Greek, Danny Allinkas, and the other, George Mojica, was about half Irish and half Cherokee. Before they stripped down, I asked Tad if it would be all right for the two to have their jumpers and hats on when I fucked with them. Tad said they could leave them on all night, if that turned me on – which, as you know, it really does. So all night they circulated wearing the upper part of their uniforms, but totally naked below the waist – really hot, with pretty cocks and even prettier asses. I got their address, by the way – and we got together whenever my ship was in port in San Diego, where they lived. I didn't have to worry about their ship being in at the same time because it turned out neither of them was even in the Navy; they just liked dressing up as sailors, and they loved fucking with real ones. Turned out they weren't lovers either, although they had started out that way. They were just two fuck-buddies who lived and fucked together and spent most of their free time tracking down sailors to get together with for sex. In fact, I got together with them only a couple of weeks ago – hotter than hell!

* * * *

At that point in Tom's narrative, Dean interrupted, laughing, "Yeah ... just three hung, horny sailors fucking each other, but really an officer and two civilians!"

Tom admitted it was probably a little strange, but the sailor-fucking mystique was so stimulating to them that they wouldn't dream of changing. "Besides, they still think I really am an enlisted man."

I couldn't help but add, "Yeah ... maybe. But I'll bet they at least suspect you're not an enlisted man, and they don't care as long as you wear that sexy uniform ... and give them a prick like that fabulous ass-reamer of yours."

He agreed I was quite likely right then returned to his tale of the big party.

* * * *

The twins were among the last to arrive; their names were Don and Ron, but everyone just referred to them as the twins, and they didn't even use their names when addressing each other. I had been told they were nineteen, but I could have as easily believed they were seventeen. Still, no matter how young they looked, they were absolutely breathtaking – tall, very blond, incredibly handsome – and indistinguishable from each other. I wondered if even they could tell each other apart! When they stripped, it was obvious they were plenty old enough to fuck. Their bodies were completely smooth, but with good muscles, extra long legs, pretty little round asses that stuck out behind them, and in spite of the blond hair on their heads, big bushes of black pubic hair over really pretty cocks, which promised to get plenty long, like Tony had promised. After they had stripped, they embraced each other before turning their attention to Tad. They played with each other's cocks, and when they turned to embrace Tad, their beautiful cocks were hard and very long – and stood straight out from their bodies, displaying a couple sets of really impressive balls. Tad knelt and took their two cocks into his mouth at the same time, Like Tony had said, their pricks were not very bulky, given their considerable length, and the two made up a really big, but still manageable mouthful. He sucked them for a while before they came over to me, put their arms around me, and kissed me on both sides of the neck. They told me they heard they were going to share a private session with me after the party. While we were kissing, I could feel their hard pricks pressing against me. One of them was groping my cock and another was playing with my ass. They were getting me really hot, but I had to hold off, so I kissed each of them and played with their asses and stroked their cocks as I told them I was looking forward to seeing them at the party, But being alone with them later was what I was looking forward to most.

Like I said, all the waiters and caterers were young and cute, and really well built, and I would have been happy to go to bed with any one of them. The one who had been at the front door, collecting clothes as the guests stripped – and handing them off to another waiter, who took them somewhere inside – was adorable, and his prick was so hard most of the time that his posing strap simply wouldn't hold it, so the head and a couple of inches of dick poked out above it.

After the last guest had arrived – all twelve of them had made the scene – I walked over to the waiter with his cock showing, and groped his pouch. I stroked the part of his cock showing and told him, "I understand all the guests are going to line up for me to fuck, and they're all gonna fuck me." He grinned and said, "That's what happens, and pardon my saying so, but you're as lucky as you are gorgeous." I grinned back at him and told him, "If there's any way you can slip in line, I'd love to fuck that pretty ass of yours and get a load of cum out of this really big dick of yours up my ass." I put my hand all the way inside his pouch when I said that, and his prick really was huge. "Wow ... that feels fantastic," I said. "No wonder you've been making me horny all this time." He groped me back and said, "Check with Tad. It's his party, but if it's okay with him, let me know. There's nobody at this party I'd rather have up my butt tonight; I've been checking you out, too, you know. My name is Johnny, by the way ... Johnny Owens." He winked at me, and I patted his bare ass as he walked away, smiling over his shoulder.

I went to bed with Johnny dozens of times after that and found out he was even hotter than I thought he would be when I asked him to join the party that night. In fact, he moved to San Diego to be near me, and we've been lovers for about a year now. The only time he fucks with anyone other than me is when we go to threesomes or orgies – which we do quite a bit, actually – but he understands I fuck around a lot, and he accepts it as long as I eventually pull my cock out of whomever I'm fucking, and stick it back in him. Come to think of it, I met a lot of guys that weekend that I later wound up fucking with regularly.

I asked Tad how he had met all those hot guys, and he told me most of them he had first picked up in gay bars, like he had me, but the high-school football player he had found hustling on the street – and he loved getting fucked as much as he loved fucking. Davey McCaslin was barely eighteen when Tad made a guest appearance on *The Arnie and Jeanette Show*, and since Davey had heard rumors about Tad's sexual appetite, and had been fantasizing about making love with him, they didn't waste time; they got together and spent the whole afternoon after the first read-through for the show having wild sex in

Davey's dressing room. After that, like I said, they sort of became lovers for a while.

He'd picked Boyd Epps up on the street, too, but he was just walking along when Tad spotted his ass – and thought (and I agreed) it was the cutest ass he'd ever seen. Boyd was mighty impressed to be meeting Tad Fisher, Tad was impressed to be meeting Boyd Epps, and the rest, like they say, is history – they'd been sucking each other off and banging each other's butts pretty regularly ever since.

The twins were another story. Tad picked up a hot guy at a gay bar and took him home; after a night of great fucking, the guy told him all about these incredibly hot twin boys he could line up for Tad. Tad was interested, of course, and it was only later that he found out that this was the twins' stepfather who was making them available. Their mother was, apparently, long gone, and Dad realized what a treasure he had at home. He had trained his stepsons just the way he wanted them. They had started sucking him off on their eighteenth birthday, and he started sucking them off a little bit later. Not long after that, Dad was fucking them regularly, and they were fucking him even more often. Tad sampled the twins in private – in an orgy with their stepfather – and flipped out. Then he paid the father to bring the twins to their first party as Guests of Honor, and they were a sensation. They loved the whole scene so much they never had to be paid to come back.

Anyway, before going in to join the party, I asked Tad if any of the waiters or caterers were allowed to take part in the orgy. He told me they didn't, normally, but they'd probably all be involved with the guests at one point or another, and as long as they did their work, that was fine – and they made a lot of money in tips for those extra services. I asked about Johnny Owens, "Could you make an exception for him? I sure would like to find his cute little butt lined up on those platforms with all the other guys, and I bet he'd love leaving a load in me like everybody else ... as much as I'd love feeling him blowing it in me." Tad agreed it would be fine, and I went to find Johnny. I told him to be sure to get in the line-up and be ready to take my cock and give me a big load. He kissed me and gave me his sexy grin again, "I've got a really big load I want to give you." I groped his balls in his pouch (a lot of his cock was showing above it again) and this time he groped back – really feeling my prick this time and getting it even harder than it was when he first felt it. "I don't think I've ever wanted anything the way I want this unbelievable cock ... if you can, please give me a load when you fuck me ... that would be so fuckin' great!" I kissed him and swore that when I got to him I wouldn't quit fucking him until I had blown a load up his ass.

After the last guest arrived, Tad and I went in to the party. I circulated around and chatted with all those hot, naked men – feeling a little strange, being the only one with clothes on, except for the two partially dressed sailors and the guys working, but they were all almost naked. Everyone was casually kissing

221

and groping as they talked, even kneeling once in a while to kiss or suck a cock or ass for a minute or so. I spotted some of the guests kneeling in front of some of the waiters and caterers, pulling their pouches down and giving them full blow jobs, or standing behind them and eating or drilling their asses as they leaned over or lay on a table.

One especially cute waiter, not Johnny Owens, came up to Davey McCaslin with a tray of *hors d'oeuvres*, and I couldn't hear what passed between them, but the waiter gave Davey the tray to hold, pulled his pouch down, got his prick hard, and jacked off – blowing a load all over the food on the tray. He pulled his pouch back up to cover his prick, and Davey put some money on the tray. He handed it back to the waiter, who grinned as he watched while the famous and beautiful Davey McCaslin proceeded to nibble on appetizers covered with his cum and share them with the other guys who had been watching the action.

After about an hour of circulating, Tad declared it was time to get down to the main order of business, and he stood on the higher, smaller platform where I was to get fucked by everybody, and called for all the guests to gather around. Then he had me step up on the platform and he said, "You've all met Tom Fox, and I'll bet you all checked out the huge piece of meat and those monster balls that are not very well concealed by those hot, tight pants. But now it's time you saw them in the flesh ... and it's a helluva lot of flesh you're about to see. Tony and I have checked it out thoroughly and I promise you you're in for a real treat. Tom, show us what we're all dying to have inside us, and what we're dying to get inside of."

Tad had briefed me a little bit on how to perform, but mostly he just told me to be as sexy as I could – so basically, I winged it. I did a very slow strip while the band played some jazzy music, and I got a big hand every time a piece of my uniform came off. By the time I was down to just my pants – I wasn't wearing any shorts, at Tom's request – the guests were all crowding the platform, and watching closely. The waiters and caterers were just as attentive, but they kept their distance. I unbuttoned my thirteen buttons, and dropped the flap, so they could see the pubic hair above my prick, then unbuttoned the belt and began to slide my pants down over my butt. It was really turning me on, and by the time I was ready to show them my cock, it was hard as hell, and when it popped out of my pants, they cheered.

I dropped my pants and kicked them off, then walked around the edges of the platform, so everyone could reach up and play with my prick and my balls – and several of them kissed the head of my dick and gave it a little lick or suck. I leaned over and stuck my ass way out and turned around so everyone could get a good look at it. Then I walked around again, putting my ass in each guy's face, so he could get a feel – and of course a lot of them also kissed my hole and gave me a quick rim. I stood in the middle of the platform and leaned way over, put

222

my hand between my legs and stuck my finger up my asshole. I began to finger-fuck myself – turning around as I did this so everyone could get a good look.

I lay on my back, spreading my legs and putting them way up in the air while I finger-fucked myself some more, telling them. "I want every prick out there doing this to me!" Then, with my finger still all the way in my ass, I rolled onto my stomach and humped the platform as wildly as I could, before rolling on my back again, planting my feet on the platform, and levering my body high in the air while I fucked my fist.

I stood, and called Tad over. I took his head in my hands as he stood there on the floor. The platform was just the right height so that my prick was pointing right at his mouth. "I want to check everybody's temperature before we start," I announced, "and since Tad's our host, I'm gonna start with him." I rammed my cock down his throat and began to fuck his mouth. Then I went around and held each guy's head tight while I fucked his mouth with about ten or twelve thrusts down the throat. A few gagged, but most of 'em held my ass and pulled me in tight while I fucked, and took almost all of my cock in their mouths. These guys were all experienced, first-rate cocksuckers, after all, and several of them – including both of the twins – gobbled every last bit of it down their throats.

Everyone "ooh-ed" and "aah-ed" and cheered and applauded everything I did, but the biggest cheer came when I pointed at the long platform and told them, "Everybody get over there and lean over. Show me where I'm going to bury this big prick ... I'm ready to fuck ass!" And they lost no time lining up and presenting their asses for me. It was truly an unbelievable sight: Tad and Tony and their twelve guests, plus the waiter Johnny – fifteen really beautiful men – all leaning over a long platform, showing a long line of hot asses, hungry to get fucked. And another twenty-five or thirty guys were standing in the background, almost every one with his posing strap pulled below his balls, and playing with his cock. They all watched as I approached Tad – the first in line – and stood behind him.

A dozen or so tubes of KY Jelly were scattered around the long platform, and I squeezed some on Tad's ass then wiped what was left on my cock and smiled at the spectators. I called out, "Saluting our host," just as I rammed my cock hard into Tad, up to the hilt. He gave a yell that turned into a moan of ecstasy as I fucked him hard for a couple of minutes. There's no point in going over what everyone said to me while I fucked them – but they were plenty vocal in urging me to fill them up.

Tony was next to Tad, and he had already lubed up his ass, so when I pulled out of Tad, I stepped behind Tony and rammed into him – and he greeted my entry as enthusiastically as his lover had. I don't remember what order they were in after that, but I gave each of them about four or five minutes of hard butt fucking and every one of them obviously loved getting big meat up the ass. Everyone backed up to meet my thrusts, and gripped my cock with their assholes and rode it hard. A few of them were unable to take all of my prick, and those I went easy on, but most of their buttholes swallowed my cock like they had no bottom, and I fucked those like a goddamned savage. The twins were absolute wild men when I fucked them, and I had a little foretaste of the private session we had scheduled for later; it was obviously going to be red hot!

When I came to Johnny Owens, the waiter, I told him to get to the end of the line before I fucked him. He looked crushed, but I whispered in his ear, "I want the very best at the end ... and I want to finish this thing up by shooting a hot load up that beautiful ass of yours!" He grinned and took his place at the end.

I whispered endearments to each guy as I fucked him, with special messages for a few: I told Davey McCaslin I'd been dreaming of getting in his adorable ass for years, and promised to give him a load if I could. Danny and George, looking especially fuckworthy in their uniform jumpers and white hats, obviously loved getting fucked, and Danny told me that he and George really wanted to get together with me later for some private fun – I told him I did, too, never guessing how often I'd be drilling those two hot little asses in the future.

When I approached Boyd Epps, he stood up, arched his back, and stuck his ass out – and it was certainly one of the most fuckable-looking asses I'd ever seen – round, and smooth, and looking like a perfect peach ready to be picked. He looked over his shoulder and down at his ass before he looked back at me and said, "This look like something you'd like to fill with that fuckin' monster piece of meat?" I told him it was the prettiest thing I'd ever seen, and I knelt behind him to kiss and caress the perfection he was proudly displaying for me, before I put my tongue as far into his asshole as it would go, and tongue-fucked him for a long time before I pressed his body down on the platform and planted my cock all the way inside that hot, magnificent butt with one fierce shove. I fucked him like a demon, and twice as long as I had so far fucked anyone; he reached behind to pull my ass in while I fucked him, and met every stroke I gave him with a grunt and a backward thrust that felt as perfect as his ass looked. Before I moved on, he said I had, indeed, penetrated his end zone better than anyone ever had. I promised him I'd be back for more.

While I fucked the twins, I told them I wasn't going to give them a load yet, but when we got together alone later, I'd be sure to have plenty for them. Judging by the way they took my cock up their asses that was going to be a really memorable session.

Probably the hottest fucker was Jacks, the high-school football player – fantastic tight ass that gripped my cock like a vacuum cleaner, and he was really insanely wild while I fucked him, telling me, "Show me how hard and how deep you want me to fuck you." Given his stupendous prick, I wanted him to fuck me like I'd never been fucked, so I kept driving into him as long as I had with Boyd Epps – I seemed to have a thing for football players that night – and I came pretty close to shooting my load up his hot butt. But I still had a few guys to fuck before I could cum, so I rested for a minute with my prick all the way inside while I promised to come back and fill his hot ass with what I wanted him to give me. He turned around to kiss me and whispered, "I'll fuck you like you've never been fucked in your life!" Big talk for a high-school kid, but he seemed to be as much man as anyone could ever ask for.

When I got to the end of the platform and shoved my cock in Johnny, he moaned, "God, Tom ... that's the biggest prick I've ever felt." But he took every inch of it, and treated it really well. I whispered in his ear, "You are the cutest, and the hottest guy here ... I'll be back to give you that load."

I started with Tad again, and by the time I got to Davey McCaslin, I was more than ready to shoot my load. I fucked hard for only a minute or two, and both Davey and I cried out as I shot my load up the butt of the cutest guy in television. All the waiters clapped and cheered, but over that I could still hear Davey telling me how wonderful it felt.

I had to slow down after my first orgasm and pace myself, but by the time I got back to Jacks, I figured I was maybe ready to shoot another load. He really worked with me like an insane fuck machine, and I had to hammer his ass about twice as long as I had before, but finally I rewarded his really expert technique with another big load, and apparently it was shot with plenty of force also, since he cried out his appreciation as soon as he felt it start. Before I went on to the next one, he turned to me and said, "That may have been the best fuck I ever got, but if you think I'm good at takin' it up the ass, wait until you find out how good I am at givin' it up the ass! When I shove this humongous dick of mine inside that honey-sweet ass of yours, I'm gonna fuckin' fill it with cum ... and baby, we are both gonna be in heaven!" I told him – quite honestly – that I was really looking forward to it, too, and to be sure he didn't beat off or exercise his monster cock on anybody else before he stuck it in me – I wanted every stroke he could give me before he shot his load up my butt.

Finally reaching Johnny again at the end, I was plenty tired, but he was so cute, and so eager to please, that I just kept fucking and fucking and fucking – and everyone, guests and workers, were watching closely by this time. They all broke into cheers when I finally threw my head back and shouted while I filled Johnny's ass with my third load in a pretty short period of time. I held him close in my arms and kissed with him, and promised him we would get together soon and make love to each other, not just fuck. He seemed really pleased, and whispered, "You can't believe how much your wanting to include me in this line-up meant to me, and how flattered I am that you gave me that huge load. When I put my prick inside you in a little while, I'm not just going to be fucking you, I'm really going to be making love to you ... think of that with every stroke I give you in your fabulous ass." I almost wanted to stop everything and take him in a bedroom right then, but the prospect of fifteen hot men all waiting to fuck my ass was so exciting, that I put those thoughts aside.

Needless to say, I was tired, but I figured I'd be spending the next hour or so on my back or my belly or my knees, getting fucked, so I saw no reason not to get started. I went over to the smaller platform and called everybody to it. "It's my turn now. I want every one of you guys, who took me up the ass so terrifically to return the favor. I want all of you to fuck me until you shoot a huge load up my hungry ass. Worship my fuckin' ass with your hard cocks and your loads. I want so much cum in me that I slosh!"

I held out my hands to Tad, and he came to me. We kissed and embraced, and over his shoulder as we held each other tight, I told the guests, "Tad Fisher is so beautiful and sexy I used to find a seat in the back row of the theatre when his movies played in Dallas, so I could jack off while I watched him." I held Tad at arm's length, and looked into his eyes. "You've no idea how slippery that floor was where I used to shoot my cum ... you inspired me to huge loads and multiple jack-offs." I took his hands and held them as I backed up toward the platform. "Sucking Tad Fisher's cock, or feeling this beautiful mouth of his on my own prick, and especially fucking and getting fucked by him, have been really intense dreams of mine for a long time. In this house recently, those dreams came true … wonderfully true. Tad, I want all your friends here to witness you giving me this incredible thrill, and honoring my lucky ass by fucking it with your beautiful prick. And I want each of you to pretend you're me for a few minutes now, and share this thrill and this honor with me." I lay down on my back at the edge of the platform, spread my legs wide, and raised them in the air. "Keep making my dreams come true, Tad."

Tad needed no further encouragement, and took hold of my legs as I lubed myself up. He thrust his cock deep into me, and the guests gathered around the platform in a tight circle to watch. I could see the waiters and caterers standing on benches and chairs to get a good view as this blond god performed for his adoring audience – screwing me with complete mastery of the art of fucking, and with genuine enthusiasm. He fucked me for a long time, often leaning over and kissing me and stroking my cock. His enthusiasm for fucking me turned into rampant savagery as he finally drove himself all the way in, and together we shouted our thrill at the huge load he blew in my ass. He kissed me again, and stood tall, with his cock still sunk in my ass. He held out his hand to Tony, and said "This hot ass is full of my cum for you, lover, Fuck it hard and deep the way you do mine, and feel your monster cock swimming in my jizz while you fuck it."

Tad pulled out, and Tony moved right in, immediately replacing Tad's cock with his own much, much larger tool – and given the workout Tad had just given my tingling asshole, he needed no added lubrication. It felt wonderful as he began to fuck, and with a lot of kissing and caressing and insane thrusting of his stupendous tool deep inside me, he reached down and picked me up bodily – still impaled on him, with my arms around his neck – and his hands cradled my ass as he continued to fuck, until I felt the enormous explosion of his orgasm.

He panted and continued to fuck while he calmed down, whispering in my ear, "That was an even bigger load than the one I gave you this afternoon. God, I love to fuck you!"

I whispered back, "Believe me, I feel the same way, and we're going to fuck each other a lot in the future, I know ... be sure we don't lose sight of that. You're a great piece of ass, Tony."

He laughed, and replied, "Second only to you, stud." And he put me back on the platform, on my back, and turned me over to the next fucker.

Three of the other guests fucked me next – and they were hot and beautiful and well-hung – it seemed that everyone at this party was – and they gave me big loads, too. By the time Davey McCaslin got to me, I had a whole helluva lot of cum in me. But Davey fucked me like a trooper, and spent a lot of time playing with my cock and kissing me while he fucked, and talking about how great all that cum felt inside me. He made that very clear when he added his own discharge to the pool, arching his back as he stayed planted deep in my ass, and shouting something like, "Yeah, Tom, take this big load from me ... I wanna fill your hot ass with my cum!" Needless to say, my hot ass was already filled with cum, but he certainly added nicely to it, and again it was great to have such a famous and beautiful star fucking me, another one I had fantasized about – along with every other gay guy in the country, most likely.

Another guest plugged me for only a short while before he shot his load, and was replaced by star quarterback Boyd Epps – and I was sorry I couldn't watch his incomparably beautiful ass while he screwed me. He was fucking me with unbelievably long strokes, so long that his cock often slipped out, but he always shoved it right back in without missing a beat. I fondled his fabulous tits while he fucked me, and visualized how the crevice between those perfect ass cheeks was opening and closing, showing and hiding his tempting little asshole while he gave me those long strokes – piston fucking me like a veritable fuck machine. I couldn't watch his ass, but I told him how beautiful it was, how great it had felt when I did to him what he was doing to me, how I adored getting fucked by him, and – when the big moment arrived – feeling him adding his load to the huge quantity of cum building up inside me.

My two sailors added their liquid love to me next, and it was great to see those uniform looming over me as George and Danny fucked me with equal devotion and expertise, and shot their hot offerings. Another of the guests was a priest; they called him Father Peter, but I think that was a joke. He followed George and Danny, and if I wasn't expecting anything special, I was surprised. He was a really accomplished lover, kissing a lot, and paying a lot of attention to my cock while he fucked, playing with my tits and crooning endearments into my ear. He had a really big prick, too, and when he came in me, he didn't shout, but whispered into my ear about how beautiful my ass was, and how big my prick was, and how much he had loved getting fucked by me.

227

The twins followed, and I cheated: as each was fucking me with his long, thin prick, I whispered in his ear, "Fake cumming in me ... we're going to be alone together after everyone leaves, and I want to be able to really appreciate the way that pretty cock feels when it's shooting a load of cum in me." They both whispered their agreement, but each also fucked me a long time, and very hard, and probably came close to actual orgasm. They were both pretty good actors, since everyone seemed convinced they had shot their loads in me. By this time, I probably couldn't have told if they had shot in me or not; they may have, but I think they didn't, because they sure had plenty to give me later on.

Johnny, my extra-cute waiter was next-to-last, and he took a long time too, fucking eagerly and deeply, but also kissing and caressing me more than anyone had, and stroking my prick as he fucked, telling me how much he had loved taking it up his ass. He finally delivered a load inside me with tremendous passion – not saying, "Take my cum," but, "Take my love!" – and lay holding me for several minutes. Before he stood up, he kissed me and whispered into my ear, "I think I'm going to wind up loving you. Is that going to be a problem?" I kissed him back and smiled at him. "I think it sounds like a good idea ... and I promise you we'll get together to explore that idea soon."

The last guy to fuck me was Jacks – the football stud, wielding the biggest cock around, except for mine – and it didn't miss being the equal of mine by much at all. He loomed over me and grinned. "I have got the biggest load you'll ever get waitin' deep inside these big balls ... see if you can tell it's in there." He got up on the platform, straddled my face and knelt, putting his balls right over my face. I stretched my mouth to take all of his monstrous ball sac inside, and began to suck. "Yeah! Hot damn," he gasped. "Suck those big balls. And how about suckin' what's gonna deliver that big load to your hot ass." He pulled his balls away from my mouth, replaced them with his incredibly big cock, and mouth-fucked me mercilessly with it. I had to use all my cocksucking technique to keep from gagging, but I opened my throat and took all he had to give me. He fucked me that way for quite a while as I played with his ass, and then he stood over me and looked down – stupendous cock sticking straight out, looking like a torpedo – and snarled, "Get that hot ass ready for the fuck of your life!"

He stepped off the platform and positioned himself behind me as I raised and spread my legs again. "Give me your cock, Jacks ... I want the biggest prick I've ever had inside me fucking me right now!" With a loud, "All right!" he put the tip of his prick up against my asshole and began to push. He had not lubricated his dick, but my ass was so distended, and awash with cum, that he needed none, He began to enter slowly, then with a grunt and a massive thrust, he was buried in me.

I'd never had such big meat inside me, and it felt unbelievably exciting. I felt hot all over, feeling utterly filled. The sensation was glorious. He was in absolute heaven, but then so was I. He was apparently as equipped by temperament to be an artist at fucking as he was physically equipped with the most perfect tool to practice his art.

When his cock had reached all the way into my ass – and I had to really relax to take all of it, but I was determined to do so – I could not only feel his huge balls and his pubic hair nestling against my ass, I could also feel streams of cum being displaced from me, and running down my buttocks and onto my lower back. Still fresh from my ass, where so many hot men had blown it, it felt hot to me as it came back out. There was, no doubt, plenty of cum still left inside me, and I knew that this masterful stud promised to give me a lot more.

As Jacks began slowly fucking me, you could actually hear his cock squishing in my assful of cum. He grinned down at me, "You've got cum runnin' out of your hot fuckin' ass, and my monster cock is swimmin' in it! God damn but that feels good! And I'm gonna replace every drop of it that's leakin' out with my big load ... 'cause I've been savin' a huge fuckin' load of hot cum for you, and I'm gonna blow it farther up this pretty ass than you've ever had it. Work with me, baby, work your ass on my cock and help me give you the best fuckin' you've ever had, just like you fucked my ass, man ... best fuck my hot ass has ever got. I'll be just dreamin' about the feel of that great big pretty cock of yours fuckin' my ass while I fuck yours. Yeah, baby ... work with me, take my cock! Godamighty, your ass is tight! Grip my cock and work it with that ass of yours ... yeah, that's so fuckin' hot ... it's like your asshole's givin' me a blowjob! Tom, baby, this is the hottest ass I ever fucked in my whole fuckin' life!" Those may not be exactly the words he said, but pretty much so; and he kept talking to me while he fucked, and if his talk wasn't quite as exciting as his fucking – nothing could have been that exciting – it was plenty stimulating. He continued to claim my ass was tight, which would have seemed ludicrous, given the fact that a dozen or so big cocks had just fucked it and blown loads there, but to a cock as big as Jacks', I guess most any ass would be fairly tight.

I did my very best to bring as much to Jacks' fuck as I could: I backed down hard on his prick with every thrust he gave me; I squeezed his big driving shaft with my ass-ring and fucked myself on it at the same time he was fucking me; and I kept encouraging him with the same kind of super-sexy talk he was using to spur me on to greater heights of passion. Between his monstrous cock, his perfect fucking technique, my own best efforts at helping him to fuck, and the wonderfully filthy talk we exchanged, I really was probably getting the fuck of my life as promised.

His slow fucking was unbelievably deep, and the length of his stroke was equally impressive – I'd never had such a big prick inside me, and so I'd never known such an absolute thrill as the feel of that colossal shaft sinking in and pulling out about nine or ten inches with each stroke. Sure, I'd been fucked with dildoes that big, but they were no substitute for the real thing.

As Jacks sped up, his talk got even wilder, and his strokes had to be a bit shorter; after about ten minutes of this savage fucking – the most intense feeling I've ever experienced – he began to whimper with lust, and he sank his prick all the way inside me and continued to fuck with extremely short and fast strokes. In a minute he blew an absolutely stupendous load deep, deep inside me. I was full of cum already, but there was no mistaking the force or the volume of his explosive eruption of hot cum, way up inside my hungry ass. As he continued to fuck for some time, and finally collapsed over me, there was no doubt that I had indeed experienced an unforgettable, watershed fuck. The thirty-five or so people watching us fuck had apparently been struck silent with awe because in the delirium of the magnificent fuck Jacks was giving me, I had completely forgotten they were there. But when he finally collapsed over me, our audience broke into cheers and appreciative whistles, which continued for a long time while they all grouped around us and congratulated us on the hottest show they'd seen.

We finally broke, and I stood on the platform to acknowledge the cheers. As I stood, a huge quantity of cum began running out of my ass and down my legs, to puddle at my feet. I looked down at it and held up my hands to silence the cheers. "You have just witnessed the absolute best fuck I've ever got in my entire lifetime ... maybe the best anyone's ever got." Everyone cheered again, and I again silenced them. "That doesn't mean that I haven't got fucked wonderfully by most of you guys here ... I have, believe me, my ass knows it! But I've never had such a huge, spectacular cock inside me as this beautiful stud just finished plowing me with!" I took hold of Jacks' huge cock – still hard, by the way – and kissed him as we got another round of applause. I reached behind me, and swiped my hand over my ass, and held it up – dripping with cum. "I thank every one of you for all the hot loads you gave me. Your cum was inside me along with Jacks' cock ... so you all shared this ... this historic fuck with me." I looked down at the puddle of cum at my feet, and grinned at everybody "My ass runneth over!"

As they started applauding again, Jacks gave me a quick kiss and stepped down. I was about to step off the platform also, when one of the waiters stepped up and stopped me from doing so. He put his arm around my waist and held up his hand for the audience to listen. He said, "Believe it or not, there are about ten of us who haven't been fucking around much with anyone yet tonight, and who have been asked to give tonight's guest of honor a very special salute. I won't tell you who asked, but he's one of us who's gonna take part in this salute." He pulled his little pouch down, and stepped out of it. "If no one objects, we're going to get out of uniform for a few minutes." A bunch of other waiters and caterers stripped off their pouches and lined up at one end of the platform – about a dozen absolutely gorgeous naked men, stroking beautiful cocks that were already hard, or well on the way. One of them was Johnny. I looked at him with a questioning look, and he smiled shyly and nodded. There

230

was no question who had lined these guys up to render whatever kind of salute I was in for, and I felt pretty sure it was going to be something really hot and extremely enjoyable.

The waiter who was addressing us took my hand and led me off the platform. "Stand on the ground right there, Tom," and he indicated a place at the edge of the platform, facing the waiters. As I stepped down, he stepped back up on the platform, standing directly in front of me, and began jacking off, with his cock very close to my face. Like every guy there, he was attractive as hell, and his cock looked wonderful as he stroked it faster and faster, until he said, "Open your mouth, Tom," and began to shoot a really spectacular load, with spurt after spurt of cum into my open mouth, on my head and chest, and generally all over me. I smiled and licked my lips where cum had landed, and swallowed the goodly amount that had actually shot into my mouth. As I did so, another beauty stepped up and began jacking off frantically in front of me – and I was shortly rewarded with another blast of hot cum in my mouth, in my hair, and all over my body.

The third guy who stepped up to jack off on me took it a little further. He put his dick at my face as he was stroking it, but he moved in close, took the back of my head in the hand not busy with his prick, and pushed his cock-head up against my lips. I happily opened my mouth, and he drove his busy cock all the way deep into my throat and began to face-fuck me. I held his legs in my hand as he fucked, and drove my lips up and down his driving shaft, sucking as hard as I could. After several wonderful minutes of this, he pulled his cock out of me and stepped back a pace; then, of course, he blew his load all over me, and again a considerable part of it went into my mouth to savor and swallow.

Everyone who followed did the same thing: they fucked my mouth hard and deep – these beautiful guys were all pretty well hung – and wound up shooting hot loads into my mouth specifically, and onto my face and body generally. I licked cocks and sucked balls as they first stepped up to me, and then I played with asses and balls, finger-fucked driving asses, fondled tits, and got face-fucked magnificently and repeatedly at the same time. After having two guys shoot their loads all over me unassisted, I sucked off another half-dozen guys in succession, and each one basically received a full-length blowjob. By the time the next-to-the-last guy had shot his load on me, I was covered with cum from the top of my head down to my cock. It was in my hair and my eyebrows, it was running down my shoulders and tits, and dripping from my belly into my pubic hair. But the greatest concentration was on my face, except where my tongue had been able to reach to lick it off. I had also swallowed an enormous quantity of those hot guys' offerings to me, and nothing had ever tasted better.

Not surprisingly, the last to approach me was Johnny Owens. He came up to me, put his cock in my face and began to stroke it – and it looked huge and unbearably tempting. But instead of driving it into my mouth as everyone had before, he knelt, and very gently took my head in both hands. He looked into my eyes for a long time, and then gradually he moved in until his lips were about an inch from mine. He smiled at me and said, "I never believed in love at first sight ... until tonight." Then his lips met mine, and we kissed very gently for a long time. He pulled back a few inches and looked at me again for some time. He asked, "Soon?" I smiled at him and nodded, "Soon, Johnny ... I swear. Now I think I want you to fuck my mouth about as much as I've ever wanted anything." Having kissed my cum-covered face, there was now a considerable amount of semen on his own. I licked every bit of it from him, and kissed him again. He stood and pressed the tip of his throbbing prick against my mouth. I opened wide and he face-fucked me for a long, wonderful time, driving his cock with incredibly long strokes. Finally, as he was about to cum, he pulled out, intending to shoot his load all over me as everyone else had done, but just after his magnificent cock had exploded a couple of hot spurts on me, I seized his ass and pulled him to me, taking his erupting cock inside – and I savored the rest of his thrilling load as he shot it deep inside my mouth. I murmured my appreciation, and sucked every last drop of cum from his beautiful tool. He continued to fuck my mouth slowly, until his cock softened, and I had swallowed every bit of his love juice. After giving eight or ten blowjobs, the last was best of all.

I stepped up on the platform, and folded Johnny in my arms. He held me tight, and we kissed again, for a long time – accompanied by the applause and cheers of everyone watching, who knew that something special and tender had passed between Johnny and me. Before we parted, I whispered into his ear, "Very soon, baby, I promise."

I thanked all the waiters for the special salute, and looking down at all the cum on my body, I announced that I needed to take a shower. Davey McCaslin stepped up on the platform and put his hand on my shoulder. He looked as adorable as only Davey McCaslin can look when he told me, "No shower necessary," and he began to lick the cum from my chest. He was licking all over me, when he was joined by Tad, and then a number of others, and I was soon completely licked clean of cum. I had even had parts of me not coated with cum – my cock, my ass, my balls – thoroughly licked also.

I witnessed all sorts of other wild sexual acts before the party broke up: I watched the two tall, beautiful blond twins holding each other and kissing while the pair of shorter, dark sailors, George and Danny, fucked them as they stood behind them – almost mirror images, but what beautiful images! There were any number of couples lying about on the deck, locked together, sucking each other off in sixty-nine. Waiters knelt behind or over guests to fuck asses, or the guests assumed the active role in drilling waiters. Davey and Tad – the two famous beauties – lay side-by-side on their backs on the platform as the golden twins rode their cocks to enthusiastic orgasm. Father Peter was getting double-fucked by two waiters and when I passed by he was sucking Tony Lopez' balls while Tony's huge prick was shooting a massive stream of cum all over the priest's hair. At least ten guys lined up while Boyd Epps of the perfect ass knelt for them to first eat his ass, then fuck it, and Jacks came back to give me another load from his mammoth cock, this time in my mouth. He wanted me to do the same for him, but I had to beg off, since I was saving myself for my session with the twins, although I promised we would get together privately soon to concentrate on each other. Later, we did – and it was fuckin' epic!

After Jacks had blown his load down my throat, he led me to the shower, next to the pool. He sat down over the drain, looked up at me, smiling, and said, "Piss on me."

One of the caterers was kneeling next to the shower, blowing one of the guests, and when he heard what Jacks had asked me to do, he sat next to him and smiled along, "Me, too, oh God, please ... me, too!" I really had to piss pretty badly, so I stood over the two, and began to take a very long piss, spraying it all over the two hot bodies waiting to receive it. Both closed their eyes, and put their heads back, asking me to piss on their faces also. I did as I was asked, and my piss splashed off their faces, and much into their wide-open mouths. Jacks was masturbating as I pissed on his cock, and it was huge and hard again, even after the monster load he had just given me. The caterer just barely touched his dick as I directed my stream onto it, and it began shooting spurts of cum quite high in the air. When I finished pissing, Jacks and the caterer fell in each other's arms kissing and fondling, and I left them there.

The party broke up around two in the morning, and everyone left except Tad and Tony – who lived there, after all – the twins, and me. Before leaving, I had exchanged addresses with Jacks, whose bigger-than-big prick I was dying to get up my ass again soon – and which I did. George and Danny, the hot pair of sailor-lovers gave me their address, and of course, Johnny did the same. I knew by the way Johnny took leave of me that something fairly serious was going to develop between us. Both Davey McCaslin (cutest guy on TV) and Boyd Epps (prettiest ass ever) promised to see me again soon at another one of Tad's parties, and both hoped to fuck and be fucked, suck and be sucked, and I assured them that would be a priority of mine, too, if Tad would invite me. Tad assured me I'd be at many parties in the future.

Tad and Tony kissed me and the twins goodnight, and went into their bedroom. Tad's blond, incredible beauty and muscular body contrasted with Tony's dark, Latin beauty and massive cock, making them a perfect pair. The twins and I were left alone in another fully mirrored bedroom.

I should have been exhausted by the activities of the party, but these two blond, identical beauties were sexually fascinating and stimulating beyond belief. Either one alone would have been a hot, fully satisfying fuck partner, but in tandem, as seemingly identical entities – two hot men doing everything, but looking like one doing double duty, an eerie feeling, in some ways – they kept me at an intense level of horniness I wouldn't have believed possible. They should have been tired also; I knew they had been very active at the party, and even though I had fucked them and they had fucked me, we had not yet cum in each other. I had recently seen them getting fucked side-by-side by two different sets of guys, however, and God knows how many other guys had fucked or sucked them or had received the same service from them. All of that mattered not at all in the bedroom with me that night – all night. They were unbelievably hot, and among the best fuckers I have ever encountered, almost at the level of the unbelievably talented Jacks with the stupendous prick. Had it not been that their incredibly pretty faces made them look like young boys, it would have been totally impossible to believe they were only eighteen years old. Their bodies were adult and well developed, their cocks were big, their balls were massive, and they performed at an almost professional level as cocksuckers, face fuckers, butt fuckers, and insatiable recipients of big meat up their asses. In addition, they were sweet and cuddly and tender, and very sharing of their wonderful charms and potency – and with thousands of kisses, some very gentle and loving, and some very, very passionate.

They occasionally giggled like kids, but the fact that this usually happened when they had cocks up their asses or were fucking an asshole or a mouth made it seem especially exciting. I felt I was fucking with boys, but boys who were mature, fully developed men sexually – and, in fact, I was. I'd fucked many barely-legal boys before who acted their age in many ways, but who just happened to adore sucking cock and getting fucked up the ass. But the twins were nothing like this; I knew I was having sex with young men when I was with them.

It would take hours to describe all the sexual positions and variations we used together. We sucked and fucked in daisy-chains, we rode pricks, we fucked in both missionary and dog style, I sucked a load out of each of their cocks as we lay in sixty-nine – first with one, and then with the other – and one of them, I have no idea which, swallowed my load just as he was erupting in my throat. I managed to blow a load up each of their asses, and they practiced their specialty on me – that wonderful dance, the Identical Twin Double-Fuck. I had been double-fucked many times, but never like this. Their pricks were very long and thin, so it was not painful having both up my ass at the same time. When I had entertained two cocks up my ass at the same time before that, it had always been a fairly precarious operation, with one of the fuckers usually having to be fairly passive while the other fucked and shot his wad – but the twins had perfected their technique through long practice.

We began in about the only way I can see that a double fuck can: one of the twins lay on his back while I rode his cock, and the other knelt behind to penetrate my ass along with his brother. The difference was that they entered me together, and the feeling of two cocks entering at the same time was indescribable, much like the fattest cock imaginable going thrillingly into your ass. They fucked really hard, and with the wonderfully long kind of strokes only possible with long cocks like theirs. At times one would fuck while the other's cock stayed still, but they also fucked together at the same time, moving their cocks in and out in perfect synchronization. The truly unique wrinkle they brought to the art of double-fucking was a sort of reverse action – one prick driving deep inside as the other pulled almost all the way out, deep and hard and fast, in rapid rotation. The feeling inside me was like nothing I have ever felt – unbelievably stimulating and sexy. When they neared orgasm while they were doing this, when one said "Ready?" and the other said he was, they smoothly switched to simultaneous movement in and out; it was obvious they had practiced this shift in attack many, many times. After about six of eight violent thrusts with both pricks, they shot their loads with explosive force – one orgasm following the other by a matter of only a few seconds. It was perhaps the most wildly erotic thing that had ever happened to me, and I thought it was no wonder the twins were more-or-less famous for it.

We slept some that night, but not much. They were as insatiable as they were beautiful, and their youth, their voraciousness, and their perfect sexual technique made it a night to be savored to the full, so I didn't want to waste much time on sleep.

The next morning, pretty near noon, we sat around the breakfast table: Tad and Tony lovey-dovey, holding hands and stark naked; the twins dressed only in little silk boxer shorts that left almost nothing to the imagination; and me wearing only my sailor pants. We discussed the party of the night before, and Tad declared it an unparalleled success. He made me promise to return for similar parties when I could, Needless to say, I promised I would. The twins were sitting very close to each other, kissing and caressing as if they were lovers – which, I gathered, they were.

The doorbell rang, and Tony went to answer it. He came back with a very handsome, well-built blond man, probably in his early forties. Tony said generally as he entered, "Allen has come to pick up the twins. Tom, meet Allen ... he's the proud father of Ron and Don here."

Allen held out his hand and smiled, "Actually, stepfather ... but plenty proud." As we shook hands, he looked down and cruised my crotch. "I can see that the boys must have had a good time. I would have, too." He joined us for coffee, and before he and the twins left, every one of us – including his twin sons – had fucked him up the ass and blown a load in him. It was a great way to formally end the party – watching my very favorite movie star fucking, seeing two beautiful youngsters fuck their own stepfather with each eating his brother's ass while he fucked, and seeing how truly sexy Tony's ass and body are – and how perfectly beautiful and enormous his prick is when he fucks. I began to think then, and later came to feel sure, that Tony – especially when he dresses for me in his old navy uniform – is probably the sexiest man I came to know at that party, even though I came to love Johnny, never saw or fucked a more perfect ass than Boyd's, and never had sex with a better hung or more savage and accomplished fucker than the incredible high-school student, Jacks.

The twins' stepfather Allen was a great fuck, by the way, and he would have fit in perfectly at the party the night before. I fucked him last, and he was almost screaming his appreciation of my prick up his ass and the big load I shot into him. As soon as I gave him every last drop of my cum, I leaned over the table and joyfully accepted his own very impressive load deep inside me. He was, incidentally, well hung, and a great fuck. I've visited him and the twins several times at their home; believe me, it's always interesting, to say the least.

The twins' college graduation is coming up, and Allen is throwing a special party for them – an orgy, of course, but with just guys the twins particularly want to fuck with. I'm flattered that they want me there, and they want Tony, too – but the really exciting part is that the other dozen or so guests will all be college boys. I guess you can imagine how Tony and I are both looking forward to that! Johnny's not too happy about it, but he understands – he's fucked the twins and got their special double-fuck a few times, so he knows I can't pass it up.

So, it was quite a party: I met and fucked one of the most famous and beautiful gay men in the country, and fucked another one again; admired and fucked the absolutely perfect ass of a famous football player; got fucked by fourteen or fifteen hot guys in a row, and fucked the same number; had ten guys blow their loads all over me before another ten or so licked me clean; welcomed the biggest prick I'd ever had up my ass; got double-fucked in a unique way by two beautiful identical twins; met several people I later had sex with on a fairly regular basis; and had a gorgeous man fall in love with me, one I shortly came to feel the same way about. And, I got paid five thousand dollars for it!

19. TOM MAKES HIS MARK

Tom's long narrative had been fascinating. For most of the telling, the three of us had lain together, snuggling on the bed and lazily playing with each other. By the time he finished, we were well rested and ready for more sex, although the hour was by then quite late.

I slipped down to kiss and admire Tom's enormous cock, and about two kisses was all it took to bring it to full glory. "I can't believe I'm kissing a prick that's fucked both Davey McCaslin and Tad Fisher," I said.

Tom laughed. "Believe me, it's fucked both of them, and it's shot more cum inside Tad's hungry ass than you can imagine." He took hold of my head, directed his prick inside my mouth, and began to fuck it. "I only fucked Davey McCaslin that one time, but he was as beautiful as you could possibly expect, and he left a really good load inside me, too. I learned from the twins that they get together to party with him frequently, just the three of them, but I'll bet their dad fucks Davey or gets Davey's cock up his ass somewhere along the way."

Dean said as he came down to help me suck Tom's cock, "Jesus, I'd love to fuck Davey McCaslin."

"He'd love to have you up his ass, believe me," Tom said, "but then so would I; I haven't had that big beauty of yours inside mine in a couple of hours. And don't forget, both Davey McCaslin and Tad Fisher have been inside there."

As Dean began licking Tom's balls and kissing the base of the monster shaft I was sucking, he said, "You know, you're gonna feel me way up inside you very damn soon ... looking for the ghost of Davey McCaslin's dick. God I love to suck cock ... and yours is the best ever, Tom."

Dean and I began what can only be described as worship of Tom's truly beautiful, steely hard, and incomparably large prick as he lay there, the two of us kissing and licking his cock together, sucking his balls and cock at the same time, and often plunging our fingers into his twitching asshole as we sucked. After a long time of his murmuring complete satisfaction at our administration of this very slow, but thorough blowjob, Tom said, "I've gotta cum ... who gets this load?" I seized his cock and began to masturbate him. "Let's watch it, Dean." I drove my fist up and down Tom's monster shaft only a few more times before his white, creamy cum began boiling out of the end, and shooting straight up in the air in a series of spurts of prodigious volume and velocity. Much of it splashed on Dean's and my faces as we encouraged Tom's massive explosion of love. Once he had finished, Dean and I lapped up every drop from his belly, his prick, and from each other's faces.

Tom's uniform jumper was by this time pretty thoroughly stained with cum, so I took it off, and sponged it clean the next morning. I climbed back in bed with the two hot men I had been worshipping – one with the biggest prick I'd ever seen, and the other with only somewhat less endowment. A total of about twenty inches of hard dick was waiting for me in that bed.

We lay there for some time as Tom expressed his thanks for our worship. He sighed, "I guess we've got to get some sleep ... but I want to get fucked goodnight." He got on his knees and smiled back over his shoulder. "Get that hot prick of your in here, John. Dean, you can fuck my mouth with that gigantic thing of yours while he does, and be looking for the ghost of Davey McCaslin in there at the same time."

I knelt behind Tom and fucked him for a long time as I watched him eagerly sucking Dean's mighty prick. Dean and I held each other and often exchanged kisses, and as I shot my load inside the hungry ass I was fucking, Tom stopped sucking to vent his excitement at the feeling.

Then Dean said, "If you keep sucking, Tom, you're gonna get my load down your throat. Isn't that what you want?"

Instead of answering predictably, Tom said, "As great as your cock feels up my ass, John, let Dean shove his in there. I want to get fucked by that monster just one more time before we go to sleep." Dean fucked him eagerly and violently, and I had my tongue up Dean's ass most of the time while he was doing it. Dean blew his load in Tom, and as they collapsed together, I put my cock in Dean's ass. I went happily to sleep that way, and I suspect that for at least a while as we slept, Tom's ass continued to harbor Dean's precious dick, just as Dean's provided a warm and familiar shelter for my own. A happy and peaceful way to end one of the hottest and most satisfying days I had ever spent.

The next morning we awoke fairly late, and started the day with a repetition of many of the wonderful acts of love and sheer animal lust that had been so delightful the day before. Before we ended our lovemaking, Tom fucked both Dean and me to full orgasm, and we each served him the same way. I lay in sixty-nine with Tom, and we both sucked loads of cum into our eager mouths; Dean and Tom later lay the same way, and I watched lovingly as their beautiful asses drove their formidable cocks deep into their mouths to achieve the same delicious results. In spite of his having shot four loads into us, Tom jacked off and shot a load on Dean's and my lips as, at his direction, we lay on the bed holding each other tight and kissing passionately.

I called home to see if Mark was back, and he was. I explained what had happened, and he regretted having not been home. I had shown Tom a picture of Mark, and he was impressed with his great beauty – as anybody would have been, but Dean told him Mark was even more beautiful in person. Tom took the phone from me and told Mark he was sorry to have missed him, and hoped that some day they might get together. Mark told Tom he'd be thrilled to have a prick like the one I had described shoved up his butt and down his throat – especially one that had fucked both Tad Fisher and Davey McCaslin. Tom laughed and said he'd really love to have Mark fill the same holes that Tad and Davey had filled for him.

Before Tom left, presumably to go back to his parents' house, and to return to San Diego the next day, I showed him Richard's picture, and gave him Richard's address in San Francisco. "I know you'd love fucking with Richard, and if Eddie is still around, you'd adore it. So, if you're in San Francisco, look him up. I'll call or write him and tell him not to turn you down if you show up wanting to go to bed." Tom took the address gladly. Richard looked fabulous in the picture, one I had taken and developed myself, showing his enormous, beautiful cock in full, very impressive erection, so Tom decided he would definitely plan to visit San Francisco soon.

It was only about a month or so later that Tom called from Richard's apartment in San Francisco. The two had just finished a marathon fuck session, and Tom was planning to spend the weekend with my well-hung ex-lover – and the supremely hung Eddie was scheduled to join them soon. Richard and Eddie were apparently no longer lovers, but they still fucked each other regularly, and Tom needed no particular persuasion to submit himself to the legendary Eddie Bliss prick.

It seemed Richard was interested in making porn videos, and Tom had promised to pull strings with some people in the gay porn industry who had long been after Tom to make fuck films for them. He was considering agreeing to appear himself in a film with Richard, fucking and getting fucked by my ex-lover, if his face were not shown – he was, after all, still on active duty with the Navy. As it happened, Tom's recommendation to the right man gave Richard the break he wanted. While Tom got sucked off by Richard, and they fucked each other in Richard's first film, Tom's face was shown only in deep shadows or silhouette.

Tom said, "Richard's told me how beautiful and hot he's heard Mark is, and you showed me his picture, of course. I really would like to come and see him, and fuck him, and get him to fuck me, and do all those wonderful things with you again, too. And maybe with Dean, too? God damn, but he is hot isn't he? When is a good time for me to fly out?" We settled on a long weekend a month or so later, and Tom promised to bring sailor uniforms for both Mark and me. When I told him I was sure I could get Dean to join us, he eagerly promised to bring one for him, too.

About a month later, Tom showed up as promised, in civilian clothes, but bringing uniforms for all of us, including one extra for the wonderful surprise he brought with him – the magnificent Tony Lopez.

Tony proved to be every bit as gorgeous facially as Tom had said, his body was smooth and extremely sexy, instead of terribly muscular, and his prick was stunning – almost as long as Dean's, extremely fat, and capable of staying unbelievably hard for hours. And as a special bonus, Tony's huge organ was a thing of smooth, dark, and absolutely perfect beauty.

Playing sailor most of the time, Mark and Dean and I all feasted for three days on Tom and Tony, and they enjoyed us in the same way. The story of that weekend would take a volume to describe in detail. Suffice it to say, it was three of the most exciting days of my life – and the most exciting days of Mark's life, according to him.

Selfishly, Mark and I had decided not to involve Cary and Mike in the visit, but seeing Cary's picture, Tom expressed great interest in at least meeting him. Reluctantly, I called, and found that Mike was out of town. Cary agreed to come out for a short time just to meet Tom and Tony, but once he saw their pricks, he was hooked. He had only a couple of hours before he had to take a test, but during that short period Tom sucked Cary off, and then he, Tony, Dean, Mark, and I in succession all shot loads into his more-than-willing, beautiful ass. By the time I had given Cary my load, Tom was hard enough to repeat his assault on the blond beauty's ass – and then Cary was hard enough again that Tony sucked him off to round out the celebration. The matchless, muscular blond went off to take a test leaving one of his copious and precious loads inside each of two of the most exciting men I have ever met, and with six loads of cum inside his perfect little butt.

Mark and I celebrated Cary and Mike's graduation that spring in much the same way we had Dean's, a year earlier. It was almost as bright a night when we gathered in the clearing in the same park, and stripped off our clothes. Wearing only a graduation cap, Cary and Mike each knelt before the other three to get his face-fucked and to suck out a load of hot cum. And using only a graduation gown as a blanket, each either knelt to offer his hungry ass, or lay with his legs spread and raised high to delight in the savage fucking the other three of us administered. It took a very long time, as we each came four times out in the park, and considerable resting was necessitated – but the kissing and snuggling that accompanied our rests was almost as enjoyable as the fabulous face- and ass-fucking we engaged in.

We then retired to Cary and Mike's apartment, and over the course of the remainder of that night and the next morning, Cary and I double-sucked each other to orgasm while Mike and Mark did the same. Then Mike and I sucked simultaneous hot loads from each other's cocks as our beautiful lovers performed the same service for each other.

That afternoon, returning home, Mark and I realized that although Mike and Cary had each taken three loads up his ass, neither of us had been fucked to celebrate their graduation, so we remedied that failing as we eagerly fucked each other in their honor.

When we had finished, I called their apartment to tell them what we had done; Cary answered, and after I explained the purpose of my call, he giggled, "Well, neither of us fucked or got fucked this morning, so Mike's got his prick in my ass right now, and judging by his breathing it won't be long before he's done and I can start in on him." Studs indeed!

Cary and Mike moved to Chicago, and rarely returned to Dowd. It was, in fact, several years after their graduation before I saw either of them. In Chicago they experimented with a number of other guys, sharing partners and having miniature orgies, but found their relationship was becoming strained through petty jealousies, so they decided to become monogamous, and my

John Butler

occasional visits with them never involved sex with all three of us, although I had sex on the sly with Cary alone, and with Mike alone any number of times during those encounters. If they were fooling each other, it was none of my business, and on those relatively rare occasions I still gloried in our love-making: the feel of Mike's arms around my waist and the massive bulk of his huge prick as he knelt behind me and filled my eager ass; gazing up at Cary's beautiful countenance as I lay on my back with my legs wrapped around his waist while his beautiful cock drove deep inside me, and I fondled his fabulous pecs; the thrill of giving my load to either of these special friends, and the wonderful taste of their treasured emissions; and all the other permutations and combinations of sexual fulfillment that we had practiced together so often and so memorably in the past.

A few years later, Mike and Cary became confident enough in their relationship that they again opened themselves up to sex with others – and on a number of visits I was again able to experience the thrill of sucking one of the two while the other drilled my eager ass.

Mark's senior year, 1968-69, was marked by a considerable lessening of our sharing of sex with others. Dean came to visit often, of course, and we both invariably thrilled to his monster cock and insatiable lustiness. Richard returned for what was to have been a two-day visit, and when he saw how beautiful Mark was, he managed to talk his way into our bed the first night – which took very little talking, needless to say. He extended his stay a week, during which time Mark and I entertained the thrill of his huge prick inside us innumerable times, and Richard offered his ass and mouth to our cocks with equal eagerness – and we often serviced both of his hot orifices at the same time.

The night before Richard returned home was incredibly hot. Mark and I double-fucked him, followed by the incomparable thrill of Mark's beautiful cock joining Richard's enormous prick already deep inside me, and their subsequent flooding of my ass. Mark doubted he would be able to take both Richard's massive shaft and another cock in his ass at the same time, but I convinced him that if I could take both Richard's beautiful monster and his own impressive cock inside me at the same time, he would do fine. Of course he did manage, and was as happy with our joint offering as I had been with theirs.

Not surprisingly, Johnny Farrar – Mark's cute soccer teammate whom he had been very interested in when we first began making love, but who had so foolishly spurned Mark's advances – came around at last. On a soccer trip, Mark and Johnny roomed together, and as Johnny began to reminisce about when he and Mark had kissed and held hands frequently in their freshman year, he began to grope Mark's ass and crotch, and soon was sucking his cock. It had taken him three years to get up the nerve, but he finally admitted he wanted to go to bed with Mark. Mark still thought Johnny was extremely attractive (so did I), and he welcomed him into his arms, his mouth, and his ass. Johnny was convinced

241

Mark was now ready to be his lover, but Mark made it clear he now had a lover, and could only sustain some kind of relationship with him if I was involved also.

Johnny came out to our house a number of times, and I was impressed with what a fine body and ass he had. While he was timid and reticent about lovemaking at first, by the time Mark and I had shown him how intense and joyous sex between men could be, he was hooked. He grew to adore the feel of our cocks up his ass, and found the taste of cum addictive. We welcomed his pretty cock and his hot load into any of our holes and loved caressing and kissing him. He became a very accomplished fucker, and shortly found another teammate to fuck with – one not already occupied with a lover. Johnny's new playmate was a very hot, very pretty Israeli, and we both felt good about having had a hand in training him to be an effective lover.

Near the end of Mark's senior year, the Selective Service System instituted the draft lottery, and his birthday was number seven – meaning he was virtually assured of being drafted very soon. Rather than face the prospect of almost surely being drafted to go off and fight in Vietnam as part of the Army, Mark enlisted in the Navy, negotiating the date of his actual induction until a week or two after his graduation.

For one week after his graduation, Mark and I saw absolutely no one else. We hiked in the nearby mountains, we swam and water-skied, we had quiet meals together, and spent a lot of time just sitting and holding each other, reminiscing and hoping for the future. We also made love a couple of times each day – and while we fucked and sucked with the kind of lustful abandon we had enjoyed so much in the past, much of our love-making was sweet also. We both discovered, for instance, that very slow, deep fucking or cocksucking – accompanied by murmurs of love rather than cries of excitement – could be fully as rewarding as the fevered kind we usually practiced.

Mark had to spend his last few days as a civilian with his family in Pennsylvania, but we managed to sneak in one night of wild, exuberant, and sometimes even hilarious sex with Dean before he left. I saw Mark off at the Atlanta airport, and just as he was about to board his plane, we held each other closely for a long time, and our last act was very daring for 1969. We kissed for a very long time in public – both passionately and tenderly – and it didn't seem to bother anyone. The man checking tickets at the gate smiled at us as Mark boarded, and winked at me and said, "He'll be fine!"

I was glad Mark was going into the Navy rather than the army; the number of soldiers getting killed was alarming (the Navy seemed to have far fewer casualties), and the stories circulating about atrocities and drug use in the ground forces were scary. He entered as an enlisted man, and considered going to Officer's Candidate School, but the additional year or two it would have added to his enlistment deterred him. Following his boot camp training at the Naval Training Center in San Diego, he was assigned to the fleet as a quartermaster trainee – a "striker," in Navy parlance. It might have seemed to be a coincidence, but he wound up stationed on the destroyer *U.S.S. Stonesifer*, whose Executive Officer was still Tom Hunt. It was not a coincidence.

At my suggestion, Mark had looked Tom up, and they got together for sex several times during his boot camp training. I knew from my own experience at the same Naval Training Center just how lonely boot camp could be, and I knew how exciting Mark found Tom Hunt – and excitement of the Tom Hunt variety is rare enough in this world. When the *Stonesifer* was in port, Tom lived with Johnny Owens – now officially his lover – and Johnny and Mark became very close friends. Tom and Johnny had what they called an "open" relationship, but in their case that basically meant that Tom fucked around a lot and Johnny accepted it as a necessary part of their union. As a couple, however, they frequently had sex with other guys – and when he could join them, they enthusiastically welcomed Mark into their bed. They occasionally called me when they were all together, and I shared vicariously in the joy – as, for instance, when I talked with Mark while Tom was plunging his monster prick into him, or heard Tom panting how much he wished I were there to share as he felt Mark's load exploding in his ass. I also got to where I felt I knew Johnny, and he seemed like an extremely nice young man.

Tom knew all sorts of people through his sexual activities – and most of them would do anything to get him to fuck them. He had fucked a personnel officer at the Training Center who managed, to show his gratitude for Tom's fuck, to get Mark sent to the *Stonesifer* upon graduation from boot camp.

When Mark reported aboard the ship, Tom got him assigned to the Executive Division, so that Tom was his division officer. Mark hadn't been aboard ship two days before he was fucking regularly with Tom. As Executive Officer, Tom was one of only two officers aboard ship who had a private cabin (the other was the Captain, of course), so they had a place to go for lovemaking, but they were both intelligent enough to practice great care in their meetings, and no one apparently ever suspected what was going on, even though a number of sailors who tried to put the make on Mark – and several of the hotter ones succeeded – told Mark how desirable they thought the Executive Officer was. Mark suspected one of them was actually fucking with Tom also, but Tom denied it.

The strange thing that happened was that although Tom and Mark loved fucking with each other, it was Mark and Johnny who became lovers. It had become increasingly clear that Johnny was overwhelmingly attracted to Mark, and one night Mark called me to say that he and Johnny were very much in love with each other, and that as much as he still loved me, he could no longer deny that it was Johnny he now most wanted to be with sexually. Tom was supportive, and the three continued to fuck when they were all together, but Tom was gone more and more, pursuing – and almost always finding – other hot cocks to suck and asses to fuck. When Tom's tour of duty on the *Stonesifer* was up, he was assigned to another destroyer, the *U.S.S. Earthman*. Mark was not surprised, nor was Johnny angry, since all had agreed in advance, when he was re-assigned to the *Earthman*.

Tom and Mark continued to fuck each other for the rest of the time Mark was in the Navy, but when he was discharged, he and Johnny bought a house together in San Diego. In that house they often entertained Tom in their bed – he was very important to them, not only as the agency that brought them together, but also as an unforgettable and incomparable sex partner. I was also welcomed to their bed on several occasions when I visited the West Coast, and found Johnny Owens to be as sexy and beautiful as Tom – and later, Mark – had claimed. For the most part, however, Johnny and Mark kept to themselves as a loyal couple. Later, like Mike and Cary, they opened up their relationship to allow for purely recreational fucking with other hot guys – like Tom and me, for instance.

Tom's separation from the Navy occasioned a party that I should love to have attended.

Before Tom left the *Earthman*, Mark supplied him with a list of eleven sailors aboard the destroyer he knew to be gay – and his information came at first hand, each one of them having either submitted to Mark's cock, or offered his own for Mark's gratification – usually both. A few days before he was to be separated, Tom called each of the sailors on Mark's list in to his office, and individually invited them to a party he was hosting at the El Cortez Hotel in San Diego. He explained that they did not have to attend – he would no longer be in the Navy by the time of the party, and could certainly not order them to do so – but he knew they would have an unusually exciting time, and would be free to leave at any time if they weren't fully enjoying themselves. Further, he told them to put in for full weekend liberty, since the party would begin at 6:00 Friday afternoon, and would not end until Sunday night. He was still their Executive Officer, and assured them their liberty would be approved if they put in for it.

Curiosity, if nothing else, brought every one of the invited eleven to the party at the three-bedroom suite Tom had rented at the El Cortez. Food and liquor were well supplied, and Tom welcomed each of them wearing civilian clothes. The eleven sailors were all, as requested, dressed in their uniforms. As they circulated, they no doubt began to suspect something of what was in store, since most of them – probably all – realized that the common denominator was their homosexuality, and that there were piles of towels and tubes of KY Jelly liberally distributed around the suite, even in the living room.

After the last guest arrived, Tom went into one of the bedrooms for a few minutes, and came back wearing only a bathrobe. He stood on a very large, solid coffee table and formally welcomed the whole group to what he hoped was going to be an unforgettable weekend. "And in case you're wondering why I asked you to be here, it's because I want each and every one of you to shove your cocks down my throat while I give you the best blow job I know how to give ... and believe me, I know how to give a blow job. After I suck every drop of cum out of those hot pricks, I want you to build up another load to give me while you fuck me up the ass."

The sailors were initially struck dumb by this announcement, but they began grinning as Tom went on. "Before you decide if you want to stay and give me what I want, I'll warn you that I expect to fuck every one of you up the ass too, and I've got a hell of a lot of meat to give you ... and I'll fuck hard, and shove every last inch of it all the way up your asses, and I won't stop until I've shot my load as far inside you as I can shoot it." At that point he dropped his bathrobe, and began to stroke his cock – which had already risen to nearly full erection while he had watched the hot sailors begin to register their excitement as he described what he wanted from them.

The eleven almost gasped as they realized what a colossal piece of meat their former Executive Officer had, and they began to grin as they contemplated how marvelous riding and feasting on that stupendous cock was going to be. One of the sailors stood up and took hold of Tom's cock as he looked up and said, "I'd be honored, Mr. Hunt ... and I'd like to be the first one to get this incredible dick inside me." Tom leaned over and kissed the sailor, promising he'd be the first, "And you'll get a load I've been carrying around for a couple of days, just to give to somebody who really appreciates it." The sailor began unbuttoning his pants as he told Tom he would definitely be one who would appreciate it. Tom reached down and got a packet of file cards and a pencil from his bathrobe pocket, removed one of the cards, and smiled at the sailor he had just kissed as he said, "I'm changing your appointment time. By the way, I'm assuming there's no one who wants to leave ... is that right?" A voice came from the group, "Jesus Christ, no, Mr. Hunt ... everybody here wants a piece of that fabulous prick!" Tom laughed, and everybody clapped, and began to chatter. Tom again silenced them. "Okay, I'm passing out appointment cards through Sunday afternoon ... then we're going to have one more sailor visit us before we break up ... and everyone, myself included, has to be able to give him one final load before the party is over."

He made some time changes on the cards and distributed them to each of the other ten sailors. "I plan to spend a full three hours with each of you guys individually ... I want to really enjoy making love with you when we're together, not just a quick fuck ... and I expect two loads from each sailor. More than two loads will always be welcome, of course! God damn, don't you love getting fucked by a sailor?" A chorus of cheers indicated full agreement. "We've got all weekend, and I planned it that way so I'll have plenty of time to work up a good load for every sailor I fuck. You can sleep, or fuck, or whatever you want to do, wherever you want to do it. There's plenty of food and beer and booze ... just don't get so drunk you can't get it up for me. I'm going to be using the master bedroom, but I suspect there's probably going to be some fucking and sucking going on in those other bedrooms while I'm busy in mine." Everybody laughed, and one sailor said, "What's wrong with the living room, Mr. Hunt?" Tom laughed and assured them they were free to use any part of the suite, "And if you want to come in and watch while I'm fucking with someone else, you'll be welcome, but don't interfere ... I want to concentrate on each of you when we fuck. Here's the only restriction: every one of you strip off every bit of your uniforms except your jumpers, and do it now ... otherwise, this is strictly a naked party. Any sailor that gets in bed with me or comes in to watch had better be wearing his jumper ... I want to be reminded I'm fucking with sailors from the *Earthman*. Of course, I know you guys are going to be such hot fuckers, you could only be sailors ... but when I look up at a guy who's fucking me, it's twice as hot if I can see he's a swabbie." This drew a big cheer, and Tom took the first sailor by the hand. They went into the master bedroom, intentionally leaving the door open to welcome admiring spectators. And spectators visited regularly during the entire time of the party, jacking off and – when more than one was watching – often playing with each other, sucking, and even fucking as they admired Tom's magnificent cock and his virtuoso fucking technique, looking forward to their time in their former Executive Officer's arms.

According to reports, Tom kissed and snuggled and lay tenderly in loving embrace with each sailor, before he sucked a load out of each cock. He welcomed getting his cock sucked in no uncertain terms, but each time he neared orgasm, he stopped so that he could save his load and explode it in each sailor's ass. He impaled some of the guys on his stupendous prick as they knelt before him, and a few as they stood, but most lay on their backs while he fucked them missionary style – and each one of them took every inch of his huge prick, and begged him to fuck faster, and harder, and even deeper. Every sailor was grinning and fully satisfied upon leaving Tom's bed, since the final part of each guy's time with Tom was shooting his last load as far into Tom's ass as he could. A number of the sailors gave Tom three loads in their three hours' time – and one even managed four. To receive this last load, Tom invariably lay on his back and reveled in the incomparable sight of a beautiful sailor over him, driving his hard cock into his ass. With his legs wrapped around his fucker's waist, he would urge as hard, as fast and as deep a penetration as possible – and each hard fuck was followed by a tender leave-taking involving some very sweet, appreciative kissing and fondling. The lovemaking in each case was thorough and unhurried, and completely satisfying. Tom treated each of these horny sailors as if he were a special lover, and every one of them as he left the bedroom was probably in love with Tom to some degree, and each definitely still sported a raging hard-on, although he had shot at least two loads into the incomparable fuckmaster.

Several lucky sailors – ones Tom had especially been wanting to fuck for a long time, and one he later revealed he had been fucking with for over a year – got to spend several extra hours in bed with their magnificently endowed, horny host, allowing Tom to get some sleep. Those chosen few lay in Tom's arms as he slept, and their luck was compounded, I later learned, because after waking Tom had those extra-time sailors fuck him up the ass one more time before leaving his bed.

By Sunday afternoon the last of the eleven sailors had fucked Tom and been fucked by him, and all had fucked and sucked with several of their shipmates as well. Right on time, as scheduled, the last sailor appeared at the suite – Mark, of course. Tom stood on the coffee table again to address the group formally, with Mark in full uniform standing next to him. Aside from several jumpers, his uniform was the only clothing in sight.

Tom and Mark kissed and caressed, and then held their arms around each other at the waist as Tom began. "I would imagine you're all wondering why Mark hasn't been a part of this group. I know that each of you has had sex with him, so you know he loves to fuck and suck as much as you do, and I don't think any of you will be angry to learn that Mark supplied me with the guest list for this party." Everyone cheered Mark wildly. Tom continued, "I first met Mark at a little college town in Alabama a couple of years ago, and I had flown all the way out there to go to bed with him. I'd fucked with his lover earlier, and had seen Mark's picture – and another guy who I was fucking out here had heard about Mark back in Alabama. Mark's lover said he was the most beautiful man he'd ever fucked, and I knew he had great taste in men, since he'd flipped his lid over me! Naturally I had to find out for myself, so I flew out there and learned that he hadn't exaggerated at all. Anyway, we spent three days fucking our brains out. Later, Mark joined the Navy, and I got him assigned to my ship, and then got him transferred to the *Earthman* when I came aboard her." He grinned broadly at Mark. "Mark and I have been fucking each other for three years ... and Mark, there's never been anyone like you." He and Mark kissed for a long time, and then he added. "I suppose I should be pissed off at Mark ... he now has a lover, and that's fine, but his lover was my lover until he realized what a sweet, exciting man Mark is. But I still get to fuck with them both, so it's okay, I guess."

Mark then spoke. "And Tom, there has certainly never been anyone like you. Has anyone here ever been fucked better, or took a bigger cock inside him, or fucked a hotter man than Tom Hunt?" A chorus of loud no's answered his question. "Neither have I, and I know you guys have all enjoyed making love with him the last couple days. I know how good it is ... we fucked each other most of a whole night earlier this week, and planned this party."

Tom again spoke. "You remember I told you all to save a load to give one last sailor? Well, Mark's the one you're going to give it to. And as a special treat for me, and for you, and especially for this wonderful guy who has meant so much to me for so long, every one of us is going to blow that load up his sweet ass and show him how much we appreciate his part in bringing us together this weekend. I once had about fifteen guys line up to blow their loads in my ass, and it was incredible, but Mark, you'll have to settle for twelve tonight. But twelve sailors from the *Earthman* can outmatch any fifteen other guys in butt fucking!"

Mark stripped seductively as he stood on the coffee table, and once he was nude, he lubricated his ass even more seductively as he grinned and announced. "This is my night to get fucked by a dozen of the greatest guys I know. I've had a wonderful time making love with all of you, at one time or another, and every one of you has shot his load in my ass any number of times. But tonight is going to be special, because you're all cumming together ... and I really do mean cumming together ... inside me. And Tom ... Mr. Hunt ... is going to be the last to fuck me, so that my ass is the receptacle that will make it possible for that special, huge cock of his to be swimming in hot cum from every one of you when he gives me his load and says goodbye to all of us. He's leaving, and while I hope and pray it's not the last time he fucks me, it could be, so help me give Tom a very special hole filled with the kind of hot sailor cum we all love."

Tom laughed as he stepped from the table. "And we're really going to enjoy watching that hole get filled up, right?" Everyone agreed, and the gang fuck began.

Mark took loads up his ass while he knelt on the coffee table, while he stood and bent over it, and lying on his back with his legs wrapped around a happy fucker's waist. Eleven guys fucking you in the ass in succession – and all to the point of orgasm – is a major ordeal for anyone. But Mark stole some rest time by hugging and kissing with most of the guys, and everyone was so horny watching, that many of them had been jacking off and were near orgasm when they first entered Mark's ass. All in all, Mark knelt, or stood, or lay there for about an hour and a half with a cock driving into his ass almost all the time.

Finally, it was time for Tom to end the marathon fuck, and he was especially gentle and loving as he entered Mark slowly, with everyone clustered around the coffee table to watch closely. They kissed and hugged a great deal, and whispered endearments to each other as Tom's massive shaft slowly went in and out of Mark – glistening and dripping with the hot cum that filled his ass. Eventually, Tom could hold back no longer, and his fucking grew more heated, until he was savagely thrusting himself in and out with strokes of incredible length. With a cry, he buried himself in Mark and locked his lips to his. His ass twitched and drove in and out in rapid, very short stokes as his massive prick exploded another enormous offering deep in Mark's beautiful ass.

As the sailors applauded and whistled, Tom told Mark to stand on the table. Mark did so, and Tom stood behind him. "Bend over a little." Again Mark did as he was told. Tom slid his big cock back into Mark's ass and began fucking rather slowly, but with absolute maximum-length strokes, and as he did so, the twelve loads of cum began leaking from Mark's ass, and coursing both down his legs and down Tom's invading cock and onto the coffee table surface. Tom continued to fuck until the flow of cum had completely stopped. Then he withdrew, turned Mark around, and held him tightly as they kissed and fondled each other.

The party had been a huge success, and the twelve *Earthman* sailors talked about it endlessly for some time. I learned all about it a couple of days later, through a telephone call from Mark and Tom that lasted about three hours. Mark concluded his enthusiastic description of the party by saying, "I remember you telling me about the five guys who fucked your ass at your birthday party, and I couldn't imagine anything like that. Now I've had twelve guys up my butt in one night, and it was fuckin' wonderful! Of course, they were wonderful guys, all of them. But just think, John, how far I've come from that night on your dock when I shot my cum all over your face without even touching myself, just because you kissed the end of my dick. But you know, that night with you was just as meaningful and exciting to me, and I'll always remember it just as fondly and clearly as I'll remember the night that the cum from twelve sailors ran down my legs while the biggest prick I've ever seen forced it out of my ass."

Tom was gone from the *Earthman*, of course, but Mark had another six months before he left the ship, at the time of his separation from the Navy. When the ship was in port in San Diego, and Mark did not have to stand duty, he spent his time with his lover in their house, but virtually every night, and many, many afternoons when he was aboard, Mark found time to have sex with the shipmates who had shared in gang-fucking him at the hotel, and even with a number of new ones who joined the crew and eagerly became part of the network of cock-loving sailors aboard the *Earthman*. A much tamer party than the El Cortez shindig was held to celebrate Mark's leaving the ship – and the Navy. Tom came down from L.A. to join the fun, and this time Mark's lover Johnny Owens did the final honors.

After leaving the Navy, Tom became a model in the Los Angeles area, working under the name "Tom Fox" – almost exclusively being photographed with his fabulous prick showing in some way, usually huge and hard. He also became an extremely high-priced escort (for which read "prostitute") in L.A., with a very selective clientele, including many of the big names in film and television. I know Tad Fisher and Davey McCaslin (until his tragic death) were frequent clients, and until Tad moved to Arizona, Tom was a regular in the orgies around his pool. By the time he was forty, Tom was mostly managing other escorts – that is to say pimping – and the hot young men in his stable were unmatched in desirability. Well into his forties Tom's prick and sexual prowess were still so legendary that he often responded to requests for his services personally.

Tom managed to talk the twins' stepfather into letting Ron and Don work for him – and I suspect Tom's huge prick was buried inside Allen when he consented. They were extremely popular with Tom's clients, and they wound up living with Tom at his Malibu beach house. When Tom entered the world of male video production, the twins also became quite well known as early porn stars; their polished sexual technique, blond beauty, and apparently unfading youth – combined with the fact that they were absolutely identical in appearance – made them great favorites. They were screwed on camera by practically all of the biggest stars and the biggest pricks of those early days of professional, slick pornography – and they never failed to fuck their partners in those films also, often practicing their "specialty." Being double-fucked by the twins on-camera became almost a rite of passage for new or young gay porn stars. Most people assumed the twins were in the Navy, because they usually appeared in Navy jumpers and white hats at some time during each film. Furthermore, a photo Tom took of the twins lying on their sides, sucking each other off with about three inches of prick still showing at their lips, and wearing sailor hats and jumpers, became very famous: with the words "Fox Hunt Video Productions" circling it, it has long been the logo for Tom's highly successful video production and distribution network.

Tom and the twins eventually became a trio of full-fledged lovers, and still share a bed. I am eternally grateful that on rare visits to Los Angeles, I have shared Tom's bed again, and met the incomparably sexy twins – and much more than just met them: their double-fuck specialty proved to be as exciting and satisfying as I had heard.

Tom became, and remains, a major force in pornographic video production, and the rumor persists that any young porn actor appearing in the many films he produces and directs initially auditioned and qualified by dressing as a sailor and taking Tom's huge cock up his ass, and then fucking him in front of at least a few of Tom's friends – and I understand that the twins Ron and Don are frequently the friends who help judge the applicant's capability. I have heard that almost all applicants are more than happy for the twins to take an active part in the audition. I was even present as a guest at one of those auditions a few years ago, along with my lover Billy, and we all fucked a young, beautiful blond bodybuilder with a huge cock and an ass that can only be described as succulent, who has gone on to become one of the hottest stars in male porn – and strictly a "top" in all his videos, even though Tom, both of the twins, Billy, and I all rotated gang-fucking his ass during an all-night marathon.

20. YOUNGSTERS AND ACTORS AND A NEPHEW

After Mark left me, I spent a few years of rootless seeking for sex – and finding an incredible amount of it, fortunately – but while a few more-or-less permanent liaisons developed, I didn't fall in love. Dean continued to visit me, and his love now meant more to me than it ever had. No one I found for sex was half as exciting as Dean, although I enjoyed plenty of fine experiences with the college students – six or eight of them fairly regularly, and a few of those extremely hot, well-hung and enthusiastic. Dave Westin and Danny Dyches were the two most memorable ones in this latter group. I could have easily fallen in love with the matchlessly cute blond Dave, and indeed we had a fairly lengthy series of fucks before he met Danny in my bed one night. The two became lovers and – selfishly, I thought – decided to keep to themselves.

Thanks to some dedicated spade work by Dean, I discovered that our local high school, from which Dean had graduated, also had a considerable pool of attractive students who enjoyed the same kind of activity in bed as I did, and I usually had two or three of them on tap when I wanted to fuck. There must have been something in the drinking water at that high school because while none of them was quite as well endowed as Dean, or quite as sexually virtuosic as that unforgettable stud – with one possible exception, to be introduced soon – all of them were at least nicely endowed, and junior studs in their own right.

Derek McCulloch, for example, was a senior, but was unbelievably talented for an eighteen-year old, with an apparently bottomless throat and ass, and an insatiable appetite to get them filled with hard cock. His own beautiful dick was equally insatiable, and among the most enjoyable ones I worshipped during those years. He showed up in my office one afternoon and asked to see me. He came in and closed the door, locking it behind him. I asked him what he was doing, and he said, "Dean Williamson told me to come and see you for help with my problem." When I asked him what his problem was, he began to unbutton my pants and told me, "I love to suck dick, but I'm not getting enough." He buried his head in my lap and proceeded to take a load from me. Then, with my cum on his lips, he looked up at me and smiled, and asked if he could fuck my ass. I agreed, of course, and serviced his cute little ass the same way shortly afterwards. It was only as he was leaving I found out how young he was. Derek and I feasted on each other for almost a year, until he went off to college.

My longest affair during those years immediately following Mark's departure was also with a high school boy. He was just nearing the end of his senior year, but he had just reached eighteen when we began our relationship. I spotted him in our city park one afternoon, where he was seated on a bench, his long legs stretched out in front of him, obviously displaying himself and dressed in the "Dean Williamson" style – wearing Levi's so tight they seemed to be painted on, with a crotch that looked like he had a grapefruit inside it. I sat next to him, and made it obvious that I was studying his basket.

"You see somethin' down there you think you might like?" he asked, with a grin.

"I think I see something I'd probably love."

"Well, maybe you could help me, then."

"I'd be glad to help you. What can I do?

He moved a little closer to me, and spread his legs wide, with one pressing against mine. "I got a whole lotta pressure built up down there, and I need someone to help me relieve it. Think you can handle that?"

"I know I can relieve the pressure, but it looks like a really big problem, I'm sure I can handle it, though ... I'm pretty good at handling problems like that ... even ones that big."

His completely winning, boyish grin grew huge, and he winked as he said, "If you've got a place to go, we can go there right now, so you can see just how big this problem really is, and I promise you can handle it all you want."

His name was Lee Anderson – a tow-headed, open faced, coltish, "Tom Sawyer" kind of kid with an irresistible grin and a Southern accent thick enough to slice. It turned out he had an adorable bubble butt and a long, slim prick, but the enormous bulk of his bulging crotch was accounted for by a pair of balls that would have been the envy of a horse. Although he was far less experienced than Derek, my other long-term high school love interest of those years, he proved to be a fuck partner gifted with unmatched natural talent when I first screwed with him – and he caught up to, and surpassed Derek in a very short period.

Unbelievably enough, I came along at exactly the right time to "catch" Lee. Before I picked him up, he had enjoyed only a few furtive, and unsatisfactory experiences with boys of his own age, but about a month earlier he had gone to stay a few weeks with relatives, and had been – as he put it – "cornholed" by his second cousin, and he had then rendered the same service to him. They had sucked each other's cocks as well. Getting fucked the first time had been painful to Lee, but the second and third times were infinitely better, and after he returned home, having been fucked six or eight times, he was enjoying it as much as his cousin obviously was. He also found fucking butt and sucking cock exciting and satisfying, but it was when his cousin's lips had first locked around his prick and sucked him off, he knew he had found what he enjoyed above all else. Getting a load of cum sucked out of his cock while he was discharging was as close to paradise as he felt he would ever get. After returning home, he had concluded that the experience was something he was eager to repeat, and he was ready to find a new partner back in his hometown.

He had not known how to go about finding a sex partner to relive the exciting experiences he had enjoyed with his cousin, and he received no encouragement from the few tentative overtures he made to those boys who he knew in his heart he was attracted to. He decided to go out looking. He put on the tightest pants he had, went to the city park, and sat there hoping someone would come along, see his considerable endowments outlined by his tight pants, and offer to make love with him. Someone did come along only a few minutes after he sat down on that park bench; thankfully, it was I! There must be a God of Good Timing, and he surely smiled on me that day.

I took the beauty home and found that his cousin had trained him well, judging by the huge grin that split his face when he first impaled himself on my hard cock ("God damn, but that does feel fine!"), his voracious sucking and the way he savored the cum I shot down his throat that first time ("Man, I used to think ice cream was the best thing in the world to eat ... shoot, it doesn't taste half as good as a big ol' load of hot cum!"), and the moans of unbridled rapture that accompanied the first blow job I gave him, with his hands fondling my head gently and sweetly as I continued to nurse on his prick long after he exploded his mammoth discharge into my mouth ("That's gotta be heaven, 'cause I can't imagine anything better!"). Yet it was not simply that his cousin had trained him well – the boy had an unbelievable natural aptitude for sex. By the time I learned he was still a high-school senior, we had fucked each other, he had sucked me off, and I had sucked him off twice. When I discovered that, I assumed he was only sixteen or seventeen, but since we had already done that much, the age problem was really academic – statutory rape was already a fait accompli, I assumed – so before I took him home that day, I sucked him off for a third time. I was relieved to find he was legal, if only barely so, and we went on to share stunningly fine sex for four years!

By the time the precocious Lee Anderson finished high school, he was a well-schooled veteran cocksucker, buttfucker, hot bottom, and face-fucker – and we had probably shot a couple of quarts of cum up each other's butts. He had probably swallowed a couple quarts of my cum also, but since he: (a) adored getting his cock sucked above all else; (b) discharged extremely large orgasms produced in those huge balls; and (c) was fully capable of having four or five of those massive orgasms in one session of love-making, I don't doubt that I probably sucked a good gallon or two of cum out of Lee's long and beautiful cock. I never made love with Lee that he didn't shoot at least three big loads into my mouth or my ass, and getting four or even five was not uncommon, if we were together for more than a couple of hours. Lee Anderson was an adorable, wholesome, boy-next-door, sexually tireless cum machine.

He also gave new meaning to the term shooting a load – the strength of his discharge was as prodigious as its volume. Even Dean had to concede defeat in a shooting contest they held on my screen porch one night when Lee outdistanced Dean by a good three feet, shooting his first spurt of cum a full fourteen feet to where it splashed down – and Lee even overcame the handicap of Dean's cock protruding about an inch or two farther into the field of flight than his. Until I quickly learned to deal with it, the initial force of Lee's orgasm almost made me choke and gag. I soon learned to let him shoot his first spurt

253

from near my lips, then move in and take his prick deep in my throat to savor the delicious, thrilling balance of his unparalleled load.

I had plenty of other sex partners during the four years I screwed with Lee, and that didn't bother him at all, but he himself fucked with very few others while we were together. He knew I was always ready to "relieve the pressure" for him, and he obviously thought I did it well enough that he felt no particular need to seek out someone else to service him. His voracious appetite to get sucked off was such that I frequently fucked with two different guys on the same day. So if, for instance, I was planning to have sex with Derek, I worked Lee in earlier or later in the day. I was always happy, ecstatically so, to attend to satisfying Lee's sexual needs, however I had to arrange it. He never objected to giving me his love in the morning or the afternoon, or even very late at night if necessary, to fit in with my schedule of working, or fucking with some other stud – since, if possible, he wanted to have sex every day, without fail.

I often picked him up at the high school, usually at the end of the school day, but occasionally even for a quick blowjob in the woods nearby during lunch or study hall. It was not uncommon for Lee to sleep over in my bed, even though he was an eighteen-year-old; apparently, his parents always accepted his stories about where he would be spending the night. He often called me in the evening, and told me – although I hadn't asked – "My folks say I can spend the night." I knew that meant his parents could hear his end of the conversation, and he wanted me to pick him up so we could fuck all night – or a good part of it, anyway. He was never upset if I was with someone else, but he always wanted to join me as soon as I could get free. I might have been "fucked out," but young Lee never was.

On then mornings of school days, after we had slept together, I played a deliriously happy Mr. Mom, making him his lunch and taking him to school – without exception after having giving him at least one morning blowjob, and often with a fresh load of his hot cum fresh in my ass as well. More often than not, he would also have a fresh load of mine inside him somewhere. When we were running late on a school morning – not at all unusual, given our late-night marathon fucks – I gave him money for his lunch, and he drove my car as we went to the school so I could suck him off on the way. He loved getting his prick sucked while he was driving; we frequently rode around just so he could experience that, and he would hump eagerly and shoot a huge, powerful load into my mouth without any loss of driving control. He usually enjoyed reaching over, as he continued to drive, and beating me off to orgasm after he came in my mouth on those occasions. I kept towels readily available in the car to clean us both up after he had held my discharging prick in his hand and continued to masturbate while he directed the spray of my orgasm all over me, him, and the front seat generally. Lee's huge orgasm never made a mess though: I happily swallowed every hot drop of it. He would invariably laugh delightedly as we cleaned up – often using his tongue to help.

And his laugh was infectious. Lee was invariably fun to be with – he truly enjoyed sex, and his innocent delight in what many people would think of as incredibly depraved behavior, seemed as natural and as wholesome as going fishing or playing catch. He truly was the boy next door, even when sucking my cock or taking it up his cute, eager little ass.

After three years as a Dowd student, Lee moved to Atlanta and began selling what he had freely given me so enthusiastically, so frequently, and so expertly for almost four years. He was enormously successful, commanding extremely high "escort" fees once his talent became well known, and he now owns a fine home in a country club in Duluth, Georgia – a suburb of Atlanta – paid for by the older man who regards him as his lover and life partner. His lover – if, in fact Lee regards him as such; there seems to be some question about that – is an investment counselor, and I understand Lee is independently wealthy now. He deserves to be.

Dean graduated from the University in 1970 and moved to Houston – occasionally returning home after that to visit his family – and, thank God, me. He is in his late forties now, and has a permanent lover back in Houston – a long-time member of the United States House of Representatives, no less – but he is still terribly attractive, and the vigor of his fucking has not diminished a whit. He thrills me and my lover as no one else can when he comes to visit.

Mark's brother Steve visited often for a year or two, even after Mark left, but his visits tapered off and finally stopped entirely. He and his wife divorced when she found him in bed with the grocery boy, but it was an amicable divorce, and she said nothing about Steve's sexual orientation to his family, which enabled Mark and Steve to continue to fuck each other any time they were together. Steve's son, Mark's nephew Randy, was to appear very briefly in my life, as will soon be noted.

In 1977 the boy who I began fucking with when he was a high school student back in Texas in the mid-1950s – now a mature and still incredibly sexy and attractive man of thirty-nine – finally divorced his wife and came to live with me and be my lover again. Billy Polk and I have been together ever since. Tom Hunt had claimed that star quarterback Boyd Epps had the most perfect, beautiful, and fuckworthy ass in history, but Billy Polk, quarterback of the 1954 Antares Texas High School squad, had at that time an ass of such incomparable beauty that I must reject Tom's claim out of hand. Billy's ass, incidentally, is still unbelievably attractive in his fifties, and I enjoy burying myself in it as much as I did when he was sixteen.

Billy and I are basically monogamous, but the occasional visit from Dean, always our favorite, or Richard – still very hot and attractive at fifty – or the even rarer visit from Cary or Mike, occasions some very hot and wonderfully nostalgic threesomes. Billy has come to treasure Dean's cock almost as much as I do, and we both agree it should be named an official "National Monument."

Heels over Head in Love

Although it would probably seem I spent all my time fucking, or working at seducing some hot young man, I managed to have a fully active and successful career at the same time, and was even able to take an active part in theatrical productions in the area – mostly amateur, but some at the professional level. I directed occasional productions, but mostly I was involved as an actor.

One of the pleasant sidelines of being in a play is the contact one has with other actors, and it is surprising that only one of my extended sexual liaisons has grown out of theatrical productions, although there were a number of rewarding shorter ones. Brief, duration-of-the-production "backstage romances" with beautiful young men who played my sons in productions of the musicals *Take Me Along* and *110 in the Shade* were especially rewarding, and I have fucked with a number of beauties in the dressing room during productions. I have often sucked cock, or had mine sucked, in the wings during rehearsals – and occasionally even during an actual performance. I was actually even fucked in the ass once while I was on stage – leaning over a fairly high fence upstage, while a very eager young actor, as a joke, plowed me with a dildo. He was later very penitent and made up for it that night by plowing me with the real thing,

One of the most attractive young actors I ever worked with was also one of the best actors. I thought, at the time, he was irredeemably straight, although he was well aware of my homosexual orientation. Thom Marks was among the most talented student actors I ever saw perform with the Dowd Players. I first came to know him when we worked together on a production of *Look Homeward, Angel*, with Thom in the lead role and me playing his older brother. It was a fine production, he was superb as Eugene Gant, and I especially enjoyed doing the play because I got to work so closely with the tempting and masculine Thom. In addition, there was another really cute, sexy student in the cast to dream about. I found Steve Heiss, a tall, beautiful blond guy who played a minor role in the show, not only beautiful and sexy, but available.

There were a few other cute guys involved in the production, but I hadn't been especially looking for sex with any of them. This was the early 1980s, and I was more than satisfied to be sharing my life with Billy, along with the occasional visit from Dean or Mike or Cary or Richard to spice up our sex life. One evening in the wings I patted Steve's ass during a rehearsal, however, and he backed up to me so that my hand was firmly pressed against him, and he wriggled his ass sexily and murmured, "That really feels good." I was soon sharing one of those "backstage romances" with Steve.

The thing that was hottest about Steve was his incredible ability to suck cock. He was able to take my entire prick and balls in his mouth at the same time, and I treasured the many times I ran my fingers through his beautiful blond hair as I looked down to see myself completely buried in his hungry mouth, and felt his tongue licking my balls while my cock drove all the way into his throat. Fortunately, we were not yet worried about AIDS as the possible result of ingesting semen, and I felt no compunction about delivering many, many loads

256

into the depths of Steve's hot throat – nor did he feel any compunction about filling mine with his copious emission on as many occasions.

One night Dean happened to be in town visiting his family, and he came to see the show. I made sure he came backstage afterward, and we lingered so we could lock ourselves in the dressing room after everyone was gone, as Steve and I regularly did – but with Dean joining us for our fun and games that night. Steve was easily able to deep-throat Dean's huge prick – his chin pressed against Dean's big balls, and his nose buried in the stud's pubic hair as he sucked the monster cock – but he wasn't quite able to take all of Dean's cock and balls in his amazingly capacious mouth at the same time, although he came close. I was treated to the sight of Steve's tongue lapping at Dean's balls as the immense cock fucking his mouth drove deep inside and deposited one of those trade-mark huge, forceful loads I had thrilled to for so many years.

Steve always pushed me down over a dressing table to fuck my ass as he stood behind, although a few times he cleared the table and had me lie on my back so he could screw me missionary style. He, on the other hand, always wanted to be fucked from behind while he stood, watching the process in a dressing-room mirror. He was so tall, however, that I had to stand on a suitcase to get the right angle the first time I fucked him. The very next rehearsal, Steve brought a wooden crate, just the right height for me to stand on to sink my prick as deep into his cute little ass as I could while he stood erect. Of course he was gloriously erect in another way every time I did it – and I did it very, very frequently during the time we rehearsed and played the show.

Given the eminently satisfying off-stage sex I was enjoying with Steve, I made it all the way through our *Look Homeward, Angel* production without seriously attempting to seduce Thom – aside from the occasional suggestive remark or the lingering friendly pat on the ass. Nonetheless I made sure that Thom was well aware not just of my homosexual orientation, but of the fact that I thought he was very, very desirable. Billy came to know Thom also and agreed that he was a hunk. He said that if Thom were gay, he would be very interested in trying to interest him in a threesome. Steve, for some incomprehensible reason, was not interested in a threesome with Billy and me – so I didn't tell my lover about my activities with the tall hot blond. I came right out and asked Thom finally, if he would consider going to bed with Billy and me. He was polite, he was friendly, and he said he was flattered and in no way offended, but he just wasn't interested in gay sex.

A few years later I shared the stage with Thom again, in a production of *The Music Man*, and he was even more attractive and sexy than he had been when we first worked together. In that show, there was another member of the cast who found Thom very exciting. He was a student named Randy Hagood, the same Randy Hagood mentioned before, son of Steve of the luscious beer-can cock and bubble butt, and nephew of my incomparable former (by then) lover, Mark. Randy was a university senior.

I had met Randy when he first reported to Dowd as a freshman; Steve had brought him by the introduce me, and returned to my house later to visit Billy and me – and he had shared his still very exciting body and delightfully fat cock with both of us. I saw little of Randy over his years as a student, and it was not until he joined the cast of *Music Man* that I learned he was gay, like his father and his uncle.

In breaks during rehearsals, Randy had made it clear that he knew I was gay, and one night made it also clear that he suspected that I had been much more than friends with his Uncle Mark. Finally, he simply asked, "You and Uncle Mark were lovers, weren't you?" When I admitted we had been, Randy said, "I don't blame you ... Uncle Mark is absolutely beautiful. But, do you know anything about my dad?" I declined to give any information, but asked why he should wonder. "There have been so many things that made me think he might be gay ... and when Mom and Dad split up, I never did understand what happened. What they told me sounded like pure bullshit, but I figured what the hell, it was their life, and they're still close even after the divorce."

Randy said he had done almost nothing about being gay, but this was his senior year, and he was coming out of the closet all the way – and he didn't care who it bothered. He apparently evinced no interest whatever in any sort of sexual play with me, or, incomprehensibly, with Billy, whom he had seen often. But he told me he was really hot for Thom; I wished him luck, but said I didn't think Thom was available – even to someone as handsome as Randy. And Randy was very attractive – hair a bit too long for my taste, but a beautiful face and a tremendous, powerful, gym-built body. I told him I suspected he was going to have no trouble getting most any gay guy he wanted into bed with him, but I thought Thom was strictly straight. He asked if I would ask him and Thom both over one night for drinks, so he could scout him out. I told Randy I'd be happy to, and that he and Thom and Billy and I could spend the evening soaking in my hot tub – a place of proven excellence for beginning, and even consummating seductions.

Thom accepted, and one evening after rehearsal, Thom, Randy and I made drinks, got naked, and got together in the hot tub. Billy had gone back to Texas for a brief visit with his daughter – now almost twenty years old, and planning her wedding. He knew of Randy's hoped-for seduction of Thom and he told me if I wound up having sex with Thom – or Randy, or even both – that was fine, as long as I told him every tiny detail later, and tried to schedule a re-match involving him as well.

Getting ready for the hot tub, I enjoyed seeing Thom fully naked, up close and for a long time. I had glimpsed his nude body and cock several times in the dressing room, and it was a magnificent body – and his cock was pretty, if not very large when soft; I hadn't seen it hard. Randy's body was even better than Thom's – carefully sculpted in the gym, a real bodybuilder's physique, with a chest that almost made me salivate; his cock was considerably longer than Thom's, and appeared to promise major meat when erect.

The three of us sat completely separated in the hot tub, with Thom between Randy and me. As the evening wore on, Randy kept moving closer to Thom. He obviously began touching him, since Thom kept moving away from him – and moving closer to me, as he did so. I kept my place, and finally the three of use were pressed close together, side-by-side, with Thom's left leg pressed against my right one. Finally he asked if I would slide down a bit; I did, but soon we had the same situation. Finally Thom said, "Randy, I wish you'd just leave me alone ... I don't mind if you're gay, I mean, John's gay, too, and that's fine with me, but I'm not interested, okay?" He stood up and went to the other side of the hot tub to sit.

Randy told Thom he didn't mean to offend him. "It's just that you really turn me on. Look!" He stood up, and his prick was standing straight out from him – and it was really impressive, probably about eight inches in length, with a big cock-head. Randy took hold of it and began to stroke it. "Just look what you do to me, Thom!"

Tom laughed. "Randy, that's a really big, nice-looking cock, but I'm not interested in guys. Why don't you give it to John? I'll bet he'd enjoy it ... and hell, I might even enjoy watching you give it to him."

Randy turned and stepped next to me, his big stiff cock right at my face. "You want it John? You want this big hot meat down your throat, huh? I think you do." He took my head in his hands and drew me in to him. "Suck my cock and let's see if we can't turn Thom on." I knelt in the hot tub in front of Randy, put my hands on his hips, and opened my mouth to admit his beautiful throbbing monster, which he began eagerly plunging into my throat.

I sucked Randy's big, driving cock for all I was worth, and he fucked face for all he was worth. I could see Thom seated across from us in the hot tub – watching, with his mouth open in shock. Randy was a pretty quiet guy, and his aggressiveness might have caused my mouth to open in shock, too, if it hadn't been so filled with his hot, hard-driving, big meat. Randy directed a litany of fuck-talk toward Tom as he drove himself into my throat. "God damn it feels great to get your dick sucked, Thom. You should feel these hot lips gripping my prick when I fuck them. No woman can suck dick like a guy can ... it takes a man to know how to really please another man. And keep it up, John, you are really doing a good job. Is your prick getting hard, Thom? Just imagine how good my hot mouth would feel if you shoved your cock inside it. I'd suck every drop of cum out of that big dick of yours ... and it is a nice big one, too. I'd love to feel that big Thom Marks prick deep inside my throat and shooting a load of hot cum for me to drink."

All this time, Randy fucked my mouth eagerly – and even though they were directed at Thom, every sexy word he uttered seemed to make his fucking more exciting for me. "Here comes my load, John ... suck every drop of it out of

259

my big cock, but keep it in your mouth so we can show Thom how much I've got to give you." And with that, he buried his prick in my throat and left it there as his cum spewed out in forceful spurts. It was all I could do to keep from gagging; he really gave me a huge load, but I managed to contain all of it. "Eat it, John ... eat it! Oh shit, that feels incredible, Thom. I'm not just shooting my load, John's sucking every bit of it out of my prick, and that feels ten times as hot as just cumming. Just think how exciting my lips would feel on your dick, and how great you'd feel when I sucked the cum out of it."

Randy asked, "Did you keep all of it, John?" I nodded my head and murmured my pleasure. "Watch this, Thom," he said as he sat down next to where I knelt and threw his head back. "Give me all my load back, John, but let Thom see it go in!" I stood, leaned over Randy's open mouth, and let his big load trickle from my mouth into it. As soon as it was all in, I told Randy, "Don't swallow all of it ... give some back to me."

Randy smiled and stood. Taking me in his arms, he kissed me, and transferred half of his load back into my mouth. He pulled back and looked into my eyes as we both smiled and swallowed happily. Still holding me with one arm, Randy held out a hand. "Come here, Thom."

Thom held out his hand to Randy, and stood. As he did so, we could see that his prick was fully erect and pointing about twenty degrees up – not terribly large, but throbbing and quivering, and looking extremely toothsome. He stepped toward us, and took Randy's hand. Randy released me, dropped to his knees. In one movement, he took all of Thom's prick deep in his mouth and began to suck noisily and greedily. Thom's arms immediately cradled Randy's head, and he fucked hard, with long strokes as Randy feasted.

I stepped behind Thom, and put my arms around his waist, with my cock pressing into him. I played with his muscular chest and arms, and kissed his neck. Thom murmured his satisfaction – whether with Randy's or my ministrations, or perhaps both, it made no difference. He was obviously enjoying this. I kissed his back, and knelt as I went down and kissed his buttocks, then reached between his legs to play with his balls. As I kneaded his balls, he spread his legs a bit to allow me better access, and I could feel Randy's chin hitting my hand as he sucked Thom's cock while I fondled his balls.

I began to kiss all over Thom's ass, and soon found my way to his asshole. As I began kissing him there, one of his hands came around to press my face deeper into him as I worshipped. He leaned forward a little, and used his hands to spread his asscheeks, presenting his asshole for me to eat. I began to eat him out, and he started to hump and wriggle his ass. Taking this as an invitation, I drove my tongue as far into him as I could, and let it dance around inside. He leaned over farther, and he pressed my face hard against his ass as I tongue-fucked him. He moaned, "Oh God, that feels great!" Whether he was talking about Randy's blowjob, or my tongue-fuck was not clear – what was clear was that he was in heaven.

I stopped rimming Thom, and as soon as I did, he again seized Randy's head and began fucking his face frantically. I quietly opened the jar of Vaseline always kept next to the hot tub, and put some on my index finger before I returned my attentions to the beautiful hot ass humping and writhing in front of me. I again tongue fucked for a few minutes then gradually began to introduce my finger into Tom's asshole. He did not object at all. Quite the contrary, he again leaned over and pressed his ass back to allow me better access. I gradually put all my finger inside Thom, and began to fuck him with it. He murmured in delight, and his asshole gripped my finger tightly as his ass-ring rode up and down it.

Soon I had two fingers all the way inside Thom's ass, and he was obviously enjoying the feeling enormously. As I added a third finger, he reached behind and grasped my wrist. He fucked his own ass savagely, using my fingers. I stood, removed my fingers, placed the tip of my prick against Thom's asshole, and gradually began to press. He humped and backed up to me, and soon I was entering him. With my prick buried to the hilt in him, he again cried out in ecstasy while Randy sucked and I fucked.

Soon Tom began to pant, and said, "I'm gonna cum," and thrust his cock deep into Randy's mouth. Both his hands came around and pulled my humping ass as tightly into him as he could – keeping me deep inside him, and gripping my cock with his asshole very, very tightly. I felt the shudders that accompanied his extended orgasm, and bit his neck while he cried loudly for Randy to take his load. After catching his breath, Thom patted my ass and said, "Let's dry off and go in the living room." Randy stood and Thom stepped away from me, causing my cock to slide from him. As Randy got out of the hot tub, Thom took hold of my cock and whispered, "In the living room, okay?" and also exited the tub.

I closed up the hot tub, and when I got to the living room, Thom and Randy were sitting on the floor, talking. As I came in, Thom held his hands out to me. "Come here," he said. He lay down on his back, spread his legs, and raised them high. I knelt between them as they clamped around my waist and his arms went around my neck. "Let's do it right," he grinned.

With one movement, I buried my cock all the way in Thom's ass, and Randy looked on in amazement while I fucked this supposedly straight beauty, who cried in passion and begged me to fuck harder and faster and deeper. Randy had apparently not been aware that I was fucking Thom's ass while he was giving him a blowjob. Randy began finger-fucking my ass, and encouraging me to heed Thom's instructions for harder, faster, and deeper fucking.

I delivered what I think was an inspired performance with my prick up Thom's ass that night. When I came, it was violent and copious, and Thom panted, "Oh, God, I can feel your prick shooting ... give me your load, John; give it to me hard!"

Heels over Head in Love

I continued to fuck long after shooting my load, and Thom continued to drive his ass down hard on my prick. Eventually, I began to get soft, and Thom said, "Don't stop ... cum in me again, that was fantastic."

"Thom, I've got to rest a few minutes, but I'll fuck you again. Take Randy up your ass; he's dying to fuck you."

Thom continued to hump his ass on my cock as he said, "Get in here, Randy ... get that prick of yours inside my fuckin' ass." I pulled out, and Randy immediately replaced me. As his much larger cock began to enter Thom's ass, Thom moaned, "God damn, your cock is big, Randy." Randy hesitated, but Thom pulled him close. "No! Fuck me hard!" Randy plunged himself all the way in with a violent thrust, and Thom encouraged him loudly as the two began a monumental fuck.

I watched the beautiful scene – Randy's magnificent body over the muscular Thom, and his cute bubble butt driving his cock fiercely into Thom's ass. Thom's manly legs and arms wrapped around Randy, and his pretty ass about a foot off the floor, clearly showing the ass-ring being stretched and disappearing as Randy's big shaft plunged in and withdrew. Randy also tried to kiss Thom as he fucked him, but Thom did not allow it. (This was no surprise to me. I have fucked many a man who refused to kiss, saying – even with my cock buried in his ass – that kissing was queer!)

Randy had shot a load in my mouth not too long before that, so he fucked Thom a long time before delivering another orgasm. When it finally came, it was obvious that both fucker and fuckee enjoyed it enormously.

Before we broke up that evening, Thom fucked both Randy and me in our asses, cumming only in mine, and we both fucked him again. With four loads of cum up his butt, one would think Thom would admit he might be queer – or at least bisexual – but he not only refused to kiss or to suck dick that night, he continually voiced his amazement that he was doing this!

For the duration of our run of *The Music Man*, Thom never mentioned what had happened. In fact, he seemed to avoid being alone with Randy and me.

I never had sex with Randy again. Of course I probably would not have had it that one night if he had not been bent on seducing Thom. It was clear he had let me blow him and share his cum so that Thom might get turned on. Neither Mark nor I told Randy about our sexual experiences with his father.

Thom was another matter. About a week after the play closed, he invited himself over to have a drink in the hot tub, and it quickly escalated into a frantic fuck session, but with my beautiful Billy as a third this time. I decided that if Thom wasn't queer, he at least had the good sense to realize what an incomparably beautiful ass Billy had, and he took special pains to fuck it long and hard – and, later sessions, even to warm it up with his tongue before fucking it.

Until he graduated, Thom came over to fuck with Billy and me at least a couple of times every month or so, and even after that he showed up

262

frequently, wanting to fuck and be fucked. We invariably obliged. I was pleased that with the onset of this relationship, Billy and I both enjoyed extremely passionate kissing with Thom. And Thom has become an expert cocksucker as well; he especially adores deep-throating Billy's long cock, but who wouldn't?

Thom still finds time for sex with us frequently. He's pretty close-mouthed about who else he's having sex with, but I suspect he may be screwing around with women also. Nevertheless, he admits he loves sucking cock or taking it up the ass – and agrees with Randy's contention that it takes a man to give a really first-class blowjob. Thom swears that fucking a guy's ass is ten times hotter than fucking a pussy.

Randy graduated only a couple months after our session with Thom, and I never saw him again after *The Music Man* closed. It was probably six months later that I got a call from Mark, from California. "I hear you fucked my nephew." I sputtered and began to apologize, explaining I only sucked him off, and neither of us had fucked the other. But Mark laughed. "Hey, it's fine ... I don't blame you, he's really cute. He came out to visit, and he started 'coming on' to both Johnny and me, and we wound up in bed together, fucking like rabbits. He's not only cute ... he's a damned fine piece of ass."

"Just like his dad, huh?"

"I was hoping you'd say 'just like his uncle.'"

"His uncle's not a fine piece of ass; he's a great lover."

Randy returned home to Pennsylvania, and I have no idea what he is now doing, although Mark told me he is currently living in New York with a ballet dancer. Mark also noted that once when he was back home and fucking with Steve, he thought Randy spied on them and figured things out. I would not be surprised to hear someday that Randy and Steve are having sex regularly – a la Allen and the twins.

So, having fucked with Mark and Steve and Randy, I fear my supply of new Hagoods has run out – although I always look forward to having sex again with Steve or possibly even Randy – but with the beautiful Mark it's not "having sex," it's making love, of course.

21. CODA IN THE FORM OF A BIRTHDAY BLOW-OUT

Billy has been the most wonderful partner imaginable. How little I would have thought, when I first kissed this incredibly beautiful man – both physically and spiritually beautiful – when he was only sixteen years old, that some forty years later we would be long-time, dedicated, loving partners in life.

Over the period of almost twenty years that we have been together since we were finally able to resume the loving relationship we had been forced to abandon by circumstances in the 1950s, Billy has done countless wonderful and exciting specific things for me, and his general acceptance of the intense sexual relationships that occasionally recur, either with those with whom I shared sex before our reunion – Richard, Dean, Mark, for example, or a few, like Thom, who shared my bed after we became partners again – has been a particular blessing. Of course, every one of them who met Billy has, with the single, totally inexplicable exception of Steve Heiss, found him beautiful and irresistible, and has insisted, whenever possible, on including him in our sex play. This has made Billy's acceptance of my fucking around with other guys more understandable, and, emphatically, much more enjoyable.

The occurrence of my sixtieth birthday, on July 14, 1992, occasioned his most astonishing accomplishment in Billy's doing things to please me – the birthday present to end all birthday presents, the perfect gift for the new sexagenarian.

I had told Billy almost every detail of my sex life, before and after and during our initial relationship and our reunion, and he had shared his experiences with me as well, but his have been fairly limited compared to mine. A year or two ago, he encouraged me to write the story of my sex life leading up to our reunion – and the present pages represent the fruit of his encouragement to continue that story, and bring it up to date. As a result, he is well acquainted with the names and qualities of the principal sex partners of my life – indeed he is personally acquainted with, and has even shared his precious body and matchless ass with many of them. Therefore, he was able to arrange the complex arrangements necessary to realize the unforgettable party that marked my sixtieth birthday.

It had taken him months to plan and arrange all the details, but its success was well worth it, according to him, and it left me in a state of euphoria I could never have imagined I would know as a sixty-year-old. Even more amazing was the fact that it was a complete surprise. I knew something was up, and Billy had promised an unusual birthday present, but the magnitude of the surprise was astonishing at the time – and even in retrospect I marvel at the logistical ability he exercised in bringing his plan to fruition.

About four in the afternoon on my sixtieth birthday, a Tuesday, Billy said we were due at the penthouse of the "Dowd House," an on-campus hotel – now mostly a dormitory, but with some rooms still used for private occasions.

Heels over Head in Love

Taking the elevator to the remote penthouse – a four-bedroom suite, actually – we entered the huge living room area, and I was astonished to find waiting for me there no fewer than twelve former lovers – all still looking great, considering the passage of time. Billy had convinced everyone there to travel to Dowd to celebrate my birthday in the way I would most enjoy it – by fucking with me again. The prospect of a lot of further intramural fucking among the guests was no doubt a much stronger factor in getting them there, of course. I later learned that he had used some windfall funds he had been holding in abeyance – which had come his way from family funeral bequests – and a pooling of many frequent flyer miles held by some of the attendees, to help fund those who wanted, or needed assistance in attending.

Most of those waiting to celebrate my birthday have been introduced in the pages preceding. lovers Cary Adams and Mike Sharp had come down from Chicago; Dean Williamson had flown up from Houston; Richard Austin had come in from San Francisco; Lee Anderson had driven over from Atlanta; Steve Hagood had come from Philadelphia; Thom Marks had to drive only a few miles to be with us; and my beautiful Mark and his lover Johnny Owens had come all the way from San Diego.

There were two former fuck buddies and the very first man I ever fell totally in love with also in attendance. Phil Baker was one; he had been a fellow student of Billy's at the Texas high school where I taught and first fell in love with my partner. Although Billy had been only a naïve, sixteen-year-old sophomore at the time, Phil was two years older, and already an extremely knowledgeable fuckmaster. Billy and Phil and I had found ourselves in all sorts of fascinating and rewarding sexual combinations during the year we shared our bodies, our love, and our unbridled lust. I had not seen Phil in at least twenty years, but his importance to the development of Billy's and my love was critical, and he certainly belonged at this party. Since he still lived in Billy's hometown, Antares, he had been easy to contact.

Like Phil, the other fuck buddy came in from the Texas Panhandle. Hal Weltmann, whom I had thought the most beautiful man in my college, and who I later found had the biggest prick and the most insatiable sexual appetite of anyone I had ever known. He and I had shared some evenings of such intense sexual rapture before I finally introduced him to Billy that they were forever etched in my memory. The three of us had actually spent only one day having sex together, in a motel in Albuquerque, but Billy remembered it as perhaps the most sexually exciting day he had ever spent. That day's excitement had been in large part generated by getting fucked, savagely, and at great length, by the biggest prick either of us had ever seen, much less taken inside us. Billy also thought Hal was the most beautiful man he had ever seen at that point, but he was second most beautiful to me – I had seen Billy! The combination of Hal's beauty and his matchless prick was potent, to say the least. Billy had worked hard to locate him and invite him to the reunion, but the sexual milestone in our

266

relationship that Hal represented made it almost mandatory that he be there, and hence well worth the trouble it took to locate him. One cannot help but add that the prospect of his also again getting Hal's cock in his hands, his mouth, or his ass made it even more certainly worth the effort for Billy. In all the years since Billy and I had feasted on Hal's titanic endowment, only Eddie Bliss' monster cock had matched it for size, and only Tom Hunt's gigantic organ was bigger or more exciting – and even that unforgettable shaft wasn't much bigger. Billy had never experienced the thrill of Eddie Bliss, but he had worshipped and compared both Tom and Hal's charms and agreed with my assessment.

The third person in attendance aside from those the reader has already met in these pages was the very first guy I ever fell in love with – my best friend from my high-school days in Chicago, Bob Coston. Not only was Bob the first guy I really loved, his prick was the first – aside from my own – that I ever saw hard, and, later, the second one I ever sucked. My first cocksucking experience – mutual, wonderfully enough – had been with the matchlessly beautiful Danny Morales, when I was fourteen and he was about eighteen. Bob's was the very first prick to ever fuck my ass, and while it had seemed to me unbelievably huge when I played with it or sucked it, it felt twice as big when he buried it in my ass. I found later, when I had begun having sex with a number of other guys as well, that Bob's prick was indeed as massive as I first thought – a cruelly and wonderfully large one to be the first up one's ass. A training size cock might have been more comfortable, but it certainly wouldn't have been as exciting. Bob was also only the second guy to ever suck my cock, and he was the very first one to ever suck me all the way off – Danny and I had satisfied ourselves by blowing our loads all over each other. Strangely enough, it was a couple of years later before I finally fucked Bob's ass and sucked a load out of his monster cock, and by then I had already tasted those thrills with a number of other guys – but if anything, the delay only made the experience more sweet and exciting. Bob was now living in Tulsa, and Billy had tracked him down through the Alumni Office at his Ohio college alma mater.

There were a number of guys I learned later Billy had either been unable to locate, or could not persuade to come for the event. They included: the sexy, gorgeous Danny Morales, the first guy I ever had sex with; the big-dicked Hispanic beauty Tony Lopez; former local high-school-student fuckbuddy Derek McCulloch; my former roommate and almost nightly fuck-mate for my last two years of college, Jim Corcoran; the unforgettable Eddie Bliss, whose epic prick was the only I had at that time even seen that could challenge Hal's for supremacy – the one that Richard fell so in love with that he left me a second time and moved to California; the muscle-stud Randy Hagood; and Mark's former teammate, Johnny Farrar.

Billy invited Tom Hunt, of course; he could have located him easily through his "Fox Hunt Video Productions," but he knew Tom's address and phone number – he had accompanied me on a trip to Los Angeles a few years earlier and sampled the matchless power and excitement of Tom Hunt's prick – still the biggest either one of us had ever feasted on – and thrilled at the unique sexual thrill the twins provided. Tom and the twins were unable, or perhaps unwilling, to come out for the party, but since he couldn't attend, Tom sent a very exciting "CARE package" along with Mark and Johnny – a box of a dozen of the new "Tom Fox Dildo," a latex replica of Tom's massive and unforgettable prick, which had just gone on the market, and ten or twelve of the latest Fox Hunt video releases. Tom also included a very special private videotape he had recorded just to send to the party – filmed in his living room, and with him and the famous twins greeting me in person, and performing sexually just for me. Predictably, the tape included the twins' trademark double fuck, with Tom as the lucky recipient – something never seen in commercial video. Fortunately there were VCR's in the suite, so Tom's videos were played a great deal during the party, and the dildos were employed ingeniously and endlessly as well. We also had Richard's videos on hand, and they were enjoyed even more than Tom's, presumably because the star was on hand in person to share in the enjoyment.

The oldest man in attendance was Hal – several months older than I – and the youngest was Thom Marks, who was around thirty. Bob was only a month or two younger than I, Phil and Billy and Steve were all in their mid-fifties, Lee was in his thirties, and the rest ranged from the early to mid-forties. So, there were no spring chickens here, but it was nothing short of astonishing to note how fit and fine everyone looked, from the youngest to the oldest. The blond, matchlessly cute Lee, the second youngest, still looked like the boy next door! Of course all these men were magnificent physical specimens to begin with, and all were aware of their beauty – and justifiably vain enough to maintain it as best they could. Through diet and exercise, they had all kept themselves well, and stayed in shape. Naturally there was some gray hair in evidence, even some thinning hair – but surprisingly little – and a slight thickening around the middle of a few waists, but again, very little. I've always been turned on by young men – but every man in the room was still very, very attractive, and some – Billy, Cary, Richard, Mark, Hal, Dean – who might now be thought of by others as devastatingly handsome, could still only be described as beautiful to me. Billy's ass, Cary's body, Hal's cock (as I was about to discover) were still matchless.

A mattress had been brought in from one of the bedrooms and put on the floor in the center of the living room, there were lubricant dispensers all over the room, and a stack of towels and a large bowl of condoms graced a coffee table – the age of AIDS had finally caught up with us. I learned later that generous supplies of lubricants, towels, and condoms were found in all the bedrooms as well. It was obvious what kind of party this was going to be.

I spent the first hour or so visiting, and trying to "catch up" at least briefly with those guys I hadn't seen or heard from in a long time. Bob, Hal and Phil all told me they were going to stay several days, so I would have plenty of time to visit and learn what had been happening in their lives; the fact that all three were invited to spend those days in Billy's and my house promised a particularly exciting reunion.

Billy told me this was my party, and I could structure it any way I wanted. I suggested that everyone should at least introduce himself to the group, and give us a bit of history. Billy agreed that was a good plan, and added that each history should include how each guy and I had first had sex. I felt that while I would love to have sex privately with any one of these wonderful guys – or perhaps share Billy in a sexual threesome with any of them – this was a celebration, and I wanted to have sex with each one in any way he felt appropriate, and I wanted everyone else to watch, so they could really share in it.

Acting as a master of ceremonies, Billy started the celebration proper – better described as highly improper to many people, I fear – by welcoming everyone. "I don't think it will surprise anyone if I say that I believe sex is the most important thing in life to John, and apparently has been since he got his first hard-on. Assuming that's true ... at that point, I loudly asserted it was ... you guys here represent the most important people in my lover's life. Every one of us here has fucked John, everyone of us has been fucked by him, we've all sucked his dick, and our dicks have all spent a lot of time in his mouth." This last sentence drew a big laugh, and an "amen" from several of the assembled studs. Billy continued, "John wants each of you to get up here, and tell us all how you first came to have sex with him – and if it's okay with you, have sex with him again, right here, and while we all watch. I know that won't be a problem for some of you ... I've heard too many stories!" After a moment, allowing for another big laugh, he went on. "We have a huge supply of rubbers, so let's be sure to keep the sex safe ... nobody fucks anyone without protection, and if anyone is ready to cum while he's getting his cock sucked, pull out and shoot on whoever is doing the honors. That way your partner will be safe, and we can get to see your cum fly. If any of you want to keep that part of this reunion private, that's fine, just tell us, and after everyone else is through, you and John can get together by yourselves. But strange as it seems, I sure hope I get to watch each one of you fuck my lover. God knows, I've seen him sucking dick and getting fucked a zillion times already. This is the most beautiful and sexy bunch of guys I've ever seen, and I've heard so much about you I feel like I've already been screwed by every one of you. Of course I'm happy to say I have had quite a few of you up my grateful ass, and I doubt John will be surprised to hear that I'd enjoy a repeat visit from all of you. And I hope I can get the rest of you inside me in the next couple of days. Anyway, I really want to watch every one of you fuck ... hell, I'm even getting hard just thinking about watching you get undressed."

I was delighted that no one opted for privacy in a sexual reunion, not even Thom, who had never really admitted he was gay – in spite of what he and

Billy and I had been doing for some time, and had done only a few days earlier –
or Bob, whom I hadn't had sex with in more than thirty-five years. I had sex
again with every one of these hot guys, and everyone else watched and enjoyed
it with us vicariously.

There were innumerable private sexual pairings during the extended
party, and a lot of widely observed pairings and orgies as well. A lot of gorgeous
guys sucked a lot of beautiful cock and took a lot of fiercely hard ones up their
hungry butts in that time. When everyone learned that Richard's birthday was
the next day, he was accorded the same honor I received. He got fucked by
every guy there, although not always in front of such an enthusiastic audience.

I thought it a little strange, as the individual reunions occurred, that
everyone stayed right there and watched attentively. I would have expected at
least a few guys to slip off to one of the bedrooms at some point for a private
fuck, to relieve the unbelievable sexuality this occasion generated. But I don't
think they were just being polite; they all wanted to see these hot guys in action.
I saw plenty of cocks being stroked, however – and by no means always by the
guy to whom the cock was attached.

I fucked everyone there during the party, but I didn't always shoot my
load when I did; at sixty, thirteen orgasms in two days or so is not possible – not
from me, at any rate. During the party I didn't cum in Billy, or Phil, or Bob,
since we would be spending time together at my house later. Hal was going to
be there, too, but after having his gargantuan meat shot a load in my ass again,
after all those years, I got so hot I couldn't stop when I fucked with him. Thom
lived nearby, and we didn't need a reunion to fuck; Dean was planning to stay
on and visit his parents for a week, so he planned to spend plenty of that time in
Billy's and my bed, fucking and getting fucked. That left eight guys, and I'm
proud to say I gave each one of them a good big load up the ass or on the face
during those two days, although only two of them got it while we were in the
"performing for the group" phase of the party – I did have to pace myself, after
all. I found both Hal's incredible, thrilling, throbbing stupendous endowment
irresistible, as I have said, and Mark's truly matchless beauty was too
unbelievably sexy to keep from having an orgasm as I made love with him.

I asked Bob, as the first guy I ever had sex with, to introduce himself
first, and asked that the others follow in something like chronological order. My
first love stepped up to me and enfolded me in his arms. We kissed very
tenderly, and for a long time. Then Bob began unbuttoning my shirt as he talked
– and the rest of my clothes followed, until I was totally naked, with my hard
cock clearly showing how I still felt about him.

He began to speak, "Johnny and I were in high school together in
Chicago, and the first time I ever showed him my prick hard was in a tent
alongside a highway. That night we did what we continued to do for the next
several years – we sucked each other's dicks. If it hadn't been for a chance
occurrence with a fellow member of the school swimming team, Johnny's would

have been the first ass I ever fucked. It was certainly the first one I fucked over and over and over again, though – and I was the lucky guy who was the one to do it. The first guy who ever shot a load in my mouth was Johnny, and I swallowed a helluva lot of his cum after that. It was a long time before he finally sucked a load out of my cock, but he worked on it for a long time, and he did a fantastic job of sucking me – the fault was all mine, and I wasn't even able to get fucked until after I had gone off to college. I'll never forget the Christmas vacation when I finally gave him a load and took him up the ass; we made up for a lot of lost time in the space of what was probably the most intensely exciting week I ever spent."

By this time Bob had begun to take his own clothes off. "We drifted apart, and I got married and raised a family. I thought all along I was straight ... and I guess I was for all those years ... but I also knew I loved Johnny and had wanted to keep making love with him. My wife died about five years ago, and the kids were grown and on their own, so I decided to give in to what I had known all along I craved. Since that first time Johnny's lips closed over my hard cock, I'd known what I really wanted was a man or boy to fuck with, so I started looking around Tulsa ... and I found plenty of hot, young guys to give me what I wanted. So Johnny, I've been practicing up for our reunion for the last couple of years, although I hadn't known it."

Bob now wore only his shorts, and it was obvious his cock was fully erect. He slid his shorts off, and stood there with arms akimbo, and his prick bobbing and swaying as it projected outward. It was as large as I remembered it: at least eight inches long, and fat, and throbbing with anticipation. He said "Take me inside you, Johnny ... where I've wanted to be again all these years." I sank to my knees and my lips again closed over my first love's magnificent tool.

Bob and I sucked each other; we lay on the mattress and double sucked. Then I put a condom on my cock, and he knelt before me while I fucked him from behind, and then, with me lying on my back, my arms around his neck and my legs around his waist, he drove his enormous cock into me and fucked my ass with all the fierceness and dedication I remembered from our youth. I all but screamed, "Jesus Christ, Bob, I've wanted your big dick up my ass again for so fuckin' long!"

As I won't bother to detail all the putting-on of condoms, I won't clutter this narrative with all the impassioned cries of "Fuck me hard!" or "Take my load!" or similar shouts of enjoyment I and my partners uttered as we made love for the next two days. I have always been very vocal in expressing my joy and excitement while making love, and have found that most sex partners react to that with similar shouts of appreciation and encouragement – so that means a great deal of dialogue will not be reproduced here!

My first lover and I encouraged each other all the time, and when he finally shot his load in me, he panted and kissed me and cried his love for fucking and his love for me. I could feel the cum coursing through his prick as his orgasm burst forth, but I missed feeling the cum shooting into me when he discharged his load, as I had so many times in the past – but the use of condoms was simply necessary by that time. Bob and I lay together for some minutes before he withdrew from me and removed the condom from his still huge, quivering prick. He inverted it, and let his impressive load drip into a bowl sitting next to the mattress. Billy had placed the bowl there, and directed everyone to empty their rubbers in it if they shot their loads inside me. Bob had received a round of applause when it was apparent he was shooting his load, and as the copiousness of his orgasm became apparent when he emptied the condom in the bowl, he got another ovation. It had been close to forty years since I had made love with this unforgettable man, and it seemed as wonderful when I was sixty as it had when I had been sixteen.

Acting on a tip from Dean, Billy found a coffee-warming unit, which he switched on from time to time over the next two days, to keep the bowl of cum warm.

Billy was next, and he told of having fallen in love with me when he was a sophomore at Antares High School in Texas, where I taught, and where I became the first person he ever really had sex with – a sixteen-year old who became my full-fledged lover. He had stripped naked before he started telling his story, and that set the tone for the rest of my reunion encounters – each came to me naked, and after a few introductory remarks, made love with me for the entertainment of all in the room.

Billy was still wonderfully handsome, and his ass was as smooth, as round, as unbelievably beautiful as it had been when I first saw him skinny-dipping in a stock pond in Texas. I ate his asshole and fucked it with the same passion and appreciation I had been bringing to that joyous task since I was twenty-two years old and he sixteen. His long cock felt as wonderful in me as I sucked it, and as it shot his precious load deep inside my ass, as it had thirty-eight years earlier – and as it had only the night before, when he had rendered the same loving service in the privacy of our bedroom.

Phil recalled having discovered sex with me in that same high school through his attraction to, and seduction of Billy. He reminisced about his wild life in high school, fucking or sucking with several different guys almost every week. "I got married and raised a family, too ... but I never stopped picking up guys and fucking with them whenever I could. With all the hundreds and hundreds of guys I've screwed around with over the years ... I dunno, maybe thousands ... I never even saw an ass that was as cute as Billy's, though. And those times when John and I and Billy fucked together were probably the best I ever knew." Phil's cock felt just as big and as fine as I remembered it, also – and I didn't miss the force of his orgasm, because just before he shot his load while he was fucking me from behind, he pulled out, stripped the rubber off, and blew a series of huge spurts of hot cum all over my back. He licked my back clean, and spit what cum he could gather into the bowl. Then we kissed to end our session – and his cum tasted as fine on his tongue as it had in the 1950s.

While I was kneeling on all fours with Phil ramming his cock in me from behind, I noticed a stranger in the room! He was a very tall young man, with tousled, straw-colored blond hair and a huge, engaging grin that would have made him attractive even if he had not been as naturally cute as he was. He was naked, so his fine, muscular body was on display, but I couldn't tell anything about his cock, since Richard had his head buried in the young blond's lap – which probably explained his huge grin. The blond cutie was fondling Richard's head as it bobbed up and down on his cock, but his attention seemed to be focused on what Phil was doing to me.

The blond's grin turned into an "o" of delight, and his eyes squeezed shut in thrill as Richard's head sank all the way down his cock, and froze there as the kid apparently delivered a load – about the same time Phil was blowing his load on my back. As Phil was retiring, and Hal was stepping up to take his place, I saw the blond kiss Richard, and slip out of the room, his cock swaying and bobbing – only semi-hard, after having just been drained, but still impressive.

Billy later explained who the blond boy was. He had cruised Billy at a gas station a few weeks earlier, and then followed him into the bathroom, where he produced a large and very pretty cock, which he stroked until it was hard, and told Billy, "It's yours if you wanna suck it, but you gotta let me blow you first." Billy accepted the offer, as I would have done, and the boy sucked his cock with the same expertise Billy then brought to bear on the boy's prick. The blond was Jerry Steele, a twenty-year-old ex sailor, who had returned home to Dowd after separation from the Navy only a week earlier, and who explained he had been in the habit of sucking dick almost daily for the last three years, and was really missing it. Billy needed to hire someone to take care of bringing food, ice, and towels in at the big sixtieth birthday party he was then planning, and who could be discreet. Billy had arranged to procure those supplies, but he needed someone to handle distribution at the party itself, and he thought Jerry could be trusted to be understanding. He sounded Jerry out, and Jerry was extremely enthusiastic about getting involved when he learned what was going to be happening at the party, and he promised he would not tell anyone about it – then, or later. Meeting a few times with Jerry to finalize details, Billy discovered that he enjoyed a lot more than just swapping blowjobs!

I only spotted Jerry at the party once more, while I was kneeling behind Lee and fucking him. At the time, the blond ex-sailor was kneeling behind Richard, and doing to Richard what I was doing to Lee – and, judging by the look on Richard's face, doing it very, very well! That Richard had been servicing the new kid on the block both times I saw him did not surprise me at all. I knew from experience – some of it painful – that Richard was always first in line for the latest available cock or ass.

Hal recalled the night he was fucking my college roommate in our dorm room when I found them together, and how he subsequently became a fairly regular fuck partner. He was actually a bit older than I, but he could have passed for thirty years younger – still a spectacularly beautiful man. His cock and balls were impressive as he stepped up, but he was not erect when he took me in his arms, kissed me, and began introducing himself. By the time he had recalled our sex play back in Texas – including having shared an incredible birthday party with his equally gorgeous lover/roommate Dan, and having a marathon threesome with Billy and me in a New Mexico motel – his prick was fully erect, and pressing hard against my stomach. As he turned to face the group, the enormous dimensions of his prodigious cock were finally revealed to them, and rather than applauding or cheering, his magnificence, every one in the room gasped or murmured – and I imagine every one of them salivated as well. He and I sucked each other's cocks athletically and at length, and Hal took me up his ass as he stood and leaned over while I stood behind him to plow his still wonderfully tight hole. He drove his unforgettable monster cock fast and hard and deep in my ass when I knelt before him, but it was as I lay on my back with my legs and ass raised to admit his huge shaft that he held me tightly in his arms and kissed me while he blew his load inside. After he pulled out, he was still hard and huge, so I had him lie on his back and I impaled myself on his still-sheathed prick. He stayed rock hard as I rode him fiercely, and continued to do so for some time after I had shot my own load all over his chest – unable to stop myself in the delirium of having this champion cock up my ass again. He fucked for a long time, driving himself up into me, and finally it was obvious that he shot a second orgasm inside me – about as flattering (and enjoyable) a thing as I could imagine.

When Hal, grinning, emptied the rubber into the bowl, the two-orgasm amount of cum that flowed from it was extremely impressive. The gasps and soft exclamations of admiration that had greeted the first sight of his gargantuan hard cock turned into wild cheers and applause. Hal smiled and bowed low, and I knelt behind him to kiss and eat his ass while he bowed.

Richard later remarked – after he had been fucked by Hal's gargantuan shaft – that taking that huge meat up his ass was as thrilling as the time that Eddie had first fucked him at our joint birthday party, years earlier. All four of the guys who had been there, and who had been fucked by the mega-hung Tom Hunt – the famous "Tom Fox" – also got fucked by Hal at my sixtieth birthday party. That was no particular distinction, since Hal managed to get around to fucking everyone in attendance at some point. And all of that four – Richard, Dean, Mark, Johnny – remembered how thrilled they had been with Tom's magnificent screwing, but swore that Hal's masterful fuck at the party was equally exciting and memorable. I was one who had been fucked by both, of course, and I knew even when Tom Hunt first buried his gargantuan rod inside me that as astonishingly big and thrilling as it was, Hal's stupendous equipment

274

had been a close match. With his matchless good looks and stupendous endowment, Hal could easily have become a greater superstar in gay porn than even Tom Fox, had he wanted.

Johnny, who had been Tom's lover for some time, until he and Mark fell in love with each other, remarked that he wished Tom could have been there to take Hal also. "I'm getting Hal's address, and he says he'll be glad to fly out to L.A. to fuck Tom if he wants it. Maybe we could even work it out so that Hal comes out when Mark and I visit Tom and the twins in L.A., which we do fairly often. Now that would be fun!" I had to agree that it indeed did sound like fun – two identical twin sex-gods and two super-endowed fuckmasters to feast on.

Before he fucked me, Richard mused on our first meeting, when he was nineteen – a day which began with my taking pictures of his huge hard cock on a remote lake island, and ended with his cum splashing all over my face while I feasted on his balls, He reminisced about our fabulous joint birthday party, and admitted that as much as he loved sex with me – he mentioned our tradition of always starting each day with joint blowjobs – the spectacularly hung stud Eddie who fucked us both so magnificently on that occasion drew him out to California. "And having seen Hal's cock in action, Eddie is really on my mind today. Hal ... I need to see you later; tomorrow is my birthday!"

Hal laughed and said, "Give John what I just gave him, and I'll be sure to observe your birthday the same way. My birthday's still eight or ten months away, but you can return the favor as an early present." He stepped up to Richard, kissed him quickly, and squeezed his hard prick. "I don't get many cocks as big and tempting as this!" This exchange really got Richard hot, and he fucked my ass like an absolute savage – but that was the way he had always plowed me. His enormous prick penetrating my grateful ass felt like a great big, exciting, hot and hard friend who had come home where he belonged. Before he blew his load, Richard pulled his prick out of me, and exploded a hot, white gusher all over my face – an action very well appreciated both by me and by our audience. With his cum dripping from my chin, I knelt between my ex-lover's raised legs and came very near shooting my load as I fucked him almost as fiercely as he had me.

Cary and Mike joined me as a couple, and we reminisced about Cary finally relenting and letting me suck him off in my car one night, and Mike waking in an Atlanta hotel room, with a couple of straight guys in the next bed, to find me sucking his prick. They both said they had thought they were straight until they each began fucking regularly with me, but I knew I had merely been a lucky bystander when those two studs discovered their appetite for dick. And then when Mike caught me fucking Cary in a hotel room in Florida one night, he joined in. He and Cary have been lovers pretty much ever since, close to twenty-five years, and while they stay pretty much to themselves sexually these days, we have never failed to enjoy plenty of hot three-way sex every time I've visited them. The two lovers knelt side by side, and I took turns fucking them from

275

behind, after which I knelt while I sucked Mike's enormous rod and Cary fucked me, without orgasm. Then they changed places, and Mike's wonderfully satisfying fuck culminated in his holding me very tightly as he humped frantically and filled his rubber with cum – almost at the same instant that Cary pulled his prick out of my mouth and shot a massive load of hot white cream all over my face.

Dean – still unbelievably beautiful, and with his truly huge cock rivaling Hal's for "best of show," was as sweet and tender as always – so strange, coming as it did from such a raging stallion. He was in no hurry to get his part of the celebration out of the way; we kissed and embraced often as he told how he had tempted me by displaying his prick to me the first night we had met, how we had become very frequent fuck buddies throughout much of his high school career, and how we had shared some particularly exciting sexual experiences – like Richard's and my joint birthday party, the two-day fuck session with Tom Hunt in Athens, etc. "John and I were never lovers as such, but we've loved each other for a very long time ... and made love to each other literally thousands of times. My cock has to be almost as familiar to John as it is to me. And it's interesting to note that I had my prick up Richard's ass before John did."

At that point, Richard laughed and called out, "It's a long story." Dean laughed also, and said, "And it's a long cock, too!" as he shook it toward Richard, who answered *"Amen!"*

Dean had me lie on my back and he rode my prick slowly, smiling and murmuring in delight as he did so. As his riding grew frenzied, he raised up, causing my prick to slip from his ass, and knelt between my legs. He raised them in the air, and with one grand and thrilling thrust, buried his huge prick to the hilt in my ass. My ass was so full of lube and come that no one had needed lubrication to enter my ass for some time that evening. He started slowly, and his fuck lasted a very long time, but his tempo and thrust had increased to ecstatic heights by the time he put his arms around me, picked my body up – still impaled on his magnificent cock – and kissed me fiercely while he shot a long and apparently massive load inside me, When he emptied the rubber later, all could see that it was indeed an impressive amount of cum.

Mark and Johnny, like the other pair of lovers, Cary and Mike, also joined me in tandem. Johnny said, "Tom Hunt is very much here in spirit today."

A big laugh ensued when someone brandished a "Tom Fox" dildo and said, "And in hard rubber, too!!"

Johnny continued, "He fucked with Dean and John a long time ago, when he was visiting his parents, and as a result of that visit he wound up fucking Richard." Richard interjected another, even louder *Amen!* at that point. "Since all three of those guys had talked about how beautiful Mark was, Tom decided to fly all the way across country to go to see if he could possibly be as handsome and sexy as his picture and his fans had made him out to be. Naturally, he found that Mark was the most beautiful man in the world ... and when Mark went in the Navy after that, Tom saw to it that he served under him on two different ships."

Mark retorted, "Every one of the hundreds of times I was under Tom, he was serving, and I was receiving!" Those of us who had also served under Tom in that way laughed.

Johnny also laughed as he continued. "Thank God Tom liked to serve under us that way, too! Anyway, I had fallen in love with Tom some time before that, and we were lovers when I first met Mark. Gradually, Mark and I fell in love with each other, and we've been together ever since ... and with Tom's blessing. It's a shame Tom couldn't be with us. Of course those of you who know him, know that if he was here, we'd probably all be wearing Navy uniforms!" Veterans of Tom Hunt's lovemaking obsession laughed at that.

"I first met John out in San Diego when he visited Mark, and the three of us wound up in bed almost immediately. I knew that he and Mark still loved each other, but it was wonderful to see how they could share their love together without my ever feeling left out or in the way, or in any danger of losing my wonderful Mark. I soon came to love John, also, and I'm really happy to be here sharing this special occasion with all of you."

Mark reminisced about our formal courtship, and got a good laugh when he talked about the first load he gave me – all over my face, without touching himself. "After I went in the Navy, time and distance kept us apart, and even though I fell in love with Mrs. Owens' beautiful boy Johnny, I never stopped thinking of John, not only as the first love of my life, but also as someone I'll continue to love all my life." We kissed and hugged, and Johnny joined us. Mark and Johnny continued to stand there and embrace as I stood behind each of them, respectively, and fucked them. I lay on my back with Mark over me as he and I sucked each other in sixty-nine while Johnny joyfully fucked Mark's ass. Then Mark and I changed positions as we double-sucked, and Johnny fucked my ass. As he was about to cum, Mark and I stopped sucking each other and lay together so Johnny could shoot his big load all over our faces. It had been so much fun, that Mark and Johnny sucked each other while I fucked them – first Johnny as he was on top, then Mark. The sight again of Mark's beautiful body before me, and the feeling of his matchless ass 'working' my prick expertly was so exciting I could not stop; with my head thrown back in rapture, and with a huge cry of lust, I drove myself as far in as I could, and held there while I shot my second load that day into his hot, still tight, perfect ass. Mark stood and told me to lie down next to Johnny; he loomed over us and masturbated until he bathed us in a very satisfactory gusher of hot, white cream.

Steve still looked great, and his beer-can cock and bubble butt were as exciting as ever. He reminisced about coming to visit his little brother, and winding up fucking his little brother's lover. "If it hadn't been for John, it's possible that Mark and I would never have done what we both had secretly wanted for a long time ... to make love together. I know there are some guys who would say it's disgusting, but what the hell, there's no way either of us is going to get the other one pregnant with an idiot child!" Oddly, he never mentioned that he and Mark were adoptive brothers. He walked over and knelt in front of Mark, who was sitting on the floor, leaning against the chair where Johnny sat. He put both hands on Mark's face and said, just before they kissed very sweetly, "And looking at my incredibly beautiful little brother, how could the word disgusting even be mentioned if he was involved? I've known all his life how beautiful he is inside, too ... so there was no way I could have resisted. I can't imagine how anyone in the world wouldn't want to make love to him." Their long kiss was very touching, and when Steve returned to me, there were tears in his eyes as he said, very quietly, "Thank you, John." He kissed me for a long time, then sank to his knees and took my prick in his mouth. The tenderness with which he began to suck gradually evaporated, and he was soon devouring me noisily and hungrily as I held his head tightly and fucked his mouth. He stood abruptly, turned and bent over, then spread his asscheeks with his hands and panted, "Fuck my ass!" He had apparently lubricated himself before he first approached me, and there was no time for me to put on a condom before he backed up on my cock, and pushed until I was buried in his wildly undulating ass. I held his waist, and he bent all the way over and urged me to fuck hard and fast. I was getting close to another orgasm, so I pulled out and bade Steve to fuck me. He stood, turned my body around and pushed my head forward as he buried his prick in me – again no condom. Billy called out, "Steve, use a rubber!" But Steve, fucking like a demon as he pulled my more-than-willing ass even tighter to him, panted, "I'll pull out before I cum!" His fucking was nothing short of a frenzy of lust – and it was wonderful, I might add. He barely pulled his cock out of my ass before he shot his load – and his huge spurts of hot cum covered my ass, shot up along my entire back, and even got in my hair as Steve yelled, "Oh fuck! Take my load, baby!" It was apparently quite a sight, since it drew a very healthy round of cheers. I fell to my knees, my back dripping with Steve's cum, as he sank down on top of me and kissed my neck, telling me how much he loved fucking me.

We had taken a number of breaks, of course. During one of these, Lee Anderson took my arm and said he needed to talk to me privately. He pulled me into the bathroom, and shut the door. We kissed and rubbed crotches and played with each other's asses for some time before he got to the point. "Look, you know better than anybody in the world how much gettin' sucked off means to me ... I don't mean just gettin' my cock sucked, either, I mean shootin' my big ol' load into a guy's throat while he's suckin' it out of me." I had to admit I knew he loved it, since I had performed that service for him hundreds, if not thousands of times, He went on. "I do everything I can to do really safe sex, and I get an HIV test every couple o' months, so I know it's safe to give my cum to somebody to swallow. I usually don't need to explain all this, because I've got two young guys down in Atlanta ... one is barely sixteen and the other one is almost seventeen ... and they both love to suck me off as much as I love their doin' it ... and like you know, I need my dick sucked off at least two or three times a day. So, I keep me completely safe for their sake, and I don't really need anybody else for sex, anyway. I almost never turn tricks anymore. Oh, I've got a couple o' old clients I still let suck me off ... and they know I'm safe ... but they never fuck me, and I never suck them." He giggled. "Shit, I've turned into a top ... well, professionally, anyway. Anyway, these two kids're both as cute as they can be, and they are sure-as-hell hot ... I mean fantastic cocksuckers ... and I take care of them. They live with me, and they stay safe and tested too, so I never worry about suckin' 'em off, and we all fuck each other all the time, too. Anyway, to get to the point, I really want to blow my load in your mouth ... because I love gettin' sucked off, of course, and I haven't got my load since this morning, but especially because this is kind of for old times' sake, you know? Basically, what I'm sayin' is, will you suck me off up there? We can pretend I'm not comin' when I do, and I'll keep fuckin' and then shoot another load on your face or up your butt, and nobody's gonna know it's the second one. What do you think?"

I sank to my knees and kissed the tip of Lee's throbbing big cock. I looked up at him as I licked it, and asked, "What about cumming three times ... can you still handle that?" He grinned as he began to push his prick into my mouth, "You know I can! It might mean the third load takes a while longer, but hell, that'll be that much more fun." He began fucking my mouth in earnest, and I deep-throated his beautiful cock and sucked and licked as hard as I could. It had actually been quite a while since I'd swallowed a load, and I really looked forward to it, and to be sucking another load out of this sweet, sexy Lee's prick was especially exciting – as he said, "for ol' times' sake." We took our time to make it last, but finally he could hold it in no longer, and with a muffled cry he seized my head in his arms and thrust himself in as far as he could while his cum filled my throat with the violent eruption I had thrilled to so many times. He continued to fuck, murmuring his satisfaction, and I sucked every drop from his prick, I savored the huge load he had given me before swallowing – it was delicious. He sank to his knees and took me in his arms. "Goddam, you're the absolute best. I can hardly wait to shoot another load in you." We kissed, and I assured him I could hardly wait either.

It was nice to hear a widely experienced, complete stud like Lee to say I was 'the best,' just as it was nice to hear all the compliments I had been receiving – and would soon receive – from my current and former sex partners assembled at the Dowd House that weekend. Furthermore, most of that praise and tribute was spoken for all to hear, and much of it was very effusive, if not even hyperbolic. Still, as pleasing as those comments were, I fully realized I was not hot enough, hung enough or young enough – to say nothing of sufficiently well-built or handsome enough – to deserve such praise from such Adonises and fuckmasters. I felt sure that much, if not most, of the praise for my sexual ability was offered in the spirit of celebrating my birthday. The fact that this dozen of studs had even taken the trouble to attend was compliment enough to please and thrill me, but I was also well aware that their attendance was worth it because of the prospect of the fucking and sucking they were going to enjoy with the other attendees, not with me. It was true that circumstances accompanying my earlier sexual adventures with these boys and men had brought most of them together – just as this sixtieth birthday party brought about some new, exciting couplings – and a large degree of the tribute they accorded me was actually tendered in gratitude for that fact. Still, I don't think I'm being immodest when I say I can give an absolutely first-rate blowjob, and I've never had a dick up my ass – even monster ass-reamers like Hal Weltmann's or Eddie Bliss's or Ton Hunt's – that I didn't take fully, and treat extremely well; my ass can milk a dick for all it's worth!

After that break, Lee was next in line. With his prick barely dry from shooting a load, and with the taste of his cum still in my mouth he began to reminiscence. His dry country wit drew plenty of amused reaction, but the sight of his boyish face and beautiful body, his long prick, and the enormous balls hanging down below his prick kept everyone much more than just interested or amused. "One Summer, when I was a kid, I went to visit my cousin on a farm. I'd never done any serious sex before that, but even though my cuz was about the same age as I was, he knew what he wanted, and by the time I got home, I'd been fucked up the butt so much I'd learned to love it. And I loved fuckin' my cousin's butt as much as he loved me doin' it. I learned to suck my cousin off, too – and he had such a good time shootin' his load down my throat, I couldn't do anything but let him do it." He grinned, "I was a guest, after all! But it was when he first sucked a load outa my dick that I found out what my favorite thing in the world was! I couldn't get enough o' his hot mouth, and when I got back home and had to start school for the fall, I knew I had to find me somebody to suck my dick. So, about the second week of school I got dressed in my tightest jeans after school one day and went and sat in the park with my legs wide apart. I hadn't been there fifteen minutes when a horny guy walked up and started starin' at my basket – and it wasn't more than an hour later that he'd already sucked two loads outa my cock and shot a load of his own up my butt. I was just a kid, maybe, but I knew I'd found a friend for life." He put his arm around my waist. "You probably figured out ... John here is the guy who came along and took what I was offerin'." He pulled me to him, kissed me very sweetly, and grinned in my face as he continued to talk.

"For the next four years, except for a day or so here and there, John sucked me off at least twice a day, and lotsa times he sucked three or four loads outa this big ol' dick o' mine. Don't get me wrong, he took plenty o' loads up his butt, too, and if he didn't give me as many loads down my throat as I gave him, he didn't miss it a helluva lot ... and next to havin' him suck me off, I loved him fuckin' me up the ass. Hell, we used to screw each other just about anyplace you could name. Jesus, John, I wonder how many times you sucked me off while I was drivin' your car? And I used to spend the night sleepin' at his house a lot of the time, and I was probably the only kid in my school who got a blowjob with his baloney sandwich when he left for school. And he helped me a lot, too ... he was a lot like an uncle to me ... just happened to be an uncle who loved for me to fuck his mouth or his ass! John ... I'm just glad to be here to help you celebrate your birthday, and I think it's about time I gave you your present."

Lee fell to his knees and began to suck my cock. Soon he lay on his back and held out his hands to me. "C'mere and suck it for me." I positioned myself over him in sixty-nine, and with a gulp he took my cock in his mouth as he drove his into mine, and his huge balls filled my vision. We changed top and bottom, we rolled on our sides, and we often released each other's cocks for a few minutes to tongue fuck each other's asses. After a long time, Lee reversed his body, and straddled my head as I lay on my back. He held my head up off the mattress and fucked directly into my mouth. He fucked vigorously and very deep, and I could tell he was near orgasm. Apparently remembering how the extreme force of his load shooting into my mouth sometimes made me gag if he was all the way in my throat, he pulled back just a few inches as his hot cum began to flood my mouth. Then he drove his cock all the way into my throat again while the rest of his big load filled my worshipping mouth, as it had done only fifteen or twenty minutes earlier in the bathroom. Lee was a pretty good actor – he continued to fuck as vigorously as he had before his orgasm, and I doubt anyone except he and I knew that he had shot an enormous load in my mouth, which I had swallowed surreptitiously.

After a few minutes, he took his prick from my mouth and reversed his body. He had blown two loads in the previous half-hour or so, but his cock was still huge and hard. Kneeling on all fours, he grinned back over his shoulder at me. "Fuck my ass, okay?" I needed no further invitation, of course, and I knelt to penetrate his cute, and still very youthful-looking butt. He bucked and squealed in delight while I fucked, often smiling at the guys watching us and commenting something like, "God damn that feels fine!" Nearing orgasm, I stopped and lay on my back and told him, "Give it to me up the butt, Lee." He winked at me as he donned a condom, then entered me in one thrust as he said, "Oh yeah, I'll fuck your butt!" And he began to plow me savagely. My legs were wrapped tightly around his waist, and my ass was far off the mattress as he held his arms locked around my neck and kissed me passionately while I felt his fine big dick hammering my ass, and heard the sound of his incomparable ball sac slapping against it. He fucked me fiercely for a very long time, and finally he pulled out and quickly positioned himself over my face, yanked the rubber off his prick, and moaned loudly as he shot a load of unbelievable size, given the fact that I had swallowed two of his loads only recently. He directed it all over my face, lips, and forehead; I wanted to open my mouth to at least some of it, but knew it would upset Billy's "safe sex" plan. (If he only knew!) When he had finished, Lee collapsed over me, and began very obviously licking his cum from me. He cupped my face in both hands and kissed me as he finished cleaning me up, so that no one could see when he transferred all the cum he had lapped up into my mouth. What a stud!

As Lee stepped aside to turn the reminiscences over to Thom, Hal stepped up to him, cupped his monstrous balls in one hand, and put the other one on his shoulder. "Damn Lee, with these balls and my prick, we could rule the world!" Lee stroked Hal's colossal cock in his hand as he kissed him lightly. "I dunno about rulin' the world, but we sure as hell can get your prick and my balls together later tonight and see what happens!" Hal released Lee's balls, put both arms around him and drew him tight as he said, "That is definitely a date," and gave him a very long, passionate kiss while Lee's hands fondled his ass. I suspected a number of those who overheard that conversation were looking forward to watching.

Thom was last on the program, so to speak. Considering how uptight he had once been about anything gay, he was remarkably open and at ease. "I used to think I was strictly straight, but a few years ago, when John and I were doing our first play together, there was a really hot guy named Steve who came on to me, and really tried to get me to go to bed with him." Thom laughed. "Well, I don't really mean bed – that's just an expression – what he really tried to do was give me a blowjob in the dressing room. Steve was tall and blond, and really hot looking, but I told him I wasn't interested, but still he kept after me, and later that year we did another play together, and I decided what the hell, I wouldn't mind getting my cock sucked – it would be the first time I'd ever had a guy do it, but I figured a blowjob's a blowjob. So anyway, Steve sucked me off, and it was really amazing. He was sucking my cock better than any woman had ever done, and then he opened his mouth more, and he even took my balls in at the same time; I tell you, the feeling of getting your balls licked while your cock's all the way down a hot throat and getting sucked is unbelievable." It was certainly believable to me; as he said this, I remembered Steve's uniquely exciting talent only too well, and watching Thom's hard prick stand straight out and throb as he recalled it, I looked forward to getting it down my throat in a few minutes. "Pretty soon I shot my wad down Steve's mouth, but he wouldn't stop, and I stood there while he just kept on sucking, and I didn't lose my hard-on until I gave him another load.

"I was convinced I'd found a treasure, and it wasn't long until Steve convinced me to fuck his ass ... and he was almost as good at taking it up the butt as he was at taking it down his throat. I got hooked, and the whole time we did that play I fucked Steve at least once every day. One night he was sucking my prick, and he turned me around and bent me over the dressing table, and began to eat my ass. Now, nobody'd ever done that to me, but it felt great. He actually started fucking me with his tongue, and I guess he could tell from the way I was moaning how much I was loving it, because pretty soon he had a finger in my ass, and then a couple of fingers, and before I knew it, he was standing behind me, and I was backing up on his cock. I couldn't believe I had a guy's prick up my ass – and Steve had a big one, too. It felt so great, I worked with him, and pretty soon I felt him shooting his load all the way inside me, just like I'd done to him so many times – and I knew then why he liked it so much. I figured, what the hell, if I liked getting fucked that much, I might as well try it all, so later that same night I sucked his cock, too – and I couldn't do it anything like as well as he did, but he gave me another great big load that way, and I not only loved the feeling of his big prick fucking my mouth, I loved the taste of his cum.

"I still thought I was straight, but until Steve graduated a year or so later, I was sucking cock regularly and getting fucked up the ass by a hot, great-looking blond stud who was just as eager to suck my cock as I was to give it to him up the ass. And we spent long hours lying in each others' arms, kissing and hugging like regular lovers, but after he left, I decided it was just something special I felt about Steve, and I wasn't going to do that anymore. And I didn't, until one night when I was over at this guy's house." Here he put his arms around my waist and kissed me lightly. "I knew John was gay, and he'd made it pretty clear he was interested in doing something with me. Sorry Billy!"

Billy laughed, "Big surprise, huh?"

Thom went on. "We even had some pretty sexy work to do together in the play, and I really liked John a lot, but I'd decided no more gay stuff. Then one night I was over at his house, in the hot tub, with another cast member – this really handsome, incredibly built guy named Randy, who I knew was also gay, since he'd been coming on to me from the first rehearsal. I guess it wouldn't be giving anything away if I said that Randy's uncle was in this room."

Steve Hagood laughed out loud, "I guess it might give something away if anyone knew his father was in the room, too!" It took a moment for it to register who Randy was, but everyone finally whooped with laughter, and Thom continued.

"Randy kept trying to play with me in the hot tub, but I didn't respond, and finally he told me to watch while he got John to suck his cock, and talked to me about how he great it felt. I got really horny, and by the time I'd watched Randy blow his load in John's mouth, I was hotter than the devil, so in a minute I was standing there with my prick down Randy's throat, fucking it like there was no tomorrow. Then I felt John's hands on my waist, and he knelt behind me and started kissing me all over. By the time he got to my asshole and started to tongue-fuck me, I knew I wanted a hard cock up my ass again, and It wasn't long before he was as far up my ass as I was down Randy's throat. Randy sucked out my load, and we went to the living room, and before the night was over they each fucked me twice, and gave me big loads every time – and I had a helluva good time fucking them, as you can imagine.

"It took me a few more visits to John's house before I decided to hell with it, I must be queer, and began to kiss and suck cock like I'd done with Steve – and like I guess I'd always wanted to do, but never admitted to myself. It didn't hurt that Billy was there, and you can all see how hot he is! Jesus, if I've ever fucked a prettier ass than Billy's – hell, if I've ever even seen a prettier or sexier ass than Billy's, I sure can't remember it." Dean responded with a hearty Amen. "Not that there aren't a bunch of pretty asses here tonight." Several Amens' were heard. "Anyway, that's how I came to be here, and I'm really happy to be a part of this celebration. This is kinda like a testimony for me: I want every one of you to see how much I enjoy taking John's cock inside me, and how eager I am to give him mine." He grinned, and looked around, "And I've seen some fuckin' big dicks tonight that I'd like to try and take, if they'll let me know they're interested. But right now, it's all for John."

Thom faced me and put his arms around me while he kissed me very sweetly for a long time, and then as our kiss grew impassioned, our hands began to fondle each other, and almost at once we were on the mattress locked in sixty-nine, with our cocks deep down each other's throats. He was extremely excited, and as he knelt over me when we double-sucked, he gave himself completely to fucking my mouth with savage abandon. He pulled out, saying he was close to cumming, and positioned himself over my cock; he impaled himself on it, and smiled down and caressed my face as he rode up and down as hard as he could. On each cycle, he drove down onto me as far as he could, and rose up as far as he could without allowing my cock to slip from him. I too was close to cumming when he stopped, disengaged himself, and raised my legs. He leaned down and kissed me as he plunged his prick into my ass and began to fuck me with the same kind of wonderful ferocity he had shown when he had fucked my mouth only a few minutes earlier.

My legs rested on his shoulders, his arms cradled my body, and he lifted my ass in the air while he plowed it so thrillingly. He sat back, and pulled my body up and into his lap as he did, so I was impaled on his prick while he knelt there. Then, using the great strength his magnificent body clearly showed he possessed, he stood, holding me in his arms with his cock still buried to the hilt inside me. My legs were locked around his waist and my arms around his neck as he smiled and kissed me, and then carried me to a table. He lay me on my back there, and put my knees up to my chest to allow him maximum access to my ass, which he proceeded to fuck passionately and gloriously for some time while I played with his massive tits.

Then he picked me up again, still fucking my ass as he did so, turned around, backed up to the table, and rested his ass near the edge; with his throbbing prick still inside me, he lay back on the table and urged me to fuck myself on his prick as hard as I could. My ass had been fucked a lot already –

obviously – but Thom looked so wonderful lying under me, his massive chest heaving with passion as his cock plunged deep into me, and his face a beautiful mask of complete rapture, that I planted my feet on either side of him on the table, and rode as hard and as fast as I could while he humped upward into my ass. Shortly, he began to clutch my waist and with a loud cry of "I'm cumming ... take my load, John!" he shot his load in a long series of violent spasms, accompanied by groans of utter ecstasy. When he calmed down, I leaned over and we kissed for a long time, with his now-softening prick still a very large and very welcome presence inside my ass.

I dismounted, and Thom relaxed completely, his back still on the table. I removed the rubber from his softening cock, and he grinned up at me. "Big load, huh? I've been saving up to give it to you." The bottom of the rubber was filled with a load of cum that might have done two horny guys proud. As I held it up so that everyone could see it run from the rubber into the bowl, they applauded and whistled. I went back to kiss him, and said, "That was an incredible load, Thom. Thanks for being such a wonderful fucking stud!" He stood and took me in his arms, and hugged and kissed me again without a word said – or needed. The glow in his beautiful eyes clearly showed his affection and love.

Billy approached us, and as we separated he kissed Thom and pulled me away from him. "It's been a long day, but it's been exciting as hell. By my count, John, you've been fucked by thirteen men, and every one of us loves you and loves fucking you ... as much as every one of us loves getting fucked by you. We're all going to be around tonight and all day tomorrow and tomorrow night, so there's plenty of time to visit, and plenty of time for you to fuck and suck with everyone, and for everybody to mix it up and fuck and suck with whoever they want to. As far as I can tell, every guy here wants to have sex with every other guy here ... right?" Lots of enthusiastic affirmation greeted his question. "It's after midnight, so it's already tomorrow, and in case you don't know it, it's now Richard's forty-seventh birthday ... and he's told me he'd be happy to get a birthday fuck from every guy here if they can work it in."

Hal stepped up to Richard, holding out his gargantuan cock – amazingly beautiful and hard. "Can you work this in, Richard?" Richard took it and kissed Hal . "Believe me, we'll work it all the way in as soon as we're finished here."

Billy continued. "But before we finish, and start pairing off ... and don't forget that larger groups than pairs are always fun ... we're going to finish giving John his birthday party the way I told you we would. John, lie down on the mattress." He smiled at me, and took me by the hand as I lay down on my back as directed. Everybody began to gather in a circle around me and they were all stroking their hard pricks as they did so. I gazed up at thirteen beautiful men, with thirteen big pricks standing out and being stroked – a forest of exciting meat! Billy grinned at me. "One more load from everyone for you before they start giving them to anyone else."

They all grinned down at me, and many of those grins were soon turning into looks of ecstasy as they masturbated fiercely. It was only a couple of minutes before Steve Hagood's fat cock shot a big load of his white, hot cum all over my face and my chest, and his load was soon covered with an even bigger one erupting from Dean's beautiful monster prick. Every guy there worked hard to bring himself to the most explosive orgasm he could achieve, because most of their emissions splashed violently all over me as they coaxed them from those wonderful cocks I had worshipped and feasted on so many times over the years. All moaned with passion until they came, and all urged me to "Take my big load, John!" or words to that effect. Everyone continued to stroke his cock after he had shot his load, to give me every possible drop. Everyone then watched those who continued to work at getting their loads, and urged them on excitedly. Even Thom, who had just given me a massive load up my ass, coaxed a number of very creditable jets of hot cum from his fine dick.

By the time all had finished, I was literally covered with cum – and in absolute heaven. Billy leaned over me and kissed me – ignoring the fact that my lips were covered with cum from someone. "Now I'm going to give you all this cum that was shot in you before, while you beat off and add your load to ours." He picked up the bowl containing all the cum we had drained from the rubbers that had been filled inside me earlier, and held it over me. "Beat off, and show us your load, baby!"

My cock was covered with cum, and slick as hell, and I was so excited by the animal lust that had inspired the copious coating I wore – and which was still almost palpable in the room – that it took me little time to bring a fountain of my own cum gushing out of my prick to further coat me. As those thirteen beautiful faces and excited bodies filled my vision, Billy poured the cum from the bowl over my prick just as my cum began to erupt from it.

I looked up at the guys generally and said, "I have never been happier, or felt more satisfied than I am right at this moment. You are the most exciting, most beautiful, most wonderful men in the world. Thank you ... each and every one of you."

Hal leaned over and rubbed his hand in the cum puddled on my chest. He walked over to Richard and grasped his huge, still very hard prick with a cum-covered hand. "I want to fuck you, birthday boy." Richard kissed him, then came over to me and coated his hand with cum before he returned to Hal to take his matchless shaft in his wet hand and say, "I want this beautiful monster cock as far up my ass as you can put it." Hal grinned at him: "You've got it, but my ass is looking forward to this big thing of yours showing me the same courtesy." They put their arms around each other, and went into a bedroom.

I didn't pay much attention to who paired off with whom, but Richard and Hal's example was soon followed, and all the cum on my body was shortly scraped off and deposited on cocks that would soon be inside appreciative asses and mouths. I personally was too happily tired to fuck any more that night, but I bedded down with Billy and Bob on one side of one of the king-sized beds where Hal was plowing Richard's ass as he knelt before the big-dicked fuckmaster – who, shortly after that, reversed roles and took Richard's hard-driving monster into him with delight fully equal to Richard's. The three of us snuggled and watched Hal and Richard in awe. I also watched Bob and Billy making love to each other. It was obvious they liked each other a great deal, and were doing more than just fucking – and both were careful to touch me and hold me as much as possible, so I felt I was sharing in beautiful lovemaking between the first guy whom I ever loved, and the wonderful guy I was then in love with.

I later learned that the two "married couples" – Mark and Johnny, and Cary and Mike – spent the night changing partners in another bed, and that Lee had convinced several other guys that his cum was "safe," and had shot loads down Thom's and Dean's throats while they were getting fucked by Steve and Phil. Those five spent the night together in one king-sized bed, and the loads Lee gave Thom and Dean were only the first of many that erupted in that bed that night. Before morning, Lee came to my bed and woke me to ask me to suck another load from his cock. He said Thom and Dean were all tied up in each other, and that Phil and Steve looked like they'd fallen in love.

I was happy to drain Lee's beautiful hose, and he joined Bob and Billy and me in the bed – where, incidentally, Hal and Richard were still at it. I asked them if they planned to get any sleep, but Richard ecstatically said he hadn't enjoyed anything as much as this since his birthday so many years before, when he and Eddie Bliss had fallen totally in lust with each other. I knew how he felt, of course – Hal's cock was only matched, in my experience, by those fabled organs Tom and Eddie had given me. Fortunately, Eddie and Tom and Hal all knew how to employ their prodigious endowments for maximum effect.

Even though he had pretty much fucked the whole night with the indefatigable and astonishing Hal, Richard and I traded our traditional blowjobs the next morning. Bob woke to find Lee eating his big cock, and Billy had an even more exciting reveille as he found that Hal had gradually, but inexorably slipped his monster cock into his ass to fuck him awake. Whether advisable or not, I let Richard shoot his load in my throat, and he took mine in his. I knew I was safe, and I thought he was – and in the light of subsequent testing, he obviously was. After Richard and I finished, we lay there and watched Bob and Lee suck each other off, while Hal fucked Billy like a demon, and shot an apparently monstrous load into him, using a condom.

Bob expressed his unqualified admiration for Hal's cock and his technique – and everything about him, really – and Hal acknowledged the compliments by rolling Bob on his back and burying the immense shaft Bob was admiring all the way up his admirer's ass. Bob's legs wrapped around Hal, and they hugged, kissed and moaned passionately for a very long time before Hal –

who had, after all, just shot a load in Billy – delivered another copious orgasm inside Bob. Bob declared he had never been fucked so wonderfully, or by such an astonishing prick. Hal asked him to reciprocate, using his own very impressive cock. Bob had blown a load in Lee shortly before, but he also applied himself at length and with great enthusiasm, finally saluting Hal's ass in the finest manner.

The day was not structured as the previous one had been, and all sorts of combinations of guys emerged. I got fucked several times again, including a joyous ride on Hal's prick (thank you, Jesus!), and I shot my load in Phil – as he and Billy and I held a threesome reunion – and in Cary, as he and Mike and I held another special reunion. We had the videos Tom Hunt had sent playing, and there was a lot of horseplay with the "Tom Fox" dildos – and a lot of very serious play with them as well, especially with Mark and Johnny, who had enjoyed the model for them so very, very often. We all lay around and reminisced and joked, and watched appreciatively and admiringly as Richard – the new birthday boy – held court on the mattress in the living room; I believe everyone there fucked him at least once during the day, I seem to recall that Thom fucked him twice, and I clearly remember that Hal returned to him later in the day for a requested repeat – and he sucked at least two loads out of Lee's eager prick. When I fucked Richard that afternoon, just after Hal's second invasion, I did not use a condom – we had, after all, sucked each other off only that morning. I assumed he had also taken at least a few other loads up his ass without a rubber, since I would have sworn his ass was full of cum already – it certainly was hot and wet, and felt absolutely wonderful, even though it had probably been fucked fourteen or fifteen times that day. I couldn't say how many loads Richard himself shot – but he certainly seemed to fuck everybody. After all the years, and all the ups and downs of our relationship, Richard's still felt absolutely right when he buried his prick inside me. He was also both sucker and suckee with about everyone in attendance.

Strangely, given the enormous variety of hot studs I could have paired off with, that second night found Billy and Bob and me still basically sleeping together. Richard had discovered all over again the incredible stamina and excitement of Dean's fucking, and had concluded his birthday of fourteen or fifteen fucks by going to bed in the next bed to ours, locked in Dean's arms as they kissed passionately. Dean had for a long time been appreciative of the glories of Richard's fucking equipment and fucking ability, and apparently they drifted off to sleep with Richard's cock buried in Dean's hungry ass. So, since Richard was not in bed with us, Hal decided to spend the night with us, and without the glorious distraction of Richard, Billy and Bob and I had Hal all to ourselves – and we shared his stupendous endowment and power. Bob, availing himself of Hal's magnificence again, declared him the most exciting lover he had ever known – by light years. "God, Johnny, I think if you'd had a cock like that back in high school, I would never have let you out of my sight!" I reminded him that he had not let me fuck him until he was almost out of college, but he said if he had been presented with such a formidable challenge as Hal's titanic prick, he would have strained every muscle to achieve it.

The next morning, Richard faithfully came to my bed, and as we always did when we were together, we sucked each other off – and Mark and Johnny appeared just about the time we were swallowing each other's cum. Mark and Billy made love for quite a while – and it was awesome to watch a pair of such unbelievably beautiful men kissing and embracing, and sucking and fucking each other. I remembered how Dean and I had delighted in watching my beautiful Mark having sex with the almost-as-beautiful Cary, and went in to bring Cary and Mike into the bedroom with us. Cary joined Mark and Billy in their love-making, and the rest of us – Hal , Richard, Bob, Mike, Johnny, and I – watched the three Adonises explore each other in every possible way – as inspiring, as beautiful, as exciting a sight as one could possibly imagine. Johnny and I knelt to watch, while the four other watchers took turns fucking us from behind – and they were the four with the truly huge pricks, which seemed especially hard and huge that morning as they wielded them on us. They were probably as inspired by watching the three beauties at play as I was. None of us shot our loads yet, though. We sucked cock in all manner of combinations, and if Johnny's cock wasn't quite the monster that Bob's, Mike's, Richard's, and especially Hal's was, it was plenty large – and my mouth felt like it had been fucked by an elephant after I had been sucking those five magnificent pricks for a while. When it seemed we were probably all near orgasm, we stood over Billy and Mark and Cary as they were involved in a three-way daisy chain, and jacked each other off to shoot our loads all over the love-making trio of beauties. They got so excited at that point, that they lay on their backs and jacked themselves off, to fountain their own loads onto their cum-covered bodies.

Dean had spent the night having sex with Richard, but had not followed him into my bedroom; it turned out he had been waylaid by Lee, wanting to get sucked off, so Dean obliged, and the two spent a long time sucking and fucking with each other on a couch in the living room, where we found them locked in sixty-nine, with Thom and Phil and Steve going at each other on the mattress in the middle of the floor.

Our party broke up early that afternoon – but it had been an unqualified success, toasted by all as the horniest occasion they could remember. I believe everyone took addresses and phone numbers from everyone else, and an accounting of sexual pairings that resulted from that exchange would probably fill volumes. Hal and Phil and Bob were all going to be spending the rest of the week at my house – this was only Thursday – and Thom lived nearby. Lee left, but he went to visit for a day or two with his parents, who lived in the country just outside of Dowd, and said he's come back to my house before he returned to Atlanta.

A couple of shifts of rental cars took everyone else back to the airport to fly home. As Mark and Johnny prepared to leave, I kissed Johnny and told him to be good to his beautiful lover and treat him well – I loved him deeply also. Billy and Mark were kissing goodbye, and Mark told Billy basically the same thing. Mark and I kissed very tenderly for a very long time before I was finally able to let him go. As much as I loved Billy, Mark was also my lover in a way, and always would be. To a somewhat lesser extent, the same thing was true of Richard, who was very reluctant to go, having discovered the wonder of Hal, but I heard the two of them promise to get together very soon. I knew I would probably hear sometime soon that Richard had convinced Hal to move to San Francisco, or that he himself had re-located in Texas. I knew from experience how Richard pursued truly gargantuan meat – and Hal's stupendous cock was unquestionably that.

The three days or so following the big party were not a continuation of the wild sexual orgy we had enjoyed at the hotel. Rather, we all relaxed and reminisced. We had plenty of sex, and Hal reined supreme as fuckmaster, of course – servicing Billy and Bob and Phil and me equally well – and we all pretty well shared our love and our passion with everyone. Phil and Billy spent a whole night together alone, reliving their high school experience, while in another bedroom Bob and I relived some of ours, but were also stimulated immeasurably by the presence in our bed of the incomparable Hal.

The morning after the party Lee had called to say he had to get sucked off, so he came out for a short while and Hal and I both drained his cock before he shot a load up Billy's ass just after Bob fucked his. He returned that same night and the next morning as well, and pretty evenly distributed his pretty body, his ready cock, his stupendous balls, and his prodigious ability to produce large and numerous orgasms. Finally, he decided he missed his two teen-age fuck partners in Atlanta too much to stay away any longer.

Phil and Hal flew back to Texas together, but Billy and I convinced Bob to stay another week; after all, he really had nothing in Tulsa he had to get back to: he was retired, his wife was gone, and his kids were on their own. Furthermore, I could tell that Billy and Bob were growing very, very close. I didn't feel left out, however – quite the contrary – I thought they related to each other as lovers of mine who were probably also falling in love with each other, and who enjoyed sharing their love with me as a team.

The whole week Bob and Billy and I spent together was idyllic. Bob felt right at home, and Billy and I both felt it seemed natural to have him around. We hiked, we had quiet dinners, we watched movies, and we slept in the same bed together every night – making love sweetly, and making love wildly and ferociously. Not only were they wonderful, sweet men, but between Bob's sublime huge prick and the matchless perfection of Billy's ass, I was in heaven – and I somehow knew, without their saying so, that they were in heaven also.

Strangely, I was sharing my life that week with the only two people I had ever known who did not call me "John." Although he had been very careful to call me by my proper name around everyone at the party, Billy reverted to calling me "Pete" as soon as the party was over. Why he began calling me Pete in the first place is another story – and for that I refer you to my book *Playing with Fire*, which details my romance with the sixteen-year old Billy. Bob had always called me "Johnny."

When Bob finally left, he promised we would be together again soon. Billy and I later visited him in Tulsa, and had a wonderful time. He returned to Billy's and my house in Dowd, two weeks on his first visit, and over a month the next. Every night we were together, we shared our bed and our love, and although the bed was occasionally a bit crowded for some of our more athletic activities, we seemed to have reached a symbiosis that promised great mutual satisfaction.

In a birthday card Tom Hunt had enclosed with the video he sent for my birthday, he had urged me to give him a call if I ever planned to be on the West coast. I called a few days after the party – before Bob returned to Oklahoma – to thank him for the video and for the dozen "Tom Fox Dildos," which I assured him had proven to be very popular "party favors." Tom suggested Billy and I practice with them and come out to see him and enjoy the real thing. Since Bob was still in residence, I suggested he be included in the invitation; Tom happily agreed, and said he'd be sure the twins were on hand also to practice their "specialty" on all of us. We agreed to set a date soon.

On Bob's first return visit, we set a date with Tom, and the three of us had a wonderful time practicing for our upcoming meeting with Tom and the twins. Each of us got double-fucked by the other two – Bob's monster shaft and Billy's long beauty fit perfectly in me – and we spent considerable time in a circle, holding hands or masturbating each other, and grinning in thrill and anticipation as we bobbed up and down on three "Tom Fox Dildos" suction-cupped to the floor. We also lay in a daisy chain and sucked cock as each fucked the guy he was sucking with one of the dildos. Our latex toys became 'good friends' in short order, and while Bob and Billy keenly anticipated getting the original down their throats and up their butts soon, I looked forward just as eagerly to a repeat of the thrills Tom had provided me when I first met him – perhaps even more eagerly, given the vividness of my memory of his sexual mastery.

On several of his ever-more-frequent visits, Thom Marks brought his "Tom Fox Dildo" along and joined in the circle and the daisy chain. By the time we were ready to go to California to meet with Tom, Thom had also been invited, and had especially enjoyed the practice sessions. Billy and I had made sure he was well trained for the twins' double-fuck!

Our visit with Tom and the twins was unforgettable, and the twins were amazing: their special double fuck was unbelievably thrilling. Tom was just as wonderful as I remembered him, and we all agreed his huge dick was much more enjoyable in the flesh than in the latex reproduction. For a special treat, the four of us also enjoyed an exciting visit with Mark and Johnny while we were in California.

By Bob's third visit to our house, he declared he felt perfectly at home with Billy and me, and we felt his presence was fully as natural. Separately, Billy and Bob each confessed his love for the other to me before he expressed it to the other, but each was careful to reassure me that he still loved me not the least bit less because of that. I loved both of them, of course, and each knew that well. Billy had known of my lasting love for Bob almost as long as I had known him. If Bob and Thom show a little extra attention to each other when the latter visits, Billy and I both think that's fine – especially since Thom still shows plenty of interest in sex with Billy and me as well.

I ran into the blond ex-sailor Jerry Steele on the street one day, and he told me how much he had enjoyed his limited participation at my birthday party – adding that he would like to get together some time for some private action. He grinned hugely as he added that he would also be especially interested in hooking up again with "the guy with the big dick that I fucked, and who sucked me off" at the party. I explained that Richard lived in San Francisco, but I promised Jerry I would show him some of Richard's videos when we got together.

Talking with Dean on the phone, I told him about Jerry, and he was amused. It seems that Jerry's father was a classmate of Dean's at the local high school, where he was an aggressively heterosexual, ladies-man, super-jock who only loved one thing better than sucking Dean's monster cock – and that was taking a load up the ass from that same prodigious instrument. Dean laughed, "And he fucked me pretty regularly, and I probably blew him a hundred times. Cute guy, fantastic body, nice dick, big load. I remember seeing the kid fucking Richard at your big birthday party. If I had known who he was, I would have caught up with him to reminisce about his dear old dad."

"Yeah, reminisce," I said. "And you'da had your cock all the way up his cute little butt while you did."

"You know me too well," Dean said.

At any rate, I made a date with Jerry to come out to my house for the 'private action' he was interested in. We watched Richard's fuck videos while we made love, and Jerry was blown away. He beamed his enormous grin, and said, "Hey, I fucked a movie star!" I found that particularly endearing, since he was fucking me at the moment he said it. He was as enthusiastic about the prospect of sucking Richard's cock and taking it up the ass as he was about having fucked Richard or getting blown by him.

Naturally, I never told Jerry what Dean had revealed to me about his father.

On his next visit, I introduced him to Billy and Bob. We've been seeing a good bit of Jerry ever since, whose two clearly favorite things are fucking Billy's luscious ass (when he isn't eating it out – the boy clearly has good sense), and getting fucked by Bob's big ass-reamer. He particularly enjoys the latter when Billy or I suck him off at the same time. He doesn't ignore me, either, but I get almost as much pleasure watching him doing his favorite things as I do when I fuck or suck with him. He may love Billy's ass and Bob's dick best, but he tells me I'm the best kisser in our little household; knowing what great kissers both Billy and Bob are, I think Jerry is just throwing me a bone, but that's fine with me – I'm happy to take young Jerry's bone any way I can get it!

Billy and Bob and I think of ourselves as a fairly monogamous *ménage à trois* (if such a threesome can be described that way), but we still enjoy visits from Jerry and some of our old fuckbuddies.

So, my first love has returned to me, my latest love is still very much just that, and each of us is very much in love with the other two. As both the earliest and most recent strands of my love life have apparently joined, I suppose I could feel a kind of closure, but instead I enjoy a kind of completeness in my life I had never expected to know, and the prospect of continuing happiness with my two lovers.

Bob's house is on the market, Billy is shopping for a king-sized bed, and I firmly believe I am the luckiest man alive!

The End

ABOUT THE AUTHOR

John Butler retired after a thirty-six year career in music teaching and administration, ranging from elementary and secondary school music, to Dean of Liberal Arts at a major American university, where he also served as professor and department head for twenty-seven years.

He has published widely in his primary career field, but his first publication in the field of interest that has occupied his mind since he started fooling around with the little boy next door at the age of nine or ten came with the publication of the erotic novel *model/escort* in 1998. Since then he has also published the novels, *WanderLUST: Ships that Pass in the Night*, *Boys HARD at Work (and Playing with Fire)*, *The Boy Next Door* (in the anthology *Any Boy Can*), *The Year the Pigs Were Aloft* (in the anthology *Seduced II*), *This Gay Utopia*, and *Teacher Is the Best Experience*, as well as novels and short stories in the anthologies *Any Boy Can*, *Taboo!*, *Fever!*, *Virgins No More*, *Seduced II*, *Wild and Willing*, and *Fantasies Made Flesh*.

Following the death of STARbooks Press founder, John Patrick, he completed editing the anthologies *Seduced II* and *Wild and Willing*. He also edited an anthology of John Patrick's best writings, *Living Vicariously*.

All these are available from the publisher, STARbooks Press.

The author welcomes comments or questions through the e-mail address NotRhett@yahoo.com.